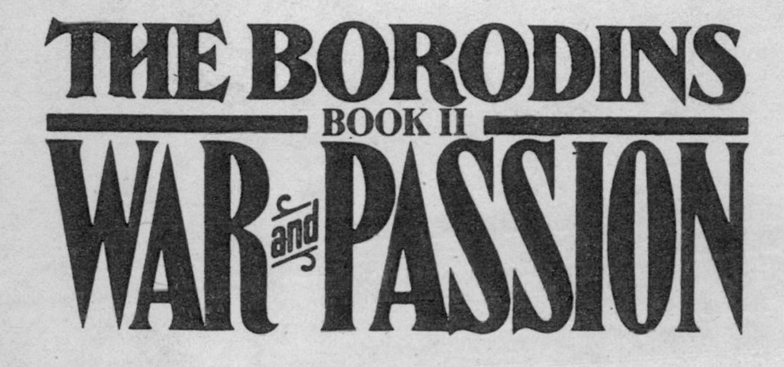

LESLIE ARLEN

A JOVE BOOK

First Jove edition published February 1981

10 9 8 7 6 5 4 3 2 1

Printed in the United States of America

Jove books are published by Jove Publications, Inc.,
200 Madison Avenue, New York, NY 10016

Verna

"DO YOU NOT KNOW," SAID THE GRAND DUKE, "THAT THE GRAND DUCHESS AND YOUR SISTER ARE DISCIPLES OF THE BEAST, RASPUTIN?"

Judith stared at him.

"Nor are they the only ones. The list of his conquests stretches into the royal family. Mademoiselle Stein, we have determined the country must be saved, and it can only be saved if Rasputin is removed. Will you help us?"

"Your highnesses, how can *I* help?"

"The holy father adores your sister," Yusupov pointed out. "Now then, suppose he discovers that Rachel Stein has a sister who is even more beautiful."

"But . . ."

"You see, mademoiselle, our only hope is to discover him alone. At a private party, perhaps . . ."

Judith looked from one to the other. The three most honorable men in all Russia.

"Now listen very carefully," Dr. Purishkevich said. "This is what we plan to do . . ."

JUDITH . . .
A dark Jewish beauty—three years of harsh exile had failed to crush her brilliant spirit.
THE COMMISSAR. *His rebel destiny had led him to the foot of the gallows—and then to the highest circles in the land—and Judith's arms.*
THE AMERICANS. *He, the crusading journalist; she, the Borodin princess—they were the only friends to Judith, cast adrift in a battle-scarred land.*

WAR AND PASSION

By Leslie Arlen
from Jove

THE BORODINS

BOOK I: *Love and Honor*
BOOK II: *War and Passion*

THE BORODINS

BOOK II

WAR and PASSION

Chapter 1

FROM THE WINDOWS OF HIS OFFICE ON THE EIGHTEENTH FLOOR of the *American People* building, George Hayman could look across the East River towards Long Island City. Since his office extended the entire width of the building, he could, by taking a short walk, also look north to the new Queensboro Bridge. This was the more attractive prospect. But George Hayman preferred to stand and think, looking east. For beyond Long Island there was the Atlantic Ocean, and beyond the Atlantic there was Europe.

And beyond Europe there was Russia.

He recognized that his fascination with that great, brooding, tragic country was almost a disease. It was easy to explain: he was married to a Russian and he had undertaken the greatest adventure of his life three years earlier, when he had matched wits with the Okhrana, the tsar's secret police. But he often felt guilt in that so much of his very valuable, and equally limited, time should be spent in remembering the past, the people he had known and the incidents that had occurred.

George Hayman was thirty-seven years old, and looked younger; his dark hair was untouched by gray, his six feet and two inches of height carried no excess weight—he golfed in the winter, played polo every Saturday in the summer. Nor had the three weeks spent in the Peter and Paul prison fortress on the outskirts of St. Petersburg, in the summer of 1911, marred the youthfulness of his face. It was a pensive face in repose, long and serious, dominated by the softness in the large brown eyes and the firmness of the flat mouth. The eyes smiled easily even when in the act of rebuking an employee—and George Hayman employed well over a thousand people, from the humblest messenger boys to the editor-in-chief he himself had appointed. Even though old Mr. George Hayman was still president of the company, it was George junior who was the active executive, and it was George's ambition and determination which had expanded the original Boston *People* into this nationwide, and indeed worldwide, publishing concern. Given financial control of the corporation by his father on his return from Russia in 1911, he had decided to buy a controlling interest in the declining New York *Morning Mail* and to rename it. The success of that venture had led him to purchase newspapers in London, Paris, and Tokyo.

He would explain, when asked, that it was a natural progression for a great newspaper. But those who understood him knew it was much more than that. His grandfather had been a penniless English immigrant. His father had progressed from selling broadsheets on a street corner to owning the *People*. This was too familiar a pattern, with an immediate decline setting in during the third generation; George Hayman was determined to be an exception to the rule. If his earlier ambition, to be the greatest war correspondent in the world, had been dissipated in the drama of his elopement with a Russian princess and the pleasures of his marriage, he had redirected all his earlier determination toward success at this higher level.

And yet, he retained this youthful concern for his wife's people, for that contrast of omnipotent splendor and bitter antagonism which she had abandoned to live at his side.

This concern with Russia was frequently demonstrated in his work. A knock on the door admitted his secretary, who would place the prominent news stories of the day on his desk, with appropriate comments from the paper's editor. But there were always two piles; one covered most of the world, and dealt only in leading items; the other covered Russia, and included every single snippet of news.

"Anything of interest today, Mrs. Killett?" George sat at

his desk, absently clipped the end from a cigar.

"I don't think so, Mr. Hayman. Save for the scandal in France."

"What scandal?"

"You remember, back in January, Mr. Hayman? The *Figaro* newspaper made accusations of fraud against Monsieur Caillaux, the Minister of Finance? Well, yesterday—you won't believe this, but Madame Caillaux marched into the office of the *Figaro* and shot Monsieur Calmette, the editor, stone dead."

"Good God." George idly turned over the papers. "An emotional people, the French."

"Yes, sir."

Mrs. Killett waited, but her employer was clearly not in the mood for conversation, so she turned to leave the room, when she was halted by another muttered, "Good God."

"Sir?"

George Hayman pushed back his chair and got up. "I'm taking the rest of the day off, Mrs. Killett. Have the car brought to the front."

"Yes, sir, Mr. Hayman, but there was that appointment—"

"Cancel it, Mrs. Killett. I'm going out to the house." He picked up one of the papers from his desk, folded it, and put it in his pocket. He crammed his hat on his head and ran past her, heading for the elevator.

Mrs. Killett leaned over the desk to glance at the papers. The one he had taken was from the Russian file. Something must have happened over there. But for the life of her she couldn't think what it was.

George Hayman took the wheel of the Duesenberg himself, leaving his chauffeur to sit beside him. He raced eastward on his way out to Cold Spring Harbor, and the huge house with its sprawling lawns. Driving fast always exhilarated him, but today he felt like a boy again. The impossible had happened. He could go back. Ilona could go back. And Johnnie . . . his smile faded into a frown, and the car slowed. John Hayman had been three years old when his mother had fled husband and family and Russia, and therefore he could remember that his name was really Ivan Sergeievich, and that he was supposed to be the only son of General Prince Sergei Roditchev. To take him back to Russia might make it essential to tell him something different. But he could never be told the truth about his parentage.

And yet, if they returned just for a visit . . . the car gathered speed again. They were unlikely ever to have to meet Sergei Roditchev again. And if they did . . . George Hayman smiled. The last time he had faced his wife's first husband he had knocked him senseless. That was only three years ago. But it seemed like a lifetime. Brawling with a Russian nobleman might be acceptable for a foreign correspondent of the Boston *People*. It was not a practical possibility for the vice-president of the *American People*.

The car swung into the willow-lined drive, scraped to a stop before the Corinthian pillars of the porch. Gravel flew, the Labradors barked, and Harrison, the butler, came down the steps to open the door. "Mr. Hayman?" Harrison was English, and could convey all the necessary questions in the smallest variations of tone.

"There's nothing wrong, Harrison." George stepped down, and stripped off his driving gloves and goggles. "Where is Mrs. Hayman?"

"Gardening, sir."

George nodded, and walked around the house and through the little maze into the flower garden that surrounded the croquet lawn like the crowded seats of a Roman amphitheater. He paused to enjoy the scene in front of him. The Labradors were not allowed in this part of the garden because of the damage they inflicted during their boisterous games, but the dachshunds were, and the pair of them trotted behind their mistress like an escort. That a Russian princess should never wish to be separated from at least some of her pets was probably not unusual; that she delighted in being surrounded by her children was a part of her determination to be more American than her husband. This morning Felicity was hanging out of her pram, waving at the dogs; she was just a year old. George the third, a year her elder, was crawling up and down the lawn in a series of assaults upon the croquet hoops. These were the true Haymans. But John Hayman filled the role of big brother as if born to it. He was actually playing croquet, manhandling the mallet which was almost his own height, clipping the wooden balls with accurate strokes, patiently easing his half-brother out of the way when they encountered each other. At six years of age John was already a serious, thoughtful boy, with fair hair which kept flopping over his forehead. His features were undeniably Russian, at least to George's eyes.

Ilona was slowly straightening, turning, and pulling off her gardening gloves, allowing them to fall onto the pile of weeds she was accumulating on the path. Even after three years of marriage, whenever he came home George felt a new sense of amazement that so lovely a creature could have become his, and his so completely. He remembered the first time he had seen her, on the terrace of her father's house in the doomed city of Port Arthur, with the Japanese guns already thundering in the background. That had been ten years earlier in 1904, and she had been eighteen. He had thought, then, that in her he was looking at the accumulated splendor of six hundred years of Russian aristocracy. He had never discovered any reason to alter that judgment. Her magnificent golden hair was loose today, instead of piled into the pompadour she still wore on social occasions; her figure had filled out, but since she was a tall woman she merely seemed the better proportioned; and no passage of time, however tragic some of it had been, could alter the flawless bone structure she had inherited from her Borodin ancestors—the small nose, the soft chin, the breathtakingly deep blue of the huge eyes. Only the seriousness of her expression suggested some of the memories which must always be lurking on the edge of her consciousness; but then, she had always been a serious woman.

"George?" Her tone was soft. "What is wrong?"

"Nothing," he said, and took her in his arms to kiss her on the forehead. "Something has happened. Something marvelous."

She held him away from her, her frown deepening. John Hayman ceased hitting croquet balls and watched them. His face was as serious as his mother's. "What is it?"

"This." George released her, reached into his pocket, and took out a piece of paper. "Came in on the wire this morning. 'In recognition of the fact that 1914 will be the twentieth year of his reign, his imperial majesty Tsar Nicholas II is pleased to announce an amnesty for all political prisoners except those actually convicted of civil crimes.'" He kissed her again. "What do you think of that?"

"Oh, George." Her eyes filled with tears. "I'm so happy. It means Peter can return to his career."

"Of course it does."

"And that poor girl, Judith Stein . . . she'll be allowed to go home."

George Hayman frowned. He did not wish to remember Judith Stein, a crumpled heap of naked flesh on the floor of Sergei Roditchev's cell. But her fate would no doubt haunt Ilona for the rest of her life; she knew her ex-husband's brutality better than anyone.

He held her close.

"Of course she will. And a lot of others besides. But I was thinking of you and me."

"Us?" The frown was back.

"Well, I was deported for helping a wanted revolutionary escape from prison. Now would you say that was a political or civil crime? I'm sure as hell going to find out."

She freed herself, walking to the bench by the side of the lawn, and sat down. Her children watched her.

"Don't you want to?" He sat beside her.

"Go back?" she asked. "Could it be possible?"

"I don't see why not. Starogan, certainly. We could visit your mother and grandmother, see Peter, the house . . . and Tatiana."

Ilona raised her head. "She's going to be twenty-one," she said. "In July."

"Well then." He kissed her on the nose. "There's an occasion. The children will love Starogan in the summer. You told me that once, remember? And you were right."

"Starogan in the summer." She sighed, and leaned back, and as quickly sat up again, her gaze drifting past George to Johnnie.

George shook his head gently. "There's nothing to worry about there, my love. Michael Nej was convicted of murder. There is no chance of *his* ever going back."

Three men and a woman walked the gentle slopes of the lower Jorat, looked, when they troubled to do so, past the rooftops of Lausanne at the sparkling waters of Lake Geneva. But it was a view they had seen too often. They preferred to argue. This was their daily entertainment, their very reason for being.

"An amnesty," Nikolai Kalinin insisted. He wore glasses and had wavy dark hair; his beard was neatly shaped although his mustache, which possessed some of the wave, was allowed to roam free and gave his face a somewhat lopsided appearance. "You must admit that there is style. And power. And decision. It will make a difference. Mark my words."

"Don't be absurd," said the man beside him. Here was a complete contrast, for Nikolai Lenin was stocky where Kalinin was slim; he wore his red hair clipped short, and his beard and moustache were scanty. "It is another of the Romanov tricks. You'll note he has specifically excluded anyone convicted of a civil crime. How many of our people, do you suppose, have *not* been convicted of a civil crime as well as a political one?" His voice was hard and strangely harsh, yet for that reason the more commanding, and his companions were usually prepared to defer to his opinions—except, perhaps his wife. He turned to her now. "Don't you think it is a trick?"

"Of course." Krupskaya spoke quietly. Her entire demeanor was quiet, as compared with Lenin's abrasive loudness, just as her looks, delicately lovely and dominated by full, somewhat pouting lips, might have been designed as a perfect complement to his blunt features. "Those released will be the dross of the movement, the hangers-on. Never the ones that matter. Michael Nikolaievich, here, cannot return."

Kalinin gave a brief laugh. "Michael Nikolaievich is lucky just to be standing here. He should have been hanged. Eh, Michael Nikolaievich?"

Michael Nej hunched his shoulders. He was the biggest of the three men, being both tall and sturdily built; his strong features, the thrusting nose and chin, were surprisingly alleviated by the softness of the brown eyes and the wide mouth. He walked a little behind the others. Although Michael was the only one of them who had ever pulled a trigger in anger—he had shot a policeman on the day, in 1911, that Prime Minister Stolypin had been assassinated, and had been convicted of the crime—he never forgot he was their inferior in social status. Fifty years before, the Nejs had been serfs; even after emancipation they had risen no higher than to become servants of the Borodin family. Michael's apogee had been as valet to Prince Peter Borodin, so far as Lenin and Kalinin were aware. He had his secret, his true achievement, but it was not one of which he ever spoke. To have held Princess Ilona Borodina in his arms was sufficient memory for any man; he could afford to keep it private.

"Well?" Kalinin thumped him on the shoulder again. "What

do you think of the tsar's amnesty?"

"I think that Krupskaya is right," Michael agreed. "It surely does not extend to me. But I would still like to go back."

Lenin stopped walking, and thrust his hands into the side pockets of his jacket. He thrust his chin forward, as he always did when he was preparing to win an argument. "Go back? What for?"

"Well—" Michael always felt diffident when arguing with this man. And there was no point in confessing that he would give a year of his life to be able to visit Starogan again; to see his mother and father, Ivan his brother, and Nona his sister; even to see the Borodins again—Prince Peter, and Tatiana, always laughing, so unlike her serious sister, but so like her in beauty. Lenin would not understand sentiments like these. "There will be thousands of people set free," Michael said. "People who believe in the things we do, in democracy and the overthrow of the tsar. But as you said, they will be on the fringes, they will lack leadership, initiative. It occurs to me that if we were to return to Russia now—"

"Nonsense," Lenin declared. "Listen, comrade, the Russian people do not *want* leadership, initiative, revolution. They are sunk into a slough, the whole lot of them. Do you not suppose I have tried? I was there in 1905. I led the people of Moscow against Roditchev's Cossacks. I made them build barricades and I manned them. And what happened? When the prince turned his guns on us, they ran away. You would be putting your head into a noose, for nothing."

"Nevertheless," Michael insisted, glancing at Krupskaya for support, "we must keep working, and it cannot be done merely by printing a newspaper here in Switzerland and arguing among ourselves. There are good people in Russia, people who believe in what we are doing and who can work with us."

"Who?"

"Well, what about the girl, Judith Stein? You remember her. Was she not on the Moscow barricades with you?"

"Briefly."

"Well, then. She was sent to Siberia not just for helping Bogrov and me—she never really did that—but for what she was writing, a complete history of revolutionary tactics."

"She was sent to Siberia because her lover, Prince Peter Borodin—your master, Michael Nikolaievich—interceded for her. Otherwise she would have been hanged."

Michael chewed his lip. "I don't believe she was ever Prince Peter's mistress. She was a well-born Jewess, not a slut. And besides, I was *there*, some of the time."

"What difference does it make if she slept with him or not?" Krupskaya said. "She was certainly saved from the noose by his intercession, just as you were saved by the American, Hayman. You have never told us why he should do that, Michael."

"It is a personal matter," Michael mumbled.

"Which is unimportant," Lenin pronounced, "except that you *were* saved, Michael Nikolaievich, and are now here with us, where you belong. I know you miss your family. I miss mine. But we are called to more important things than families. We shall return to Russia, I promise you that. But when we do, it will be as masters, when the people send for us. Until then, you belong here." His face broke into a charming smile, all trace of harshness disappearing. "As for Judith Stein, let her return, and resume writing her treatise on revolution. Who knows? We may find it useful one day. And let her go back to her prince, down in Starogan. That too may be useful, one day."

"How do I look? Is it sitting right?" Rachel Stein peered at herself in the mirror, and adjusted her hat for the fifth time. It was a mass of red velvet, gathered with its band to make it fit close around her head, but it was inclined to slide.

"It looks fine," Ruth Stein assured her daughter. "You are as pretty as a picture. Judith will be proud of you."

Rachel bit her lips to add a little color; Momma did not permit cosmetics. She wondered if she *was* as pretty as a picture. Judith had been pretty, even lovely. Had been. Why use such words? Judith *was*, and she would soon be home.

Would she still be as pretty as a picture, after six weeks in General Prince Roditchev's cells, and then three years in the empty waste of a Siberian labor camp? Rachel straightened, and again regarded herself. She was twenty, therefore Judith would now be twenty-five. Rachel was a tall girl, but Judith had always been taller. She was slender, with breasts that hardly disturbed the crisp poplin of her orange-and-white summer dress, hips that scarcely measured more than her waist; Judith had always been more voluptuous. Rachel possessed the straight dark hair, the long and serious features of the Steins, the enormous dark eyes. Not much difference there, save that Judith's face had always been even more serious. Judith had seldom smiled, and when she had laughed it had been with contempt. Would she still laugh, with contempt?

"Oh, stop preening yourself." Joseph Stein pulled on his gloves. He was two years older than she, halfway between her and Judith.

"Nervous?" Rachel inquired.

"Why in the name of God should I be nervous?"

"Well . . . you could have gone with her. Couldn't you?"

Joseph straightened his tie. "I went to a couple of meetings. Nothing more than that. I was young and foolish. I wish you'd stop bringing it up. Here's Poppa."

Jacob Stein stood at the head of the stairs. Although he was just past fifty, he looked much older; that was Judith's doing. It was not merely the shock of realizing that his daughter was an anarchist involved in the plot to assassinate Prime Minister Stolypin and the tsar that September day in 1911, nor even the disgrace of having to leave Moscow and his thriving law practice and make a fresh start in St. Petersburg; he had managed to create another thriving practice here, and had succeeded in securing election to the Duma. But Jacob Stein had been allowed to see Judith while she was still in the hands of Roditchev's Okhrana. That day he had become an old man.

What had he seen? He had never told anyone. Not even his wife, so far as Rachel knew. But the rest of the family were about to learn something of what had haunted him these three years.

"Are we ready?" He slapped his hands together.

"Ready, Poppa. Do you like my hat?"

Jacob Stein inspected his youngest daughter, and nodded. "I think it is very fine. Momma?"

"We should go," Ruth Stein agreed.

They trooped down the front stairs, very conscious that their neighbors were watching them from behind chintz curtains. Although Jacob Stein, in his frantic climb towards what he considered respectability, had escaped the pale in which so many of his compatriots were forced to live, he had not been able to buy a house in one of the more fashionable parts of the city, on the Nevskiy Prospekt, for example; instead he had had to make do with a modest dwelling here on Petersburg Island, facing the city proper, in the very shadow of the Fortress of

St. Peter and St. Paul, where the tsars were buried, and where, in its new role as state prison, Judith Stein had spent the weeks of her trial. Perhaps this too had contributed to his aging, Rachel thought.

But at least they possessed a motor car, which Joseph was preparing to drive, Rachel beside him, holding her hat on her head with a chiffon scarf, while Momma and Poppa sat in the back.

"Smile, Jacob," Ruth Stein begged. "Today should be a joyous occasion."

"Do you really suppose so?" Jacob Stein muttered. But he raised his hat at the people across the street.

"Three years is not so long a time," Momma insisted.

From the corner of her eye Rachel saw the expression on her father's face, for just a moment. Momma had not seen Judith since she was arrested, except at a distance, in court. What was it she could expect to see now? She glanced at Joseph who was concentrating on the traffic, the carriages and bicycles that shared the bridge to the mainland with the cars. Joseph's lips were tight, his entire face concentrated. He was not looking forward to seeing Judith again either. Despite his denial, he *had* been involved with the anarchists, and more than briefly. Rachel could remember that man Bogrov, who had actually shot down Peter Stolypin, coming to their house, looking for Joe and especially Judith. Bogrov had been hanged. But the other assassin, Michael Nej, had escaped, mysteriously smuggled from Russia by an American newspaper correspondent, George Hayman. That had been the talk of the country, at the time. Why hadn't the American been able to smuggle Judith from the country as well? Because he had not known she existed?

The car approached the station, slowed, and eventually Joseph found a parking place. There was a huge crowd here today, thousands of people standing and gossiping, jostling each other as they pushed their way towards the barriers. Many, like the Steins, were relatives of returning exiles. But most were simply curious. And some were more curious than others. Rachel watched her brother's gaze sweep across the crowd, and come to rest on a group of three men, dressed in silk hats and well-cut suits, standing a little apart from the throng and inspecting it. Even Rachel guessed the men were members of the Okhrana. But the Steins were here today on legitimate business, and in any event, what did she have to fear? She had never been involved in any anarchist plots. Even Prince Roditchev knew that.

Joseph pushed his way into the crowd, making a corridor for his parents. Rachel came behind, her brain teeming with jumbled thoughts. She was for the first time realizing that Judith's return might be more important to her than she had ever imagined. She had completed school two years before, and yet was treated as a schoolgirl. Her parents had blamed Judith's tragedy on the freedom she had been allowed, so no risks were to be taken with Rachel. She had dreamed of a career. Women did have careers, certainly in the West. Uncle Abe lived in the United States, and she had hoped that Poppa would send her there to study; all her life she had dreamed of being a surgeon, and such things were possible, even for women, in America. But Poppa had never agreed, had always put it off, was clearly hoping she would marry some nice Jewish boy and not give her parents any trouble as her brother and sister had.

But with Judith back, Poppa might let her go. Her heart started to pound with anticipation, and she clutched her hat tighter on her head as someone jostled her and it threatened to slip away altogether. Then they were at the barrier, and Joseph was showing the tickets they had secured a week before. The inspector studied the pasteboard with great care. He always worked at his own measured pace—all bureaucrats did, as far as Rachel could tell—but today he clearly had a reason. In addition to the Okhrana, there were uniformed policemen here, determined that only the relatives of returning exiles should be allowed onto the platform. There was already a huge crowd of relatives, and the train was not due for another ten minutes. But at last he was satisfied, and allowed them through, to stand together under the clock, smiling nervously at those who greeted them, exposing themselves to all the world as the family of an anarchist, exposing themselves to the searching eyes of the Okhrana—as if the Okhrana did not already have files on all of them.

But they were exposing themselves to even more than that, for suddenly Joseph stiffened, and clutched her arm. "Oh, my God," he muttered. "It's Roditchev himself."

General Prince Roditchev was in his mid-forties, tall and strongly built; he wore his green uniform with careless arrogance. But then, he was clearly an arrogant man; he allowed his mustache to curl rather than tame it with the fashionable wax, and he looked at human beings beneath his own rank as if they were especially annoying insects. He had cleanly etched features with prominent nose and chin, and a gracious smile, when he cared to use it. He was smiling today as his gaze swept the Steins, suddenly huddled together—like frightened sheep, Rachel thought.

"Monsieur Stein. Madame." The Prince saluted with his cane and allowed his gaze to drift over Joseph, where it rested for a moment, and then to Rachel. Suddenly she felt cold. "This must be a joyous day for you."

"For all Russia, your excellency," Jacob Stein ventured.

The prince frowned at him. "I doubt that, monsieur. I doubt that." His gloved finger flicked out, pointing at the lawyer. "What do you say to the news from Sarajevo?"

"The assassination, your excellency?"

"The murder of the Archduke Ferdinand and his wife by *anarchists*, Monsieur Stein. It is a cancerous growth spreading through our society. But I rely upon you, at the least, to impress upon your daughter that she will receive no second chance. Next time it will be the noose. Remember that. Madame." He nodded to Ruth Stein, looked again at Joseph and, lingeringly, at Rachel, then turned away.

"Swine," Joseph muttered. "*He* should have been assassinated long ago."

"For God's sake be quiet," Ruth Stein begged.

Rachel watched Roditchev receding into the throng, being saluted by his men as he went, touching the peak of his cap with his cane. She wondered what it must be like to possess such all-embracing power, to have enjoyed it for so long. Did he not fear assassination? There could be no more hated man in all Russia. But presumably men like Sergei Roditchev did not fear anything. That was the source of their strength and their power.

A whistle sounded in the distance, and the crowd sighed, and stirred, and surged forward to the edge of the platform, before retreating again as those in the front found themselves pushed too close to the rails.

"We will wait here," Jacob Stein decreed. His wife held his hand. Rachel wanted to hold hands with someone, but Joseph was showing no disposition to hold *her* hand. He was looking past the crowd at the train. which was slowly creeping into the station—an odd train, this, because there were no first-class and no second-class compartments. This train had come all the way from Irkutsk, and the passengers would have been sitting and sleeping on bare boards the entire journey.

But they were not sitting or lying now. Every window was filled with a happy face, a waving hand. Rachel could not identify anyone, partly because she did not know where to look, and partly because her vision was obscured by the waving hands and handkerchiefs and hats of the people in front of her.

"Where is she?" Ruth Stein kept asking. "Where is she? She's not there, Jacob. She has not come. They have kept her behind."

"Now, Momma, she will be here. We were told she would be here. Just be patient, Momma. Just a little while longer."

Ruth Stein began to cry, and Joseph gave her his handkerchief. Rachel tried standing on tiptoe, for the train had now stopped, and the doors were opening, and people were getting down. Men, and women. But she realized that she would have recognized none of them, even if she had known them all. The men wore beards and their clothes did not seem to fit. The women wore kerchiefs round their heads, and *their* clothes seemed hardly more than sacks. She could not tell about their faces, because they were all smiling or crying as they greeted their relatives, but she had a sudden feeling that she would recognize none of those either.

"There she is," Joseph said.

Rachel craned her neck, but could not see her sister.

"I will fetch her over here," Joseph said. "Don't move." He pushed his way into the crowd.

"Where is she?" Ruth begged. "Where is she, Jacob?"

"I can't see her," Jacob said. "But she will be here in a moment. Just a moment, Momma."

The crowd, which had closed behind Joseph, was parting again to let him through. He was followed by a woman, whose hand he held, and she in turn was holding the hand of another woman. They were just like all the other women who had got off the train, their dresses obviously homemade without the benefit of patterns or even sewing machines, their hair concealed beneath well-worn kerchiefs. And Rachel realized with a start of horror that her presentiment had been accurate. This was clearly her sister Judith, tall and handsome. But this too was a stranger, behind the so familiar face, who did not weep as she embraced her mother and then her father, kissed Joseph, and held open her arms for Rachel. But then, she remembered, Judith had been a stranger since that night, seven years ago, when she had first been interrogated by the Okhrana. By Roditchev.

She was hugged between strong arms, kissed on both cheeks. "You are a woman now," Judith said. "You are so pretty." She held Rachel at arm's length to look at her. "You must show me where you buy your clothes."

The others were waiting in embarrassed silence, as the woman who had accompanied Judith from the train was also waiting in silence. But she was not embarrassed, merely patient. She was younger than Judith, dark and small, with features that might have been attractive but for the hate that seemed to fill her eyes, to tighten her mouth, and a figure that was nonexistent beneath the shapeless dress.

"Oh, I am sorry," Judith said. "Momma, Poppa, this is Dora Ulyanova. Dora, my mother and father. My brother Joseph. My sister Rachel."

The girl shook hands with each of them in turn.

"But my dear," Momma said. "How long have you been in Siberia?"

"Three years," Dora Ulyanova said.

"But . . ."

"I was nineteen, Madame Stein."

"My God."

"Ulyanova," Joseph said, half to himself. "I know that name. Vladimir Ilich Ulyanov—"

"Who calls himself Nikolai Lenin. He is my uncle," the girl said, and shrugged. "Was my uncle. I have not seen him for eleven years. But I will see him again."

"For God's sake," Jacob Stein begged, "do not use that name here. There are policemen everywhere. Come, we must leave. Mademoiselle Ulyanova, it has been a pleasure."

The girl glanced at Judith.

"I . . . Dora has nowhere to go," Judith said. "She has no family in St. Petersburg. I have said she could stay with us."

"With . . ." Jacob Stein looked at his wife.

"Of course she may," Ruth Stein said. "Until she can make contact with her family. Of course she may. Where are your bags?"

The two women looked at each other, and Rachel realized

that each of them carried a small bundle under her arm. A terribly small bundle.

"Let me have those," Joseph said.

"No," Judith said, while Dora Ulyanova merely held hers tighter. "They are not heavy."

"Well . . . the car is this way."

The crowd was starting to thin as people made their way out of the station, forming a long line to pass the inspector and his flanking guard of policemen—and General Prince Sergei Roditchev. Judith, her arm round her mother's shoulders, did not notice him until she was actually at the barrier. Then she stopped, and her face froze.

General Prince Roditchev inspected her from head to foot. "Judith Stein," he said.

Judith stared at him, as a rabbit might stare at a snake.

"You must be pleased to be home, after only three years," the prince remarked, "especially since your original sentence was for life. Do you not agree that his majesty is merciful?"

Rachel, standing immediately behind her sister, could hear the whistle of the air being sucked into Judith's lungs.

"Yes, your excellency," Judith said, in a low voice. "His majesty is merciful."

Roditchev nodded, and then made a peculiar gesture. His right arm, which had been hanging at his side, moved to bring his cane up almost into a salute. But it was not a salute. He was showing Judith Stein the cane, and Judith had seen it before. She took a step backward, and all the color fled from her cheeks.

"I would hope you have learned your lesson, Judith," the prince said. "You will not wish to be arrested again, I am sure." He too stepped back, and the Steins could go on. But Judith could not immediately move, it seemed. Her mother had to drag her forward. Then Dora Ulyanova drew level with the prince, but he made no remark to her. And a few moments later they were in the car and driving out of the yard, Judith in the front seat now, beside Joseph, Dora and Rachel crammed into the back with Momma and Poppa.

"I am sorry that Prince Roditchev had to be there," Poppa said, to Judith.

She did not turn her head. "I knew he would be. But I . . . I had not prepared myself."

She and Poppa were having a private conversation. No one else in the car fully understood what they were talking about, except perhaps Dora Ulyanova. "One day," she remarked, "I am going to sit on his chest and pick out his eyes. I swear it."

Ruth Stein poured tea and made conversation. Joseph fussed. And even Jacob kept talking although he could not take his eyes from Judith's face. Despite all that had happened over the preceding half-dozen years, they were not used to such intense hatred. Dora Ulyanova was a stranger to them. But not to Judith. Did Judith also hate, so deeply?

Rachel sipped tea, watched and listened. This was really a world outside of her knowledge. She could remember the day Judith had been arrested, the policemen knocking down the door of the house in Moscow. It had not been necessary to knock down the door; it had not been locked. But it had been their way of showing their power. She could remember Judith screaming as they had dragged her out. She could remember the policeman on his hands and knees gathering the scattered sheets of the manuscript on which Judith had been working, her study of revolution. And before then, she could remember the assassin Bogrov coming to the house, and talking with Judith in her room. Judith had always denied any complicity in the assassination plot, even any knowledge of it. That denial, together with Prince Peter Borodin's intercession, had saved her from the gallows. Had she confessed to complicity in the murder, even Prince Peter could not have helped her.

But she *had* spent many hours closeted in the bedroom with Mordka Bogrov. What had they talked about, if it had not been murder?

That was the sum total of Rachel's knowledge of what really happened in the world outside, as opposed to the world she read of in her romances, where everything always ended happily; or the world she heard of from Moses Lewin, the rabbi, where one could rely on God for everything; or the world she observed at her mother's side, where one was treated according to the number of roubles in one's purse—and Momma's purse was always well filled with roubles.

But presumably all of them—Momma, and Moses Lewin, and even the men and women who wrote the romances—knew that there was darkness behind the light, gall beneath the sugar coating on their messages. They knew, without having experienced. So what did you say to two girls who had experienced? And who had only their hate to sustain them?

Certainly you did not ask questions about life in Irkutsk,

however much you were dying to know. You prattled on about people who had once been, talked about clothes, grew suddenly embarrassed when you looked at Judith's own clothes, and then could recover with a smile because at least Judith would be able to buy new ones. And you talked about the weather, which was always good for half an hour of conversation in St. Petersburg, where if it was not snowing it was probably raining, and if it was neither snowing nor raining, it must be the five or six weeks of midsummer, when it was so hot as to be unbearable. And you could gossip about the doings of the starets, Gregory Rasputin, wondering if it was true that he kept a harem of noble ladies to do his every carnal bidding, and that the empress was his absolute slave. Because you had to keep the conversation in the present. The future—even the immediate future, even tomorrow—was hardly any easier to discuss than the past. What did the future hold? What *could* the future hold, for Judith Stein and Dora Ulyanova?

"And Hannah Janowska," Ruth said. "She was there. My dear, wearing the most ghastly pink dress. You have never seen anything like it. You remember Hannah Janowska, Rachel? At the Meyer boy's bar mitzvah?"

"Yes, Momma," Rachel said obediently, and watched Dora Ulyanova. She too was listening, but she was obviously not interested. She seemed more interested in the house, in the heavy, overstuffed furniture, the photographs of the Stein family in their silver frames, all the evidence of solid middle-class prosperity and respectability. Was she wondering how on earth Judith, with such a background, had become a revolutionary?

But since they had lived together in the most frightful of conditions, for three years, she would have to know the answer to that. So was she wondering how this wealth and this respectability could be made to work for her cause? Dora had not abandoned *her* beliefs; that much was certain. But had Judith abandoned hers?

Rachel watched her sister. The face was quiet, composed, but not relaxed. It was impossible to imagine Judith Stein's features as other than watchful. And when she was startled, as now with the entrance of Hilda, the maid, her face seemed to close like a trap, shutting off her mind from any prying eyes.

Hilda was in a state of some agitation. "A visitor, madame," she stammered. "There is a gentleman."

"A gentleman?" Ruth frowned at her.

"To see Mademoiselle Judith." Hilda gave a nervous half curtsey, and cast a fearful glance at Judith. "It is Prince Peter Borodin."

There was a moment of absolute silence, then Judith and her parents rose together. "The Prince is *here*?" Ruth asked.

"Yes, madame. And asking—"

"But, isn't he—" Judith stopped, her mouth still open, as Peter Borodin himself filled the doorway behind the maid. Rachel had seen him before; he had called at the Moscow house more than once, before Judith's arrest. She had then thought him the most elegant of men. Now, even after three years' banishment to his estate in Starogan, a punishment for his assault on Rasputin, Rachel could find no reason to alter her opinion. He wore civilian clothes; according to Judith, he was even more elegant in uniform. But in his pale gray suit, with the crisp white collar and the diamond pin piercing his tie, he might have stepped straight from the pages of a fashion magazine. Not that it would have mattered had he worn sacking, like Judith's. He had the height of all the Borodins, and the Borodin pale blond hair. His features were big and bold, his mustache a gentle fair wisp on his upper lip. His eyes were pale blue, his tanned complexion evidence of the open-air life he enjoyed in the South. And he was smiling. When he smiled, Peter Borodin was not only elegant, he was handsome.

"Madame Stein," he said, and kissed both of Ruth's hands. "Monsieur," he greeted Jacob. He gave a brief smile to both Rachel and Joseph, glanced at Dora Ulyanova, and then concentrated on Judith. "An amnesty extends even to princes, Judith," he said.

"I'm so glad," Judith said, and Rachel was amazed to observe a tear trickling down her cheek, where none had escaped earlier. "I'm so glad."

He held her hands, kissed them, did not release them.

"Yes," Ruth said. "Well, I'm sure you have lots to talk about. We'd better see about supper. Rachel, you'll assist me. Joseph, Mademoiselle Ulyanova . . ." She ushered them from the room, into the hallway, and closed the door.

They gazed at each other.

"Judith," he said.

"Your excellency."

"Peter," he suggested.

"Peter," she agreed, and watched him lean towards her. He held her shoulders lightly, and when she turned up her face, kissed her softly on the lips. He had kissed her like that before; it was the only way he had ever touched her. He had wanted to do more, but because he was Prince Peter Borodin he had always waited for her invitation. And because she was Mademoiselle Judith Stein she had always refused him.

They had known each other for seven years. He had met her for the first time in his sister's house in Moscow, when Ilona had still been the Princess Roditcheva, and when she had been dabbling, in her own way, in socialism. Ilona was not and had never been a socialist, but she had, for a brief period in her life, considered it important to understand the socialists, and perhaps help them, much as she considered it necessary to understand and help the poor and the sick. Her well-meaning fumblings had brought disaster on the Moscow Socialist Party, and ultimately on herself, but from the ashes she had climbed as resplendent as ever, triumphing over every obstacle. That was because she was Ilona Borodina—and because she had managed to suppress her upbringing and her morals and her religion and run away with the man she loved.

Judith Stein had been able to make herself do none of those things, and so her disasters had merely accumulated. Prince Peter had met her, and had wanted her. Judith had not supposed then that love came into it at all. She had been an attractive girl, and he had been an attractive young man whose marriage had reached a crisis. He had invited her to his bed and she had refused. She had supposed that to be the end of the matter, but when her world had collapsed in the debris left by Mordka Bogrov and Michael Nej's insane attempt to set Russia on fire, Prince Peter had come to her rescue. He had persuaded the tsar to commute her death sentence to exile, even though he himself was already disgraced for his assault on Rasputin, and must have known that he could only complete his social obliteration by taking on the defense of a Jewish anarchist. She had thought then, as the train had carried her away from St. Petersburg into the snowbound wastes of Irkutsk, that she had been an utter fool. Had she said yes to Prince Peter in 1907, she would have known nothing but wealth and comfort, however much her parents and friends, her own conscience, might have despised her.

And now he was back, and he thought she was still simply Mademoiselle Judith Stein, because he was still Prince Peter Borodin. His exile had been spent on his family estate, not in Siberia. He could know nothing of what she had endured, must *never* know, if he were to continue to want her. Or would he want her all the more? She had never been able to decide what he really felt for her. Curiosity, certainly, because she was a handsome middle-class Jewess, and also a radical. Lust, she supposed. And now, male possessiveness; he *had* saved her life, and even though she had always refused him, he had no reason to believe she had accepted anyone else.

Did any of those things relate to love? And was that important? Even if he had not been married, a Russian prince could never wed a Jew.

But was *that* important, to a Judith Stein who had been to Siberia and come back again, to a world composed of frightened mothers, of men like Prince Roditchev, and only one Prince of Starogan?

"Momma," Jacob Stein said.

"She is a woman," Ruth insisted. "She is no longer a girl. And he is a prince."

"A married man," Jacob said. "And he is not Jewish."

"Separated from his wife," Ruth said, ignoring the other remark.

"But not divorced."

"There has been no reason for a divorce, up to now," Ruth pointed out.

Jacob Stein chewed his lip in indecision.

"Marriage. Divorce," Joseph said contemptuously. "What do they matter? They are lovers. They have been lovers for years. *That* is what matters."

"No," his father said. "They were never lovers. Judith swore it to me. He asked her, but she refused. My Judith has always been a good girl."

"She hates him," Dora Ulyanova said softly. "He is a prince. Judith hates all princes."

The Steins looked from one to the other.

"Well," Ruth said. "We cannot just stand here. Rachel, you'll show Mademoiselle Ulyanova to the spare room. Poppa, we'll go to the study. Joseph . . ."

"Oh, I'll go out," Joseph said. "I agree with Dora. I'm not

all that fond of . . ." His voice died as the drawing-room door opened.

The prince came out. Earlier he had been smiling; now he was beaming. "A very brief call, Madame Stein," he said. "I am sorry. The next time I will stay longer. Monsieur Stein. Joseph, Rachel." Once again he looked at Dora in slight bewilderment, then turned back to Judith, standing at his side. "My car will call for you," he said. "Two weeks from Monday. Until then."

The front door closed behind him. The family stared at one another.

"Two weeks from Monday?" Ruth asked.

"The Prince has invited me down to Starogan."

"Starogan?" her father cried.

"But . . . oh my darling Judith," Ruth said, holding out her hands. "You cannot go. You—"

"He has invited Rachel as well, Momma," Judith said quietly.

"Me?" Rachel cried with joy.

"So we will be chaperones for each other. It is to be a great party. His sister Tatiana is going to be twenty-one."

"Invited to Starogan," Rachel said dreamily. Surely this *was* a dream. Places like Starogan did not really exist, for people like Rachel Stein.

"And you have said yes?" Dora demanded.

Judith met her gaze. "Yes," she said. "I have accepted."

"To go to Starogan. To go to his home. To meet his family and his friends. You will do that?"

"Yes," Judith said.

"And become his mistress," Dora said contemptuously. "That is what will happen, you know. You may have refused him before. But if you are going to Starogan, he will ask you again, and you will not refuse. Not there."

Judith's cheeks had turned pink, but she met her friend's gaze, and she could look her mother and her father in the eye as well. "Yes," she said. "I refused him before. And went to Siberia. If he asks me again, I will say yes."

The conductor knocked on the compartment door and slid it open. "Good afternoon, ladies," he said. "Our next stop will be Starogan. It will be a brief stop, so I would ask you to be ready." He sounded like a schoolmaster, Rachel thought. No doubt he disapproved of them. Two young ladies, traveling by themselves, and Jews into the bargain, using a first-class sleeping compartment, and on the instructions of the prince of Starogan . . . not for the first time, she felt like sticking out her tongue at him.

But she didn't, because he represented authority, and Poppa had always told her to respect authority, even when it was puffed up and absurd. Besides, she was far too excited to be annoyed. She had been in a state of excitement for the past two weeks. Starogan! The seat of the Princes Borodin for more than three hundred years. And she was going there. Preparing their clothes had been like preparing a trousseau, especially since everyone knew that they *were* preparing a trousseau, of sorts, for Judith. But that was unmentionable, because everyone also knew that no Prince of Starogan would ever *marry* a Jew.

The mere fact that they were making the journey was unbelievable enough. Unbelievable that Momma and Poppa had agreed. But how could they do otherwise? Judith was twenty-five years old. Judith had spent weeks in General Prince Roditchev's torture chamber. And Judith had spent three years in a labor camp. There was no one in all the world, and certainly not in her own family, who could now tell Judith what to do with her life. Dora Ulyanova had tried, and she probably knew Judith better than anyone, now. But Judith had merely invited her to come with them, and Dora had silently given up. Momma and Poppa could only hope, and pray, and perhaps count on Rachel being always underfoot.

But of course Momma and Poppa's reaction was more complicated than a mere surrender to the inevitable. For all his life Jacob Stein had fought to overcome the stigma of being a Jew. Slowly and surely he had first qualified as a lawyer, and then pushed his way up in the ranks of that profession. He had escaped the pale of settlement and had entered into a comfortable middle-classdom. He had succeeded, only to see all his achievements ripped away from him upon the arrest of his daughter as an anarchist. But he had not accepted his fate; he had changed cities and painfully started the climb once more, knowing all the while that true success was now an impossible goal. Even as a member of the Duma, the leaden weight of Judith's crime would be hung around his neck forever.

Now that was not so certain. Judith Stein might be a convicted anarchist, but she was going to be a guest at Tatiana Borodina's twenty-first birthday party. There was no princely family in all Russia superior in rank to the Borodins. Until Prince Peter had quarreled with Tsar Nicholas, the Borodins had been intimate friends of the Romanovs themselves. And now that his banishment was officially over, who could doubt that they would be friends again? All those who would detract from Jacob Stein's achievements, and sneer behind his back, now had come to terms with this simple fact; his daughter was a close friend of the prince of Starogan. Whether she was more than that could be left to speculation; her connection to the prince could only increase the envy of others. No, Jacob Stein would never make more than a token opposition to such a stroke of good fortune. Why, Rachel thought, had Judith not returned, had Prince Peter invited *her* instead, Poppa would still probably have said yes. The thought made her feel almost faint.

But she was too excited to feel faint. After the clothes and the preparations, there had been the journey. She had been on only one long train journey before, when the family had moved from Moscow to St. Petersburg, and that had been merely an overnight trip. Now they had spent two nights on the train, and in a first-class carriage too, surrounded by plush leather and brocade curtains, with washbasins in every compartment, and the conductor constantly serving cups of steaming tea from the samovar he kept bubbling away at the end of the corridor. She wondered what Judith thought of it all; this sort of living could soon be hers for life. But Rachel's hope that such a journey might bring alive the intimacy of true sisters had quickly faded. They had never been intimate. Now Judith was more than ever a stranger. When Rachel talked of what they might expect to find in Starogan, Judith only smiled. When Rachel turned the conversation even vaguely to the past, Judith merely closed her eyes. Had it not been for the excitement of their destination, the journey would have been downright boring.

But now they were here. Rachel knelt on the chair to peer out of the window as the train started to slow, and was disappointed at the size of the place. This was a fair-sized village, but still a village like any of the others they had passed through during the morning, and it was surrounded by the same waving fields of wheat. She had supposed that a trip to the far south meant they would reach the seaside, but there was only a river, brown and sluggish.

"Brush your hair, do," Judith commanded, inspecting herself in the mirror and adjusting her hat, a huge brimmed straw that flopped over one eye.

Rachel hastily obeyed, then put on her own hat, another straw, although considerably smaller. She nearly fell over as the train came to a halt. Almost immediately there came another tap on their door; Judith opened it and saw Prince Peter himself.

"Your excellency." Judith gave a half curtsey, and in turn had her hands seized and kissed.

"At last, my dear Judith," he said. "I've wanted to show you Starogan for so long." He looked past her at Rachel. "Did you have a good journey?"

"Oh, it was marvelous," Rachel said, wondering if he was going to kiss her hands as well. But he merely smiled, and stepped back to allow them out of the compartment, into a corridor at once filled with people and yet all theirs, because everyone was making room for the prince of Starogan.

Judith hesitated. "Our bags . . ."

"Will be looked after. Ivan Nikolaievich, you'll see to the ladies' things. Judith, this is Ivan Nej, the son of my steward."

The young man was not a great deal older than herself, Rachel estimated, and was of medium height and stockily built. His features were regular enough, but were distorted by the spectacles that gleamed in the sunlight drifting through the windows and gave his entire expression a look of slyness. Now he bobbed his head and touched his peaked cap, but as she turned away from him, Rachel could feel his eyes on her back; she had a sudden irrational suspicion that he could see right through her gown, and even through her petticoats to her flesh.

"That's not Michael Nej's brother?" Judith whispered.

"I'm afraid it is," Prince Peter agreed. "But Ivan is an entirely different sort."

Rachel wanted to turn her head to look at the man again. Michael Nej, the terrorist, the assassin. And here she was, meeting his brother.

"My car is waiting," Peter said, stepping onto the platform, and holding Judith's hand to assist her. Rachel waited, but it was the station master who helped her down. Then she was hurrying across the old wooden boards of the platform, past the gazes of the locals gathered to watch the arrival and departure of the train, wondering if she should smile at them or ignore them altogether, as Judith was doing.

"It's lovely, really," Prince Peter was saying. "If only for the peace of it."

He was apologizing for his village, Rachel realized. To Judith. And then she was distracted by another official who was waiting to hand her down the steps at the rear of the platform. She realized she had never before truly understood the meaning of the word servants. Her parents had a butler, three maids, and a cook. But service stopped at the front door. Nor had she ever fully appreciated the meaning of the word wealth; there was a Rolls-Royce, almost as big as the carriage they had just left, with a uniformed chauffeur sitting rigidly behind the wheel. He did not step down to assist them or to handle baggage; there were valets and porters to do that.

The car door was opened, and Rachel was being seated first. Of course this was so that Judith would have to sit in the middle, next to Prince Peter. Rachel settled herself and watched the crowd of onlookers touching their foreheads as the prince drove out of the yard, leaving the hissing, gasping train behind, with its rows of equally curious faces at the windows. She looked for Ivan Nej, and saw him marshaling the porters as their bags were placed on a pony cart. She discovered that he was looking at her. Or at least at the car. Hastily she leaned back again.

"How far is it to the house?" she asked.

"It's just there," Prince Peter said, pointing through the windshield.

The road stretched away from the village in a straight line of yellow dust, presently still, but Rachel could imagine what it might be like should a wind spring up. The wheat waved to either side, shutting out any view there might have been, but ahead of them she could see the roof of a very large house, made of wood. It was a rectangular box four stories high, with verandas surrounding the ground floor, and great windows above to let in all possible light and air. but yet without any spark of originality in its design.

The wheat ended with some suddenness, and the river suddenly appeared again, beside the road. Now they were driving through an orchard of apple trees, and beyond there were lawns and more trees. These were peacefully beautiful. But always the house loomed larger and larger, towering above the landscape. Now she could see the outbuildings, the stables and the kitchens—built away from the main structure to lessen the risk of fire—the servants' houses, and even the farm, which lay about a mile farther on.

The car stopped at the foot of the curving front staircase and was surrounded by a small army of footmen, opening doors and bowing to the prince. "At last I can truly say welcome to Starogan," Peter said, holding Judith's hand. "Now I want you to meet my mother."

Rachel could only marvel at the ease with which Judith seemed to climb the stairs. She herself felt paralyzed. She smoothed her skirt, wondering if she should take off her glove to shake hands or not, and managed to place her foot on the bottom step.

There were four people waiting for them at the top, if she ignored the servants who stood behind. At the front, and at this moment greeting Judith, was a tall, fair woman, with features too soft to be a Borodin born; clearly she was the Dowager Princess Olga. Looking at her—at the way she stood, the way she held her head, the coldness of her face—and at the same time attempting to estimate the value of the diamond rings on her fingers, of the double string of pearls looped carelessly round her neck, Rachel for the first time wondered what Prince Peter had had to undergo in obtaining permission to invite them at all. Or was he, as prince of Starogan, immune to criticism by his own mother?

"Mademoiselle Stein, how nice," Olga Borodina said. "And this is Rachel?" Her lip almost curled. "I'm afraid you will have to share a room with your sister, mademoiselle. You do not mind, I hope. But we are going to be very crowded when the others arrive."

"I do not mind in the least, madame," Judith said. "After all, she *is* my sister."

Olga Borodina stared at her for a moment, then turned. "This is the Dowager Princess Marie."

Rachel hoped she was going to be able to remember all the names, and the titles. But Judith had at least explained the family to her. Marie Borodina was over eighty, a small, wizened woman who, in contrast to her daughter-in-law, wore no jewelry at all. She was Peter's grandmother, the wife of the previous Prince Peter.

Her grasp was limp, her eyes lifeless. She disapproves of us even more than Peter's mother does, Rachel thought. Oh, if only they hadn't come. If only *she* hadn't come. Let Judith do whatever she wished. But for her this visit had to be a disaster.

"And I'm Tattie," announced the third woman, seizing both Judith's hands, and smiling past her at Rachel. "I'm so glad you're here. I've heard so much about you."

Sunshine, at last, peering through the chill rain clouds. But then, Tatiana Borodina was like a sun herself, a glow of blond beauty. She was almost as tall as her brother, and possessed a mane of straight yellow hair which this afternoon fell free and wispy in the gentle breeze. Her body matched her height, with thrusting breasts and wide hips supported by long legs. Her nose and chin were a shade too large, her mouth a shade too wide, her eyes enormous pale-blue pools. She was exactly as Rachel had pictured her, for she had heard a lot about this young Borodin princess. Both the daughters were black sheep. Ilona, the elder—reputed to be even lovelier than Tatiana—had abandoned her husband and run away with the American (as if any woman could possibly live as wife to General Prince Roditchev, Rachel thought), and Tattie had become one of Rasputin's disciples. But Prince Peter had put a stop to that with his assault on Rasputin, and Tattie was still here at Starogan. About to be twenty-one, and about to enter respectability? It seemed so, for now the young man at her side was also being introduced.

"Lieutenant Alexei Gorchakov."

He was shorter than his fiancée, and less strongly built, but equally fair and rather nondescript in appearance. He hardly looked the part of a Borodin. Or was her family hoping that Tattie would soon cease to be a Borodina, and become entirely a Gorchakova?

"Alexei is in my own regiment, the Preobraschenski," Peter explained, smiling.

Rachel glanced at the two dowager princesses. There was no relaxation of the hostility there. My God, she thought. Two black sheep for daughters, and now a black sheep as a son as well. A man who is introducing Jewesses into the family home.

The brief feeling of welcome she had felt when Tattie had greeted her dissipated like dust before the wind—and returned immediately.

"Come along," Tattie said, taking each of their arms. "I'll show you to your room. I'm so glad you're here. Starogan is so boring. But with you here, it'll be such fun."

Ivan Nej brought the pony cart to a halt at the back of the house, jumped down, and signaled Gromek the footman.

Gromek was a big fellow, somewhat untidy. He was lucky to be a footman at all; his family had always been farmers rather than in service. But it was part of Prince Peter's vision of the future of Starogan to introduce some new blood into the household staff. Ivan wondered how long Gromek would last.

Now he peered into the back of the trap. "Two suitcases," he sneered.

"What did you expect?" Ivan asked. "They are not ladies."

"Jewesses," Gromek remarked. "I was in the hall when Prince Peter told the dowager princess what he meant to do."

"Were you?" Ivan hefted the smaller case. No doubt it belonged to the younger girl.

"There was the most terrible scene," Gromek said, taking the other bag. "Give me that."

"I'll take it," Ivan said.

"You?" Gromek frowned at him. Everyone knew that Ivan had been tried as a footman, without success. His hands had always been dirty, and he lacked proper respect. And besides, there was that business about his brother running away to become an anarchist and start killing people. So even if old Nikolai Nej was the most senior domestic on the entire estate, his sons were of no account. Ivan had no business in the house at all. But he was a difficult man to argue with. Gromek shrugged. "Suit yourself."

They climbed the staircase, entered the back hall. The huge house was quiet, any noise deadened by the gentle whisper of the breeze. And then suddenly, like the sweetest of chimes, the sound of a woman's laughter rippled through the stillness.

The two servants exchanged glances. "Tattie," Gromek remarked.

Ivan did not need to be told. But for the probability that he would see Tatiana Borodina, he would have left the suitcases to Gromek. Now, as he followed him up the back stairs, his heart began to pound pleasantly. It was all a dream, of course. But then, he had dreamed all his life about one or other of the two Borodin girls. And who was to say dreams could not come true?

They reached the landing, and the sound of the girls' voices was closer. Gromek marched along the corridor, his feet dull in the thick pile carpet. He paused at the bedroom door, but did not immediately knock. Gromek, like all servants, was a gatherer of trifles.

Ivan stood at his shoulder. "Well," Tatiana was saying. "He's all right, I suppose. I have to marry someone, so it might as well be him. And he lives in St. Petersburg. Can you imagine? I'll be going back to St. Petersburg. Peter hasn't let me go there for three years. But now he can't stop me." A giggle followed. "I'll be able to see you too. Peter won't *want* to stop me doing that."

Gromek glanced at Ivan, and then knocked.

"Come in," Tatiana called.

Gromek opened the door and stepped inside. Ivan followed him, gazing at the three young women. They made a considerable contrast. The elder Stein sister looked patient and determined. She knew she should not be here, but she was here, and she was going to enjoy it. Ivan wondered what Prince Peter saw in her. She was not what he'd call pretty. Her features were too large and too solemn, and her eyes were too opaque. She was not half as good looking as her little sister, and besides, she had spent three years in a labor camp. Would any man, especially a man like Prince Peter, who could have any woman in Russia, really want someone who had spent three years in a labor camp? The younger Stein girl was obviously still terrified by her surroundings, as she had been terrified when she had alighted from the train. But she was pretty, and she was young, and she was eager, and she had not spent three years in a labor camp. She might even be worth dreaming about. But not when he could look at Tattie, and dream of her.

"Put them over there," Tattie said, and turned back to resume her conversation. He did not really exist, for Tatiana Borodina. He was Ivan Nikolaievich, and he had been around since the day she was born. He was about as important as the paint on the walls. In that sense Tattie was not at all like her sister. Ilona, for all her beauty and her air of complete self-control, had always been anxious to be friends with everyone, including her servants. She would even pass the time of day with him, occasionally. But Tattie did not really require friends; Tattie existed in a private world of her own, a world typified by the chaotic music she delighted in playing to annoy her mother,. just as the way she was gushing over these Jewish women was also obviously intended to annoy her mother. It was impossible to say what went on in Tattie's private world, but Ivan was not troubled about that. He had his own private world, in which only he and Tattie existed. And he did not want to love, or be loved. He wanted to possess. To have all that golden beauty at the disposal of his every whim, the way General Prince Roditchev had once had Ilona.

Since that could only happen in a dream—barring an earthquake or some other unimaginable catastrophe—he did not require friends either. The dreams were enough. He put down the suitcase and backed from the room, watching her, as she smiled, and laughed, and talked about her forthcoming marriage.

Chapter 2

"WAKE UP, DO," JUDITH SAID, SHAKING RACHEL'S SHOULDER. "You can't lie abed the whole day. The grand duke arrives this morning."

Rachel sat up. She had actually been awake for some time, but had preferred to lie in bed, listening to the sounds of the estate coming to life. Starogan! And she had slept here.

She had forgotten all about the grand duke.

Judith was filling the basin with water from the china ewer, cleaning her teeth and splashing. "And you'll never guess who's coming as well. They should be here by tomorrow. George Hayman and Ilona."

Rachel hung her legs out of the bed; it was very high off the floor. "Do you know them?"

"I knew Ilona once, quite well. I've never met George Hayman. But I've heard enough about him. He quarrelled with Peter when he tried to run off with Ilona, and the family turned against him, but it seems that Peter, at least, is willing to forget and forgive. You're going to meet the whole family, Rachel."

Rachel thrust her fingers deep into her mass of curling dark hair, and rubbed her scalp. "I don't think they like us. The family, I mean."

Judith turned round to look at her as she dried her façe and hands. "Well, of course they don't. We're Jews."

"Then why have we come?"

"Because Prince Peter likes us. And so does Tattie. And so will Ilona."

Rachel got out of bed, and paused in dismay as Judith gathered her nightgown at her shoulders, lifted it over her head, and then threw in onto the other bed. She had never seen another person naked. Not even Judith, when they had been girls together. Momma said nakedness was a sin.

"And I think George Hayman will like us too," Judith said, "if Ilona does." She seized her brush and began to draw it through her hair, which was long and dark and straight. Her muscles quivered with the movement, her breasts trembled. She was a strong woman. Rachel did not know where to look, so she lay down again and looked at the ceiling. "You want to be nice to Mr. Hayman, Rachel," Judith went on. "If you ever wish to go to America, he's the man to know."

"Why should I wish to go America?" Rachel asked. She had never confided her dream to anyone.

"What is there to stay here for?"

Rachel raised herself on her elbow without meaning to. But the immediate crisis was past. Judith had stopped brushing her hair and was stepping into her drawers. But she had changed. Oh, she had changed. And yet, what Rachel wanted to ask was easier because of the change.

"I thought you *were* staying here. With Prince Peter," she said.

Judith gave her a glance, dropped her first petticoat over her head, was proper again. "I haven't made up my mind."

"Has he asked you?"

"When do you suppose he has had the time to do that?"

Rachel lay down again. That was perfectly true. She had been puzzled at dinner last night, however. Peter had been perfectly polite to everyone, including herself, and after dinner they had sat and listened to Tattie playing Chopin's nocturnes—she played quite beautifully, as well as any professional—and then they had gone to bed. Prince Peter had not invited Judith to go for a walk or to sit on the veranda, or anything. Rachel had not understood that at all.

"Prince Peter will say something when he is ready," Judith said, smoothing her skirt. "When he has seen me in his family surroundings, perhaps. He is like that. He thinks about things very carefully before he acts. And you want to remember that he is seeing you, too, in his family surroundings. So you'd better get up and dress."

She is waiting, as if it were a business transaction, Rachel thought as she obeyed, carefully putting on her underclothes before she took off her nightdress. But then, presumably becoming a man's mistress was like a business transaction.

"Come on, come *on*." Tatiana Borodina entered the room without knocking. "Xenia is here. You must come down to meet Xenia."

Rachel hastily knotted her tie. She felt almost confident in her white summer skirt and blouse, because Tatiana was similarly dressed, each wearing a silk tie and neither a hat. Ordinary clothes. When they were dressed like this, no one could tell that she was not also an embryo princess.

"Do put me right," she begged, as she followed Tattie and Judith out of the door. "Xenia is your aunt?"

"Oh, no, goose," Tatiana cried. "She is my cousin. Her father is my Uncle Igor. He's here too. They're all here." She ran down the main staircase, Judith and Rachel having to hurry at her heels. "This is Aunt Anna, Uncle Igor's wife."

Anna Borodina was a large woman, with prominent hips and bosom. She wore the inevitable double loop of pearls, and her hat was a mass of feathers, her fingers a glitter of diamonds. Rachel supposed she had never seen anything quite so vulgar in her life. But she was the Countess Anna Borodina, and vulgarity was irrelevant. Rumor also had it that she was a friend of Rasputin's. *Could* she be? "Why, Tatiana," she was saying. "You grow every day." Obviously she did not intend the remark to be a compliment. But now her gaze was drifting. "And you must be Mademoiselle Stein."

"I am Judith, madame," Judith said. "This is my sister Rachel."

Rachel felt her knees begin to threaten an impromptu curtsey. But I am Prince Peter's guest, she reminded herself. Where *was* he? She held out her hand. "I am pleased to make your acquaintance, Countess."

Anna Borodina's brows drew together in a frown. Perhaps she expects me to curtsey after all, Rachel thought. Oh, where was the prince? There, standing behind them all, and smiling. At her.

"What pretty girls." This must be the Grand Duchess Xenia, Tattie's friend. But not theirs. Xenia was a younger edition of her mother, but possibly even more vulgarly handsome and adorned, with a mass of pale red hair and the most sensual features Rachel had ever seen. "Don't you think Mademoiselle Stein is pretty, Philip?"

Just as if we were servants, Rachel thought angrily, wishing she could stop blushing. And she did not even know which of them Xenia was referring to.

But the grand duke, shorter and generally smaller than his wife, also looked vaguely embarrassed, as he tugged at his somewhat abbreviated mustache. "Stein," he said. "Stein. I know your father."

"Jacob Stein, your excellency," Judith said.

"Of course. Sits in the Duma."

"I think you are very pretty too." The speaker was another young man, this one with Borodin features, decorated by a carefully waxed mustache. He was older than Peter, Rachel thought. "I am Tigran Borodin," he explained.

"Oh, your excellency," Rachel stammered. Why was he not speaking to Judith first?

"And you are Rachel," Tigran said. "Peter has told me of you, and do you know, I did not believe a word he said? Until now."

"Tigran and I have similar tastes," Peter remarked.

"You are teasing me," she said, regaining some of her composure.

"We are both admirers of beauty," Tigran Borodin said, and tucked her arm under his. "I work in St. Petersburg, you know, at the Foreign Office. I do not know how you have escaped my notice. But you shall not do so in the future."

Rachel glanced at Judith, but her sister was looking at Peter. What was she to do? This man could not be serious. He would not even notice her existence, if Peter had not invited them down here. But now she was walking at his side, behind his sister Xenia, and her royal husband, and the Countess Anna, towards the drawing room where the two dowager princesses were waiting. This was definitely something out of her romances. Would it also have a happy ending?

Count Igor Borodin and his younger son, Viktor, arrived in the second car. The count had the family height, but was thin, and entirely bald save for a fringe of graying hair round his temples. He wore gold-rimmed pince-nez, and surveyed the two girls as if he did not really accept their existence. But then, Rachel was relieved to observe, he surveyed Prince Peter and Tatiana that way as well, and warmed only to the Dowager Princess Marie, his mother. Judith had told Rachel the story of how both Peter and his father, Count Dimitri, had been involved in the catastrophe of Port Arthur, ten years before; at the very time old Prince Peter had died, Count Dimitri had been killed. Count Igor must wish that Peter had emulated his father and got himself killed by the Japanese, Rachel thought; in that case the princedom would have reverted to him.

Not that his sons seemed distressed at belonging to the junior branch of the family. Tigran had already begun to flirt with her, however much she might distrust his sincerity, and Viktor, youngest of them all—only just older than Tattie and herself, Rachel gathered—was as unprincely a fellow as one could imagine. "You're Judith Stein," he exclaimed, kissing her on each cheek. "You were in the Stolypin plot."

There was a moment of utter silence, during which Rachel opened her mouth and closed it again, and wished the floor would open up in turn and swallow her into obscurity.

"Rachel is my sister, monsieur," Judith said quietly. "*I* was accused of being involved in the Stolypin plot."

"Oh, I say, I'm most terribly sorry," Viktor said, and kissed her hand. "I'm proud to meet you, Mademoiselle Stein."

"Viktor," boomed his mother.

"But I am," Viktor insisted. "It was one of the best things that ever happened to Russia. Stolypin was a menace. I'm sure his majesty was just wondering how to get rid of him."

Another silence followed. Then Anna Borodina started talking, and continued throughout lunch; she was determined to bury any embarrassment over her son's point of view beneath a mound of verbiage. Fortunately it was a warm day, and grew warmer after the meal, when food and wine dulled everyone's senses. And a great deal of what Countess Anna had to say was quite interesting. She talked about her majesty and the young tsarevnas, Olga and Tatiana, Marie and Anastasia, about the tsarevich, always up to boyish pranks, about his illness, a subject that was rarely discussed. Indeed, Rachel had never been entirely sure whether or not he *was* liable to bouts of illness, or whether that was just another St. Petersburg rumor.

Anna Borodina was also quite willing to talk about Rasputin, despite all the glances exchanged by the men, including her own son-in-law. But there was nothing to be learned from her on that subject. Father Gregory was the finest creature on earth, a true starets, a holy man who cared nothing for money or power so long as he could save sinners from the eternal fires of hell. "And we are all sinners, my dears," she said, looking from left to right around the circle of half-asleep listeners, as if daring anyone to contradict her.

"Of course, Aunt Anna," Peter said predictably, but producing his most engaging smile. "Men as well as women. But Father Gregory is only interested in saving women, alas."

There was another of the deathly hushes to which Rachel was becoming accustomed, while Anna Borodina stared at her recalcitrant nephew, no doubt remembering that in rescuing his sister from the holy man's salon he had actually assaulted the starets. Then she smiled in turn. "Of course, my dear Peter. Are not women the source of all sin, beginning with Eve?"

Another hush, while Peter turned pink, and Rachel tensed herself for an explosion. The day was saved by old Nikolai Nej himself, appearing deferentially in the door of the drawing room. His white beard rested neatly on his white smock, his black boots gleamed with polish.

"Yes, Nikolai Ivanovich?" Peter asked.

"Mr. and Mrs. Hayman are here, your excellency," Nikolai said.

The company rose together, to form an inchoate mass in the center of the floor, while George Hayman and his wife entered the room. Rachel, as a devoted fan of the Baroness Orczy, had already approximated this man in her mind with the Scarlet Pimpernel, and now was not disappointed, for he wore a blue velvet jacket, in contrast to the black favored by Russian civilians, and a silk hat, which he was only now removing and handing to the waiting footman. But his whole demeanor—the utter confidence with which he faced the family, the charm of his smile, his height and breadth and the flawless cut of his clothes—fulfilled her conception of a man who would challenge the Okhrana itself, meet General Prince Roditchev on equal terms.

Ilona, too, was all that Judith had ever said of her, with her almost perfect beauty, her slight air of distraction, as if she were really thinking of something other than the events around her, and the Paris original she wore as carelessly as Judith had worn her sack back from Irkutsk. Except for the tsarina herself, she was the most famous, or infamous, woman in all Russia, the scandal of whose marriage to Prince Roditchev, and subsequent elopement and divorce, was still a subject for whispered teatime conversation.

"Well," George Hayman said. "Don't all look so frightened. We did write."

"George," Tatiana screamed, and ran forward, tears streaming down her face, to throw herself into his arms. "Illy." Her hands reached behind George to squeeze Ilona's.

"Ilona." Peter kissed his sister on each cheek. "George." He shook hands. "We did not expect you until tomorrow."

"The boat got in early, and since there was no train we hired a car," George explained.

"And now you are here," Peter said. "And bygones—"

"Are bygones, my dear Peter. And I'm so glad they can be. Princess Borodina. Will you not welcome me back into your house?"

Olga Borodina stared at him for some seconds, then all the rigidity in her face seemed to dissolve. "You have made Ilona happy, Mr. Hayman," she said. He kissed her hand, but she had eyes only for Ilona, and a moment later mother and daughter were in each other's arms.

"Well," declared Count Igor. "Really. I am amazed you were not arrested on sight."

"Ah, but Count Borodin," George said. "An amnesty is an amnesty."

"And if Prince Roditchev should learn you are in the country?"

"George will punch him on the nose," Tigran said, holding out his hand. "As you did before. Welcome, George."

"Tigger, I have dreamed of this moment." George Hayman found himself facing Xenia Romanova. "Highness."

Another long stare, then Xenia Romanova decided to follow fashion, and smiled. "Mr. Hayman. It must be nine years since we met, my poor grandfather's funeral. You've not met my husband, Philip Alexandrovich."

"Your excellency." George shook hands, and at last arrived at Judith. The smile left his face as he kissed her fingers. "Mademoiselle Stein. We . . . haven't met. But I have heard enough about you."

"None of it good, I'm sure, Mr. Hayman," Judith said, with

the amazing calmness she seemed to have learned in Irkutsk.

George Hayman raised his head and gazed at her for some seconds. "Good and bad is a point of view, mademoiselle, not a fact. I'd like to discuss points of view with you, sometime." His gaze drifted to Rachel.

"This is my sister, Rachel," Judith said.

George shook hands. Why do all men shake my hand, Rachel wondered, instead of kissing it? Do I look that young?

"I am charmed, Mademoiselle Stein," he said.

"Rachel does not follow in my footsteps, Mr. Hayman," Judith said softly.

Hayman gave an almost guilty start, and then smiled. "She may be the happier for that, mademoiselle." He continued to gaze at Rachel, who started to blush.

"But Ilona," Tatiana was shouting. "Didn't you bring the children?"

"Of course I did. They are waiting with their nurse. Come in, Alice, do," Ilona commanded.

Alice carried Felicity in the crook of her arm, held George the third by the hand. But the assembly had eyes only for Johnnie, coming forward in front of the nurse, slowly and shyly.

"Ivan?" His grandmother knelt before him. "Are you really Ivan?"

"Johnnie," he said, in English. "I'm Johnnie Hayman."

Olga Borodina swept her grandson from the floor. "In Russia you are Ivan. Ivan Sergeievich," Olga declared, turning to face her family, the little boy still in her arms. "This is your home, Ivan Sergeievich. I'm so glad you've come back. George, I'm so glad you've come back."

"How could we stay away," George said, "from the greatest occasion in Tattie's life? You still haven't introduced the most important person here."

Lieutenant Gorchakov had been forgotten at the back of the throng, as he had a habit of being forgotten, for he spoke little. Now he was hurried forward to have his hand shaken and his cheeks kissed, while he flushed and stammered his greetings.

"Now," Olga Borodina said. "Now we can celebrate. United at last. All of us. This is the greatest day in the history of the Borodins." Her gaze swept across her inlaws and her mother-in-law, daring them to disagree. "The very greatest. Nikolai Ivanovich?"

Old Nikolai Nej had anticipated her command, and was waiting with a tray laden with filled champagne glasses. Olga lifted one. "I give you, the Borodins," she declared. "May the next three hundred years be as successful as the last."

Starogan! Ilona realized she had, after all, forgotten the peace of it, the feeling of security within the constant sighing of the breeze, the certainty of protection when surrounded by hordes of silent servants, anxious only to please.

And yet, it was different from her memory of it. She had lived a large part of her life here, up to the age of eleven, but then it had been her grandfather's house, molded around his enormous personality. After that she had been taken off to Port Arthur, together with her brother and sister and their servants, the Nejs, to follow her father as he pursued his military career at the very fringes of the empire. When she had returned again, seven years later, it had been in the company of George, but the delicious happiness of those two months had been outweighed by the disastrous six years that followed, when she was the wife of Sergei Roditchev. She had begun to regard her home with mixed feelings, a paradise where nightmares started.

But Starogan *had* changed, in a way that ten years ago would have been quite unimaginable. She continued to hesitate for a moment longer, then knocked on the door, and gazed at Rachel Stein.

"Hello," she said. "Is Judith there?"

"Come in, Ilona," Judith said from inside, and Rachel held the door wide. Ilona extended her arms, and Judith came into the embrace, while Rachel stared at them.

"My dear," Ilona said. "To see you again . . ." She released Judith almost guiltily, and smiled at Rachel. "Your sister saved my life," she said. "From a mob. Did you know that?"

Rachel nodded.

"And then we sort of drifted apart." Ilona said. "But now . . ."

"Why don't you go and find Tattie," Judith suggested to her sister. "Isn't that she playing the piano?"

"Murdering the piano." Ilona smiled, and Rachel hurried from the room. "At least your little sister can take a hint. We'd have had to push Tattie out." She sighed. "Rachel is very shy."

Judith sat on the bed. "She is quite overawed by her surroundings. By being here at all. And you too are amazed to see us here."

Ilona could feel her cheeks burning. "Well . . . I suppose I hadn't realized that you and Peter were so, well . . ."

"Close? We aren't in the least close. We have never been lovers."

Ilona's eyebrows arched.

Judith smiled. "He is testing the water, to see if it is still hot."

"After seven years," Ilona said. "He *must* love you very much."

"Seven years," Judith said. "Three of them in Siberia." She paused, obviously expecting a reaction, but Ilona, try as she might, could not envision those three years. *She* had crossed Siberia, going to and from Port Arthur. It was a bleak, empty country. But life in a labor camp was beyond her imagination. Ilona had experienced cruelty, but never deprivation.

"I agree with you though," Judith said at last. "He is being very foolish."

"Foolish?"

"In bringing me here. Your family do not approve."

"Well, perhaps . . ."

"And you do not approve."

Ilona took Judith's hands. "I do not approve of what he is doing to you. He will never marry you, you know. He will never even divorce Irina."

"I know that."

"But you love him too, so it doesn't matter."

Judith gazed at her for several seconds. "I don't know that," she said at last.

"But . . ."

Judith freed herself, got up and went to the window. "You will not understand. You cannot understand, princess."

"I am no longer a princess."

"You are Mrs. George Hayman. I think that is even better than being a princess. You can love, or you can hate, or you can ignore, as you choose. You see, your world has many facets, and they are all facets of *you*, your personality. My world has only four facets, princess, and none of them is of my own choosing."

"Tell me."

Judith shrugged. "One is the fact of my parentage and my upbringing. Another is the existence of your first husband, Prince Roditchev. And a third is the love, if it is love, of your brother. That love may be able to smother the first two, so I cannot afford to turn my back on it." She smiled. "Am I being too honest with you?"

"I am flattered. And I *can* understand. But you said four facets."

"Oh, yes, princess. I was sent to Siberia."

"The tsar."

They all stood, even the ladies. Rachel held her napkin in front of her gown, where a spot of soup had fallen. Disaster. She had known it would happen. Her excitement, the constant sense of exhilaration that pumped through her arteries at the very fact of being here, dining with these people, was constantly overlaid with this feeling that she was about to commit the most frightful gaffe, either by word or deed. And now it had happened. She had only two gowns for evening, and her best must be saved for the banquet tomorrow. Therefore she had worn this gown last night as well, and the others had certainly noticed. And now there was a spot on the skirt.

"The tsarina."

Once again the lifted glasses, the solemn intonation.

"The tsarevich."

Rachel touched her lip with her glass, careful not to drink any of the wine. She had had more than enough.

"The tsarevnas."

How long does this go *on*? She dared not turn her head to look at Tatiana, seated on the other side of George Hayman. Like everyone else in the room, even the butler and the footmen in their blue and gold livery, she was required to gaze at Prince Peter during the toast.

At last he was sitting down. Blessed relief. But she was not to sit down. The dowager princesses were leaving, followed by the other ladies. Rachel stepped round her chair, and discovered that she was still holding her glass. She hesitated, helplessly, until she was rescued by a footman who gently took the glass from her fingers. The ladies were already through the door, and the men were waiting for her to leave so that they could drink their port and light their cigars. She hurried, lifting her hem from the floor, and certain her hair was coming down. Unlike the Borodin women, she did not have a maid to see to it, and had put it up herself. Now she could feel a pin slipping, a curl threatening to drift past her ear.

She sighed with relief; the dining room was behind her. But

the drawing room was empty. She had forgotten that the ladies always went upstairs first, whether they needed to or not. She scooped her skirts higher yet, gave an embarrassed smile to the two footmen waiting to pour coffee, and ran up the stairs, heels slipping on each tread. Oh, why did I come? she wondered. I don't belong in this house. I don't share anything with these people. My family does not toast each member of the royal family every night at dinner.

She reached the top, and paused, frowning. Does that mean we are disloyal? It was something she must discuss with Judith. But where *was* Judith?

"Boo." Tatiana gave her a hug. "Aren't you *bored*? They're all so *boring*. And it hasn't even started yet."

"You can't be bored by your own birthday, your own engagement." Rachel freed herself and hurried to the nearest bathroom; there were two on the floor.

"I can think of better ways to spend it," Tattie said, following her inside the large room and sitting before the mirror.

Rachel closed the door to the toilet behind her. Now she could relax for a moment. Blessed relief. She peered at the spot on her dress. The light was poor in the toilet compartment, yet the stain looked terribly obvious. Dare she put water on it? That would make it worse. More obvious, anyway. How on earth had she managed to be so careless? But the dowager princess had actually addressed her, and she had been so surprised she had tilted her spoon.

"And tomorrow night is going to be worse," Tatiana said through the door. "Listen! I have an idea. Don't let's go down."

"What ever do you mean?" Rachel straightened her skirt, attempted to repair the threatening collapse of her hair, and opened the door.

"Don't let's go down. Let's go for a walk instead," Tattie said. "Just you and me."

"A walk?"

"It's a lovely night," Tattie said. "We'll go down to the orchard, and I'll dance for you."

"Dance for me?" Rachel felt a perfect fool.

Tattie did a little whirl; her skirts rose and settled again, her hair flopped. It did not seem to bother Tattie if *her* hair came down. "I love dancing. I used to dance for Father Gregory before Peter took me away. They don't like for me to dance. They think it's obscene. Mama has told me so. But after tomorrow I'll be twenty-one. And I'll be betrothed. They won't be *able* to stop me then."

"Does your fiancé like for you to dance?"

"Him? I shouldn't think so. He's the most boring of them all."

"But . . . you're going to marry him."

"Well, of course I am. You have to marry someone, my dear Rachel. And as I told you yesterday, at least Alexei Pavlovich is not years older than me, or anything like that. He's quite good-looking, don't you think? And he's taking me back to live in St. Petersburg. I'll be able to visit Father Gregory again."

"Won't he object? Your husband, I mean."

"He'd better not. I don't mean to have any trouble with him. *Shall* we go for a walk? We can take off our shoes and stockings."

Rachel thought how nice it would be to go for a walk with Tattie, and take off their shoes and stockings and dance in the dust. But what the dowager princesses would say, or even Judith . . . "We can't," she said firmly. "We must go down. I must, anyway."

The evening was fine and warm, and dusk was a long way off, even at nine o'clock. The glass doors to the veranda stood open, and a gentle breeze drifted through the house. Only the breeze made any noise—that and the occasional clink of a coffee cup being replaced. For at least ten minutes after the men had joined them no one spoke. My God, Rachel realized, Tatiana was absolutely right. This *was* boring.

Suddenly Rachel found Tigran looking at her. She flushed, and set down her coffee cup a little too hard. The noise sounded like a distant shot, and for a dreadful moment she thought she had broken the china.

Every head turned to look at her, and George Hayman came to her rescue. "If you people will excuse us," he said, "I'd like to take Ilona for a walk. It's a long time since she and I have walked, here on Starogan."

"I'd like that," Ilona said, getting up. "You'll excuse us, Mama, Grandmama?"

Olga Borodina looked at her son. She was determined to maintain the correct way of doing things, even for the Americans.

"I think that's a splendid idea," Peter said. "I'll go for a walk too. Oh, not with you, George," he smiled. "I'll take . . ." He glanced around the room with an air of indecision. "Judith. Will you take a walk with me, Judith?"

Rachel dared not turn her head. She could feel the gazes all around her, like darting slivers of ice.

"I should like that very much, your excellency," Judith said.

"Well, then . . ." Peter got up.

"We'll come too," Tatiana declared, bouncing to her feet. "Come along, Alexei Pavlovich."

"Oh, I . . ."

"You will not," Peter said.

Tattie glared at him, and it was Tigran's turn to perform the rescuing act.

"You are going to play billiards, Tattie. With Alexei against me and Rachel."

"Oh, but I don't play," Rachel said without thinking.

Tigran held her hand, pulled her to her feet. "We are going to teach you," he said. "*I* am going to teach you. Won't that be fun?"

Judith Stein slowly tied her hair in a chiffon headscarf. She was very conscious both of Peter, waiting patiently for her to finish, and of the footman, standing rigidly at attention just inside the front door. But it was necessary for her to take her time, in order to compose her thoughts. Tonight she would have to make her final decision.

Every word Judith had said to Ilona was true; this man *could* obliterate all the misery in her life, the memory of Roditchev and Siberia. To do that, however, he had to be told. So—was she going to throw it all away again, and for the last time? Only a fool would do that. And when a man is about to make a proposition, which the woman wishes to accept, the greatest foolishness of all is to be honest.

She stood at the top of the steps. "I have never seen a moon like that." It had already risen, although it was hardly dusk, and was setting the wheatfield landscape aglow.

"There's nothing like a Starogan moon." His hand slipped over hers as they walked away from the house.

"There's nothing like a Starogan anything, is there?"

He gave a guilty laugh. "I suppose we feel so." His fingers tightened. "I'm sorry they're all so . . . well, so Borodin, I suppose."

"Why should they not be?"

"No reason at all. It's just that I know what an ordeal it must be for you, to be thrust into the midst of so many strangers."

"I do not blame them for disliking me."

"Disliking you?"

"Hating me, perhaps. I wonder if I should have come."

"For heaven's sake! Well, I suppose Mama and Grandmama do find it hard to understand. I am still legally married, you see, even if Irina and I have not spoken to each other for three years. And when they were young, and a situation like this arose, it was kept very much a secret. But I don't wish to keep you a secret, Judith."

He stopped walking. The glow of the house was faint now and they were shaded from the moon by the branches of a tree. She could hear the whisper of the waving wheat and the rush of the river. She could not doubt that he still wanted her. It was really very difficult to doubt even his love, in view of the public way he was endeavoring to display it. But her instincts told her that his loyalty to her was also caused by his determination to be his own man, to defy society and convention. Because the tsar had punished him for opposing Rasputin? Or simply because he was a Borodin, and this generation of Borodins, the men as well as the women, seemed destined for rebellion against the mores of their ancestors? And did it matter? After all, she could only benefit by his devotion.

"Anyway," he said, taking her other hand so as to turn her to face him. "They will get over their dislike of you, perhaps their fear of you, as they get to know you."

"Will they get to know me?"

"I'd like you to come and live on Starogan. You must know that is what I want."

"That is what you asked me to do seven years ago," she said. Oh, my God, she thought: I *am* going to throw it all away. But she could not stop herself. "Don't you suppose that was a different woman?"

He smiled at her. "Possibly not as attractive."

"Your excellency—"

"Peter."

She shrugged. "Peter. I am a convicted anarchist."

"That is common knowledge. It did not concern me before. Why should it concern me now?"

"I have spent three years in Siberia."

"And are more of an anarchist than ever," he said. "Sending people to Siberia has never cured them of their political beliefs. But I would like to try, using *my* methods. Don't you think you should allow me at least a chance?"

Gently she pulled her hands free. She could no longer look at him. "Before I went to Siberia, I spent six weeks in Roditchev's cell."

"I know," Peter said. "Believe me, one day I will make him pay for that. I swear it, Judith."

She turned her back on him, gazed at the wheat. "I want you to know what he did to me."

"I know what he did to you," Peter said. "You told me."

"I told you that he used his cane," Judith said. "That he took away my virginity with his cane. I want you to understand that."

"Judith . . ." His hands closed on her shoulders.

She shrugged herself free, and walked a little distance away. "Have you ever thought about that?"

"Of course not. It is not something to be thought about. It is too horrible."

She turned. "It *happened*, Prince Peter, to me. Don't you suppose I have to think about it? Four of his men held me down, while he beat me. They stripped me naked, Prince Peter, and they held me down, and beat me and beat me and beat me. And when he was tired of that they rolled me on my back, and held my arms above my head, and pulled my legs as wide as they could, while he . . . while he used his cane. And all the time they laughed and joked and said things to me. Can you invite me to your bed without thinking about that?" She sighed. "And having thought about that, do you still wish to invite me to your bed?"

"Judith." Once again he reached for her shoulders, and this time she allowed him to pull her against him. Perhaps, she thought, it is going to be all right, after all. "Does anyone else know about this?"

She raised her head. But he was only being what he was, Prince Peter Borodin of Starogan. He might he prepared to defy society on her behalf, but not a society which could whisper *that*.

"Roditchev knows," she said. "And his four men."

"They are not important," Peter said, and hugged her close. She could feel his lips on her hair. But she had not finished.

If he would have her, he must have her as she was, not as he still fondly imagined her to be.

"Then I went to Siberia," she said.

"I know that. My darling, darling Judith . . ."

"And since I had been sent there for life, and I no longer had anything worth protecting, I sought to make life as acceptable as possible."

"Judith . . ."

Her lips moved against the collar of his dinner jacket, but her words were quite distinct. "I made friends with a girl called Dora Ulyanova. She was a convicted anarchist too. But she has a quality of hating which I have never been able to achieve. She provided all the strength I had, for a while. We lived together." She paused, but he seemed not to understand what she had just implied. "And then, after a while, we moved in with some young men. That way we could survive."

"Judith . . ."

"I became pregnant, Peter. I have borne a child."

Suddenly the fingers were gone from her back, and she could look into his face.

"Oh, it died. See how carelessly I can speak of life and death, your excellency? Of a life that came from me and is now gone? That is how one *must* think of life and death, in Siberia."

His back was to the moon, and it was impossible to see his face.

"And the father?" he asked.

Judith shrugged. "He had robbed a bank, to add to the party funds. The amnesty did not apply to him."

"But you . . . do you love him?"

"I do not love anybody, Prince Peter. I do not even think I love myself, very much."

His cue. To say; Then let me teach you to love, Judith. Let me teach you to laugh and be happy, to forget everything that has passed, here in the sunlight of Starogan. Let me teach you to build on what you have experienced, instead of bending under the load of it.

For some seconds he did not speak. So there it is, she thought. At the end of it all, he is not a prince—not a fairy-tale prince, anyway—but just a man.

Then he reached for her again, and held her close. "So you are not a virgin," he said. "Neither am I. And you know you can have children. I have never had a child." He held her against him, and she nestled her head on his breast, great waves of relief and happiness surging upwards from her belly into her chest. He had not said the right things, but he had not said anything wrong, either.

If only he had not hesitated.

"Aha!" Tigran Borodin walked slowly round the billiards table, absently chalking his cue. "Yes, that rather sets it up."

Rachel had no doubt he was right. He was obviously a master of cue and ball, cushion and spin. He had more than compensated for her own ineptitude, and at least she had not actually ripped the baize, which was what she had been most afraid of doing.

"Yes," Tigran said again, bending over the white, his cue already sliding up and down his hand like an extra arm. "That red in the far pocket . . ."

"Oh, bother." Tatiana picked up the red as Tigran stroked the white towards it. "I hate losing."

"But you have lost, my dear," Tigran pointed out without rancor. "You have just resigned."

"I hate billiards anyway," Tattie said. "Don't you hate billiards, Alexei?"

"I think you play rather well," Alexei said gallantly.

Tattie stuck out her tongue at him. "I'm going to dance. Come and watch me dance. Come *on*." She seized Alexei's hand and dragged him from the billiards room and towards the back of the house.

Rachel glanced at Tigran, found him watching her as usual, and promptly flushed, also as usual.

"Would you like to watch Tattie dance?" he asked.

"Well . . . should we?"

"She likes an audience. But she isn't very good. She just throws herself about the place and holds her skirts above her waist. It really is quite indecent."

"Don't you disapprove?"

Tigran shrugged. "I neither approve nor disapprove of anything, my dear Rachel. A man, or a woman, is what he or she is, and one must take them as that, or leave them. Heaven knows what poor Alexei Pavlovich will make of it. I sometimes wonder what he makes of this entire family. What do you make of this family, mademoiselle?"

"I think it's very interesting," she said cautiously.

He gave a brief laugh, came round the table, took the cue from her hand, and placed it in the stand.

"Interesting? They are the most boring people imaginable. I am the most boring chap imaginable. They are not interesting. Now, tell me about Dora Ulyanova."

"Who?" Rachel's voice rose to a squeak.

"Dora Ulyanova. Judith's friend. She lives with you, doesn't she?"

"For the moment," Rachel said cautiously. "But how do you know about her?"

"Judith told me. She wants me to give her a job in my office. Judith says she's an expert stenographer. Is that true?"

"I don't know." Dora Ulyanova, working for Tigran Borodin? "You know she was in Siberia with Judith?"

"Of course I do."

"Well, then . . ."

"My dear Rachel, she has been amnestied by the tsar. How can we say, 'Come back, Dora Ulyanova, all is forgiven,' and still treat her as an outcast? Certainly no one is holding anything against your sister."

"Aren't they?" Rachel flushed. "I didn't know the ministry employed women, anyway."

"We are just starting to." He winked. "If they are pretty. Is this girl pretty?"

"I think so."

"Well then, she should do very well. Now let's talk about you."

"There's a limited topic."

"I don't agree at all." Tigran strolled across the room and closed the door. Oh, Lord, Rachel thought. What do I do now? "You're finished school," he said. "Obviously. And I'm sure you're not a stenographer, unfortunately for me. What do you wish to be?"

"Nothing."

"Oh, come now. You, Rachel? Of all the girls I know, you must have the most ambition."

"Do you know many girls?"

"I know of only one who matters."

Tigran Borodin was making advances to her. Tigran, the darling of the St. Petersburg social scene, the future foreign minister of Russia, it was said. If only her brain would stop rushing around in circles. "You don't know me at all, your excellency. And anyway, if I told you what I'd like to do, you'd laugh."

"I won't. Promise."

"I . . . I'd like to be a surgeon."

"A—" His mouth opened.

"You promised."

"And I'm not laughing. I'm . . . well, surprised. A surgeon? A woman can't be a surgeon."

"Why not?"

"Well, think of the blood. Anyway, where would you study?"

"Not in Russia," she agreed. "Not since they've closed the Women's University."

"You resent that?"

"Of course I do. Why should women not have the right to a good education?"

"Because there are more important things for them to do." He came away from the door, and stopped in front of her. She knew he was going to attempt to kiss her, sometime soon. Whether he succeeded or not depended upon her. "Particularly women who are beautiful and intelligent, like you."

"I'm not beautiful," she pointed out. "Nor am I particularly intelligent. There were lots of girls in my class—"

"To me you are beautiful and intelligent," he said. "The most beautiful and the most intelligent girl I have ever known."

He kissed her on the lips. It took her by surprise, and she did not have the time to decide whether to allow him to or not. But she did not wish him to stop.

Rachel peered at herself in the mirror. She had not changed. But why had she not changed? I have been kissed by his excellency Tigran Borodin, she thought, who will one day be Count Borodin, and if, as seems likely, Prince Peter never has any legitimate children, might one day be Prince Borodin himself. And I have not changed.

She gave a hasty glance at the other bed. It was just past five in the morning, and already broad daylight. But Judith was still asleep. Rachel had not heard her come in, in fact, so she must have taken a very long walk with Prince Peter. She wondered what they had resolved. But she wasn't sure whether or not she wanted Judith to wake up, anytime soon. She wasn't sure she could face her, or anyone else. She only knew that she could not possibly stay in bed a moment longer.

But what to do today? Tigran had kissed her as she had never been kissed before. In fact, if that was a kiss, she had never been kissed before at all. Their tongues had actually touched. Had intertwined. But softly, with no harshness or discomfort. Other girls at school had claimed to have been kissed like that, and she had never believed them. It had seemed so indecent, so *intimate*; she had not been able to imagine any two people really sharing their saliva. But now it had happened to her, and therefore it was real. And that meant that everything she had heard about but had not quite believed, was real. Last night, standing by the billiard table, she would have accepted anything he wished to do, anything he might have asked of her. But after kissing her, he had merely suggested that they rejoin the others. Was that because he was a member of one of the oldest and greatest families in Russia, and therefore a gentleman? Or because he was one of the most eligible bachelors in St. Petersburg, who suddenly found himself kissing a Jewish lawyer's daughter, and had asked himself what in the name of God he was doing?

Either way she had been fortunate, had been given a whole night in which to collect herself, to decide on her attitude. A wasted night. But he would have to be faced. And *he* would have decided on *his* attitude.

She dressed herself and went downstairs. Even at this early hour the house was awake; there were housemaids sweeping and dusting in the drawing room, footmen carefully opening the great windows without making any noise, and the clink of cutlery and crockery being washed in the kitchen. The lower part of the house had to be just so whenever the prince and his mother and their family and guests came down. She wondered if she should apologize for anticipating that event, but the girls merely curtseyed to her and the footmen bowed, and she found herself on the front veranda, looking out at the interminable wheatfields, and enjoying the cool morning breeze that swept across the steppe.

"Early bird."

Rachel swung round guiltily, and faced Tattie. "You made me jump."

"I meant to." Tattie wore no tie to her blouse, and no hat either. She carried an enormous bathrobe over her shoulder.

"Well," Rachel said. "Many happy returns."

"Twenty-one." Tatiana pulled a face. "I don't feel any different. But I'm glad you're up early. I like early risers. And I've been the only one until now. You can come with me, if you like."

She was already going down the steps. Rachel hurried behind her. "Where?"

"To the river. I'm going to swim."

"Swim?" Rachel's voice rose an octave.

"I go for a swim most mornings in the summer." Tattie led her towards the orchard that bordered the river. "You didn't come to watch me dance last night."

"Well, I—"

"You preferred to stay and spoon with Tigger. I don't blame you."

"Spoon?"

"That's what Tigger likes doing best. He spoons with everyone. He's even spooned with me, and I'm his cousin."

"I . . . I don't know what you mean," Rachel protested, feeling vaguely sick.

"To kiss, you know. And occasionally to stroke your breasts. Did he stroke your breasts?"

"Of course not," Rachel said.

Tattie glanced over her shoulder. "Well, I don't suppose you have any, really. He adores mine. Tattie's titties, he says. The best in the world." She frowned, thoughtfully. "Do you suppose he ever felt Illy's breasts? I can't imagine that. I can't imagine anyone touching Illy." She giggled. "But I suppose George does. And Roditchev did. I don't suppose there is a girl in the world who doesn't like having her breasts stroked. By the right man, of course."

Rachel had no idea what to say. But in addition to her embarrassment there was total dismay. *Why* had he not touched her? She *did* have breasts, even if they were not nearly as large as Tattie's.

And what would she have said, or done, if he had?

They had reached the edge of the river, screened from the house itself by the trees of the orchard. But Tattie turned along it, towards the wheatfields. "There's a spot just along here," she said. "It's completely private. My favorite."

Rachel gazed at the slow-moving brown water. It was clear enough; she could see the bottom quite a way out. But she also thought she could see something moving.

"Aren't there fish?" she asked.

"Oh, yes. The servants catch them all the time. They're very good to eat."

"Aren't you afraid of them?"

"Afraid of them? Good heavens, no. What is there to be afraid of in a fish?"

Of course. Tattie Borodina was not actually afraid ot anything. That was the secret of her class's wealth and power.

"Here we are." They had arrived at a spot where the bank sloped down to the water, and the river itself had carved a little bay on its journey to the sea, where the current eddied aimlessly before setting off again. It was a place of fallen leaves and clear brown water, and it was completely shut in by a wall of waving wheat, with only the trees of the orchard just visible in the distance.

Tattie carefully spread the bathrobe on the ground, then sat on it and took off her shoes, before pulling up her skirts to roll down her garters and stockings. "Come on," she said. "We don't have much time if we're going to be back for breakfast."

"But I haven't brought a costume," Rachel explained. "I had no idea we were going swimming."

"Silly goose." Tattie knelt and unbuttoned her blouse. "I don't wear a swimming costume. Not here on Starogan. So you won't need one either."

Ivan Nej invariably awoke at the first cockcrow. There was always a great deal for him to get done before the family came down; all the boots had to be polished and placed outside their doors by eight o'clock. But in the summer there was an added reason for getting up early.

He sat up, pushed his hair from his eyes, and reached for his spectacles. Although he was not a domestic, because of his father's privileged position as Prince Peter's steward he was allowed a room in the house. Feodor Geller, the schoolmaster, had been very careful to make sure of that before he had allowed his daughter to marry; no sleeping on the straw-covered floor of some hut, with the family goat snuggling up for warmth, for Feodor Geller's daughter. Ivan's lip curled. If the truth were to be known, Feodor Geller would have insisted Zoe marry him if he had been a pigherd. Zoe had been betrothed to his brother Michael, and had been left in the lurch when

Michael ran away to become an anarchist. Michael's running away at all had been the greatest scandal the village had known within living memory; Mademoiselle Ilona's somewhat blatant love affairs had been a Borodin scandal, not a Starogan one. And thus Feodor had come up to the house to see both old Nikolai Nej and Prince Peter, and point out that since his daughter had been cruelly betrayed it was only right that the remaining Nej boy take her to wife.

Ivan had not been especially reluctant. All his life he had dreamed of sex without having had any; he had always been too shy and too conscious of the superior attractions of his brother. But here was sex being presented to him on a plate, so to speak. And she had been an attractive little thing, round in every possible direction. He had enjoyed sex with her, for a while; he had even been able to stop thinking about Mademoiselle Tatiana.

But that had been before Tattie disgraced herself in St. Petersburg, and Prince Peter brought her home to stay. When she had lived in Starogan before, Tattie was a young girl, all arms and legs. When she returned from St. Petersburg she was a young woman, all breasts and buttocks. And by then Zoe's round curves had dissolved into a succession of jellylike mounds.

He glanced down at her, and she buried her face contentedly into the pillow he had just left. She was an entirely happy woman. Actually to live in the Borodin house must have been beyond her wildest dreams. And if she had not quite achieved her father's ambitions—she had been intended to become one of the Dowager Princess Olga's maids, but had proved far too clumsy—she was probably happier as a laundress; she could laugh and gossip to her heart's content, and had plenty of time to spend with her two children.

They also shared the bed, on the far side of their mother; Ivan would not have them next to him. He had never disliked two boys more, and the fact that they came from his own seed did not in any way alleviate his loathing for them. Short and fat and inept, they took after their mother in every way. But more than that, they were living symbols of the chain that was secured to his ankles. Michael had been able to run away. But Michael had not yet been married. To desert wife and family was a deadly sin, according to Father Gregory in the village.

And yet, he remembered, Princess Ilona had deserted *her*

husband. She had taken her son with her, though. The point was, Ivan didn't *want* the two boys. And now Feodor Ivanovich was actually awake, the little termite.

"Papa?"

"Go back to sleep," Ivan said, getting out of bed and pulling on his clothes. "I have work to do."

He put on his cap, opened the door, stepped onto the landing, and stood listening to the sounds of the house awakening around him, the floorboards creaking as the servants crept downstairs to go about their duties. And not only the servants. His heart commenced to pound pleasantly as he tiptoed down the back staircase, smiling and winking at the housemaids who bustled past him, at the footmen, already wearing livery, setting off about their duties. Fools, he thought. They all considered him a failure, because he had never made their grade. But what freedom did they have to go about life as they wished, when every moment was allotted to duty, or to awaiting the call to duty? He was free as air, to do what he wished, go where he wished, see what he wished, so long as the boots were all polished by eight o'clock.

He opened the back door and stepped outside. From their pen behind the building the dogs barked. They were another of his duties, but he never let them out before ten. He snapped his fingers at them as he passed, and the borzois bounced against the rails and snuffled at him. Then he was round the corner of the building and setting off towards the apple orchard. Since he always came back to the house with his haversack filled with windfalls—a Nej privilege going back to some special service given by an ancestor to a Borodin over a hundred years before—no one ever questioned what he did in the early morning. They could see for themselves. But once in the orchard he was out of sight of the house. He could place his haversack on the ground beneath the nearest tree, and commence to crawl away from the trees and into the first of the wheatfields, with the slow murmur of the river close on his right.

This was the greatest moment of his day, the moment, indeed, on which his entire day, and most of his night, was founded. Having watched Tattie, he could spend the rest of the day dreaming, and when he climbed into his bed beside Zoe Feodorovna at night, he could close his eyes and love her. He still dreamed that one day it might be possible to love the real thing. But as he did not know how that could possibly come about, it had to remain a shadowy dream, which too often left him disappointed and irritable.

He was on his belly now, worming his way along the ground between the stalks, so that if any of them moved high above him it would look like nothing more than a whisper of wind. And then he paused, his heart pounding, as he heard a peal of laughter, and some words. Tattie was not given to talking to herself. Or laughing by herself, for all her good humor.

He moved more urgently, and arrived at the end of the wheat screen. From there he looked at the river, and watched his idol slowly wading into the water, early-morning sunlight glinting from snow-white shoulders and back and bottom, hair gathered loosely on the top of her head and secured with a ribbon, heavy breasts—already commencing a slight sag, even on her twenty-first birthday. The water slowly lapped up the long, dance-muscled legs to dampen the thick patch of hair at her groin as she eased herself forward, lay in the water, gave a few kicks with her feet, and then turned on her back, gazing at the shore.

"Oh, come *on*," she said. "Nothing can possibly harm you."

This was the picture he dreamed of all night, the picture he looked forward to every morning. He had never considered diffusing it with another. But suddenly he realised how narrow had been his dreams. There could not have been a greater contrast between the laughing, voluptuous, pale-skinned and fair-haired goddess in the water, and the slender, dark-haired girl who was hesitantly removing her clothing on the bank. Here were breasts only slightly more than mounds, although the chill morning air was doing delightful things to her nipples. Here were thighs so slender it was impossible to suppose she might ever bear a child. And here was hair as dark as Tattie's was fair. There was no comparison between them, and yet Rachel Stein was every bit as attractive. Her face was prettier, because her features were smaller and more intelligent, and this morning made even more so by the overlay of anxiety as she laid her drawers on the ground and straightened, hesitantly, as if aware that she was being watched. But of course she was being watched, by Tattie, and Ivan realized that this girl must never before have undressed in front of anyone. Starogan was doing strange things to her.

She turned her back to him to walk down the bank and into

the river. But she was as alluringly innocent from the back as from the front, every ripple of muscle in calf or thigh, every shiver of breast or shoulders as the water chilled her skin, every trace of pink blush that raced across the surface of her body, made her the most entrancing sight he had ever seen.

He nestled himself the more comfortably into the earth, eyes half closed. He hoped the Stein sisters were going to stay a long time. He thought he could spend a very pleasant summer, lying here and watching Tattie and her new friend bathe.

"Oh, you look lovely," Tatiana said.

"Do I?" Rachel asked.

"Lovely, lovely, lovely," Tattie insisted. "Doesn't she look lovely, Judith?"

Judith, fastening her earrings, turned away from the mirror and smiled at the two younger girls. "Of course she does," she agreed. "You both look lovely."

About Tattie there could be no argument. She was already beginning to look vaguely untidy, having been dressed for fifteen minutes, but her earrings contained real diamonds, and her bracelets were jade and emerald; Rachel could not imagine what other jewels she was likely to see this evening. She and Judith had had to share the jewelry their mother had lent them. They each wore a plain gold bracelet, but Judith had the gold earrings; Rachel's were costume. And Judith wore the diamond brooch on her aigrette. This was Momma's proudest possession, but the diamonds were small and a trifle yellow and not really very valuable.

So Rachel must rely on her gown, which was pale-green satin with bands of silver embroidery from her shoulder to her hem, across her square bodice, and at the hem itself. On her left shoulder she had pinned an enormous dark-green satin bow rosette, and now it was time to pull on her white kid gloves and wish she had a necklace. She did have a necklace, but it too was costume, and she had decided against wearing it. So there was nothing between her chin and the tops of her breasts. She wished she had larger breasts, or at least more of a bulge. It was something she had scarcely been aware of before this morning.

This morning. Had it really happened? Had she really taken off all her clothes and gone swimming in the river? Was this really Tattie standing beside her, looking incredibly beautiful?

She had not known what to expect after the swim, but there had been nothing to expect. They had merely dried themselves, sharing the towel, and dressed themselves and walked back towards the house, while Tattie had talked about this evening's party, St. Petersburg, about Rasputin—she always talked about him but she never really *said* anything to indicate whether the rumors were true or not. Tattie was so completely natural about everything, it was impossible ever to feel embarrassed with her. And in a delightful fashion this morning's swim had made Rachel feel less embarrassed about meeting Tigran again. But he too had been entirely natural, had merely winked at her once and then gone off riding with Prince Peter and Viktor.

She wondered if Tattie would wish to go swimming again tomorrow morning.

"Lovely," Tatiana said. "You *are* lovely. Let's go down."

"Is it time?"

"We'll be first."

"Oh, I . . ." Despite her lack of jewelry, she so wanted to make an entrance, have them all look at her. "Are you coming now, Judith?"

Judith shook her head. "I'll wait awhile."

Going swimming with Tattie had even clouded her curiosity over what Judith and Prince Peter had said to each other last night. And Judith had not been in the least forthcoming. Judith had spent the entire day in what appeared to be a daydream, except when Peter had looked at her. Then she had smiled, a slow, happy smile. Oh, undoubtedly they had come to a decision last night.

"I'll give you another lesson at billiards," Tattie promised. "It really is a fascinating game."

Perhaps they wouldn't look at me, anyway, Rachel thought as she followed her down the stairs. Why should they?

Viktor, looking uncomfortable in his black suit and high white collar, was already playing by himself. Clearly he was as expert as his elder brother. His cue slid into the white, and the ball neatly cannoned off the cushion and clicked into the red; the red rolled slowly, but surely, towards the pocket.

"Teach Rachel," Tatiana commanded.

Viktor straightened. "Mademoiselle Stein," he said, with mock courtesy. But his eyes were admiring. "Have you heard the news? The Austrians have given the Serbs an ultimatum."

"Whatever are you talking about?"

"Don't you remember the murder last month? The Archduke Ferdinand and his wife, shot by anarchists?"

"He probably deserved it," Tattie remarked. "All Austrian archdukes deserve to be shot."

"Well, there's going to be trouble," Viktor said. "Mark my words. We'll never stand by and let the Austrians invade Serbia."

"Oh, curse the Austrians," Tattie said. "I hate all Austrians. Teach Rachel." She selected a cue from the stand against the wall and presented it to her.

Viktor placed the balls. "You slide the cue between thumb and forefinger, like this."

"Remembering not to cut the cloth," Tatiana reminded her.

Like Tattie, Rachel did not suppose the news was particularly important. Serbia was an awfully long way from Starogan.

"I'm afraid you have to bend," Viktor said.

Rachel bent and squinted along the cue.

"I'll just see you have it straight," Viktor said, and walked to the other side of the table, where he also bent, and squinted back. He's looking down my front, Rachel realized and straightened. She had suddenly become aware of herself as a woman.

"What on earth . . . ?" He straightened too.

"I—" She was flushing, as usual.

"It's very simple, really."

"Whatever are you at?"

Rachel turned in relief, and watched Prince Peter and Tigran descending the stairs. "Viktor was teaching me how to play billiards."

"*I* will teach you how to play billiards," Tigran announced. "After dinner. Rachel, you look magnificent. Doesn't she look magnificent, Peter?"

Peter nodded, but he was not really interested in her, she realized. He was turning to watch the stairs.

"They're coming down," Tattie hissed.

They faced the doorway and the hall and the stairs, as first the Dowager Princess Olga and the Dowager Princess Marie descended, then Count and Countess Igor, then Ilona and George Hayman, then the Grand Duke and Duchess Philip Alexandrovich, then Lieutenant Alexei Gorchakov, and lastly, Judith. Even descending the stairs, Rachel observed, the family maintained strict precedence. And she had been entirely correct in abandoning her necklace. Rubies glowed from Ilona's hair, sapphires from her fingers; Xenia wore emeralds; Olga's rings were diamond solitaires, and Anna's tiara was a glitter of diamonds; there was not a pearl to be seen. Pearls were for day wear. And there was not even anyone to impress; they certainly would not be thinking of Judith or her.

Judith had definitely made a mistake in waiting to accompany the grand procession. She looked almost like a poor relation. Well, presumably she was. A relation-to-be? Rachel glanced at Peter, but tonight he was on duty as the Prince of Starogan, and his first responsibility was to his mother and grandmother.

"Highness." Nikolai Nej addressed Olga Borodina, as the senior female present, and she graciously inclined her head, then looked into the billard room. Tattie hurried forward to walk beside her mother, and they all swept into the drawing room, Peter falling in beside his grandmother, Tigran and Viktor taking their places at the back, with herself and Judith. They filled the end of the huge room—what are we *doing* here? Rachel wondered—while the double doors at the far end were thrown open, and in shuffled the members of the Zemstvo, the village council, and their wives, led by the priest, whose huge black hat almost brushed the top of the doorway. The scent of perfume was quenched by the scent of humanity, although every man and every woman was in his or her best, blouses sparkling white, skirts pressed, boots freshly polished, hair brushed and beards combed, and faces washed.

The two opposite ends of the social scale gazed at each other, while the space behind was filled with the Borodin servants—the valets and the ladies' maids, the upstairs maids and the downstairs maids, the footmen and the kitchen staff, the butler and the cook and the chauffeurs, the laundrywomen and the bootblack—people everyone took for granted because they were always there, even if one never actually noticed them.

The Dowager Princess Olga inclined her head again, and she and Tattie moved forward, towards their people, followed by the rest of the Borodin family. Electric light sparkled from the diamonds and rubies and emeralds and sapphires. What must the villagers think, Rachel wondered, at seeing such gems, every one of which represented more money than the entire village could earn in a hundred years?

With an enormous hushed sound, part sigh and part groan,

the assembly knelt. Cushions had of course been provided for the family, even for Judith and Rachel. But the peasants used the bare floor as they knelt, hands clasped in front of themselves, while the priest intoned the blessing. Incense seeped through the still air, and nostrils twitched and knees scrabbled to and fro, and the responses were mumbled. Viktor nudged Rachel in the ribs and winked. Then all was bustle and expectation as everyone stood, and footmen hurried in with the presents. The Dowager Princess Olga and her son and her daughter, who this day became a woman, moved about their people, smiling and talking, and the gifts were distributed. Rachel found it odd that on Tattie's birthday she should be giving presents to the villagers, but everyone seemed very happy; no one fortunate enough to be invited to the house would have cause to forget this night.

The family was also required to circulate. Since Peter was occupied, Judith took Viktor's arm. Tigran had already secured Rachel, and she was glad to stay at his side, listening to snatches of greeting and praise. The pair came face to face with Ivan Nej, looking uncomfortable and hot in his coat and tie, until he saw her.

"Ivan Nikolaievich," Tigran said. "How are those dogs of yours? I thought we might do a little hunting tomorrow."

"They are ready, your excellency," Ivan said. "May I compliment Mademoiselle Stein?"

"You may."

"Then I should like to say that she is the most beautiful woman in the room."

"Why, Ivan!" Tigran clapped him on the shoulder. "Gallantry?"

"I fear I have offended the young lady," Ivan said. "I will apologize."

Rachel felt her flesh begin to cool. "You have not offended me, Ivan Nikolaievich," she said. "I am flattered. Although I fear you have not looked closely enough at anyone else."

"Mademoiselle Stein," Ivan said, "I would like to present my wife."

Rachel shook hands with the short, plump woman. Somehow she had not imagined Ivan Nej as having a wife.

Zoe Nej simpered and curtsied, and seemed about to speak, when a great rustle passed through the room. Heads turned to face the outer doors, where the throng had suddenly parted to leave a woman standing there, a woman in a fur-trimmed cape over her beaded gown, a woman who glittered with precious stones, whose rich dark-brown hair was gathered in a pompadour surmounted by a tiara that outdid even Anna Borodina's, and whose bold, cold features were arranging themselves into a terrible facsimile of a smile as she moved forward.

Rachel felt Tigran's fingers suddenly tighten on her arm. But she did not need to be told who the new arrival was. The Princess Irina Borodina had come home.

Chapter 3

IRINA BORODINA SHRUGGED HER CAPE FROM HER SHOULDERS. She might have intended to drop it on the floor, but Gromek the footman darted forward to take it. Thus relieved, the princess walked into the room. Her gown had the deepest décolletage Rachel had ever seen; it appeared to be slit to the waist. It left no doubt that she was a remarkably handsome woman.

And a very confident one. "Madame," she said to the Dowager Princess Olga, at the same time extending her arms. Olga hesitated for a moment, then allowed herself to be kissed on each cheek. "I have come home for Tatiana's birthday," Irina announced. "Peter?"

Peter Borodin's face had turned scarlet. Now he glanced to right and left, perhaps seeking Judith, perhaps wondering what his tenants thought of it all, before stepping forward. Irina waited, a half smile on her lips, as he hesitated again. At last he took her hands to bring her close to him, and kissed her on the cheek. He would have stepped back then, but she presented her other cheek. Then she let him escape and began to survey the room. "Welcome to our home," she said to the assembly. "I must apologize for not being here to greet you, but the train was delayed. Tattie, many happy returns of the day, and my congratulations on your betrothal."

Tattie chewed her lip for a moment, in as much indecision as her brother, then she too accepted an embrace and a kiss.

"Dreadful woman," Tigran muttered. "Why did she have to turn up and spoil everything? See how they fawn?"

"But why?" Rachel whispered. "Is she very wealthy?"

"She is not wealthy at all, compared with the Borodins. But she is the Princess Borodina. She may have chosen to live apart from her husband for the past three years, but then, she always did prefer St. Petersburg to Starogan. Brace yourself."

For the princess was moving through the guests, greeting each one, smiling and talking, but sometimes glancing at the little group by the door. Rachel glanced at Judith. She looked mesmerized as she watched her rival approaching. Does she hate or fear? Rachel wondered. Or merely envy?

A movement on her other side caught her attention, and she discovered Ivan Nej, slowly backing away from the center of the room to regain the safety of his own people. He was pushing his wife before him. But he was also watching the princess, with glowing eyes.

"Why, Tigger," the princess remarked. "It must be at least a fortnight since we met. Will you not introduce your young friend?"

"Mademoiselle Rachel Stein," Tigran said. "The Princess Irina Borodina."

"*Rachel* Stein?" Irina frowned at her.

Rachel could think of nothing to say, and looked at Tigran for support.

"Mademoiselle Stein is here with her sister," Tigran explained. "Mademoiselle Judith Stein, the Princess Borodina."

"Ah," Irina said, smiling. "The anarchist."

"I have that privilege, madame," Judith said in a low voice.

"Privilege?" Irina inquired. "My dear girl, you have no privileges at all. Not even the privilege of remaining on Starogan. I do assure you, now I have returned, Prince Peter will have little time for you. And *no* need of you."

Judith's mouth had opened as if she would have replied. Now it closed again while pink spots flared in her cheeks, and she looked at Peter, who had followed his wife. Irina had a penetrating voice, and there could be no one in the room who had not heard. Rachel looked at Peter too, and was horrified at the indecision she saw there, the uncertainty. So she looked for George Hayman, and found him standing alone, away from his wife. His expression was the picture of distress, but he was not prepared to interfere. How could he, she thought, in a quarrel between two women, especially where one was so clearly in the wrong? But why did Tattie not come to their rescue? Tattie was her friend; they had bathed together that very morning. And now she merely observed the scene in front of her, a slight smile on her lips.

"Then I will depart, madame," Judith said, still speaking in a very low voice. She turned and left the room.

Rachel pulled her arm free of Tigran's. "Wait," he said. "Rachel! May I call, in Petersburg?"

Not, may I defend you now? May I leave the party with you? she thought angrily. She ignored him, and walked towards the door. The faces to either side were a blur, and she knew she was about to cry. But not until she reached the hall, surely. Ivan Nej was holding the door for her. Was there sympathy in his face, or amusement? Or contempt? The tears were too close for her to be sure.

She reached the hall, heard the door close behind her, and stood still. Judith was already halfway up the main staircase, but now she too paused and looked down. Not at her, Rachel realized. For the door behind her had opened and now was being closed again.

"Judith . . ." Prince Peter moved to stand at her elbow.

"Have you come to ask me to stay?" Judith inquired.

"I . . ."

"But you do not wish to antagonize your wife," Judith said. "And besides, you have had what you wanted, have you not, your excellency? I have nothing more to offer you."

Oh, my God, Rachel thought, wondering what she should do. Oh, my God.

"You can't leave now, Judith," Peter said. "There is nowhere for you to go. There is no train until tomorrow morning."

"It is a warm night," Judith said. "Rachel and I will spend it on the platform. I spent most of last night out as well, your excellency, and have not yet caught cold. I am sure we shall survive. Rachel?"

Rachel gathered her skirts and ran for the stairs.

"May we beg the use of one of your cars, you excellency?" Judith said. "It will not take us long to pack."

"Judith . . ." Peter said once more, and stepped forward. And then halted. The door to the drawing room had opened again, and the Princess Irina had stepped through. Judith gazed at her for a moment, and then turned and continued up the stairs, Rachel at her heels.

Peter Borodin took another step towards the stairs.

"If you go after that girl now," his wifc said, "you will be a fool."

He hesitated, his hand on the banister. All I have to do, he thought, is turn and slap her on the face. Slap her hard, so that her lip is cut, her beauty is tarnishcd. In that one movement I can send her back from whence she came. Not even Irina would stand for that.

And then he could climb the stairs and regain Judith, prevent her leaving, defy his family all over again. If he wanted to. If he could be sure of his emotions, of his love. If he could be sure of anything.

The death, in rapid succession, of both his father and his grandfather, had pitchforked him into the princedom—the senior princedom in all Russia—at the age of twenty-one. That was ten years ago, in the aftermath of the defeat of the Russian army by the Japanese, and he had been one of those forced to surrender at Port Arthur. He could still remember the mixture of shame at what had happened, and detcrminaton to rise above it, to make Russia rise above it, with which he had come home. And what had he achieved? He had quarreled with the family's friend, George Hayman, ordered him from Starogan rather than permit him to marry Ilona. Why? Simply because Hayman was not a prince. And what had *that* accomplished? He had driven Ilona into marriage with Sergei Roditchev, had realized his mistake and been unable to do anything about it, and at the end, had been forced to sit back and watch while she had taken her destiny into her own hands and fled her home and her family. Was that record anything to be proud of?

And he himself had been married—to the woman standing behind him—had been made to feel like an inexperienced little boy on his wedding night. No doubt he was an inexperienced little boy, to Irina Golovina; she was four years older than he, a sophisticated woman. From that start their marriage had never recovered, and in his misery he had turned to Ilona's friend, Judith Stein. She had refused his advances, and he had watched, with growing dismay, her involvement in the Moscow socialist movement. He had felt responsible for her, for her misfortunes, and when all Russia had been rocked by the murder of Prime Minister Stolypin, he had gone to the tsar to beg for her life. He had already quarreled with Nicholas, over his assault on Rasputin; his support for a socialist Jewess had been the last straw, as far as his majesty was concerned, even if he—or rather, Peter supposed, his wife—had relented and sentenced Judith to lifelong exile rather than the gallows.

After such a record there had been nothing for the disgraced Prince of Starogan to do but return to his estates, and live out the rest of his life in best-forgotten misery. He had been prepared to do that, been prepared to concentrate on his three hundred thousand acres of wheat, his thirty thousand sheep, his horses, his dogs, his motor cars, and his family, prepared to do what he could to alleviate the grief of his mother, to protect Tattie from the excesses of her own nature until he could find her a suitable husband. He had worked at all of those tasks with some success, until the news of the amnesty had acted like a bucking horse in hurling him from the seat of duty and common sense he had adopted. His resolutions had been scattered like so much dust.

Why? Even now he could not answer that question. Judith had never been willing. Had he really wanted a mistress, he could have found someone far more suitable in his own class and his own race. And yet the very thought of her, the memory of her as he had seen her, standing defiantly before Roditchev as that scoundrel had been about to whip her, or standing just as defiantly in the dock in St. Petersburg as the judge had pronounced the sentence of death upon her, could make his heartbeat quicken.

Besides, he had known that, after three years' exile in Siberia, she would no longer refuse him. He had known, without being prepared to recognize why. She had confessed, in effect, to having become a whore. She had even had a child by one of her protectors. She was truly, as she had pointed out, as far removed from the girl he had attempted to seduce as it was possible to be. Had he known, then, that he had made yet another mistake? And yet he had made love to her. After waiting for seven years he had not been able to stop himself, and she had been prepared to accept him. Her response meant nothing more than that; he had known that at the time. They had lain on the ground, on his cloak. It had been dark, and he had not been able to see, and she had not undressed. It had been a meeting of knees and groins, a limited function. He had no means of knowing if she had enjoyed it; she had at the least seemed pleased to see him again the next day.

He had not enjoyed it. He had had to remind himself that it was a first time, that when they were together again it would be in a bed and in a warm room, that he would be able to use all his senses, that she was the woman he had always wanted above all others, and that she was his, at last.

If he still wanted her.

A hand touched his arm. He turned, and faced beauty, and poise, and confidence, and wealth, and arrogance, and a voluptuousness he had forgotten existed in his wife.

"I ought to—"

"Ssssh," she said, and turned her head. Gromek the footman had come into the hall.

"What the devil do you want?" Peter demanded.

"I thought you might have instructions for me, your excellency."

"And you do have instructions for him," Irina said. "Did you not offer the young ladies the use of your car?"

Peter glanced at her. But she was right. If he was not going to climb those stairs, then he must give Gromek his instructions.

"Shall I order the car, your excellency?" Gromek inquired.

"I suppose you had better."

"I shall do it now, your excellency." Gromek bowed, and went towards the pantry. Irina walked down the hall, away from the drawing room.

"Where are you going?" Peter asked.

"I think we should have a little talk. In your study."

He went behind her, inhaling her perfume. She had always worn the most exquisite perfume. "I ought to break your neck," he said.

She went into the room, and turned to face him. "Would that not be a waste? Close the door."

He pushed it shut behind him, and she smiled.

"But I agree that I behaved quite impossibly. Oh, not in returning to save you from yourself. But in leaving you in the first place. I am surprised you do not beat me."

He frowned at her.

"Sergei Roditchev would beat me, if I were his wife," she said.

"I wish you wouldn't talk nonsense," he said.

"I am not talking nonsense. I have come back to you. After three years, I have come back to you. I wish to be your wife. In every way. I wish you to treat me as your wife. I realized that the fault in our marriage is entirely mine. You married too young, and you were confused by the tragedy of your father and your sudden inheritance. And I, like a fool, merely sat back and expected you to be my husband. I should have shown you what being a husband means." She gazed at his bewildered frown, and sighed. "If you won't beat me, then will you not at least kiss me?"

Peter looked down at his hand. Strangely, he did wish to hit her. But he knew he was not going to. That would mean complete surrender. And yet, he could not stand here and look at her without touching her. Before he could make up his mind, she was in his arms, her tongue stroking his, her scent clouding his nostrils. His fingers slid up the soft contours of her back.

Her mouth moved, her lips touched his ear. "I think, my darling," she said, "that I like this punishment better."

The Rolls-Royce drew to a halt, and a dog barked. The sound was taken up by others, and the ripple of growls and woofs seemed to surround them. But the village slept; most of the adults were up at the house, celebrating Mademoiselle Tatiana's birthday.

The chauffeur stepped down to take the two suitcases and place them on the platform. Rachel held the door for Judith. They had not spoken during the drive. They had been spirited from the house by the servants' staircase—at last established in their rightful place, Rachel thought—while only an hour earlier she had walked on the arm of Tigran Borodin of the Foreign Office. There was nothing to talk about.

Although it was a warm night, there was a breeze, drifting across the wheatfield. Rachel pulled her coat tighter as she climbed the steps. The chauffeur had placed the suitcases next to the single bench; there was no waiting room at the Starogan station. Now he returned to his car. He did not salute the two women, and a moment later the sound of the engine faded away.

Judith sat down and crossed her knees. They had changed

from their evening gowns in such a hurry that she still wore her gold earrings. "The train will not be here for several hours," she said. "You may as well come and sit down."

Rachel remained standing at the edge of the platform, listening to the soughing of the wind, and gazing at the wheatfields and the track running through them, revealed by the brilliant moon. Starogan. The most beautiful place on earth, and the most peaceful.

"At least," Judith said, "we have first-class return tickets."

Rachel turned. "Is that all you feel?"

Judith appeared to consider; it was difficult to be sure of her expression in the darkness. "That is all I *shall* feel," she said at last. "It is not a good thing to feel at all, in Siberia. I thought perhaps I might be able to again, but I was wrong. I'm only sorry I exposed you to such a humiliation."

Rachel sat beside her. "Oh, don't worry about me," she said. "I only wish they hadn't been so friendly. Tigran. And Tattie herself. So hypocritical. Not one of them—"

"What did you expect them to do?" Judith asked, her voice suddenly brittle. "They only do what Peter tells them to do, by his example. When he welcomed us, they welcomed us."

"But Tattie . . . I would have said she would make her own decision."

"She is a Borodina," Judith said. "That is all that . . . what's that?"

Rachel was on her feet again, gazing at the headlights cutting through the darkness. "A car," she said. "Oh, Lord, a car."

Judith got up and went to the back of the platform, to stand at the top of the steps. "Who is it?" Her voice trembled.

"Ilona Hayman." Ilona got down and approached the steps. Behind her Rachel saw the tall figure of her husband, also getting out of the car. Her entire body seemed to be suffused with warmth, and she started to cry again, even as she knew how terribly disappointed Judith must be.

"You should not have come," Judith said. "They will never forgive you."

Ilona smiled as she came up the steps. "They've forgiven me for worse. Judith—" she held her friend's hands. "I wish I could make you know how sorry I am. How I wish we could do something."

"It is no fault of yours," Judith said, returning to her place on the bench. "I was a fool ever to accept. I am always being a fool." She shrugged. "I suppose I shall go on being a fool."

Rachel, still standing by the steps, discovered George Hayman beside her. Her very own Scarlet Pimpernel. Why could he not help them?

He might have been able to read her mind. "We can do something," he said. "Not here in Starogan, I'm afraid, mademoiselle. But if there is anything within my power..." It was his turn to pause. "I'm fairly well-known in the States."

Judith said nothing.

"Could we...do you think we could go to America?" Rachel asked.

Judith looked up.

"I mean..." The darkness hid Rachel's flush. "I think it would be better there."

"You told me once you had an uncle in New York," Ilona said.

"If it's a question of money—" George Hayman said.

"I should think Poppa could afford the passage," Judith said. "We would not be traveling first class."

"Judith," Rachel said.

"I'm sorry," Judith agreed. "It is very kind of you. Too kind of you, Mr. Hayman. But..."

"But you cannot desert Russia? Your socialist friends? Your family?" Ilona demanded. "Have you anything left to offer them here, Judith? Have they anything left to offer you?"

"I...I cannot think at this moment, princess. Really I cannot. But I'm grateful. Believe that."

"Well, come back with us," Hayman said. "You cannot spend the night on this platform."

"It is not your house, to invite us to," Judith said.

"We'll manage it."

She shook her head. "We will spend the night here. Now go back to the party. It is Tattie's birthday, and her betrothal. We are the guilty ones, for having spoiled it. You must not stay out here with us."

Hayman looked at his wife. Ilona sighed. "I suppose we must. But Judith..."

Another shake of the head. "No. No more offers of help, princess. We will manage. We always have."

Ilona hesitated, then went to the steps. George Hayman felt in his pocket and produced a card. "You keep this," he said to Rachel. "Just remember you have friends." He put out his hand, tucked his forefinger under her chin, and raised her head. "Just remember."

He went down the steps, got into the car, and reversed it.

"I feel ashamed," Ilona said.

"I imagine most of us do."

She watched the ribbon of dust road unfolding before the headlights. "Could this happen in America, George?"

"Of course it could. The difference is that in America Judith Stein would have been entitled to say, well, if you don't want me, you can go to hell. Here she simply has to take it, and crawl away into the night."

"Will you help her?"

"If she wants me to. And her sister."

"Yes, there's Rachel too," Ilona mused. "I never met Rachel, back in Moscow. Did you?"

George shook his head.

"But you did meet Judith."

"I saw her, but she'll never remember it. Roditchev took me down to his cells when he was questioning her. That night he made me come to your home for dinner."

"I remember. Was it very unpleasant?"

"He was a very unpleasant man. I must say, I was so surprised that he'd want to show *me*, an American correspondent, what he was capable of, I didn't perhaps take in as much as I should. I wouldn't like that girl ever to know that I saw her."

"She's not likely to." Ilona hugged herself. "Why should some people—you and me, for instance—have so much, be so happy, and others, like those two girls, have so little? Who decides that, George?"

"I don't think anyone does, my love. I imagine these things happen in cycles. You know, life must have looked pretty grim to Granddad. Yet here I am at the top of the tree. I suspect the Haymans will go down again after a while, maybe just as the Steins are coming up. As for whether any particular individual is born during a down-cycle or an up-cycle, that has to be luck."

"That theory doesn't hold," Ilona said. "Because what about the Borodins? They've been at the top for three hundred years. What of the Roditchevs and the Gorchakovs? What of the Romanovs themselves? Always at the top."

"Well, maybe when their particular crash comes, it'll be bigger than ours."

"I wish we could all just go upwards," Ilona said. "The Steins as well. George, what are we going to do?"

The glittering windows of the house were rising in front of them, and now the music was starting, the balalaikas and the drums, the cymbals and the flutes.

"I guess, since it *is* Tattie's birthday, we go in and enjoy ourselves, my love. And get drunk. I think that's our best plan."

And try not to think about those poor girls, he thought, sitting on their platform, waiting for the train that would take them back to nothing. Oh, their family might be prosperous enough, but what of their futures? The girl Rachel had not yet suffered, though, not yet been crushed into the ground. There was hope there, as well as charm and looks. Perhaps Rachel would be the Stein to climb the tree. He hoped so.

It was easy to get drunk, as he danced with Ilona and with Tattie, with the Dowager Princess Olga and the Grand Duchess Xenia, and several of the women from the village, plump and perspiring, and then, without warning, with the Princess Irina herself, who was a glow of dark excitement. For it was her night far more than Tattie's. She had returned to claim what was hers, and she had won.

I should hate you, he thought, as she waltzed in his arms, her smiling face only inches from his own. I should hate the whole rotten society that keeps this incredible system alive. But he had thought that before, and wound up marrying one of them. His grandfather had been a Chartist, one of those who had agitated for an end to the British monarchy, the British system of aristocracy and class dominance, and he had suffered for his beliefs. Just as Judith Stein had suffered for hers. That was too easy to forget.

But as he lay in bed that night, Rachel's face haunted him, with its mixture of innocence and bewilderment, of sorrow and anger. He suddenly wanted very much to help her. To help her avoid the catastrophes into which her sister had fallen again and again. He wondered if Ilona would have any objections to that.

George awoke with a blinding headache to see the late morning sun streaming through his bedroom window. The train would have come and left again. He did not suppose he would ever see the Stein sisters again.

He sat up and looked down at his sleeping wife, golden hair clouded across her face, arms thrown in front of her. Better not to wake her up, he supposed, since she would undoubtedly also have a hangover. It must be quite late, though, and he heard an unusual amount of stirring in the house.

He got out of bed, pulled on his dressing gown, draped a towel over his shoulder, and was opening the door, when he was nearly bowled over by Tattie, hurrying along, hair flying and skirts too, for she was fully dressed.

"George," she cried. "Have you heard the news? Peter has been called to join his regiment. Alexei too. They're off to fight the Austrians."

The villagers gathered in the square, facing the railway line. They shuffled their feet, and the dust rose into the still July air. The members of the Zemstvo stood at the front, their wives at their sides. All looked suitably serious. Already the rumors were spreading.

The Rolls-Royce came to a stop, the chauffeur stepped down to open the door. Prince Peter Borodin moved slowly, as if uncertain of what he had to do. He was accompanied by his wife, his mother, his sister Tatiana, and her fiancé. Behind them the two other cars came to a stop, and the Grand Duke and Duchess Philip Alexandrovich, as well as Count Igor and his family, and the American and his wife, also got down. This was in itself a sign that something quite remarkable was happening. Only last week the village had gone to the house to fete these same poeple on Mademoiselle Tatiana's birthday. Now the mighty had come to the village.

Slowly the Borodins climbed the steps to the platform and faced the crowd. Their faces were equally serious, even Tatiana's. The prince advanced to the edge of the steps, gazed at the assembly, and gave a little tug to the end of his mustache. "My friends," he said. "Our country is at war."

A ripple spread through the crowd. More feet shifted, sending more dust eddying. George Hayman frowned. Hyperbole was all very well, but it was necessary to be accurate at a time like this.

"A general mobilization has been decreed," Prince Peter went on. "To meet the threat from the oldest and bitterest enemy of our Motherland—the threat from the blood and iron of Germany."

The members of the Zemstvo exchanged glances. In their

limited knowledge they had thought he was going to say the Turks. The Germans posed no threat, here in Starogan. The Turks were too close for comfort.

"It is a just war we undertake," the prince said. "The Germans, and their Austrian lackeys, intend to invade Serbia. They intend to wipe Serbia from the face of the map, and make that staunch little country—that country of our brothers, my friends—into nothing more than an Austrian province. And that is but the beginning of their plan. After Serbia, all the Balkans would lie at the foot of the conquerors. And so our tsar has determined to resist this naked aggression, to hurl the Teutonic hordes back where they belong. He has asked for our support. No, he has *called* for our support, demanded it, as is his right to do, for is he not our Little Father, God's chosen representative in this fair land of ours? He has commanded, and we shall obey.

"I shall be leaving here in a few days to join my regiment. My future brother-in-law, Lieutenant Gorchakov, will be accompanying me. My cousins and my uncle, and his highness the grand duke, will be leaving as well, to take up their posts in the face of those who would oppose our country. I expect nothing less from my people. For those of you who are reservists, a train will be arriving the day after tomorrow. Take your places. Rejoin your units. And be sure of the blessing of our Father in heaven. For those of you who have not yet had the privilege of bearing arms, the train will take you to Rostov-on-Don, and there you will be recruited. Any man under the age of forty who is sound in wind and limb will be welcomed there, and will be honored by me as he leaves. More, he will be honored by his wife and children, and their children and their children after them. For how better may a man—" He changed his mind about the word he would use. "—serve, than in the uniform of his country?"

He paused, took a silk handkerchief from his pocket, wiped his face and lips. The crowd waited uncertainly, and their priest stepped forward.

"Your people wish only to obey you, your excellency," he said. "But they ask, what of the crop that is soon to be harvested?"

"The nation is at war," Peter repeated. "There is no duty greater than serving Russia in her hour of need, Holy Father. The harvest will be gathered by the old and the infirm, the young and the women. My wife—" He turned his head to look at Irina, standing at his side in an attitude of martial fervor. "—and my mother—" Olga stood on his other side. "—will be remaining here to supervise your labors. The harvest will be gathered, I promise you that."

Once again there was a brief hesitation, while George Hayman studied Irina's sudden frown. Then a young man stepped from the ranks of the crowd, face burning with embarrassed enthusiasm. "I shall be on that train, your excellency," he shouted. "Who will come with me to fight for tsar and Motherland?"

"I will," shouted another. "And I," shouted a third, and then there was a mass movement forward. Women started to weep, and children to wail. Men embraced each other, hats were flung into the air. The square became a place of heated passion. Not even Prince Peter, raising his arms for silence, could command instant obedience. But gradually the noise settled along with the dust.

"I thank you," Peter shouted. "I thank you all. But I expected nothing less of Starogan." Once again he wiped his brow. "What is the name of that fellow?" he asked the priest.

"Rauzer, your excellency. Stefan Rauzer."

Peter nodded. "I shall remember." He walked through the crowd to the cars, looked into the one that had been driven by George Hayman, where Johnnie, not allowed out by his mother, had rolled down the window.

"Will the Germans come to Starogan, Uncle Peter?" he asked. Taught Russian by his mother almost from birth, he had slipped naturally into his native language.

Peter rubbed his head. "No. We shall go to them, Ivan Sergeievich. Oh, indeed, we shall go to them. But no German will ever come to Starogan, I promise you that. Not in a thousand years. Well, George? Once more into battle. Why so solemn?"

"It's a solemn occasion, wouldn't you say?"

"George is concerned," Ilona said, seating herself beside her son, "that you have misled the people."

"Misled them? How have I misled them?"

"It's only that we are not actually at war yet," Ilona said. "Nor, as I understand it, have we yet declared a general mobilization. It is only a mobilization against Austria."

"Oh, rubbish. Where the Austrians go the Germans will

follow. And how old is that news? Two days? By now we are at war. You may be sure of it. What you mean is, George is remembering that Japanese fiasco. Tell the truth now, George."

"Well . . ."

"Things will be different this time," Peter insisted. "That was a colonial war. Colonial wars often mean disaster. What of your General Custer, eh? But this is a European war. The honor, as well as the safety, of Russia is at stake. Why, did you know that his majesty has decreed that all sales of vodka must cease? You will see a different nation this time, if you care to stay and watch."

"Of course he must go." Nikolai Nej dried the tears that were trickling from his eyes. "It is just that . . . you will understand, your excellency, I no longer have an elder son, and now to lose my younger son . . ."

"To war," Nadia Nej wailed, openly crying.

"He will be killed," Zoe Nej cried. "We shall never see him again. Never."

"Oh, I say, please don't take on so," Peter begged. The other servants were looking equally embarrassed; he wished he had started with them instead of Ivan. But the son of the steward had to show the way. "He won't be killed. No one will be killed. The French are fighting with us. How can the Germans fight both us and the French at the same time? We shall simply roll up their armies, occupy Berlin, and make them pay an indemnity. It will be over by Christmas, I promise you."

"Of course he must go." Nikolai threw his arm round Ivan's shoulders; he was disturbed because the boy had not said a word. "Of course you must go."

"I shall expect you at the train tomorrow morning, Ivan Nikolaievich." Peter smiled at the two women. "He will wear a medal when he returns. I promise you." He turned to the footmen, waiting in line. "Now then, I think we can spare four of you. Who will volunteer to fight for his tsar? Gromek?"

The big young man stared at his master in consternation.

"It will be the adventure of a lifetime," Peter explained. "Say good-bye to your parents, Gromek, and be at the train tomorrow morning. Petrov? You too will make a fine soldier."

Two others were selected, and Prince Peter said a few more words about the honor and glory that would be theirs when they did their duty, and then he dismissed them. It was time to serve luncheon.

Ivan watched the door close behind the prince and listened to the sudden murmur of conversation on either side. He was going to war. He had been singled out, just like that, and told to leave the warmth and the security that was Starogan, and march off to war. Instead of lazy days picking up windfalls in the orchard he would be beaten by drill sergeants; instead of lying by the river watching Mademoiselle Tatiana bathe, he would be trapped in a barracks or a tent filled with other men; instead of lying next to Zoe at night he would be being shot at, and blown out of existence. Often he had dreamed of escaping Zoe, escaping Starogan. He had never considered joining the army as a means of escape. As was often the case, his resentment turned to his older brother. Had Michael been here, *he* would have been the one sent off.

When they had been together in Port Arthur, before the war with the Japanese and the death of Count Dimitri had changed their world, Michael had read all sorts of books, surreptitiously, in Count Dimitri's library, and had talked about socialism, about the injustices and inequalities of being ruled by the tsars and their henchmen. Ivan had always been bored by such absurdities. The tsar was there, and that was the end of the matter. But who was to say Michael had not been right?

"Of course you must go." Nikolai frowned as he watched his son. "Do you not want to go?"

"It is not my war." Ivan stepped away from his father and stood against the wall, while everyone stared at him. "It is not your war either. It is a war decided on by the tsar in St. Petersburg, by the Kaiser in Berlin. They wish to fight, for reasons of their own, for their own profit." He unconsciously echoed his brother's words. "I will bet you whatever you like that there is no ordinary German who wishes to fight, no ordinary Austrian or Frenchman. They are being driven to it, just like we are."

"My God, that is treason," said Alexei Alexandrovich, the butler.

"It is the truth. Are you all so afraid of the truth?"

"You are sounding just like your brother Michael," Nikolai said.

"And if you do not go, you will be put into prison," Nadia Nej said, practical as ever.

"Oh, I shall go, Mama. I shall go because I am commanded to do it, but do not expect me to sing songs in praise of the tsar. Why should I not sound like Michael, Papa? He is my brother."

"He is a foul traitor," Nikolai Nej growled.

"A traitor?" Ivan cried. "How can he be a traitor? He killed a man who was stamping Russia into the ground."

"Count Stolypin was the tsar's prime minister," Alexis Alexandrovich declared. "How could he stamp Russia into the ground? Russia belongs to the tsar."

"Russia belongs to us," Ivan said, now realizing that he *was* quoting Michael. "The Russian people. Not one man."

"My God. My God." Nikolai Nej held his head in his hands. "If Prince Peter heard you—"

"I do not care what Prince Peter hears," Ivan shouted. "I do not care what he thinks."

"But you will go?" Mama insisted.

"I'm going," Gromek said. "I'm looking forward to it. I would like to kill Germans."

You would like to kill Germans, Ivan thought contemptuously. What is the pleasure in killing anyone, compared with the horror of being killed yourself? Suddenly he was quite desperate. He had not intended to speak out. But now that he had, he was realizing how alone he was. There was no one here who understood, or wished to understand, the truth. Did that mean he was really just a coward? He dreamed of violence, often enough. In his mental adventures, with Tattie at his side—or better yet, Tattie *and* the Jewish girl—he was prepared to take on the earth, and to deal out death with brutal determination. He had never supposed he would actually have to do it.

"But you will go?" Nadia Nej pressed her point.

Ivan sighed, and shrugged. "I will be at the station tomorrow morning. There. I will go." He went out the back door, slammed it behind himself. I will go, he thought. And fight. And kill men I have never seen before in my life, who will be trying to kill me. Suppose they succeed? Suppose I am to die? What a life. Twenty-six years of blacking boots, of bowing and scraping to idiots like Prince Peter, in order to become a lump of putrefying flesh on some empty field. No, the field would not be empty. There would be other lumps of putrefying flesh all around him.

"Ivan Nikolaievich?"

He thrust his hands into his pockets and went down the back stairs. He splashed through a puddle—it had rained during the night.

"Ivan." Zoe had followed. She was confused. Being a woman, he thought, she could not understand how any man did not wish to put on uniform and hurry away to kill and be killed. But then, she understood nothing about him. She could not understand why he did not make love to her every night, as he had for the first year of their marriage. She knew nothing of his dreams, of course. They could not be shared with anyone.

"Ivan." She caught up with him, and held his arm. "To-morrow morning you are going away."

He glanced at her. She was smiling, even though she was sad and bewildered. Zoe would always be smiling.

Zoe rested her head on his shoulder. He began to walk again, but she still kept her head on his shoulder. "I did not think we would ever be separated," she said. "Mama and Papa, your mother and father, in all their lives they have never been separated. And now you are going away. Ivan, will you . . ." She bit her lip.

Love you tonight? he thought. Slip your nightdress about your waist and put my hand on your mound? Simple to do that, with Zoe Feodorovna. Why, since they were nearly out of sight of the house, he could do it now. There would be no obstacles, even from her clothes. No frilly white linen drawers here, slowly sliding over long white legs, like Tattie's, or smooth light buttocks, like Rachel Stein's. Or even Ilona—he closed his eyes then, remembering the time he had seen Ilona. That had been years before, in Port Arthur, when she was a girl no older than Rachel Stein; he had been passing by when Tattie threw open the bedroom door at a moment when her sister was undressed. For the next few years he had dreamed of Ilona, because at that time Tattie was nothing but a scrawny kid. But after Ilona had run away with her American—how he hated that American—there had been no one but Tattie.

Zoe held his other arm and turned him to face her; they had walked round the stables and were completely isolated. "Ivan Nikolaievich," she said, "tell me you will come back. Tell me you will not be killed."

He watched the happy mouth dissolve into misery as she waited for his answer, the tears begin to spring into the huge brown eyes. When she was miserable, Zoe lost all her looks, and became what she was, what she would be, increasingly, as she grew older—a peasant from the steppe.

He smiled, and kissed each eye in turn. "Of course I shall not be killed. You heard what Prince Peter said. The war will be over by Christmas. I shall be back for Christmas."

"Oh, Ivan . . ." The tears had stopped. He had accomplished that much. But he had awakened that much more. He found himself being pushed into the stables, where there were several stalls filled with hay. "But you must love me, Ivan, again and again and again, if you are to go away until Christmas."

A peasant from the steppe. But even she could feel romantic, could wish to recapture some of the thrills and the pleasures of their courting days, to hoard against the uncertainty of the future. Zoe Feodorovna, who loved him. Why could she not be tall, and slender, and innocent? With dark hair, or yellow?

"You may serve the champagne, Alexei Alexandrovich." Prince Peter Borodin relaxed at the top of the long table, looked down the twin lines of rather uncertain faces, to his wife at the far end.

"Champagne?" inquired the Dowager Princess Olga, seated as usual on her son's right. "Is this a celebration?"

"Well, of course it is, Mama. It is the moment we have all been waiting for. You will see. All the grumbling and discontent we hear about will disappear just like that." He snapped his fingers. "There is nothing like a just war to make people rally behind the tsar, the government, the country." There was a gentle pop behind him, and he waited while Alexei Alexandrovich filled his glass. Then he stood. "I give you, a quick war, a triumphant war."

They rose and drank, while George Hayman studied their faces. They did not really believe anything their prince was saying, any more than George did. But they wanted to believe. How desperately did they want to believe! And did it matter what they believed, or even what happened to them? He had wanted to come back to see them again, because they were the most fascinating people he had ever known. But not the most sensible. Did they really suppose the country would rally behind a small group of aristocrats who treated the rest of the population like dirt? Did they really think the Steins, for example, would rush to serve? In the week since the two girls had left, they had not been mentioned. He could not even tell if they had been thought about. They had been an aberration of Peter's, and now Peter had returned to sanity. Irina had seen to that. In the week she had been here she had not left her husband's side for a moment, and no one could doubt that she was similarly attentive in bed. She glowed with righteous sexuality, and when Irina Borodina did that, she was a very attractive woman indeed.

They sat down again. "Even George must agree that the odds are in our favor this time," Tigran said, a trifle slyly.

"I don't think he does," Peter said. "George keeps looking over his shoulder to Port Arthur. We lost to the Japanese, George, because we could not transport sufficient men and matériel to Mukden in time. There was no other reason. Those were mistakes of the high command. I admit it freely. They took the whole thing too lightly. They did not make any mistakes like that this time. Sukhomlinov is no Kuropatkin."

"I agree with you there," George said.

Peter frowned at him. "Just what do you mean?"

"I mean that General Kuropatkin was at least a professional soldier who had seen service before he was sent to fight the Japanese. General Sukhomlinov, as I understand it, is a political appointment."

"As you understand it," Igor Borodin said contemptuously.

"Ah, but George has a point, Papa," Tigran said seriously. "I too am not entirely happy with the general staff. But fortunately the general staff have to do nothing more than plan. The actual campaign will be conducted by the generals in the field, and they will be commanded by the Grand Duke Nicholas Nikolaievich, God bless him." He rose and raised his glass. "I give you the grand duke, the finest soldier in Europe."

Once again they drank, while the ladies looked from face to face, anxious to understand this talk which only two days ago they would have found inexpressibly boring, and said so.

"Would you argue with that, George?" Peter asked.

"I'd prefer not to."

"But you don't agree."

"I don't see why we have to argue about anything," Irina said. "The situation is far too serious for argument. Regardless of what happens at the end of it, the fact is that we are at war. You are all marching off tomorrow morning. There is so much to be discussed."

"Exactly," Peter agreed. "There is a great deal to be discussed. Which is why I am glad we are all assembled here."

"For the last time," Viktor remarked.

"What a silly thing to say," his mother snapped.

"Well, it could be," Viktor said defensively.

"Alexei and I are catching the early train tomorrow," Peter said, ignoring the altercation further down the table. "The Preobraschenski are on duty in St. Petersburg. We must get there as rapidly as possible."

"There is no possibility that we shall be kept on garrison duty, sir, is there?" Alexei Gorchakov asked anxiously. "And not be sent to the front?"

"Men," Tatiana groaned. "Do you *want* to get your head shot off? If you're in St. Petersburg we'll be able to live together."

"Tatiana!" Olga boomed.

"Well, Mama, aren't we going to get married? I thought that was what we were going to discuss today. Why, we could get married this afternoon. All we need is a special license, and Peter could give us that."

Heads turned to look at the prince, who had obviously not considered the matter.

"I never heard such nonsense in all my life," Olga declared. "Your marriage must be an event, in St. Petersburg, when the war is over. Ilona's marriage was an event." She gazed at her elder daughter with her mouth open, realizing what she had just said.

"Her *first* marriage, you mean," the Grand Duchess Xenia huffed.

"I think, Mama, that in time of war," Ilona said, ignoring her cousin, "exceptions could be made."

"Nonsense," Olga said again. "I will not have it. Peter says the war will be over by Christmas. We'll have the wedding next spring. And if . . . well . . . we'll have the wedding next spring." She glared from left to right as if daring anyone to challenge her.

"You nearly said that if Alexei is killed, then it won't matter," Tattie said.

"Oh, I say—" Alexei protested.

Olga did not even blush. "These things have to be considered, in time of war. Your father was killed on the parapet at Port Arthur, Tattie. It is a possibility I am not afraid to consider."

"He'll be dead," Tattie wailed, "and I'll still be a virgin."

There was a startled noise from farther down the table, and Anna Borodina gave a shriek. "It's the dowager princess. Grandmama. She's fainted."

"Smelling salts," Olga shouted. "Irina . . . Ilona . . . Xenia . . . oh, ring the bell, somebody. Tattie, how *could* you?"

"I only said—"

"There are certain words which one does not use," Olga pointed out severely. "I do not know why they were invented at all. Is Mama all right, Anna?"

Anna was patting the old lady's hand. "I think so. Her eyes are opening. Where are those salts?"

Viktor had rung the bell, and Alexei Alexandrovich had arrived. Anna waved the salts under the dowager princess's nose, and Marie Borodina opened her eyes.

"It's all right, my dear," Anna said. "It won't happen again."

"*Are* you all right, Grandmama?" Peter asked. "Would you like to lie down?"

"No," said the dowager princess. "No. I want to stay. As Viktor says, it may be the last time we shall all be together."

Everyone glared at Viktor, giving Tattie a momentary respite. George and Ilona exchanged glances, and she raised her eyebrows to warn him not to laugh.

Peter endeavored to regain control of the discussion. "We are having a serious talk," he said. "Will everyone just listen for a moment. I think Mama is quite right, and weddings should be put off until this business is finished." He wagged his finger. "If you interrupt, Tattie, I will send you to your room. Now, Alexei and I will be off tomorrow morning. Uncle Igor?"

Igor Borodin sighed. "I think I should come with you. I must get to the ministry. Tigran?"

"Oh, I'll be on that train."

"Philip?"

"I must get back," the grand duke said. He was Tigran's immediate superior in the Foreign Office.

"Well, then," Peter said. "That takes care of the men. Save for George. I imagine you'll want to get back to America as rapidly as possible, George."

"I've been thinking about that." George said.

"George!" It was Ilona's turn to be sharp.

"Well," he said, flushing, "here we are at the start of what could be quite a scrap, and I happen to be on the spot. I don't think I'd ever forgive myself if I didn't write up a first-hand report. I think I should be on that train as well."

"You have a correspondent in St. Petersburg," Ilona pointed out. Now it was the family's turn to watch them indulgently.

"Crawford doesn't have a lot of experience," George said. "No, I think it's my job—"

"Then I shall come with you," Ilona declared.

"Now, my love, you can't. What about the children?"

"They can stay here, on Starogan. Can't they, Mama?"

"Of course they can. I should adore to have my grandchildren to stay. But do you wish to return to St. Petersburg, my dear?"

Ilona blushed as she glanced at her husband. "I don't care whether or not I am accepted socially. I just want to be with George." She smiled. "And I would so like to see it again."

"I think we should make a list." Peter snapped his fingers, and Alexei Alexandrovich hurried forward with a pen and a piece of paper. "That's six places on the train for tomorrow morning. Now for the ladies—"

"I beg your pardon," Viktor said. "What about me?"

Heads turned.

"I am in my last year at the university," Viktor said. "Surely I should join up."

"You?" his mother demanded. "You are just a boy."

"I am twenty-two years old," Viktor said. "All those lads from the village, they're no older. I want to fight."

"Oh, stuff and nonsense," Igor Borodin said. "There are other things for you to do. Leave the fighting to the professional soldiers, and the . . . ah . . . volunteers. We need people like you in St. Petersburg. I'll find you a job in the ministry."

"I want to fight," Viktor said.

"You'll do as your father tells you," Anna Borodina said.

"Still, he should come with us tomorrow," Peter agreed, still writing.

"I shall come with you," Xenia said. "I think it's going to be terribly exciting, St. Petersburg at war. I shall work as a nurse. Yes. I shall like that. The tsarina and the girls will probably be nurses. They are trained for it."

"And you are not," Viktor pointed out.

Xenia regarded her brother as if he were a beetle. "I will learn. Ilona, you worked as a nurse in Port Arthur. You can do it again."

Ilona looked at George. They both remembered the horrors of the hospital during the siege.

"Of course," Ilona said. "If I am required."

"Aunt Anna?"

"I shall come too."

"A full-scale exodus," Peter said, writing. "Well, then, that will leave you, Mama, and Grandmama and Irina and Tattie to hold the fort here, so to speak, with the children."

"Four women?" Olga Borodina demanded.

"There'll be nothing to worry about. Nikolai Nej and Alexei Alexandrovich will take care of everything. And Father Gregory in the village. Feodor Geller the schoolmaster is a good man as well, and you can rely entirely upon the village headman. I have thought of everything."

"Peter," Irina said. "You can't really mean that you wish me to bury myself down here in Starogan just as the season is starting . . ." She paused, and looked at the accusing faces. "Well," she said, "there *will* be a season. There is always a St. Petersburg season. It would be the height of defeatism to allow the Germans to put a stop to that."

"There is too much to be done here," Peter said.

"Well, I'm not staying here," Tattie declared. "I'm going to St. Petersburg. I'm going to be a nurse too, with Xenia. And you can't stop me," she said to Peter. "I'm twenty-one now. So there."

"Now, look here—"

"I do feel, since time is short, that we have some packing to do." George finished his champagne and pushed back his chair. "You'll excuse us, Peter . . . Princess." He waited for Ilona to join him. Alexei Alexandrovich opened the door, and they climbed the stairs together.

"Aren't they impossible?" Ilona's hand strayed into his.

"I don't suppose they're very different from any other family," he said. "Only their circumstances are different. Sweetheart, do you really want to go to St. Petersburg?"

"I think I do. I'm quite excited about it."

"And suppose you're cut by everybody?"

"I expect to be cut by everybody."

"Suppose you run into Sergei?"

"That's hardly likely, if I'm not going to be invited out. Suppose *you* run into him, George? That's far more probable."

He smiled. "Then I'll cut him dead. Sweetheart . . ." His

fingers tightened on hers. "You do understand that I must go, and see for myself."

"I suppose I do." They had reached the landing, and paused in front of their suite. From within they could hear the sound of the children playing. "George . . . there's no chance that anything could go wrong, this time?"

"I hope to God there isn't."

"But you think there is."

"I don't think it is going to be half as easy as Peter supposes. The Germans are reputed to have the finest army in the world."

"So we could lose. Again."

"It is possible that you might not win, again. And what's this *we* business? You're an American now."

Ilona turned away from him and looked out the window. The harvesting was about to begin, and the fields had never looked so filled with food. "What will happen if Russia does not win, George?"

"To Russia? Not a great deal."

"To my family, George."

"Now, that I can't say." He held her shoulders, and pulled her back against him. "They'll survive, my darling. They'll survive anything, if they really want to."

"It's true." Kalinin as usual was waving pieces of paper. "Germany and Austria against Russia and France. Oh, and Serbia, of course."

"What about England?" Krupskaya, Lenin's wife, wanted to know.

"No word on that. Yet. But the rumor in Geneva is that they will sit back, unless provoked."

"The English always sit back," Lenin remarked. "They are the parasites of history, anxious only to inherit others' wealth."

"Well." Kalinin stood before them. "I think this calls for a drink. A celebration drink."

"What have we got to celebrate?" Lenin inquired.

"The war. You always said—"

"I always said that were Russia to lose another war, that would be our opportunity," Lenin said.

"Well, then?"

"How can she lose this one? It is the Germans who are going to lose. Of all the absurdities, to go to war with France *and* Russia. How can she defend both her frontiers?"

"The Austrians—"

"Are useless. Believe me."

"Well, then, the Italians. They are tied to Germany and Austria by treaty. When they come in as well—"

"When," Lenin said. "And if. The Italians are like the English. They prefer to pick up the pieces. No, no, comrades. This war is a disaster for us. The people—even the proletariat, my friend—will march off to war singing songs and praising the tsar. And when they have won, they will sing that it is the tsar who has won, and settle down without a murmur to another hundred years of repression. Do you know why Nicholas sits on his throne so omnipotently in 1914? It is because Alexander I defeated Napoleon in 1814. That is how long a victorious war will support a crown."

"I must go back," Michael Nej said.

"Oh, don't start that again. Here, Krupskaya, pour us all a drink. We *do* have something to celebrate—that we are not in Russia to be conscripted."

Krupskaya got up and fetched the bottle of vodka. Their only real link with Russia, now, Michael thought. But Russia was at war, and they were Russians.

"Surely you don't *want* to go and fight for the tsar?" Kalinin was curious.

Michael got up, thrust his hands into his pockets, and gazed out the window. "If you are right, Vladimir Ilich," he said, "then all of us are wasting our lives. Would it not be better to go back and fight for the Motherland; and in that way try to ensure a better life for our families?"

"No, it would not be better," Lenin said. "Apart from the fact that we would be hanged—you most certainly, Michael Nikolaievich—there can never be a better time for our people while the tsar lives, and that woman dominates the country. We must wait, and be patient. They say the tsarevich is not strong. His father will die eventually, and perhaps his mother as well. Perhaps then . . . who knows. We must wait, and be patient."

"Wait!" Michael shouted, turning on them. "Wait and be patient. That is all you ever have to say. Russia is at war. Starogan is at war. Do you know what will be happening at Starogan? All those men I grew up with will be marching off, shouldering their rifles and singing songs. My own brother, Ivan, will be going, I suppose." He frowned. He could not imagine Ivan a soldier.

"The more fools they." Lenin finished his vodka and held

out his glass for Krupskaya to refill. "I know what is troubling you. You have always dreamed of being a soldier. In the name of God, why?"

"I served a family of soldiers," Michael said. Prince Peter would be going off too, riding at the head of his regiment.

"You served," Lenin echoed. "Why should you wish to serve again? Why should you wish to get yourself killed for the tsar? Or even kill other people for the tsar?"

"I would not do it for the tsar," Michael said. "I would do it for Russia."

"For Russia. That is a boy's dream, Michael Nikolaievich. I am ashamed of you. If you could be a commander, well, then, perhaps I could understand. But to set off as a private soldier being whipped along the road by your sergeant, to be blown full of holes at the end of it—all so that the tsar and his woman can slap themselves on the chest and say, We won a war . . . Not you, you understand—you will not have won the war for them, they will have won the war for themselves, by sitting in St. Petersburg and sending people like you off to be killed. Sit down, comrade, and have another drink, and thank God that you are here and not there."

Chapter 4

THE CROWD BAYED. IT SWAYED TO AND FRO, AS THOSE IN FRONT surged up to the window, pushed by those behind, and then retreated. Umbrellas waved in the air, together with walking sticks. Rachel Stein, pressed into a doorway on the far side of the street, realized that the crowd had ceased to be a collection of human beings, and become instead a single entity, a mob. And there were women here as well. She could not believe it. But the women were the worst. Their voices were the loudest, and they urged their menfolk on. Well-dressed women, who would return home to drink tea from china cups, now called for destruction and even more than that.

"Germans!" they shouted. "They should all be hanged!"

Someone had prized loose a paving stone, and a moment later there came the tinkle of shattering glass. Hans Freiling peered from an upstairs window and shook a fist. The crowd shrieked at him, and surged forward. More glass shattered, and there came the even more sinister sound of splintering wood. It was suddenly overshadowed by the rattle of hooves on the cobbles, the blaring of a bugle.

Rachel gathered her skirts and ran, heels slipping on the rain-wet street, hat threatening to slide away to be trampled in the rush. Around her, everyone was running. They had had their sport, and Hans Freiling's windows had been broken; they were not going to wait to be trampled by Cossacks.

Rachel found herself pushed down a side street, and paused for breath. She fumbled in her handbag for her handkerchief, and patted sweat from her lips and forehead as she watched the horses scatter the crowd at the corner. But since they were dispersing a mob who were venting their hatred against the Germans, no swords were drawn, and even the sticks were merely being whirled above the heads of their supposed victims. Poor Germans. To have all this hate directed at them. She found herself flushing. Why should she feel pity for the Germans? But those that she knew, the considerable number of successful merchants who lived in St. Petersburg, had always seemed pleasant enough people.

Why, she thought, the tsarina herself is a German. Was that a disloyal thought? But the Jews were well treated in Germany, not subjected to continuous pogroms at the whim of every district governor. She thought she might be happy in Germany.

She left the street by the other exit, caught a tram, and stood on the platform, watching the people. War had been declared a week before, and still the excitement had not died. Men kept grabbing other men by the arm to talk, heads close together; women huddled in little groups on corners. The tram itself was full of whispered gossip.

"The Austrians have bombarded Belgrade."

"Oh, that was days ago. They have crossed the border by now."

"But the Serbs have defeated them."

"What nonsense! How could the Serbs defeat the Austrians?"

"They have, I tell you. Captain Dimitrov told my brother. The Serbs are good fighters."

"What of the French?"

"They are invading the Ruhr."

"Already? Impossible."

"They are. I have it on authority, from Captain Dimitrov. Do you know the British are going to fight too, on our side?"

"Why should the British fight for us? The British are allied to the Japanese."

"Oh, they will fight against the Germans. They hate the Germans. Everyone hates the Germans."

And do the Germans hate everybody? Rachel wondered as she stepped down.

She hurried up the street, and through the Steins' wrought-iron gate. The drive was paved, though short, and to either side the half-dozen great elms that were Poppa's pride and joy dripped onto the flowerbeds, a blaze of carnations with blue rhododendrons guarding the inner end. Then she was in the shelter of the porch itself, and bursting into the front hall, which extended right through to the croquet lawn at the back, and the rose garden. Perhaps the house was on Petersburg Island and not the Nevskiy Prospekt—it was still a lovely house, one of the best in the area. So why should she feel ashamed of it? Because it was the only house they owned, and she was on foot, and there was no horde of servants waiting to welcome her? Presumably the Borodin town houses, each of them, contained such hordes.

But she knew that Poppa could not really afford even this house, had indeed recently taken a second mortgage. It was good for a leading lawyer who was also a member of the Duma to have a house like this, good for business, whatever the strain. Rachel wondered if the Borodins were in debt. Could princes get into debt? It was something to ask Poppa.

"Rachel! Where have you been?"

Momma looked unusually severe, and Judith stood peering over her shoulder.

For all her pretended insouciance at the railway station in Starogan, Judith had been crushed by what had happened. She had been stony-faced nearly all the way home. And since returning she had not gone out. Nor had she told her mother what had happened, although Momma could obviously guess that the visit had not gone well. But her curiosity, and her concern, had been smothered in the excitement of the war.

"I went to Madame Louvier's, for lace," Rachel explained.

"But there has been a *riot*," Ruth Stein said. "Your father is very worried. And very angry."

Rachel took off her hat and began to climb the stairs. "I saw it."

"You . . . my God. You're not hurt?"

"Of course I'm not hurt, Momma. But they were stoning poor Herr Freiling's store. Really, I don't know what will happen next."

The front door banged, and she joined them in peering over

the banister. Joseph stood there. His hat had come off and his black hair was streaming in the wind. He too had not been the same since their return. It was nothing to do with Starogan; he had tried to join up and been refused because he could not hold his breath for sixty seconds. As if that was necessary for a soldier.

"Joseph!" Ruth Stein cried. His coat was covered with mud.

"Cossacks," he said. "Charging up and down the street. My God, you'd think we were Germans."

"They didn't catch you?" Judith asked.

"Not me. But I slipped and fell in the gutter." He took off his coat and attempted to brush the mud from his shoes.

"Your father is very upset," Ruth Stein said, becoming severe again as she understood that neither of her younger children was hurt. "He asked everyone to stay home, unless it was absolutely necessary to go out. And you have both been out. Buying lace, indeed. He is *very* upset."

"I shall make him smile." Rachel continued her way up the stairs and opened the door to her father's study. Immediately the chair at the desk creaked, and he frowned at her.

"Rachel."

"Poppa." Rachel sat on his lap, put both arms around his neck, and kissed him on the nose.

"I asked you not to go out."

"But I had to, Poppa. It's so—well . . . there'll never be another war like this, will there?"

"One sincerely hopes not. But Rachel, I'm told the Cossacks were out."

"Charging up and down," Joseph said from the doorway. "Behaving like madmen. The whole nation has gone mad. Perhaps the entire world."

"War is a necessary evil, from time to time," Jacob Stein said gravely. His arm went round Rachel's waist; she had always been his favorite child. "There comes a time when people must fight for what they believe."

"And what do *we* believe?" Joseph demanded, hands on hips. "Do you really suppose that Austria means to occupy Serbia? And would it harm us if they did? What harm can Austria do us? What harm can anyone do us? They tell us we are the greatest nation in the world. What reason can we have for fighting anyone?"

Having been turned down for the army, Joseph had become a pacifist. Rachel looked at her father, who looked at his wife, who looked at Judith.

"There comes a time—" Jacob Stein said again.

"Oh, please, Poppa," Joseph said. "People are going to be killed. Don't you understand? Think of that. You think of that, Judith. Your prince is going to have blood all over that pretty uniform of his."

Judith had not even told Joseph what had happened at Starogan.

"Prince Peter is not my prince," Judith said quietly.

"Oh really? He took you home to meet his family."

"It was a visit," Judith said. "I do not think his family approved of us. We shall not be invited again."

"Blood," Joseph said. "He'll have a great hole in the center of his tunic, and that will be the end of him."

"Joseph!" his mother protested.

"Serve him right, too," Joseph declared. "It's his sort who got us into this war. His sort at the Foreign Office, and the War Office, whispering into the ear of the tsar. They want to fight. They have nothing else to do with their lives."

"Well, it's not your problem," Rachel said, angry because she could see he had upset Judith. Then she heard footsteps on the stairs, and hastily got off her father's lap.

Dora Ulyanova appeared on the landing, wearing the new suit Jacob Stein had bought for her. "I got the job," she said. "I got the job."

They stared at her.

"At the Foreign Ministry," she said. "I'm to be secretary to Monsieur Borodin."

"But . . ." Judith glanced at Rachel. They had forgotten to tell Dora that she could no longer apply.

"He was very kind," Dora said. "He knew all about me. But do you know what else? He brought me home. He's downstairs now."

Rachel found that both her hands were clasped round her throat. Tigran Borodin? She didn't want to have anything more to do with him. Why should she? He hadn't come to their support down in Starogan. Only the Haymans had done that. Tigran had stood back and let it happen, let them be humiliated. Why should she ever wish to see him again?

Then why was her heart now leaping about her chest? She looked from Poppa to Momma to Joseph. She did not wish to look at Judith.

"You applied?" Judith whispered.

"Well, of course I did. Think of it. Me, Dora Ulyanova, working for the ministry. What a joke."

"You can't," Judith said. "You mustn't. You—"

"Why shouldn't I?" Dora demanded. "You went off with your prince. Leave me to work out my own salvation."

"For heaven's sake be quiet, both of you," Ruth Stein snapped. "Monsieur Borodin is downstairs, and you are quarreling like a pair of fishwives. Joseph, run down and show Monsieur Borodin into the drawing room. Judith, it must be you he wishes to see. For heaven's sake, girl, wash your face and brush your hair."

Judith looked at Rachel.

"May I come down too, Momma?" Rachel asked. But why? *Why*? What could he now want with her?

"Of course you shall come down," Judith decided as her mother hesitated. "It is nothing more than a call."

"Well, don't be long." Jacob Stein got up. "I have no idea what to say to him."

"Yes, hurry up," Joseph said, going to the stairs.

"If you say a word about it being silly to fight—" his mother warned.

"I'll let him do the talking."

Rachel raced to the bathroom, got there before Judith, splashed water on her face, peered at her teeth to be sure they were clean, and brushed her hair; she had released it when she took off her hat, and there was no time to put it up again. But he had seen her with her hair loose, at Starogan. Starogan. He had kissed her at Starogan. But according to Tattie he kissed every girl he could lay hands on, and then he also . . . but he had never actually laid hands on her.

She was already running down the stairs, leaving Judith behind, hurrying on to the hallway before she could check herself, to get her breathing under control and smooth her skirt. And arrange her thoughts. She should be ice-cold and rather disdainful. At Starogan it had been possible for the Borodins to treat them as inferiors. But this was her own father's house. Even a Borodin had no rights here.

Why hadn't he touched her, if Tattie was telling the truth, and he liked to touch everybody? Her stomach seemed entirely filled with butterflies.

Vasili Mikhailovich, the butler, was waiting to open the door for her. She stood just within the doorway, blinking, because the drawing room was filled with afternoon sunlight that made Momma's pale chintzes seem even less inspiring than usual; but at least the lawn beyond the french windows was neatly cropped, and the beds were a mass of yellow roses. He'd have realized that they lived in some style.

She had forgotten, in little more than a week, how elegant he was. Not as elegant as his cousin Peter, to be sure, nor as handsome. But elegant enough, and handsome enough; with his so neat mustache, waxed at each end, and his black business suit. He stood with one hand under the tail of his coat, the other tucked, by means of its thumb, into a pocket of his pearl-gray waistcoat. His striped trousers, his bespatted shoes, the jeweled pin that held his tie in place, all made both Joseph and Poppa, standing beside him, look like nobodies.

"Rachel?" he said, and held out both hands.

She hurried across the parquet floor, her heels sounding to her ears like a cavalry charge, and gave him her hands. He kissed them, one after the other.

"I don't know what to say," he said. "About—"

Rachel shook her head. "Don't say anything. Please, Tigran." Had she ever used his name before? She could not remember. But that would show Joseph and Poppa how well she knew him.

He gazed at her.

"Tell us about the war," Poppa said. "If it is possible."

Tigran released Rachel's hands slowly, and sat down, bringing the tails of his coat forward over his thighs. "It is straightforward enough," he said. "Our armies are already on their way into Poland. That is where we shall meet the enemy. Better to fight them there than in Russia proper."

"Poor Poles," Joseph remarked.

Rachel gave him a glare, but Tigran continued to smile. "They are an unfortunate people. The Poles and the Belgians. You have heard that the Germans have invaded Belgium?"

"Only a rumor." Jacob Stein sat down. "But that is incredible. They seem eager to fight the whole world."

"And they may well find themselves doing so," Tigran said. "I can tell you that England has come in on the French side, and that means on our side."

"I heard that on the tram." Rachel bit her lip. She didn't want to confess that she had been chased home by the Cossacks. "I mean, it seems so absurd. They're all related. I mean, the tsar, and the Kaiser, and the king of England—even the emperor of Austria is related. Isn't he?"

"I doubt that has anything to do with it," Tigran said, smiling at her. "Kings and tsars don't make wars, nowadays. It is the people who make wars. The Germans are growing and growing. They have been growing for two hundred years. Now they must be shown their proper place."

Rachel looked at Joseph, who opened his mouth, understood her expression, and closed it again.

"Of course they must," Jacob Stein agreed. "And the response is very gratifying, is it not, your worship? I have heard the whole nation is rallying to arms."

"Indeed it is," Tigran agreed. "Why, nearly every able-bodied man between the ages of eighteen and forty from our own village of Starogan has volunteered for the colors. We shall be putting armies of ten, twelve million men into the field. The Germans will rue the day they started this war."

"Twelve million men," Joseph said, with apparent concern. "Quite a lot to feed. And arm."

Rachel glared at him again, certain he was preparing some trap.

"Indeed it is," Tigran said. "This is warfare, movement, logistics, on an unprecedented scale. Why—" He stood up as Ruth Stein and Judith entered the room. "Madame Stein. Please accept my thanks for welcoming me into your house."

"It is we who should thank you, your worship, for being so kind to Mademoiselle Ulyanova."

Tigran smiled at Dora. "It is my pleasure, madame. Mademoiselle Ulyanova types better than any of my male secretaries. And it is so nice to have a pretty face about the office. Mademoiselle Stein."

"Your worship." Judith's face was expressionless as Tigran bent over her hand.

"I am so sorry that we cannot stay to entertain you," Ruth Stein went on. "But we were all about to leave to pay a call on Grandmother. She is terribly upset by all the excitement.

Rachel, fetch your coat. Come along, Jacob. You too, Joseph."

"Oh, but—"

"You too, Joseph," his mother said with the sweet sternness that had ruled her family for years.

"You'll excuse us," Jacob Stein said. "Dear Grandmother—I had quite forgotten. You'll offer his worship a glass of wine, Judith. Vasili Mikhailovich is right outside the door. You'll remember that."

"If you'll excuse me," Tigran said, raising his voice. "I have called to see Mademoiselle Rachel."

The room was silent as the family looked from one to the other. Rachel's cheeks became so hot she thought she might burst into flames.

"As Momma said," Judith said softly, "we are on our way to see my grandmother. She merely mixed up Rachel and me. Do excuse us, your worship."

"But —" Jacob Stein began.

"Come along, Jacob," his wife snapped, seizing his arm to pilot him through the door. Rachel turned her back on them. She did not wish to meet any of their gazes at this moment.

"They are very good to me," Tigran said, when they had left. He sat beside her on the settee.

"You embarrassed them," she said.

"I did not mean to, believe me. But I *did* come to see you. I'm not sure what Judith and I would have to say to each other. I'm not sure what I can say to you. About last week."

"Then why say anything? *Would* you like a glass of wine?"

"Not at this moment, thank you. Perhaps later."

Oh, dear, she thought. He has come to flirt. And they have gone out. *Have* they gone out? Or are they just lurking upstairs? "Later?"

"Well, later, perhaps, we shall have something to drink to."

"It is impossible to have anything to celebrate, in a war," she pointed out.

"War is terrible," he agreed, without conviction. "But sometimes it is good for people. For individuals. It makes one realize the shortness of life, the importance of living now, instead of just planning. Rachel . . ." He bit his lip.

What to do? He is about to make some kind of a proposition. My God, what to do?

"I have to say this," he went on. "My family behaved abominably, in Starogan. Oh, myself included. The fact is, as you must have gathered, they did not approve of what Peter was doing." He gave a little shrug. "I don't suppose in his heart he approved either, which is why he surrendered to that woman without a murmur. On the other hand, he has always been a trifle weak. He has such lofty ambitions, such lofty ideals, and yet he makes a mess of everything because he goes about it in the wrong way. Had he truly had the courage of his convictions, had he truly been of the stature of a prince of Starogan, he would have divorced Irina long ago, and married your sister. I think he *does* love her."

"That is in the past now," Rachel said. "And it is between the two of them."

"Of course. I just wanted you to know . . . well, I was equally weak. I should have stood up to Irina, there and then. But you see, well, it was Tattie's twenty-first, and also her betrothal party, and for me to go against the family on such an occasion . . . do you understand?"

"Of course I do," Rachel said, staring into the fireplace.

"And can you ever forgive me?"

"Who am I, your worship, to forgive you?"

"Just now you called me Tigran. And you also looked at me as you spoke."

She turned her head. "It is very kind of you to come here and explain the situation to me, Tigran. Now—"

He took her hand. "I didn't come here merely to explain the situation to you. There is to be a dance. Tomorrow night. A ball, to say farewell to the Guards' officers before they go to the front. His majesty is to be there. Will you accompany me?"

She stared at him. A ball? With the royal family present? And if it was held as a farewell to the Guards, then no doubt Prince Peter would also be there, and Alexei Gorchakov, Tattie's fiancé, as well. And she would go with Tigran Borodin? A rake? A man who wished only to flirt and kiss and touch girls' breasts? But he had never touched *her* breasts, and she had never been to a ball.

"I've nothing to wear."

"Wear what you did for the banquet in Starogan. The green gown. Wear that, Rachel. You were the most beautiful woman there."

"Monsieur Tigran Borodin, and Mademoiselle Rachel Stein." The major-domo's voice echoed across the crowded room; no doubt, Rachel thought, he was appointed entirely for his stentorian tones. Her knees touched with apprehension, and Tigran gave her gloved hand a quick sqeeze before releasing her so that she could precede him and join the line of those waiting to be presented to the tsar.

Why was she here? Why had she come, betraying Judith, betraying herself? But Judith had uttered no word of reproach, had pretended, like Momma, to be excited at the prospect, had helped her get her gown ready. And tonight she was the one who wore the gold earrings and the diamond aigrette. Only Dora had openly sneered, but that she could understand; Dora must have hoped to be invited herself.

But now she *was* here, and tonight, surely, there could be no disasters. Before her was a dazzling kaleidoscope of electrically lit chandeliers, of brilliantly clad men, each one in uniform except for the few black-suited members of the government, of scintillating necklaces and rings and tiaras, of gleaming bare shoulders and throats, of glittering teeth as women smiled, and equally glittering eyes as they inspected their rivals, tore them apart in their minds, and awaited the opportunity to tear them apart with their tongues as well. Certainly they would wish to tear Rachel Stein apart. She could hear some of the whispers coming from those who did not bother to wait.

"Rachel who?"

"Stein, my dear. Jewish. Her father's a lawyer."

"Member of the Duma. Rather a firebrand, I believe."

"Sort of fellow the country could do without."

"Certainly now."

"But she's a pretty little thing."

"Far too skinny. I can't imagine what dear Tigran sees in her."

"He took her to Starogan in the summer."

"Did he? Good heavens. I wonder what Prince Peter thought of that."

"Perhaps he means to set her up in a house somewhere."

"Ah, now there's a likely possibility. Lucky fellow."

"Mademoiselle Rachel Stein, your majesty." The aide-de-camp spoke in a hushed voice.

Rachel curtseyed. For a dreadful moment she thought she was going down and down until she could find herself sitting on the floor. But the tsar was really a very friendly-looking man, surprisingly short, with twinkling blue eyes above his neatly trimmed beard. His uniform jacket was the whitest she had ever seen, and the stars and ribbons displayed on it seemed to wink at her.

"Rachel Stein." He kissed her hand. "Truly do our soldiers fight for beauty as well as home, Mademoiselle Stein."

He had released her, and it was time to pass on. She should have said something. But her tongue seemed cloven to the top of her mouth.

"Rachel Stein."

Another curtsey, and this time it was her turn to do the kissing, and then straighten to gaze at the stern face, still almost beautiful in its perfect regularity, and utterly regal in the tilt of her chin, the gleam of diamonds in her tiara, the flawless translucence of the pearls at her throat; the tsarina wore pearls on *every* occasion.

"Have you left school, Rachel Stein?"

"Yes, your majesty."

"Just in time for the war." The tsarina's lips twitched in the semblance of a smile. "What will you do for us?"

"I . . ."

"The country needs nurses," the tsarina remarked. "I intend to nurse, as do my daughters." Her gaze drifted to Tigran, and Rachel found herself facing the eldest tsarevna, Olga, who closely resembled her father; the cold beauty of her features was only slightly alleviated by the softer contours of the Romanovs. She did not speak, merely nodded her head in response to Rachel's curtsey. Then it was on to the next sister, Tatiana. But here was a smile, and laughing eyes; she looked like her father and was clearly as boisterously good-humored as her Borodin namesake.

"Rachel Stein," she said. "Oh, do become a nurse, Rachel Stein. It will be such fun."

"Then I shall, your highness," Rachel agreed, and passed on to Marie and then Anastasia, the youngest of them all. They each gave her a smile, and then Tigran was steering her into the packed ballroom.

"Such fun, indeed," he remarked. "I don't suppose those girls have ever seen an injured man in their lives."

"Oh, but . . ." Everyone had heard how the tsarevnas slept on hard beds and took cold showers every morning. Surely they were much more suited to tending wounded men than she, who slept on a down mattress and liked her baths to be as hot as she could stand.

As Tigran perhaps understood. "And I'm not at all sure that it is a good idea for young girls to go nursing in any event," he said. "It really is not a very nice profession."

"Is there such a thing as a nice profession, in wartime?"

"Some are better than others."

"But I do want to do something worthwhile," she explained. "And if I am ever going to be a doctor—"

"What nonsense," he said. "You remember my sister, Xenia?"

Rachel looked up to see the Grand Duchess Xenia, who was actually smiling at her. "My dear mademoiselle," she said. "I had not expected to see you again so soon. Tigger has kept you a secret."

Rachel blushed and glanced at Tigran, who merely smiled indulgently.

"I never had an opportunity to say good-bye at Starogan," Xenia said. "But then, you left in such a rush. My dear, you look as pretty tonight as you did then. The same gown, is it not?"

Rachel bit her lip and gave Tigran another glance; was she to be humiliated all over again? Had he deliberately suggested she wear the gown so that his sister could tear her composure to shreds?

"And why not?" asked the Grand Duke Philip, taking her hand to kiss it. "When it is so becoming. Besides, as I keep trying to impress upon you, my dear Xenia, the nation is at war. Thrift is the order of the day. Perhaps you could take a lesson from Mademoiselle Stein."

Xenia raised her eyebrows, but did not seem offended, and the grand duke was immediately deep in conversation with Tigran.

"They'll wish to talk soldiering," Xenia remarked, and to Rachel's utter surprise, tucked her arm under her own. "My dear, I simply have to say how much I admire your courage."

"My—"

"In coming here at all. After the dreadful business down in Starogan. Peter's fault, of course. He is the greatest oaf on earth. But I would have supposed you would—"

"Crawl into a hole and die?" Rachel demanded.

Once again Xenia worked her eyebrows. "I was going to say, have seen enough of us Borodins to last a lifetime, my dear," she said.

"I'm sorry." Rachel flushed. "The quarrel was between my

sister and the Princess Borodina. I did not think it included your family."

"A family is a family, my dear," Xenia pointed out. "And besides, coming here with Tigger . . . you do *know* about him?"

Rachel stared at her.

"I mean," Xenia said, still smiling, "he wants to go to bed with you. You do understand that? Just as Peter wanted to go to bed with your sister, and having accomplished that . . ."

I'm going to slap her face, Rachel thought. I'm going—

"Hush," someone said. "The starets."

Everyone turned to face the ballroom's entrance. Either all the guests had arrived, or those coming late were going to miss a presentation. The tsarina was walking into the ballroom itself, and at her side was a huge man dressed like one of the Starogan peasants, except that his white smock was made of silk and was spotlessly clean, the belt at his waist was leather, and Rachel decided that his black breeches were also made of silk. She had never seen such highly polished boots. But the clothes hung awkwardly on the shambling frame, and beneath the shaggy hair was an even shaggier beard that reached to his chest. His features were large and brooding, his mouth pessimistic.

He moved down the line of bowing and curtseying guests, talking easily to the empress, giving an occasional smile or remark to one of the people he passed. Rachel glanced at Xenia and saw that her handsome face had paled, and yet pink spots had blazed up in her cheeks; the bodice of her gown rose and fell with the urgency of her breathing. Rasputin was smiling at her before moving on, to stop immediately in front of Rachel. Oh, my God, she thought, and was overwhelmed by his body odor, which quite eliminated the tsarina's perfume. She watched his hand move, and felt paralyzed with a mixture of fright and anticipation. His fingers settled under her chin, the way George Hayman had held her, raising her head and turning it from side to side.

"Russian beauty," he remarked. "There is none to match it, majesty." His voice was a fascinating growl.

"Let us pray our soldiers remember that, Father Gregory," the tsarina agreed.

Rachel found herself staring into those huge brown eyes, while her knees went weak. Then the fingers left her chin and he had moved on.

"He touched you," Xenia said. "My God, he held your chin.

If he likes you, you are made for life."

"The dancing will be starting in a moment," Tigran interrupted. "Let me fill your card."

The music stopped, and Rachel smoothed perspiration from her temples, while Tigran held her elbow and led her from the floor, through the pattering applause. He had danced with her all night, allowing only his brother-in-law one concession. And he danced superbly. They had waltzed, and waltzed, and waltzed, and even indulged in the tango, while the empress had gazed at them in disapproval and Father Gregory had clapped his hands in time to the music. Dancing with Tigger, whirling time after time through all the beautiful men and women who surrounded her, had made them all seem no more important than herself, and Xenia's words of no special significance. No doubt Xenia was right about Tigran's motives, but on the other hand, she had met the tsar and the tsarina, and Rasputin. She had this night moved in the highest circles in the land. Let everyone look at her and sneer and suppose she was on her way to Tigger's bed. She had no doubt she could look out for herself. Her only disappointment was that neither Prince Peter nor Lieutenant Gorchakov had attended the ball, after all.

"Three o'clock," Tigger said, releasing her to secure two glasses of champagne from a passing tray. The royal party had left at midnight, and Father Gregory had started to get drunk, as he apparently always did once the empress had left. Just over an hour ago he had had to be removed, with some scuffling. "My word. Do you know, I think we should leave. I do not believe I could dance another step."

She gulped at her drink and bubbles traveled up into her head. She had not expected to have to look out for herself quite so suddenly, and her brain was still whirling from the dancing and the champagne.

"Don't you think that is a good idea?" he asked.

"I . . . I thought we were staying to the end," she said.

"Good Lord, no. That won't be until dawn."

"Isn't the regiment marching off at dawn?"

"You've seen soldiers before," he pointed out. "It's been impossible to look at anything else, this last week."

"But isn't the tsar going to bless them? I'd like to see that, Tigger."

"The tsar is safely home in bed. When he gets up he's going

to be fresh, while we are going to be walking corpses. I tell you what, we'll see how we feel. But I really must get out of here."

He had guided her to the end of the ballroom, where he gave instructions to the waiting footmen. What am I to do? Rachel wondered. But now that they had left the heady atmosphere of the dance floor itself, she was realizing that she too was very tired. Too tired to resist him? He was a rogue. Perhaps he would have counted on that.

She was wrapped in her cloak, Tigran in his, and they walked down the great staircase together. Rachel was stiff with dread. It had been the very finest evening of her entire life, despite Xenia, and she did not want it to end in unpleasantness.

The car was waiting for them, and the chauffeur assisted her into the back seat. "Where would you like to go?" Tigran asked, getting in beside her.

"I thought we were going home."

"And I thought you wanted to go on until dawn. Have you ever seen dawn in St. Petersburg?"

"Of course I have."

"But not from the park overlooking the harbor, I'll bet."

"Well . . . I'm not a very early riser."

"The park," Tigran told the chauffeur, and leaned back beside her. "It is very lovely there."

She had expected him to suggest his own apartment. But nothing could possibly happen to her in a car with the chauffeur in the front seat. Why, he could not even *say* anything indiscreet. Momma could have no objection to that. She decided to enjoy the drive and the cool air, and made no objection when he held her hand.

"Did you enjoy the party?"

"It was wonderful. I'm so grateful to you for asking me."

"I'm so grateful to you for coming."

"I've never been to a state ball before," she said, and wished she could shut herself up.

"You were superb." His fingers tightened on hers. "Everything I had dreamed of. My family thinks I'm a scoundrel, you know."

She had been looking out the window, because their heads were very close together. Now she turned without meaning to, and their lips actually brushed for a moment. Hastily she leaned away from him.

"With justice," Tigran said. "I have been a scoundrel for a great part of my life. As regards women, I mean. And of course, with you . . ." He hesitated. "Well, you know their attitude."

Was he patronizing her? She did not think so. It occurred to her that in his own odd way he was stumbling towards some sort of a confession. Would it involve her? Her heart was sounding like a bass drum; she was amazed he could not hear it.

He released her hand and leaned away from her in turn. "I will tell you something I never imagined I would confess to any girl," he said. "My family were absolutely right regarding me. In the beginning, that is. I was as shocked as everyone else when Peter announced he was having two Jewesses down to Starogan for Tattie's birthday. But even then I thought, well he can't mean to bed them both at the same time. There'll be one left. Am I disturbing you?"

Rachel shook her head, and wondered if he could see the movement in the darkness.

"And when I saw you," he went on, "I was even more pleased. You were the answer to a prayer. Such beauty, such innocence . . . but there was something else. I don't think I recognized it at first. It was not until that night—you were so dignified, so composed, while Irina was insulting your sister. I knew what you must be feeling, and I wished—well, that I had gone to the station to say good-bye."

"George and Ilona did." She was surprised at the calmness of her voice.

"George and Ilona make up their own rules as they go along. I'm still Tigran Borodin. A coward, if you like, when it comes to family affairs. So there it is. I didn't go. But you have given me a second chance."

"To take me to bed?"

What a conversation to be having with a chauffeur only a few feet away. And the car was stopping on the brow of a hill, with the twinkling lights of St. Petersburg beneath them.

"To say that I am falling in love with you," Tigran said.

Again Rachel's head turned, as if it were attached to a string that he had just pulled. Dimly she heard the sound of the chauffeur's door opening and shutting again. They were alone in the car, her last protection gone.

"Because I am," Tigran said.

"I . . ." Words. How desperately she needed words. For he was moving towards her, slowly but inescapably. "I don't really think we have known each other long enough," she said in a rush.

"Quite true." She could feel his breath, and then his lips brushed hers again. "But that can be rectified."

His hand was on her arm, sliding up towards her shoulder. His eyes were only inches away. She gazed at him in petrification. He was touching her after all, and there was nothing she could do about it. The chauffeur was gone, and besides, he was Tigran's chauffeur. And there would be no one else within earshot, even if she could summon the courage to scream.

"I think what I am really trying to do," Tigran whispered, as his lips touched her, "is ask you to marry me."

"Rachel?" Ruth Stein was standing on the steps, hair in pigtails, dressing gown clutched about her.

"I'm engaged, Momma. I'm to be married. I'm to be Madame Tigran Borodina."

The words came out as if memorized. She had to keep saying them to make herself believe them. To make herself sure that she wanted to believe them.

Madame Tigran Borodina. The Countess Borodina, in the course of time. Was that what she wanted, more than anything else? Not the title, but the chance to be friends with people like Xenia and Tattie, to be able to smile and talk with the tsarina and tsarevnas, to be one of *them*, even if on a lower scale? The right to visit Starogan for Christmas and Easter and during the summer holidays, even if she would always have to play second fiddle to Irina?

Or merely the right to see the prince from time to time, to belong to his family. If Prince Peter had been at the ball, would she have said yes?

But she *had* said yes, and they had kissed each other. They had kissed and kissed and kissed. His mouth had roamed over her forehead and her eyes, her nose and her chin, had sucked down wisps of her hair, had scoured the flesh on her neck. And she had done the same to him.

His hands had slipped up and down her back, becoming entangled with the straps of her petticoat. Then they had come round in front and she had wanted him to do that. He had squeezed her breasts, so gently, but through the material of her gown. He had made no attempt to unfasten the gown while she had clung to his shoulders and waited, uncertain what she wanted, uncertain what rights their engagement gave him, what duties it gave her.

"Oh, my dear, dear girl." Momma ran down the stairs, and Rachel was hugged and then released. Momma was frowning, suddenly realizing that her daughter's hair had come down, her clothes were disheveled; Rachel held the aigrette in her hand. "You have been at the ball until now?"

"No, Momma. I have spent the past hour in his car."

"In his . . ."

"Talking, Momma. Talking. We're engaged. He is going to come and see Poppa today." And he touched my breasts and my bottom. But he is going to be my husband.

"Of course he will," Momma said, reassuring herself. "My darling girl, I am so happy for you. Judith, Rachel is engaged to be married to Monsieur Borodin."

Judith was fully dressed and wrapped in a cloak. She gazed at her sister, and Rachel looked back, attempting to apologize with her eyes. But she had not known how to say no.

"Darling Rachel." Judith gave her a hug. "I'm so happy for you."

"But . . . where are you off to?"

"I . . ." Judith flushed. "I want to see the Guards leave. They're to be blessed by the tsar."

"Wait for me," Rachel said. "I'll come with you. I want to see the Guards leave, too."

Tigran opened his eyes and gazed at his mother. The Countess Anna Borodina stood by his bed, back stiff; with her choker of pearls and her formidable chin she looked like a queen, Tigran realized, and realized too that he had never thought so before, and yet she must have looked like this often.

But never before had she invaded his apartment in the early morning. She came here very seldom.

"This place looks like a slum," Anna remarked. "And smells like one. What is the name of your man?"

"Efim Alexievich, Mama." Tigran sat up and scratched his head, then hastily pulled the sheet over his naked body.

"He was alseep when I rang the bell," Anna pointed out. "Should he not be working, cleaning up this mess?"

"Efim understands that he is not to awake until I do, Mama.

Would you like some coffee?"

Anna Borodina regarded her son as if he were an inferior species. Which, he reflected, he probably was to her.

"I have had a telephone call from Xenia," she said.

Tigran nodded, lay down again, and closed his eyes. "I saw her and Philip at the ball."

"Their majesties were there," Anna pointed out.

"I saw them too."

"Xenia tells me you took that Jewish girl, Rachel Stein."

Tigran opened his eyes and then closed them again. Rachel Stein. He had spent the night with Rachel Stein in his arms, and strangely, for him, he had wanted to do nothing more than that—to feel her, and smell her, and look at her. Until . . . his eyes opened again.

"I would have supposed," Anna said, "that you had seen enough of her on Starogan."

"She is a very nice girl."

"I am sure she is," Anna agreed. "Therefore it is in her interest as well as yours that you leave her alone. There is a war on. Only an hour ago Peter marched off to the front, while you lie here like a wallowing hippopotamus. That is by the by. The important thing is that it is our duty to lead, in this crisis, not to lie down with the herd."

Tigran sat up again. He had known that there was going to be a scene, eventually, and had decided to approach the matter slowly. But suddenly he was angry.

"It is our duty to unite the nation as never before, Mama."

"The nation is united by his majesty, God bless him," Anna said. "He does not require us for that. He requires us for leadership. I shall be obliged if you do not see this girl again, and then I will not even have to inform your father of the matter."

"Mother . . . I have asked Mademoiselle Stein to marry me." The words came out in a terrible gabble, to his regret.

The Countess Borodina had turned away from the bedside as she had prepared to take her leave, but now she turned back to face him. He watched a frown gathering between her eyes. All his life Tigran had been afraid of that frown.

"I . . . well, I love her."

Still the brows were lowering.

"I can't think of anyone I'd rather marry. And she comes from a good family. Her father is a lawyer."

"And a Jew. And, I believe, a very troublesome member of the Duma."

"Well, Mother, he was elected to represent the people—"

"Stuff and nonsense. The people? The people do not need representing. They do not *wish* to be represented. Do you suppose anyone at Starogan wishes to be represented? They put their faith in Prince Peter, and there's the end of it. Stein is a troublemaker. All the members of the Duma are troublemakers."

"I am not marrying Monsieur Stein," Tigran pointed out.

"Bourgeoisie," the countess remarked in a tone of utter contempt. She walked across the room and sat down in a chair. "I presume you have not discussed this with your father?"

"There hasn't been time. I only decided yesterday."

"You mean you decided last night, when you were filled with wine and anxious to get your hands on the girl. You are a remarkably stupid young man, Tigran Igorovich."

"I only became sure last night," Tigran said, keeping his temper with difficulty. "I am sure now. I have thought of nothing else for the past week. Rachel is beautiful, and intelligent, and well-educated, and she has a mind of her own—"

"Bourgeoisie," Anna Borodina said again. "Admit it. You wish to sleep with her, and she is bargaining with you. You don't have to marry a girl like that to sleep with her, Tigran."

It was his turn to frown—an angry frown—and she had the grace to flush.

"You must see that you cannot marry her."

"I shall marry Rachel Stein, Mother, or I shall marry no one."

For a few moments they glared at each other, then Anna smiled. "It is something you should think about a while longer, Tigger. Think about the consequences. Your father would most certainly disown you. But think also of the war. You have work to do, to see that our country is victorious. I am sure even Mademoiselle Stein has a part to play in our victory. Talk of marriage is absurd until the war is over. Why, not even Tattie is getting married until then." She got up. "Think about those things, Tigger." She left the room.

Even after the Guards had marched away and the sound of the band had faded, the crowd remained gathered in front of the Winter Palace, cheering and waving hats and scarves. After a while their majesties appeared on the balcony, accompanied by their daughters, and to the delight of the crowd, by the tsarevich himself, held on high by his father while his mother looked on with anxious eyes. The people surged forward against the railings of the palace to kiss the icons that had been hung there, while the palace guards looked at each other and grasped their rifles tighter. Did they remember, wondered Judith Stein, that nine years ago they had been commanded to open fire on just such a mob?

But that was nine years ago. Today Russians were adoring their tsar, their master, the man who commanded, and whom, today, they were happy to obey.

Then what of Judith Stein? She had always been prepared to obey the tsar. There was the tragedy of it. She had sought only to remove that corset of aristocratic and reactionary advisers that surrounded him. Assassination and violent revolution had always been abhorrent to her. But because she had dared to oppose at all, the revolutionaries and reactionaries had been drawn to her, and when their world exploded, she had become one of the flying fragments.

It was instructive to remember where those fragments had flown. Nikolai Lenin had fled to Switzerland, and there had been joined by others, including, eventually, Michael Nej, who had sought the death of Prime Minister Stolypin. Mordka Bogrov, the actual assassin, had been hanged. And Judith Stein, among others, had been sent to Siberia. Had that made her more or less of a revolutionary?

Rachel squeezed her arm. "We'd better be getting home." She smiled, and blushed. "Tigran will be coming this morning, to see Poppa."

Dear Rachel. Thank God Rachel had avoided all the disasters of socialism. And now she was about to become an aristocrat herself. Was she jealous of her sister, Judith wondered? She had never dreamed so high, because she had known it was impossible for her. She had dreamed only of the security and comfort of being a prince's mistress. That was what Siberia had done to her—forced her to settle for life as a fallen woman; the only alternative was to hate, as Dora Ulyanova did. How she wished she could hate. But she could not even hate the unkind fate that had robbed her of her child. She had never expected it to live, in Siberia. She squeezed Rachel's arm in turn as they left the palace and made their way back towards the bridge to Petersburg Island. Dora had been still asleep when Rachel came home this morning. What she would say when she heard about the engagement did not bear thinking about.

As if it mattered what Dora Ulyanova said, or thought. But hatred was undoubtedly a satisfying emotion, Judith thought. Lacking hatred what *did* she have now, herself? She had given Prince Peter what he wanted, and she supposed he had been satisfied. If she had not lain on the ground beneath him, would he have defied his wife? That was an unworthy thought, and an improbable one. He had defied his family, and no doubt his own instincts and judgment, because he could tell himself that his marriage was at an end. Once that marriage was resurrected, he could no longer justify an affair with her, not even to himself.

But despite her rationalization of his actions, she still wished she could hate him. Had he not reappeared in her life, she might have been able to pick up the pieces she had left behind, perhaps even start her history of revolution again. Instead, in his selfish search for pleasure, he had sent her whirling through the air and she still did not know where she would settle, now that he had carelessly let go of her again.

And yet she could not blame him. She was even glad that she had seen him again, sitting his horse as he led his men. It had almost been possible to imagine she was his wife, come to see her husband off to war. In that moment his weakness, his splendor, his arrogance, his elegance, his selfishness, and his courage personified everything that was wrong with the Russian aristocracy. But she almost loved him.

The people thinned, and Judith and Rachel reached the bridge. Rachel paused for breath, and to look down at the water slowly surging beneath them on its way to the Baltic. She glanced at her sister as a tear plummeted down to join the river.

"He looked very handsome," she said.

Judith dried her eyes.

"I almost wish Tigger were a soldier," Rachel said. "He would make a splendid soldier. Not so good as Peter, of course, but—but then he'd have to go to war."

Judith turned away from the bridge, and Rachel realized how carelessly she had spoken. She hurried to her sister's side.

"Judith, I'm so terribly sorry."

"About what?"

"About, well . . . he asked me. I couldn't say no."

It was Judith's turn to look at her. "What a remarkable thing to say. Didn't you want to say yes?"

"I—well—of course I did. I mean, I didn't want to offend you."

"Goose. How on earth could you offend me? I'm happy for you. I suppose I still can't believe it. Tigran Borodin, well . . . he has quite a reputation, you know."

"I know."

"He didn't, well . . ."

"No, he didn't," Rachel said quite firmly. "I wouldn't have let him. But he didn't try to, either. We kissed. And we . . . well, we kissed. Judith—when we're married, you'll be able to come back to Starogan too. If you want to."

"Will I? He's marrying you, not your family."

"But if I want you to come, he'll have to invite you. If you want to."

"Let's wait and see," Judith said, and turned through the wrought-iron gates into the drive.

"I wonder if he's been here yet," Rachel said, hurrying on ahead, up the stairs, half pushing Vasili Mikhailovich, the butler, out of her way.

"Has anyone called?" she asked. "Monsieur Borodin, from the Foreign Office?"

"No, mademoiselle. No one has called."

"Oh." Rachel stood still, biting her lip. Judith took off her coat and hat. "He's probably still in bed," Rachel said, smiling. "I know that's where I'm going. Judith, the tsarina suggested I become a nurse. Do you think that's a good idea?"

"I think that's a very good idea."

"Will you become one too? We could nurse together. It's the thing to do. The tsarevnas are going to nurse, and so is Xenia. All the ladies are going to nurse."

"All the ladies," Judith mused. "Yes, I'd like to, if they'll have me."

"Of course they'll have you," Rachel said. She went to the foot of the stairs, hesitated, and looked over her shoulder. "He will come, Judith? He will come, today?"

Judith smiled at her. "Of course he'll come, Rachel. He asked you to marry him, didn't he?"

"Well," Ilona asked. "How was the parade?"

"Parade?" George Hayman asked. "It was a religious service." He took off his hat and coat and hung them on the hook by the door; the apartment was very small, but it was all they had been able to secure at short notice, and with the entire country in a buzz. Nor had Ilona as yet been able to find any servants. "This whole thing is starting to look like a Muslim Holy War."

Ilona led him into the tiny living room, and poured coffee. "And you don't think it should be a Holy War?"

"For heaven's sake, my darling, it's a war like any other." George accepted a cup of coffee, sat down, and crossed his legs. "Austria has had her eye on Serbia for years. They're after a general expansion through the Balkans, as Turkey weakens. France has had her eye on Germany for years, to get back what she lost in 1871. England has been keeping her eye on Germany for the past ten years, because Germany is showing too many signs of becoming a naval and colonial power."

"And Russia?" Ilona asked.

"Is out to regain top place among the European nations. It's a tragic thought that if the Japanese had never taken Port Arthur, this war might not have happened."

"You could say such things about all history," she pointed out, sitting beside him.

"But this time there's a difference. In the past when we've talked of England or France or Germany or Austria going to war, we've been speaking of their governments. The poor old common man, the soldier, has been told by his government to go and fight, and off he's gone. But your tsar is invoking heaven in this one. He's talking as if it's God's war."

"You have to invoke heaven to make men willing to leave their families and go off to the chance of being killed. Don't you?"

"The trouble with invoking heaven, my love, is that if you don't win, your people start to think that maybe God is on the other side."

"I think you're being far too pessimistic," Ilona said. "The papers are saying we are going to put thirteen million men into the field. For heaven's sake, George, that's more than all the other armies in Europe put together, on either side. How can the Germans and the Austrians stand up to that?"

"Did the papers say how many modern rifles there are in Russia today? Or how many are being produced every day? Did the papers say anything about the fact that Samsonov and

Rennenkampf can't stand each other? And that Jilinsky, who's in overall command in Poland, can't stand either of them?"

"Well, the war caught us unprepared."

"It didn't catch Germany unprepared. Don't misunderstand me. I agree that thirteen million men is a lot of people. I don't think Russia is going to lose this war. But I'd suggest you prepare yourself for one or two shocks before she wins it. And it certainly isn't going to be over by Christmas." He put down his coffee cup and squeezed her hand. "Happier thoughts. Peter looked splendid at the head of his company. So did young Gorchakov."

"Who else was there? From the family?"

"I saw Aunt Anna."

"Nobody else?"

"Roditchev."

"Oh, my God. I didn't even know he was in St. Petersburg. Did he see you?"

"Nope. And by the way, no more of this St. Petersburg stuff."

"What do you mean?"

"An imperial decree, my darling. As from today St. Petersburg is to be known as Petrograd. Petersburg is too German, you see."

"My God. Isn't that rather, well . . ."

"Childish? I agree. What do you think will happen to England if they start to change every place name with a Saxon derivation? Anyway, I assure you that Roditchev didn't see me. Although you can bet your bottom dollar he knows we're here. He's still commanding the Okhrana, so far as I know. I imagine he'll have a lot to do, interrogating spies. And suspected spies. Do you know who else I saw there today? Those two girls."

"Which two girls?"

"The Steins."

Ilona bit her lip. "Did they look all right?"

"Happy enough. They were holding hands, staring at Peter."

"It must be nice to have a sister with whom you can really share," Ilona said.

"Have you never, with Tattie?"

Ilona shrugged, and got up. "We were six years apart. And anyway, how could anyone share, with Tattie?"

"She helped you and me get back together."

"Of course she did, and I'm eternally grateful. But even

that was part of a scheme on her part to avoid being taken back to Starogan by Peter. But you know, that music she likes to play—well, once she played me that thing called 'Alexander's Ragtime Band,' by Irving Berlin."

"Good stuff."

"Very American stuff, to be sure. But it wasn't enough just to play it. She wanted to dance to it. She wanted to leave home and go dancing. You've seen her dancing, with her skirts about her waist, and nothing on . . . How can one share with a person like that?"

"Don't sound so disapproving," George said. "Compared with you, Tattie is the apple of her mother's eye. Let's hope she remains that way." He turned his head. "Was that the bell?"

He got up and opened the door, and stood frowning at Tigran. "You don't look very well, old man."

"Too much champagne." Tigran took off his hat and coat, and kissed Ilona's hands. "And a problem."

"Not trouble at the Foreign Office?"

He sat down and accepted a cup of coffee. "I need this. I haven't had any breakfast. Trouble at the Foreign Office. For me, maybe. Will you advise me?" He looked from one to the other.

"If we can," George said.

"I've asked the Stein girl to marry me."

"Good Lord," Ilona said.

"Good for you," George remarked. "I assume you mean Rachel?"

Tigran nodded.

"And Aunt Anna is not pleased," Ilona said. "What does Uncle Igor say?"

"He doesn't know yet. Mama says she will not tell him if I am sensible about it."

"Reconsider, you mean?" George asked. "What did Mademoiselle Stein say?"

"She said yes."

"But why?" Ilona asked.

Tigran raised his eyebrows.

"I don't mean why did she say yes. Why do you want to marry her?"

"Has it occurred to you that he might be in love with her?" George asked.

"After knowing her a few weeks? What have those two girls got, that they can set both you and Peter by the ears?"

"I don't know." Tigran finished his coffee. "I don't know about Peter and Judith. But as for me, I didn't mean to do anything like this. I took her to the ball last night, and I assumed well . . . that we might sort of get together afterwards." He glanced at Ilona, and flushed. "But then . . . it's difficult to explain it, to someone else. She dances divinely. And she smiles . . . she really is the most adorable thing I have ever met."

"Thing?" Ilona asked.

"I meant young woman. Anyway, I didn't . . . well, take advantage of the situation. I meant to. But instead I wound up telling her that I loved her and asking her to marry me."

"And *do* you love her, in the cold light of day?" George asked.

"Mama says I don't. The fact is, you see, I don't really know what it's like to be in love. I never have been."

"If you don't know, then it's reasonable to suppose that you aren't," Ilona pointed out.

"I can't get her out of my mind. I want to be with her. I . . . but Father will cut me off. I know he will. He hates Jews." He shrugged. "I've no income of my own. I couldn't possibly live on what they pay me at the F.O."

"You'll have to join the army," Ilona suggested wickedly. "And go and fight."

"*Can't* you advise me?" Tigran asked.

"No," George said. "Except to say that for both your sakes, you must be very sure of what you're doing. But I can give you a prophecy, for what it's worth."

"What?"

"I don't think Russia is going to be same after this war. I think it will have to be more liberal. Perhaps even the Borodins will have to be more liberal."

"Hm." Tigran got up and went into the little hall, and put on his hat. "You know, I suppose proposing to Rachel Stein is about the first decent thing I have ever done." He gave a half smile. "Must be the war. Do you know, I almost wish I *were* in the army, and marching off to fight. That way there wouldn't have to be any decision until after I got back."

"Bread?" demanded Monsieur Halprin. "There is none left, Mademoiselle Stein. I sold out half an hour ago. You should have come earlier."

"You have never been sold out this early," Judith said.

"Ah, well, there is a war on, you see. Perhaps you have not noticed." Monsieur Halprin saw no reason to be polite to an amnestied terrorist who was also Jewish.

"I do not see how a declaration of war can immediately cause a bread shortage," Judith said. "Well, then, sell me some flour and we shall make our own."

"Flour? I have no flour. None to spare, anyway. It is the flour shortage that has caused the bread shortage. The trucks, the railways, mademoiselle—they are needed to carry our armies to Poland, not to transport flour."

He was making some sense at last. But she was sure he did have bread to spare, hidden away at the back of the shop for his favorite customers, or for the housekeepers of the aristocracy. Well, she thought, shall I tell him that we are soon to be related to the aristocracy? No. He would not believe her, and besides, she had promised to keep it a secret, as Tigran apparently wished. So much for that. But it might still happen. There was so much change in the air, so much excitement, it was difficult to believe that Russia could ever be the same again.

"Then I shall come earlier, tomorrow morning, Monsieur Halprin," she said. She went outside and stood listening to the bustle of the city all around her—undoubtedly there would be another parading regiment to be blessed by the tsar this morning, before setting off for the front—when she suddenly noticed two men standing beside her, one on either side.

She lost her breath, as if she had just been hit in the stomach. The last time she had been arrested, she *had* been hit in the stomach. It was no surprise to realize Russia would never change.

"You are to come with us, Mademoiselle Stein," said one of the men, raising his hat. But they were always scrupulously polite, on the street.

"Where?" she asked, fighting to keep her voice from revealing her fear.

"General Prince Roditchev wishes to have a word with you, mademoiselle."

"Do you have a warrant?"

"Of course we do not have a warrant, mademoiselle. We are not arresting you. We are inviting you to discuss certain matters with the prince. That is a compliment, mademoiselle."

Judith supposed she could turn away from them and hurry down the street. But even without a warrant, they might still arrest her; the Okhrana did not always bother to follow the letter of the law. And who among the crowds around her would dream of coming to her rescue?

But could she go to see Roditchev in his office without a protest? Could she willingly put herself once again in his power? She had never been out of his power, though. And she had done nothing, absolutely nothing, since her return from Irkutsk. Except visit Starogan. That could not possibly be a crime against the state.

"Our car is over there," said the other man, and she allowed herself to be guided across the road. No one stopped to stare. Rather, after a quick sideways glance, they hurried about their business with more haste. It did not pay to be curious about the workings of the Okhrana.

The two men smiled pleasantly at her as she was whisked through the streets. The last time she had shared a car with members of the Okhrana they had beaten her up, and smiled while they were doing it. This morning they were endeavoring to be polite. But she could hardly restrain a shiver as the car drove under the archway of the so familiar, so hated building.

No one watched her with any curiosity, neither the men nor the women, for there were female secretaries here as well. As she was taken up the stairs she felt amazingly cool, even relaxed, with only a slightly uneasy feeling in the pit of her stomach. Before, when she had come here, her brain had teemed with possible defenses, with possible names, such as Prince Peter Borodin's, that she could use to alleviate her fate. And none of them had done her any good at all with Roditchev. So this time she could only be patient, and keep her nerve, and wait. She had done nothing wrong. Not even Sergei Roditchev could pretend otherwise.

The men knocked on a door, and received a command to enter. They stepped into a large office with four male secretaries and one female. One of the secretaries nodded and they walked across to an inner door. With another knock, another command, one of her escorts opened the door.

General Prince Roditchev leaned back in his chair and smiled at her. He did not rise. "Mademoiselle Stein," he said. "Would you close the door?"

Judith realized that the two men who had accompanied her from the bakery had disappeared. She stepped into the room, and closed the door behind her.

"Sit down," Roditchev suggested.

There was a straight chair in front of the desk. Judith perched on the edge. Roditchev continued to smile as he leaned forward.

"Are you afraid of me?"

Judith sighed. But what was the use of lying to this man? He probably knew her better than anyone else in the world. "I am afraid, your excellency."

"There is no reason to be. You have committed no crime recently. Have you?"

"No, your excellency."

"Just as I thought." His chair scraped, and he got up. His cane lay on the desk beside him, and it required an enormous act of will to prevent herself from looking at it. But he did not pick it up. "What are your emotions, regarding this war?"

Judith raised her head. "I pray for a Russian victory, your excellency. A speedy Russian victory."

"I will say amen to that." He walked round his desk and perched on the edge. His knee was close to her shoulder. "Did you enjoy your visit to Starogan?"

She met his gaze. "It is a lovely place, your excellency."

"Indeed it is. It is some years since I was there. But if you are going to become a regular visitor, it will be very pleasant for you."

Judith had to check a frown. Was it possible that he did not know what had happened there?

"The Borodins," Roditchev mused, "are a strange family. One wonders . . . this fellow Tigran, for example. Would you not agree that he is a complete layabout?"

"That has been his reputation," Judith said cautiously.

"Yet he holds an important post in the Foreign Office. How nice it must be to be brother-in-law to a grand duke. But now, employing this reprieved anarchist as a secretary . . . but I forget. She is a friend of yours."

At last, Judith thought. And the situation is not as dangerous as I had supposed.

"I met her in Irkutsk, your excellency. It is necessary to have friends, in Irkutsk."

"I'm sure it is. And did you recommend her for Monsieur Borodin's secretary?"

"He knew she was my friend when he employed her, your excellency."

"Of course he did. He would have found out when he was

at Starogan. Was it at Starogan that he met your sister? What a pretty girl. Do you know, I saw her for the first time at the station, the day you came home, the month before last. I thought then, what a pretty girl. You are both pretty girls, Judith. But then, she is not as experienced as you."

Judith's heart was pumping hard, and she was having trouble with her breathing. But he was only trying to frighten her. Surely.

"You can have nothing on Rachel," she said.

"God forbid that I should ever have anything on a future Madame Borodina. A future Countess, no less."

"You . . . how did you know of that?"

Roditchev smiled. "It is my business to know. People tell me things, Judith, because so often I can help them."

"Rachel has the misfortune to be my sister, your excellency. Tigran Borodin knows that. She has not and never will be a socialist. And Tigran knows that too."

"She has more sense," Roditchev agreed. "But not enough. Sometimes young girls aim too far above themselves. A wise sister, a loving sister, would advise her younger sister not to do that."

So, it came down to a simple case of trying to frighten her, and through her, Rachel. What contemptible people these princes and princesses were.

"I would think about that," Roditchev said. He eased himself off the desk, walked round it, and sat down again. He placed his elbows on the desk, his fingertips together. "People who climb too high so often lose their balance, my dear Judith. They fall. It is a terrifying business. And then they come down to earth. Often they find themselves in places like this office. Now of course, speaking for myself, and for my men, I could imagine nothing more pleasant than to have your sister Rachel come to see us. We would enjoy that. Just as we enjoyed having you come to visit us, Judith."

Judith refused to lower her gaze. You are despicable, she thought, and hoped he could read her mind. And yet, he *could* frighten. He could frighten just by making her remember what he had done to her, and then suggesting that one day he might be able to do as much to Rachel.

But he would never succeed in that. Not if they could trust Tigran. And surely they could trust Tigran, now.

She got up. "I will remember what you have said, Prince Roditchev."

"I was sure you would. Go home and think about it."

"I shall," she agreed. So she could, after all, hate; because she hated this man even more than she had hated him before. What had Dora said? "One day I am going to sit on his chest and pick out his eyes." Well, that was an unlikely event. But she had suddenly remembered that even General Prince Roditchev could be hurt, if she dared. She turned as if to go, then looked back to him. "You have not asked me about the people I met at Starogan."

"I know who you met at Starogan."

Judith looked at him, half over her shoulder. "George Hayman? And Mrs. Hayman?"

"The interview is finished, mademoiselle."

Judith smiled at him. "Mr. Hayman remembers you, your excellency. He was telling me about the last time you met. He tells things so well. I suppose it is because he is trained to it, as a journalist."

"Get out," Roditchev said. "Get out of here, Mademoiselle Stein. And by God, if you ever enter this door again, I will strip the skin from your bones."

"I shall remember that too, your excellency," Judith said. "I shall tell Mr. Hayman what you said."

Chapter 5

WHAT DO YOU THINK ABOUT, WHEN MARCHING INTO BATTLE? Certainly you dare not think that you would rather be somewhere else; and to utter such a thought would be to risk a lynching on the spot. Ivan Nej found the consuming patriotism, the spirit of Victory-or-Death, that pervaded his company quite nauseating. He had anticipated that the army—his part of the army, composed of recruits rather than seasoned soldiers—would be entirely of his mind, would agree that it was utter tyranny on the part of the tsar to send them off to a distant battle when there were so many better things to be done at home. Instead, he was surrounded by an amazing military fervor. These men, and some of them were now his friends, actually wanted to fight. They wanted to kill, for the Motherland, for the tsar. He wasn't sure any of them wanted to kill for the tsarina, but they were willing to admit it was not her fault she had been born a German.

They had trained briefly, with unflagging energy. They had taken their turns at the rifle range with deadly seriousness, however laughable their efforts might have seemed to an outsider: one rifle to every ten men, one cartridge per head. He lay on his belly and sighted down the barrel and squeezed the trigger and listened to the click and slapped the barrel and withdrew the bolt, then he slammed the bolt home again and squeezed the trigger once more. And when he had done that a dozen times, the sergeant said "Load," and the precious cartridge was thrust home, and this time the rifle jerked in his hands and against his shoulder, and the distant target remained as virginal as when it had been taken from its box.

"A German is much bigger than that target," Sergeant Rimski had told him reassuringly. But he had been uneasy. The rifles promised to the regiment were late in arriving. Ivan wondered what the sergeant thought now, for they were marching through Poland, and it was April, and still the rifles had not arrived in sufficient quantity. There were two to each ten men, now. Ivan still carried a wooden facsimile on his shoulder; who would have supposed that a neatly carved piece of wood could possibly weigh so much? And what was he supposed to do with it, when he saw the enemy?

On the other hand, perhaps the enemy would not wait to find out. There were many soldiers marching towards Germany, and the enemy was not to know that only twenty percent of them actually had rifles and ammunition, and that none of them at all had had any real practice in shooting. The Germans had gained a victory, or perhaps several victories, last autumn. No one knew for certain what had happened, because news was scarce. It was obvious, however, that if the Russian armies of Generals Samsonov and Rennenkampf *had* won, there would have been no necessity for this long-prepared spring offensive. Indeed, there were rumors that Samsonov had blown out his brains at the magnitude of his defeat. But now they were going to wipe out that defeat. The Germans were totally committed on the French front, they had been told, and there was only a token force in Poland. Certainly not a force sufficient to withstand the assault of thirteen million men, however poorly armed.

What would the enemy look like, Ivan wondered? The enemy would be a man like himself. But he would be dressed differently. Ivan wore khaki tunic and breeches, tucked into black boots, and a khaki peaked cap on his head. He suspected Zoe would say that he made a very handsome figure, and Mama would clap her hands with joy. His bedding roll crossed his shoulder and settled on his right thigh; the roll contained more than just bedding—in it were his spare shirt and his spare drawers, and he would have carried a spare pair of socks too, had he been allowed to. But socks were forbidden to the Russian soldier. His knapsack, on his left thigh, contained his entrenching tools and his emergency rations, and his water bottle bobbed next to it. His useless rifle was slung on his right shoulder, next to the bedding roll, and his bayonet slapped his thigh next to his water bottle. It was at least a real bayonet. If any German came close enough to be reached, he could do some damage with that bayonet. If only the whole kit didn't weigh so much. He wondered if he'd have any strength left, when they finally went into battle.

How would he feel, if he had to stab a man with a bayonet? But that was an unthinkable thought, because it immediately led to another: how would he feel if he were stabbed *by* a bayonet? But maybe he would be hit by a bullet instead, and die instantly.

He did not wish to die, though. And maybe he would not. His head was filled with a mass of statistics, that Michael had quoted from the encyclopedias he had read when they were boys in Port Arthur. The figures hadn't seemed important then, but they were important now. According to Michael, in any battle, any war, casualties mounted to only one in ten, and of those ten percent, only about a quarter were actually killed. There were an awful lot of men around him. He had never imagined so many men in one place at the same time. They made an endless brown column, stretching into the distance across the Polish plain for as far as he could see. Most of the marchers were dressed as he was, but their ranks were interspersed occasionally by groups of men in the blue uniforms of the artillery; they sat cheerfully on their bouncing caissons and scattered mud on the unfortunate infantry. To either side the artillery's flanks were guarded by the Cossacks, fierce mustachioed fellows in fur caps, and with elaborate cartridge belts and great curving swords to accompany their enormously long lances. The Cossacks were at the least a source of entertainment, for every so often they would climb out of their stirrups and stand on their saddles, apparently quite as comfortable and secure in that absurd posture as when sitting down.

"Fall out!" The command came down the line, and the long snaking mass of men came to a halt. Corporals showed them where they could sit, allowed them to brew tea in the samovars carried by every tenth man... Perhaps only the men who carried the samovars would be killed; Ivan had a sudden vision of a battlefield littered with the dead bodies of men hugging battered samovars to their chests.

"Do you realize," Vygodchovsky asked, "that the sea is only about fifty miles to the north of us? We have crossed the frontier. This is Prussia."

"Can't be," Ivan objected. He polished his spectacles. "We haven't reached Warsaw yet."

"East Prussia," Vygodchovsky pointed out. "Warsaw is to the south. The Germans are in Warsaw." He pointed to where he claimed was the south; it was impossible to be sure, so consistent were the cloud cover and the endless drizzle. "Over there. We are engaged in surrounding them."

"General told you so, did he?" inquired Taimanov, sitting on Ivan's left.

"The sergeant told me."

"Is that a fact?"

"Well . . ." Vygodchovsky rubbed his nose and drank tea noisily. "I heard him telling another sergeant, and he said he'd got it from the lieutenant. They don't have a chance. They're outnumbered, you see, by about five to one, and they're not even sure where we are. We've seen no cavalry scouts."

"But we know where they are?" Ivan asked.

"Of course. The Cossacks know. They're the eyes of the army."

Vygodchovsky was a walking military manual. His eyes burned with dedication whenever he saw an officer, and he crossed himself whenever the tsar was mentioned. And presumably his information was right. They had marched a very long way since crossing the Polish frontier, and they hadn't heard a shot.

"Fall in!" They had only been resting for five minutes. Tea mugs were hastily put down, and the men scrambled to their feet, forming lines to either side, shoulders back, faces rigidly facing forward, while the staff trotted briskly down the road. They were led by Grand Duke Nicholas Nikolaievich, a huge man, well over six feet tall, who seemed to dwarf his horse. His breast was a glitter of stars and medals, his cap was braided with red and gold, his epaulettes gleamed against the khaki of his tunic. He looked neither to left nor right; his expression was one of composed hauteur, his long nose and chin seeming to meld into the continuous frown on his forehead. No doubt,

Ivan thought, he was a man with a great deal on his mind.

His staff were no less resplendent, and their demeanor was an imitation of that of their commander.

"It won't be long now," Taimanov whispered. "If the nobs have arrived."

Distant thunder rumbled across the early morning. Sergeant Rimsky was moving among the men of the company, waking them, kicking them when they would not immediately respond. "Up, up," he said. "There's a war to be won."

What war? Ivan looked at a gray sky, felt the drizzle settling on his face. Around him he could see only his own company. He watched his captain and the two subalterns, heads together as they peered at their maps by the light of a lantern. No doubt they knew where they were, where they were going, perhaps even where the enemy was. But they were not going to tell him. They were not going to tell anyone. It was his business to march and kill. With a toy rifle?

And eventually it would be his business to die.

Vygodchovsky thrust a tin mug of steaming tea into his hand. "Hear that?"

"Thunder," Ivan explained. "No doubt there's going to be a storm."

Vygodchovsky gave a brief snort of laughter. "Thunder? That's artillery. You wait."

Ivan stared into the distance. Artillery? He had never heard such a continuous sound before, not even in Starogan, where the autumn thunder storms were fierce. Starogan! It seemed like another world.

"Fall in." Sergeant Rimsky marched up and down, slapping recalcitrants with his stick; the sting seldom had to be repeated. They were going into battle. But first they must march. Captain Dolgurovsky mounted, then the lieutenants, and the company fell into a column, feet splashing through the puddles, rain settling on heads and shoulders, dampening caps and knapsacks, increasing their weight. The wooden rifle bumped on his shoulder. At least he was between friends. Thank God for Vygodchovsky and Taimanov.

The morning exploded. Ivan trembled with the sound, lost his hearing for a moment, and staggered against Vygodchovsky, who had bumped against the man beside him. The noise was unbearable, the echoing crashes being followed by a high-pitched whine that penetrated his already tortured eardrums.

Slap, sting, went Rimsky's stick. He was shouting as well, but Ivan could not hear what he was saying. He had managed to regain his balance and his place, and gradually order was restored. "Those are our guns," Vygodchovsky said. "They'll know we're coming now."

My God, Ivan thought; what does it feel like to be on the receiving end of such a bombardment? But that was the Germans' problem. Now it was broad daylight, and he could see that they were not as isolated as he had supposed. The other companies of the regiment were to either side of them, and there were some cavalry over to his right, splashing their way through the endless morass into which this country turned whenever it rained. But the blue-trousered artillery had disappeared. They were behind, firing off their guns. Oh, lucky artillerymen, to be behind, firing off their guns.

Captain Dolgurovsky had dismounted and was drawing his sword.

"Company will fix bayonets."

With a great clatter they drew their weapons. Ivan thought of himself as the equivalent of a medieval pikeman, and they had done well as soldiers, until the invention of gunpowder. There were nearly a thousand men in the regiment, and he was in the very middle. He could hardly be any safer.

But where was the enemy? He could not see past the men in front of him. He seemed to have been looking at their backs ever since he had left the train. Perhaps he would spend the entire war just looking at their backs.

There was a sudden sound from in front of him, a ripple down the rank and through the column. Someone had fallen to his knees, and as Ivan watched, he fell to his face as well, his comrades obligingly stepping aside to let him down. Oh, there was going to be trouble about that. Sergeant Rimsky would be after the man with his stick. He must have missed his footing; Ivan could see no evidence of injury, except that the man's cap had fallen off and his face looked suddenly gray and remarkably uninterested. Then he saw the red mixing with the water that was slowly absorbing his body. Ivan realized that the bullet must have passed right through the poor chap and lodged in his knapsack.

The bullet? He stared into the distance, saw another flash of light. There were men over there, firing. Firing at *him*.

"Close up there, close up." Sergeant Rimsky continued to march up and down the line. Presumably he had been fired at before. He did not seem very worried.

"Company will advance." Captain Dolgurovsky took his place before them. He too was not apparently disturbed by the distant flashes. "Company will maintain dressing."

"Dress there, dress," one of the lieutenants barked; his face was pale, but then he was only a boy. Ivan hastily extended his left arm to touch Vygodchovsky's right shoulder, then found himself marching forward, rifle thrust in front of himself, bayonet gleaming. It was necessary to step over the body of the dead man. He felt his belly roll.

Through the mist on his glasses he could see a whole fireworks display of flashes, and suddenly he could hear them too, even above the rustle and clump of nearly a thousand men hurrying together. And this was a dreadful sound, a mechanical ratatatat.

"Company will advance on the double," shouted Captain Dolgurovsky, and began to run. Ivan also found himself running, tripping and stumbling. The man in front of him gave a sudden shriek and threw up his arms, wooden rifle flung into the air. He came backwards so suddenly and with such force that Ivan nearly stabbed him in the back. He had to stop quickly, and was hit by the man behind, shoulder to shoulder, sending Ivan to his knees. He stayed there for a moment, while the others hurried past him, gazing at the dead man. His name, he recalled, was Kuslov. They had never been friends; Kuslov was from the north, and despised muzhiks from the steppes. But they were friends now. If that bullet had not made such a great hole in the very center of Kuslov's chest, it would have made an equally great hole in the very center of Ivan's chest. He stared at the hole in fascination; the center was red, and welling upwards, but the edges were gray, mingling with the tattered khaki of the jacket. Had Kuslov felt anything? The old soldiers always claimed that no one ever felt the bullet that killed him. But how did they *know?*

"Up, up." The stick stung his shoulders. "Up, by God, or I'll blow your brains out." The rifle barrel was thrust forward, the shining tip of the bayonet only inches from his ear. Ivan scrambled to his feet and ran forward, almost immediately stumbling over yet another body, and then another. His comrades were perhaps thirty yards in front of him, running and shouting and falling, and now he could see the Germans, their uniforms almost the same color as his own; the only way he knew they were Germans was by the spiked helmets they were wearing and the different arrangement of belts and equipment. They stood up to fire; no wooden rifles there. Ivan gasped for breath, stumbled, staggered, expecting every moment to feel the thud that would mean he was hit. He ran so fast he all but caught up with Vygodchovsky as they reached the enemy line. A man stood immediately in front of him, rifle held to his shoulder, squeezing the trigger. Amazingly, Ivan felt nothing. The man was amazed too. He lowered the rifle, his mouth wide. The German was shouting something, but Ivan did not know what it was. He was hurtling forward with all the impetus of his hundred-yard-long dash, and his bayonet had entered the exact center of the German's stomach. Blood spurted out, almost as if expelled from a hose, splashed onto his wooden rifle barrel, and as he cannoned onwards, onto his hands as well. The German fell backwards, and the bayonet was so deeply embedded Ivan found himself going right over the dead man's head, still hanging on to his rifle, which then broke with a loud crack to land him on his back, winded, staring at the gray drizzling clouds. I have killed a man, he thought.

The first of many. "Up, up," shouted Sergeant Rimsky. "The bastards are running. Up, up."

"Are they beaten?" Ivan asked. "Do you think they're beaten?"

Vygodchovsky chewed the end of his pipe. "Not quite, or we'd still be advancing."

Ivan had imagined they had stopped advancing because they were tired. They had burst through the first two lines of Germans and charged through a wood, and now they were on the far side of the wood, where there was a farmhouse—or rather, where there had *been* a farmhouse, because the Russian barrage had crept across this landscape, turning it into something out of a nightmare. Water and blood filled great crater-like holes, and all around him were shattered houses and the remains of animals, and of men, too. But no women, and no children. They had been withdrawn. He felt cheated. But would he, in his so strange mixture of fear and exhaustion and revulsion, have been able to do anything about the woman, anyway?

And now it was dusk. Was it only this morning they had

been awakened and sent forth on their dreaded mission? Was it only this morning that Taimanov had been smiling and joking? No one knew what had happened to Taimanov. He was not here now. Of the eighty-nine men who had formed the company this morning, only fifty-two were here now. That was not at all right, according to the statistics Michael had quoted from the encyclopedia. Something was wrong, somewhere.

But he was here, and so was Vygodchovsky. And so was Captain Dolgurovsky, even though he had charged at the head of his men. And so was Sergeant Rimsky. Only one of the lieutenants remained. No doubt the other one, like Taimanov, like Kuslov, like so many of the Germans, was a festering mess somewhere behind them. And in front of them, and to either side of them. The spring rain had stopped for the moment, and in place of the cloying dampness there was another smell. My God, Ivan thought. Suppose we are still here come tomorrow morning? But of course they would still be here tomorrow morning. They had stopped for the night.

"Good men." Rimsky was actually smiling, and pulling his mustache. "Good men. You fought well, and tomorrow you will fight better. The captain is pleased."

Then why does he not come and tell us himself, Ivan wondered?

"Good men," Rimsky said a third time. "Private Vygodchovsky, Corporal Selesniev has been wounded. You will take the rank of corporal as of this moment. Understood?"

Vygodchovsky scrambled to his feet and saluted. Then he smiled at his comrades. "You heard that? I'm a corporal now. When I speak you had best—" He never finished the sentence. For once again the skies had opened.

Ivan lay on his face in the mud and the water. He had wet himself and he had excreted. Not from fear. He was sure of that. His system was too shocked to produce fear. There was nothing but sound—crashing, booming, thudding, catastrophic sound. Occasionally something was hurled across him—mud, or blood, or brains, he supposed. Occasionally he heard a scream of pain or terror or despair. Perhaps some of the screams were made by himself. How long had it been going on? The Germans obviously had no shortage of ammunition. And now it was really dark, except that it could never be truly dark again, not with the star shells lighting up the sky, or the vast explosions of kaleidoscopic brilliance as one of the enormous missiles crashed into the ground and turned itself into a volcano spewing forth molten steel.

I will go mad, he thought. My brain will burst its way out of my ears. Perhaps I am mad already. We are all mad. Only men who are mad can willingly march into such a situation, and die in such a situation, in so much filth and fear and horror.

Something struck him on the shoulder, harder than a piece of mud. He rolled onto his back, gazed at Vygodchovsky. Could he really be alive? Could any of them really be alive?

"Up," Vygodchovsky shouted. "Up."

Even more amazing than the fact that Vygodchovsky was alive was the fact that he could be heard. Ivan sat up and realized that the barrage had stopped.

"Up," Vygodchovsky shouted again, and then made a curious whistling sound, did a slow pirouette, and fell into the crater. Ivan did not waste time looking after him. He knew by now when a man was dead. He rose to his feet and watched the shadowy figures running towards him, some of them firing as they ran. Russians? Or Germans? Where were the men from their own battalion, who had gone in front of them? Where were the men with whom he had marched this morning? He could see no one save the approaching enemy, their image blurred because there was mud and water on his spectacles. The Russian army seemed to have disintegrated. And he was alone. Before he could stop himself he had jumped into the hole beside Vygodchovsky, sliding into the mud, tossing his rifle to one side. And this was a real rifle, taken from a dead man, not just a wooden toy. But it was no good to him now. Water rose about his ankles, and seeped into the tops of his boots. He stared up at the ring of lighter darkness that was the sky. Perhaps they would not look into here. Perhaps they would go rushing by. They had not been beaten, after all. Now they were going to win.

But they were going to look into holes as well. Ivan saw the faces peering down at him, the gleam of the bayonets. And there would be bullets in those rifles; *they* were not made of wood.

He threw his arms into the air, and hoped they could see him.

From the window of his office Tigran Borodin looked across the Nevskiy Prospekt at the harbor, and beyond at the islands, with the Fortress of St. Peter and St. Paul in the foreground. He did not suppose there was a better view in all Petrograd, not even from the Winter Palace itself. He liked it best in winter, when the Neva was choked with ice, and it seemed possible to walk all the way to Helsinki without getting your feet wet. But it was attractive in summer too. Except that as this summer approached he was haunted by the idea that one fine day he might look out this window and see the German High Seas Fleet steaming into the harbor. Which was absurd. The Germans had the British to think about, at least at sea.

In looking at the Peter and Paul Fortress, he was, of course, also looking in the direction of his fiancée's house, although he could not see it from this distance. But merely to be looking in that direction was enough to induce a feeling of disbelief at what he had done, at what he was daily doing, in fact. No doubt his friends, of both sexes, shared his emotion.

It was simpler in wartime, of course. Everyone was, for the first time in their lives, busy. Most of his male friends had gone to the front with their regiments, or like himself, were at their offices ten hours a day. His female friends were no less occupied with their nursing and their various other occupations that it had suddenly been discovered were quite acceptable for ladies to perform. Balls and parties had become things of the past, so much so that Irina Borodina, disobeying her husband and coming up to Petrograd for the season, had soon returned again to Starogan. Petrograd society seemed to have shut down for the duration of the war, at least publicly.

This situation meant that he also saw less of his family, and thus was spared constant reminders of their disapproval. When he had told his father what he intended to do, Count Igor had merely stared at him and then turned and left the room. But his allowance was still being paid into his account every month; that was the important thing. No doubt Mother had persuaded Father that the engagement was a temporary aberration brought on by the war, and that since it had never been officially announced, there was still time for him to come to his senses. As for the others—well, Viktor was enthusiastic about the idea, while Xenia . . . it was difficult to be sure about Xenia. But she worked in the same hospital with the Stein sisters, and seemed to get on well with Rachel at least.

So . . . was it an aberration? If it wasn't, why did he constantly feel this sense of unreality? Had he really hoped, when he had called on Jacob Stein and asked for his daughter's hand—but at the same time pointed out that it was impossible for them to be properly betrothed, much less married, until the end of the war—that he might be refused? He had not been sure at the time. But now . . . he was filled with a sense of honor, a sense of virtue, which was at once unaccustomed and delightful. He knew himself for what he was. He had been born into the highest family in the land, except for the Romanovs themselves, but into a junior branch of that family; never having had to bear the full responsibility of his name, he had taken from life everything he could think of, ever since he had left school. His allowance had been spent on cases of champagne, Havana cigars, horses and a car, ladies, who had ranged from prima ballerinas to card-bearing prostitutes, and gambling soirees with his male friends. He had wallowed in dissipation, and been aware of what he was doing, relying always on the belief that one day he would find something he really wanted to do, or someone he really wanted to love, and that would be that.

That she would be a dark-haired Jewess, and that it should have happened in so odd a fashion, without any real intention on his part, was what was amazing and a little disturbing. But it had happened, and he was happy. More happy than he had ever been. Happy at his courage in going through with it, and at his forbearance when he was with her. They were betrothed, even if unofficially. Presumably she loved him. It was difficult to be sure of this, because she was not a very communicative girl. But she had said yes, and she seemed happy to be in his company. She was a delight to hold, to kiss, to caress, and undoubtedly she would be a delight to do much more to than that. But he never had. He had never even tried. He was Tigran Borodin the New Man. He had honor, as he had courage. In an incredible fashion, Rachel Stein had made him into a gentleman. Of course no one believed it. He could not believe it himself. They were all waiting for her belly to swell so that they could nod wisely to one another. Well, they could wait. When he crawled into bed beside her on their wedding night, she would still be a virgin.

Of course, since he was in a mood of complete honesty, he admitted that he was only succeeding in his self-imposed perfection because of the war. It was easy to be honorable in wartime, when one's friends were being shot to pieces in Poland and Galicia. One had a duty to oneself and one's class, to be above the temptations of the flesh, to work only for the victory of the Motherland, to look forward to all the good things that would result from that victory. One needed to hold out a reward for oneself. And Rachel Stein, daily growing more beautiful as she grew more confident and aware of herself, was a superb reward.

And in another surprising fashion, he was growing to like the Steins as a family. He had never really considered the Jewish question before, had not really supposed there *was* a Jewish question. There were certainly more Jews in Russia than in any other country in the world, but five million Jews was still a very small percentage of the entire population of the country. That they had always chosen to stand outside the mainstream of the country's culture, with their own religion and their own food and their own Sabbath, had never seemed particularly important to him, and that the government should find it necessary to herd them together in the pale had seemed pointless. Not that any of that applied to the Steins. Jacob Stein, as his elder daughter had once remarked contemptuously, had Medized. Well, his assimilation might not have pleased Judith, but it was most certainly a sensible attitude. But for that, he would never have met Rachel. And Judith, as a convicted revolutionary, could not really be considered a true representative of her family. Thank God Rachel had no sympathy for revolutionary or indeed any anti-government activities.

The door opened to Dora Ulyanova's knock. For the office Dora wore horn-rimmed spectacles and bound her hair in a very tight bun, but for all that she was an extremely attractive girl. She had a large bust and narrow thighs, both amply demonstrated by the white blouse and the contour-clinging black linen skirt that composed a secretary's summer uniform. Tigran often thought about her in bed at night, when he was not thinking about Rachel. Dora was another example of the thinking of the new Tigran Borodin. It was incredible that he worked with this girl every day, and had done so for nearly a year now, and had never touched more than her hand. The old Tigran would have had a female secretary on the settee within minutes of her arrival on her first day.

But even if Rachel did not exist, he was not sure he would have made advances to Dora Ulyanova. There was a quality about her that disturbed him. Her eyes, which seemed to gleam behind her glasses, possessed an opaqueness that frightened him, and sometimes, when she did not know he was looking at her, her face wore an expression that was almost demoniacal. A result, no doubt, of her years in Siberia. She was not the sort of secretary of whom everyone approved. A reprieved anarchist working in the Foreign Office, even if only for a junior official? He had had to twist Philip's arm to have her accepted at all, had had to explain that Dora was a Russian first and an anarchist second, that her sole concern was the defeat of Germany, and that—his favorite theme—this war was their chance to unite the nation solidly behind the tsar, not perpetuate senseless divisions. Fortunately Philip's arm was not difficult to twist—he was completely under the thumb of Tigran's sister—and fortunately, too, Dora had proved both loyal and efficient.

She stood by his desk now, waiting for him to sit down. "Good morning, your excellency."

"Good morning, Dora. Is it a good morning?"

"The advance continues, your excellency."

"So I believe." The advance always continued, until they ran out of bullets or food, then it stopped and the Germans advanced in turn. And another million men would be left wasted on the bloodstained fields of Poland. This had been the pattern last autumn when the Russian armies had been chopped to pieces at Tannenberg and in the Masurian Lakes. So in this spring of 1915 things were going to be different; the Grand Duke Nicholas had personally taken command of the armies on the western front. Well, that remained to be seen. But the Grand Duke at least had a reputation as a soldier.

"And there are still bread lines," Dora said.

Tigran nodded wearily. The incredible thing was that according to the reports that arrived on his desk, food production in the country had never been higher; he knew there was no starvation down on Starogan, for example. But very little of it got to Petrograd, and apparently Moscow was equally desperate. The nation's railways—the nation's entire transport system—were not geared to fighting a war *and* moving food. He did not wish to think what next winter might be like.

"Did you get any?"

"A loaf." She waited.

"Well done. I have some despatches to read, then there will be some letters. Come back in half an hour."

She remained standing, her hands clasped in front of her, frowning at him.

"Is something the matter, Dora?"

"I would like you to return the cipher file, your excellency."

Tigran leaned back in his chair. "The cipher file?"

"You know it is against the rule for the file to be kept out overnight, your excellency." How severe she looked. Like a schoolmistress, he thought.

"I don't have the file, Dora."

Her frown deepened. "It is not there, your excellency."

"That is impossible."

"I have just looked."

"My God." Tigran scratched his head.

"We must inform the minister," Dora said. "And then the police. This is a very serious matter."

"I'm sure there is some reasonable explanation."

"For taking the file out of its drawer, and for an entire night?"

"Hm."

"We *must* sound the alarm," Dora insisted. Now she sounded like a medieval chatelaine, with wild Turks about to attack her castle.

"I will go and discuss the situation with the grand duke," Tigran decided.

"But . . ." Dora looked doubtful.

"I am sure there *is* an explanation." Tigran got up and patted her on the shoulder. "Nothing for you to worry about." He hurried out of the office and down the corridor to his brother-in-law's room. Dora was so utterly dedicated. He supposed that was an essential part of her job. He should be similarly dedicated. But there was no point in panicking. There *had* to be a reason.

In his office Philip Romanov was smoking a cigar. "There is no bread to be had, anywhere," he announced.

"I know that," Tigran said, and waved the grand duke's secretary outside. "Philip—"

"I think something is going to have to be done about that," Philip said. "Or we are going to have riots. And the last thing we want is riots on the home front. The people may be willing to put up with food shortages in the winter, but they will never stand for it in the summer. We need organization. Trains will have to be diverted from troop-carrying to food-carrying, that is certain. I have spoken to Sukhomlinov, but he says he has no power without the signature of the tsar, and his majesty is waiting to discuss the matter with the tsarina, and she is waiting for a decision from Father Gregory. My God, what a way to run a country."

"Listen." Tigran sat on the desk. "The cipher file is missing."

"Of course it isn't."

"It is, I tell you. It was apparently taken from its drawer last night, and has not yet been replaced."

"I know that."

"What?"

"Well, Protopopov wanted it. After all, he *is* the prime minister. I couldn't very well refuse."

"But for God's sake, even prime ministers must obey the rules. And what the devil does he want with a cipher file? Is he sending private messages?"

Philip shrugged. "Very probably."

Tigran stood up. "Well, I'm damned if I'll stand for it. I shall go to the minister."

"Who was appointed by Protopopov."

"Well, then, I shall go to . . ." He hesitated.

"His majesty? Now, he appointed Protopopov on the advice of her majesty, and with the blessing of Father Gregory." Philip pointed with his cigar. "And don't forget you are not the most popular fellow in royal circles. You will find yourself posted to Kabul as junior attaché with the Afghanistan mission."

"But in the name of God, do you know what they are saying?"

"They," Philip mused. "I have always wondered who *they* are. But I know what the gossips are saying. That because her majesty is a German she must be in the pay of the Kaiser, and that therefore everyone she recommends for office must also be in the Germans' pay. Has it ever occurred to you that that includes you and me, Tigger? Certainly me."

"But my God—"

"So my advice to you is to go back to your office and pretend that you have not noticed the file is missing. It will be returned. I give you my word. And Tigger, I would rather you did not repeat any of this conversation, to anyone."

Tigran gazed at him for some seconds, then turned and left the room.

In his office Dora was still standing before his desk. "Well?"

"The matter is being taken care of." He sat down.

"But, your excellency—"

"I said, the matter is being taken care of, Dora. You have done well. I congratulate you for noticing that the file was missing and for reporting it to me. Now the matter is closed, as far as you are concerned."

It was Dora's turn to stare for some seconds. Then she turned and left the room.

"Nurses." The orderly stood in the doorway of the rest room, heels together, face rigid. These women were all nurses. He enjoyed remembering that. They might not deign to notice him on the street, but once they were in here, they were just nurses.

"Another train." The Grand Duchess Tatiana, second oldest daughter of the tsar, led the others up the stairs; Xenia Romanova was at one elbow, Rachel Stein at the other. They were all friends now. Good friends. They had worked at each other's sides for more than twelve months, and in those twelve months many of those who had been girls had become women.

The three women filed into the ward, waited in a group at the end, straightening their starched white aprons and caps, watching the stretchers being wheeled in, wondering what horror was going to be thrown at them this day. Rachel supposed these men were more fortunate than most. Wounded men worth bringing all the way to Petrograd were supposed to recover. Not all of them did, but they were at least hopeful when they arrived.

"Your highness, bed three." The staff doctor had a pad in his hand, and began to tick off the names. Tatiana hurried forward. "Your highness, bed seven." It was Xenia's turn. "Mademoiselle Stein, bed eight."

Rachel stood beside the bed to which she had been assigned and uttered a silent prayer of thanks. The man's injury was to his head. No doubt she was very wrong to be grateful, because the entire head was bandaged, and the white cloth covered his right eye as well; he had evidently received a severe wound. But it was to his head, not his legs or his belly. It was the body wounds she hated most. The first time she had looked at an exposed intestine she had wanted to vomit on the floor. That had been nearly a year ago, and her response would be different now. But she hated having to wash their genitals. She had never seen a male penis until she came here to work, and had been alarmed and disgusted; she had looked at the Grand Duchess Tatiana to see what her reaction was. Tatiana had not even blinked. Presumably being the tsar's daughter inured one to such things. But she could only think, Tigger has one of these, and he will want to push it into me. Had Prince Peter ever pushed his into Judith? It was not a question she could ask, but she could think of nothing more unpleasant. And then the penis had moved as she had touched it, quivered and hardened, and the man, for all his pain, had smiled at her. She had wanted to run from the room. That had also been several months ago, but she did not suppose she would ever get used to it.

She smoothed the sheets over him, and held a glass of water to his lips. He had a mustache. Half a mustache. The other half had been shaved away by the field surgeon. Now he licked his lips, slowly and painfully. "You are an angel," he said. "An angel."

"Sssh," she said, for his remaining eye had flickered as he spoke and she knew his head must be very painful. "I am here to see that you get well."

The inspecting surgeon had reached the next bed, where Xenia was standing at attention.

"Name?"

"Gromek, your worship. Michael Gromek."

"Regiment?"

"One hundred and eightieth regiment of foot, your worship."

"Home town?"

"Starogan, your worship."

Rachel tried to see his face. Starogan! How far away Starogan seemed. The doctor was consulting his pad.

"Hm," he muttered. "I shall inspect him this afternoon, Nurse Romanova."

"Of course, doctor."

He came to Rachel's bed, and went through the same rigmarole. But Rachel hardly listened. She wanted him to move on, and eventually he did.

"Xenia." She hurried round the bed. "Could we switch?"

"Whatever for?"

"I'd like to talk with Gromek."

Xenia's face broke into that enormous smile of hers. "About

Starogan? You'll never live there, you know. And he was only a footman." She did not bother to lower her voice. "Besides, he's wounded in the thigh." Xenia knew all about Rachel's likes and dislikes.

"Please."

Xenia shrugged. "All right." She came round the bed. "How's your head, then?" she asked Rachel's patient. Despite her loudness and her arrogance, Xenia could make the most desperately wounded man smile. But then, Rachel thought, it must help to be outrageously beautiful.

Rachel smoothed Gromek's pillow. "Do you remember Starogan, mademoiselle?" he said.

"Me?"

"I remember you," Gromek said. "You came down with your sister, last July. I carried your bags. Me and Ivan Nej."

"Ivan Nej?" Rachel realized that she was flushing at the mention of Ivan's name. There had been something about the way he looked at her, especially on that last dreadful night, just before the Princess Irina had arrived. "Is he still there?"

"Ivan?" Gromek snorted. "The prince sent him off to war as well. You should have heard him whine. He's a socialist, of course. Everyone knows that. His brother was sentenced to death for socialism. Ivan is just the same. Only he has no courage."

Rachel waited patiently for the tirade to end. "Were you in the same regiment?"

"Oh, no. They split us up. Mademoiselle, will they be able to save my leg?"

She smiled at him. "I'm sure they will, or they would not have brought you here."

"Nurses will stand at attention," came the command from the doorway. Rachel hastily turned away from Gromek to stand by the foot of the bed. As she watched the tsarina come in, followed immediately by Gregory Rasputin, her stomach did a roll. He inspected the hospital quite often, and every time he came he would stare at her with those enormous eyes of his, so that she felt quite weak. But he could want nothing of her. He was interested only in those ladies who could assist him in his growing domination of the government—those with husbands in positions of importance. Xenia? She glanced at her future sister-in-law. Xenia's face had changed, as it always did when she saw the starets; her nostrils flared and her eyes seemed to catch fire. Definitely Xenia. But what did they *do*, these ladies, when they went to visit the holy man? Petrograd was alive with rumors, but they simply could not be believed.

The tsarina was talking with the surgeon in German. Rachel wished she wouldn't do that, not only because she did not understand the language, but because she knew the men resented it. Whether or not they believed the preposterous rumors that the tsarina wished the Germans to win the war, they were here because Germans had injured them, and it was not very pleasant to be reminded that their empress was an enemy by birth.

She did not think Father Gregory much cared for it either. He had moved away and was coming closer. He stood next to the Grand Duchess Tatiana, put his arm round her shoulder, and gave her a hug. As if he were the tsar himself. And she did not seem to mind, but merely smiled, and even gave him a kiss on the cheek. He was her mother's friend.

Now he stood in front of Rachel. He had not touched her since the night of the ball last August. Perhaps, with his intuition, he could tell that she did not wish him to touch her. But he always gave her that appraising stare.

"Rachel Stein," he said. "Rachel Stein." Then he moved on to Xenia's bed. He always touched Xenia.

"You really should remind Tigger to come see his family occasionally," Xenia remarked, inhaling the night air, so crisp and clean after the stench of the hospital. "Surely he can spare some time away from you."

"We see each other very seldom," Rachel pointed out, descending the steps beside her, "since I am on shift duty, and he has such terribly long hours at the Foreign Office."

"And when you do get together there is no time for conversation," Xenia said with one of her high-pitched laughs. "Only time for bed."

"I . . . we never go to bed," Rachel protested. "We never have. We're engaged, not married."

Xenia stopped at the foot of the steps and turned to stare at her. "Tigger, my brother Tigger, has never taken you to bed?"

"Of course not." Rachel was grateful to the gathering darkness for hiding her flush.

"You don't expect me to believe you?"

"It's the truth. Why, I . . . I would never dream of it, until I'm married."

"Ah. So he *has* asked you."

"Well . . . no, he hasn't."

"You should at least tell the truth to your future sister-in-law," Xenia said severely. "It wouldn't go any further."

"I . . ." Rachel frowned. Had he expected her to give him a lead? He couldn't have. She had anticipated something of a struggle on that first night, and instead he had proposed marriage. Since then he had seemed content with holding her in his arms, with touching her, but always through her dress. *Had* he been content, though? Had he expected more of a response, and perhaps been disappointed? Was that why he so seldom seemed able to spare the time to see her?

"Oh, very well, keep your secrets," Xenia said with good-humored irritation. She waited while the chauffeur opened the door for her; the Rolls came for her every evening when she left the hospital. "I'll give you a lift, if you like."

Rachel was taken by surprise. Xenia had never before offered her a lift. "That would be very nice of you." She sank into the soft cushions.

"Have you heard from Tattie?" Xenia asked.

"No. Why?"

"I thought you might. She is writing letters to everyone she can think of. Can you imagine, being trapped down on Starogan, with so much going on here? And with only those two old biddies to talk to? Oh, and Irina, of course. I suppose Irina and Tattie are company for each other. They can reminisce."

"I suppose they can," Rachel agreed, looking out the window and not understanding a word of what she was saying.

"Oh, yes," Xenia said. "Irina and Tattie and I used to have such good times when Tattie was at school here in St. Petersburg—oops, I meant Petrograd. Do you think they'll change back the name after the war?"

"I have no idea," Rachel said, head twisting. "We've passed the bridge to the island."

"I know, my dear," Xenia said. "But you don't want to go home right away, do you? I was telling you about Irina and Tattie and me, in the good old days, before Peter spoiled everything."

"Where are we going?" Rachel demanded.

"Ah . . . a party."

"But . . . like this?" Rachel cried. "I haven't bathed, and there's blood—look!—and my hands smell of disinfectant—"

"You've been working—for Russia. It wouldn't be right for you to be all prettied up. Father Gregory used to let Tattie play whatever music she wished, you know. And then she would dance for him. Oh, it was quite entrancing. She dances beautifully. Have you ever seen her dance?"

"No, I . . ." Rachel's brain was tumbling. It was nearly midnight, and she was terribly tired. She only wanted to get home and go to bed. And besides, she couldn't go to a party without Tigger along, even if she were being escorted by his sister. Tigger was always suggesting that Xenia lived as misspent a life as he had, before meeting her.

The car was slowing. "Is this where we're going?"

Xenia looked out of the window. "Yes."

"Oh, but . . ." The car had turned down a tree-lined drive and was coming to a stop before a high-porticoed house. "Look, please take me home and let me at least wash my face and change into a gown. I won't be long."

"Stuff and nonsense," Xenia said.

A footman was opening the door, and Xenia was already out. Rachel sighed, and followed. She saw that already there were several other cars here, their chauffeurs gathered in a cigarette-smoking group. They did not seem interested in the new arrivals. "Xenia . . ."

"Stop *worrying*. I haven't changed either." She seized Rachel's hand and dragged her through the open doorway.

"I'm not sure Tigger would approve."

Xenia gave one of her shrieks of laughter. "Then don't tell him. You must get into practice. No wife tells her husband where she goes when he's not around."

Rachel chewed her lip in consternation as she gazed at the furs hanging in the closet beside the door. The other guests hadn't come straight from a hospital.

Another footman was opening a door, and Xenia was leading her into an antechamber. Rachel paused in dismay. There were at least twenty women in the room, all of them, judging by their clothes as well as the coats outside, very wealthy indeed. But they were just sitting, sipping tea which was being served by two waiters, and staring at each other and the wall. Now their heads turned towards the two new arrivals. And the stares were hostile.

"Xenia," Rachel whispered. "Are we *invited*?"

"Of course we're invited. These people are always here," Xenia said loudly, and marched across the room to the major-domo, who was lecturing one of the ladies. "Anton."

The major-domo sprang to attention. "Your highness." He seized Xenia's hand and kissed it, then looked at Rachel.

"Mademoiselle Stein."

"Mademoiselle Stein. Of course, mademoiselle. Of course. The starets is waiting for you."

"The starets?" Rachel cried. "Xenia . . ." But the door was already swinging open, and she was gazing at Rasputin.

He wore the same peasant garb she had always seen him in, but tonight his shirt was not as clean as usual; he had spilled red wine down it, and as he came closer she could smell the liquor on his breath, mingling with the body odor that always surrounded him like a cloud. But there was nowhere she could turn; the door had closed behind her, and Xenia was holding her hand.

"Rachel Stein," Rasputin said, his low voice seeping around her. "Welcome to my home."

She allowed him to kiss her hand. But he did not kiss her knuckles; he licked them. "I . . . it is my pleasure, holy father."

"Good," he said, and put his other hand on top of hers, to draw her further into the room. It was a big room, high-ceilinged but sparsely furnished, with just a couple of settees against the wall, a Persian rug in the center of the parquet floor, and a table on which was placed a bottle of Madeira wine and several glasses. Despite the heat of the summer night, a porcelain stove glowed with heat against the far wall. Rachel could feel herself immediately begin to perspire, and wondered if living in this constant oven might not be responsible for his smell.

"You look very smart in your uniform," Rasputin commented, and at last released her to seat himself on the settee. "The grand duchess tells me you are to marry her brother."

"Yes, holy father." She glanced at Xenia, who remained standing beside her, apparently unoffended at not being invited to sit down. But then, as always when in this man's presence,

Xenia had lost all her arrogance and appeared like a nervous little girl.

"Then I do congratulate you. You have kept the secret well. But your engagement is the reason I have asked Xenia to bring you here tonight. We must talk."

"Holy father?" Does he mean that we should stand here all evening, she wondered? Like a couple of errant schoolgirls?

"You are engaged to be married, Rachel Stein," he said severely, "to a member of one of the greatest families in the land, a family related to the imperial house itself." He smiled at Xenia. "Are you ready for such a responsibility?"

A sudden warning tick seemed to develop inside Rachel's brain. Of course she had been surprised at the way the Borodins had apparently acquiesced in Tigger's engagement. Perhaps they had not acquiesced. Perhaps they had merely been waiting to see if the engagement would last, and meanwhile been laying their plans. And now they had brought out one of their biggest guns to fire at her. Well, hadn't she half-expected something like this, all along? She met his gaze. "I think so, holy father."

"You think so. That is not enough, girl. It is your mind that concerns me. It must be uplifted, beyond the reach of sinful thoughts. It must have reached the grace of God. Has your mind reached such a state?"

"Holy father?"

He snapped his fingers. "Take off your cap."

"Holy father?"

"Do as the holy father says, my dear," Xenia commanded. "Free your hair."

Rachel hesitated, then slowly put up her hands and released the pins holding the cap. A moment later her hair tumbled about her shoulders.

"You are very beautiful, my child," Rasputin said. "Show me more of you. Take off your uniform."

"Father?" Her voice had risen to a squeak.

"She is shy. Xenia, pour her a glass of wine. Pour us all a glass of wine."

As if mesmerized, Rachel watched the grand duchess obediently go to the table, where she filled three glasses, placed them on a tray, and brought them back.

"Now drink," Rasputin commanded, and Rachel obeyed. Her head was spinning, as much from the hypnotic power of his eyes as from either exhaustion or alcohol.

"You think it is wrong to take off your clothes before me, a holy man?" he asked.

Rachel licked her lips. "Well, holy father . . ."

"You think it is a sin?"

Rachel looked at Xenia helplessly. But Xenia was smiling, a smile she had never seen before. Xenia would know all about that morning swim down in Starogan; Tattie would have told her. What am I to do, she wondered?

"Have you never sinned before, Rachel?"

Rachel gazed at him. "I suppose so, holy father. Everyone has sinned."

"Little sins," Rasputin said contemptuously. "Have you never committed a great sin?"

"I . . . I hope not, father."

"Then how can you hope to know God's greatness, God's forgiveness? God is not concerned with little sins. He wishes his children to commit *great* sins, and then pray to him for forgiveness, that he may know they *are* his children."

Rachel found her mouth was open, and closed it again. She had never considered that point of view.

"That is a priest's business," the guttural voice continued. "To intercept such terrible sins, and intercede with God our Father for the forgiveness of the transgressor. No one can commence to live—and you are but commencing to live, Rachel Stein—without the blessing of God. Drink your wine."

Rachel drank.

"Now take off your clothes. You are right, it is a great sin to take off your clothes for any man but your husband. Yet must you sin, that I may pray to God to forgive you, and make you strong for the trials that lie ahead."

Rachel stared at him. Think, she told herself. What to do? She couldn't possibly undress before a man, even if he were a starets. He was not her starets, and she didn't believe in anything he stood for.

But suppose he was right about sin? Why had no one ever before suggested to her that way of thinking? Rabbi Lewin, for example?

"She is shy," Rasputin said again. "Keep her company, Xenia."

Xenia put down her glass, giving a little shiver as she did so. She took off her clothes with an exuberant abandon that suggested she had done this often before. Tunic and petticoat and drawers fell to the floor and she did no more than stoop to roll down her stockings and garters, and kick off her shoes. She was a glowing goddess of pink-and-white beauty, and as she took off the last garment, her cap, she loosed a cascade of auburn hair; Rachel could only stare at the big, thrusting breasts, the pouting belly, the thatch of surprisingly dark hair that coated her groin, the long powerful legs. . . . Xenia *was* a goddess.

Rasputin snapped his fingers, and Xenia draped herself across his lap, on her back. Rasputin's hand immediately slid over her breasts and down her stomach to sift the silky hair on her groin. Rachel thought she was going to faint. But she had never fainted, and anyway, she would not dare faint now.

"Her highness is committing a sin," Rasputin said, his voice lower than ever, while Xenia sighed and allowed her legs to spread, one heel dropping to the floor, "for which she will receive the blessing of God. Now, Rachel, you must resist me no longer. I command you, take off your clothes."

The power of the eyes was irresistible. Rachel released her buttons and shrugged the tunic from her shoulders.

"And then," Rasputin said, "you can come and replace Xenia. No, you must come now."

He seized Xenia by the hair, pulling her off his lap and onto the seat beside him. She did no more than moan her pain. Then he released his belt and his breeches fell to his ankles, and Rachel gazed at the most terrifying sight she had ever seen, twice the size of any man who had ever been sent to the hospital. And with that she knew why she was really here, why she had been lured by Xenia, who was nothing more than a procurer for the devil she worshipped, a man who wanted only her body to satisfy his lust. And he had wanted her body since their first meeting, when he had had the tsarina on his arm.

She wanted to turn and run. But there was nowhere to run to, and besides, she seemed paralyzed by the power in those enormous eyes, the even greater power in the erect penis coming towards her. And now Xenia had turned on her knees, still on the couch, but gazing at her with liquid eyes and drooping mouth. I am dreaming, Rachel thought. But it was the most fascinatingly obscene dream she had ever known, extending far beyond the boundaries of her feeble imagination, her half-afraid anticipations. She was being assaulted by demons, but the demons knew exactly what she wanted done to her, what she had always desired, in those recesses of her mind she had never even dared explore.

She was on the settee, her clothes scattered behind her across the floor. She sat on a huge lap, a devillike lap, and she fondled an immense member. His hands encompassed her, one cupping her buttocks, the other between her legs, so that his fingers touched. His beard tickled her breasts and stomach as he lowered his head to kiss her mouth, with a consuming, devouring thrust of tongue and lip such as she had never known. And all the while Xenia was helping him, holding her hair and stroking it through her fingers.

It might have lasted an eternity, or it might have lasted only seconds. Then it was submerged in the explosion of passion which seemed to overtake Rasputin and herself in the same moment, left them each damply spent, her brain whirling round and round as it descended deeper and deeper into a pit of despair and alarm, horrifyingly tinged with ecstasy. But if she was exhausted, the starets was not. With a great shout of laughter he stood up, and as Xenia had done a few minutes before, Rachel tumbled off his lap and onto the floor.

"Now," he said, looking down on her and pulling Xenia into his arms to give her a squeeze. "Now you shall bathe me."

The Grand Duchess Xenia Romanova gave an unladylike stretch, and then covered her mouth with patting fingers in an extremely ladylike yawn. "I am exhausted," she said. "Utterly exhausted. Look at the time." She peered at her diamond-encrusted buttonhole watch. "Half past two. Isn't it lucky we are not going on duty again before noon?" She attempted to squeeze Rachel's hand, and Rachel hastily withdrew hand and body to the far side of the seat.

She could not believe it. Could not believe that she was sitting here, in the back of the Rolls, beside Xenia, when they had both so recently been . . . she dared not even think the thought. And the chauffeur. He studied the road as he drove towards the bridge to the island. But he had remained, waiting, gossiping with all the other chauffeurs, for more than two hours, while their mistresses had been busy within. Did they not know what all those haughty women had been doing, or waiting patiently to do?

"You will sleep well tonight," Xenia said.

Rachel turned her head. Even in the darkness she could see the gleam of Xenia's teeth.

"I shall never sleep again," she said.

"Don't be childish," Xenia said. "But of course, you are a child. Or you were, until tonight. I suppose that is what Tigger likes about you."

"I shall never see Tigger again," Rachel muttered.

"Now you *are* being childish. Although there's no doubt that would please Mama and Papa. Why, if I told them how it had happened, they'd give me a present."

"And isn't that what you intended?" Rachel cried, forgetting the chauffeur in her anger. "To make me so ashamed I . . ." She sighed, and subsided into the darkness.

"Silly goose." Xenia moved across the seat and put her arm round Rachel's shoulders. "I wouldn't do a thing like that. Well, I might, if I thought it would do me any good. But I don't give a damn who Tigger marries. If it wasn't you it would probably be some ballerina from the opera, who'd be quite impossible. But you . . . Father Gregory likes you. He has told me so, often. He has suggested I bring you, but I have never really had the opportunity." She gave a little laugh. "Or the courage, I suppose. But now, we are going to be such friends, you and I, Rachel. After tonight, how could we not be?"

"Friends?" Rachel cried. "After you have had me . . ." She did not know the necessary words.

"Had you what?" Xenia demanded. "You have not been raped. Your hymen is as intact as the day you were born. So he gave you an orgasm. My God, that's what sex is all about. Not that Tigger will know that. You'd better count your blessings. What do you suppose I've had to put up with from Philip? My God, he's royalty. It's in and out, in and out, wham wham, and then puff puff in my ear. Thank God I'd already become a disciple before my marriage, or I'd have gone stark raving mad. I've done you the greatest favor of your life, my darling girl."

"Favor," Rachel muttered.

"You're overtired," Xenia said, and gave her another hug. "Tomorrow morning, when you wake up, you are going to have the most wonderful feeling in the world. And after the next time . . ."

"There isn't going to be a next time," Rachel said.

"Don't be silly. We shall go again next time we are both on the late shift."

"No. Never. And if you try—"

"If *you* try, my darling girl. How can you stop visiting the starets now? You are a disciple. Father Gregory would be angry were you not to come again. He might well command me to do things I should hate to do. Like telling Tigger that you have become a disciple. Tigger does not understand these things. He thinks I go there to pray. Tigger would hate to know the truth about Father Gregory, and about us. Especially about you, since *he* has never done the things to you that Father Gregory did. We'll go again, next time we're both on the night shift."

Spring rain. Presumably, if it was raining in Germany it was raining in Poland and Galicia, and on the Western Front as well. Ivan approximated war with rain. He had never known anything different. Not that he had known a great deal of war, he thought, staring beyond the barbed-wire fence at the undulating Bavarian countryside. He had known a great deal of *war,* but not a lot of actual fighting. He had been here for months, sitting beside this fence, watching the green hills turn brown and then white with snow, and then brown and then green again with spring.

He did not suppose he had any cause for complaint. He was alive, and he had not even been wounded. He was far better off then Vygodchovsky and Taimanov, than Captain Dolgurovsky and Sergeant Rimsky. Even their bones must be gone now. But he was alive, and he was reasonably well fed; the Germans were not at all bad, when one got to know them. Most of them didn't like this war any more than he did. It no longer seemed to have any meaning, and no one had any idea when it would end. Well, it had never had any meaning to him.

"Good morning, Private Nej."

He stood up, as he had to for Korlov. But theirs was an odd relationship, for although Korlov was a sergeant, he was a new prisoner in the camp. As the longest inhabitant of the camp, Ivan therefore commanded respect from him. They were polite to each other.

"It is not a good morning, sergeant. I think it is going to be a damp summer."

"No doubt, no doubt," Korlov agreed. "But that is a good thing, do you not agree, private? There will be lots of mist, lots of low clouds on the hills and in the valleys. I think that is a good thing."

"Bad for the rheumatism, sergeant."

"Haha." Korlov looked around to make sure there was no one within earshot. "A young lad like you does not have rheumatism. How old are you, Nej?"

"I am twenty-seven." And what have I done with my life, he wondered? I have moved from the prison that was Port Arthur to the prison that was Starogan to the prison that is Germany. This is not much to have accomplished in twenty-seven years.

"Too young to spend the rest of your life sitting looking through this fence," Korlov observed. "Do you not agree?"

Ivan shrugged. Am I any worse off here than in Starogan? he asked himself. At least I have only my own boots to clean, when I feel like it. I do not have to salute the Borodins. As the oldest inhabitant I am not expected to salute anyone, except the German officers, and they do not count. So what if I do not have the comfort of Zoe's arms, the softness of her belly—I have never enjoyed having those, because I have always been dreaming of someone else. Well, I can dream of that someone else just as well here.

"Too young," said Sergeant Korlov. "We are all too young. Private Nej, there are some of us who are not going to stay here the rest of our lives."

"What?"

"There is a tunnel," Korlov said, lowering his voice. "And Switzerland is only fifty miles away. There'll be mists on the hills and in the valleys, once autumn comes."

"Where is this tunnel?"

Korlov laid his finger on his nose. "When the time comes."

"Why are you inviting me?"

"It was a unanimous decision. You have been here longest of all the prisoners. We would like you to accompany us."

Switzerland. Michael was in Switzerland, with his friend Lenin and all the other escaped terrorists. But what were they accomplishing? What was anyone accomplishing? Lenin had forecast this war in his newspaper, according to Michael, years ago. But he had also forecast that it would be a short war, and it would bring the collapse of capitalism and the birth of international socialism. Well, he had been wrong there, as he had been wrong about so many things. The only result of this war was that millions of potential socialists had been killed, were being killed every day. The casualty lists did not contain many names of actual capitalists—Prince Borodin or Lieutenant Gorchakov, for example. None of *them*. What would he achieve by escaping to Switzerland? He would very likely starve, if he was not shot on the way.

"Well?" Korlov demanded.

"I am happy here," Ivan said, and walked towards the gate. He had seen the truck coming in, the German soldiers snapping to attention. Mail. A letter from Zoe, as usual, telling him all about Starogan, about how miserable they all were because their menfolk had gone away. But she would also tell him how beautiful it was. He did not wish to hear how beautiful Starogan was. If there was one thing this war had made him determined on, it was that he would never return to Starogan. So he put the letter in his pocket unopened, and reached for the newspaper. For with the mail there came a newspaper, a German newspaper, but printed in Russian for the benefit of their prisoners. Oh, the Germans were kind. Every misfortune, every problem on the home front, every catastrophic defeat suffered by the Russian armies, was carefully catalogued and reported. And every death that could be identified. He knew all this, knew that more than half of it was pure propaganda, yet he waited from month to month for the newspaper, and as the senior prisoner he got to read it first.

He leaned against the wall of his barrack, glanced down the casualty list. No Borodins, and the B's came early on. They would survive this war as successfully as they had survived every other war; it would make them even richer and more powerful. It occurred to Ivan that he hated the Borodins. No doubt he had always hated them, but sitting here with nothing to do but think about life on Starogan, his hate had crystallized.

And he hated Prince Peter Borodin most of all.

Idly he turned the pages. Bread riots in Moscow; next winter would be worse. Changes in the ministry, all for the worse. Social events, describing how the rich were living it up while the poor suffered in the trenches. Rasputin.

"Here is a list of the fashionable ladies seen patronizing the salon of this *holy* man," said the paper. Ivan ran his eye down the list of countesses and ladies, smiled cynically as he came across the Grand Duchess Xenia Borodina, and stopped reading as he arrived at the next name: Mademoiselle Rachel Stein.

He found himself staring at the wire fence. The newspaper had already devoted much space to describing, in every possible detail, the orgies that were conducted in Rasputin's house. These articles had never meant much to him. But Rachel, that tall, slender beauty, with all that hair, giving herself to such a foul monster from the steppes . . . and no doubt she'd been introduced to him by the Borodins. Had not his own Tattie also been a disciple in her time?

He found he was crumpling the paper in his hands, and had to make himself stop with an effort. Others had to read this paper. Others had to read about Rachel Stein's shame. He would not stop them. That would be unfair to all the men in this camp. He could only hate, and wait for the day when people like this Rasputin, and his ladies-in-waiting, would be brought down by the will of the people.

But he could no longer just sit here, waiting. It might be possible to bring that day closer. He left the barracks wall, and went in search of Sergeant Korlov.

Chapter 6

THE TRAIN CAME SLOWLY INTO THE STATION, AND MAJOR PRINCE Peter Borodin stood up and adjusted his cross belts. He supposed Petrograd was the one remaining bastion of sanity in the entire country, after Starogan. But Starogan had a quality of unreality, a too-peaceful peacefulness which belied the state of the world. Petrograd was equally far removed from the bloodstained horror of the front, but it seethed. With war fever? Or with discontent?

The door was opened for him by his orderly, and he stepped down. The platform was crowded with soldiers, but few of them saluted the officer. The army certainly seethed with discontent. Nearly two years of defeat accounted for that. But it would be different after this summer campaign.

And despite all the rumors, there were still taxis for hire. He took one from the station yard, and was driven through the crowded streets. It was early in the morning, and the housewives of the city were out searching for food. They wandered from shop to shop, and at every shop where there was food available they had to join lines that sometimes stretched for an entire block. They chattered at each other, heads close together. They seemed good-humored enough; rationing and standing in line had become a way of life. How they would hate me, Peter thought, if they knew I have just come from Starogan, where there are no shortages and no lines, where life is continuing as it has done for the past three hundred years, regardless of what might be happening in the Carpathians or Poland.

The cab came to a halt, and Peter climbed the stairs of George and Ilona's building. He banged the heavy brass knocker. He would learn the truth about Petrograd from George Hayman.

George wore a dressing gown and smoked a breakfast pipe. He at least represented continuity. Peter could not imagine George ever changing from the confident, good-humored, and yet utterly determined man that he had first met during that earlier war, twelve years ago. "Peter? Good Lord, how wonderful to see you. Come in, come in. Natasha, there'll be two for breakfast." He took Peter's cap and cross belts, and hung them by the door. "How *very* good to see you. I'm afraid Ilona isn't here, you know."

"I know." Peter stepped into the small living room, where he inhaled the scent of last night's brandy and of the good cigars George was now offering.

"But if you're on your way down to Starogan you'll see her."

Peter sat down. "I have just come from Starogan."

"You mean you're on your way *back* from leave?" George waited while the housekeeper hurried in with coffee and strange-looking rolls. "Home-cooked," he explained. "With corn flour. And there isn't too much of that about."

"I should have brought you some," Peter said.

"You'd have been mobbed. How is Ilona? The children?"

"They are fine," Peter said. "Everything is fine at Starogan, as you might imagine."

"It's good to know that everything is fine somewhere." George poured coffee. "She told you why she decided to go back?"

Peter nodded. "I knew it would be that way." He shrugged. "You can't altogether blame these people who rule our society. Propriety is everything. Even nowadays."

"Propriety is meaningless," George said, "in a war like this. Illy is a trained and experienced nurse. And they wouldn't have her. She tried several times, and they just did not want to know. If I may say so, Peter, that attitude, which is so typical, is what is losing Russia this war."

Peter raised his eyebrows. "Losing us the war?"

"You're not going to pretend that you're winning it. I don't even think the British and the French would pretend that. I had some hopes for the Mediterranean campaign, but now they've evacuated Gallipoli . . ."

"We are going to win this war, George, and we are going to win it this summer. Shall I tell you why?"

"I wish you would."

"Well, you'll agree that the Germans are pinned down at Verdun?"

"I'm not altogether sure I'd put it that way. But go on."

"And the Austrians are pinned down on the Isonzo."

"I'll give you that one."

"Well, can't you see, after that business at Lake Naroch last February, they regard the Eastern Front, as they call it, to be stable for the rest of this year. With reason, I suppose. We lost nearly a quarter of a million men in that one engagement."

"As you say," George agreed, "they have reason for supposing your people will need time to recover."

"Well, we are not going to wait to recover," Peter said. "We know now where we have been making our mistake. There is no question that the Germans, because of their discipline, and their homogeneity as a fighting force, are far superior to the Austrians, composed as they are of so many races and languages and religions. But we have always been assaulting in Poland. Now we are going to march through Galicia, and before the Austrians know where they are, we shall be in Vienna. Knock Austria out of the war, and Germany will *have* to make peace."

George sighed, and buttered the cornbread. "You'll forgive me for saying that I seem to have heard all that before."

"Of course you have. War is a choice of options, and one must *expect* to succeed in every option one adopts. Of course mistakes have been made. This time will be different."

"Tell me why. Tell me why those poor sods out there are going to fight any better in 1916 than in 1915, when they still don't have enough shells or enough bullets or even enough rifles. After two years of war. I suppose you don't see it, at the front, but when they come home to Petrograd on leave, they look like a defeated army. And sound like one as well. Okay, all soldiers grumble. But some of these grumbles are damned near to mutiny. They come home, having been shot to hell without a chance of returning the beating, and they find their wives and families half starving, and the tsarina in charge. You know the biggest mistake your tsar has made in this war? Taking over command of the army from the grand duke. The only thing that could possibly save the situation now would be for him to hand over again and come home to run the country. I've no doubt her majesty is doing her best, but it just isn't her forte. She was never trained for it. And her association with our old friend Rasputin isn't doing her reputation any good at all."

Peter leaned back. He did not look disturbed by George's lecture. "Who do you suppose his majesty should hand over *to*?"

"Ah. Well, I imagine it would be a mistake to recall the grand duke from the Caucasus. He's doing well, and it would be an admission of his own incompetence. I suppose someone like Brusilov—"

Peter snapped his fingers. "I thought you'd say that. Brusilov has been appointed to overall command. Last week."

"Of all the armies? Now you're talking."

"Of the armies for the offensive," Peter said.

"But . . . you mean his majesty is remaining as commander-in-chief?"

"He *is* commander-in-chief, George. It is his duty. The discontent here and in Moscow—it is not caused by food shortages. There are food shortages in Berlin and Vienna and Paris and London as well, you know. It is caused simply by lack of success in the field. You watch. After this coming offensive, after we have smashed the Austrians, all discontent will disappear like a puff of smoke."

"I hope you're right. I hope to God you're right. And of course I'll wish you every possible success. I hate to confess it, but I'm getting just a little tired of this war myself. I suppose a little fearful, if you want the truth. But I tell you what, since you're in Petrograd, no more war. Tell me about Starogan. I didn't ask after your mother."

"Fine," Peter said. "Absolutely thriving. She enjoys running the place. Even Grandmama is thriving."

"And Irina? Tattie?"

Peter sighed. "Well . . . Irina was never really a country person. She's bored, I suppose. There's no use pretending. And when she gets bored she gets petulant. As for Tattie . . . but of course I can see her point. Here she is, engaged to be married, just about to be twenty-three years old, and as far as she can see she's wasting her life down there. Oh, I can see her point."

"Young Gorchakov is all right?"

"Of course he is. But you see, we received only a week's leave before the offensive is due to start, and he felt he had to go to his mother and father. Tattie hasn't seen him in a year. It's very sad. But this will be the end, I promise you. After our offensive—"

"When *does* it start?"

"In a week. The fourth of June."

"Should you have told me that?"

"You won't publish it, George. That I know."

"Maybe. But you're only a major. Does every major in the army know the date?"

"I suppose so."

"And most of them have been given a week's leave?"

"Russian officers are not usually blabbermouths, George."

"Don't take offense. It's just that, if I were fighting a war, I wouldn't trust *anyone*. Not even my best friend. Not even my brother."

"Ah, well, it makes no difference. The point is, even if the Austrians know we are coming, they can do nothing about it. They just don't have the men anymore. It's as simple as that." He finished his coffee, and wiped a crumb from his mustache. "That was a magnificent breakfast. Now George, I am not due to leave for the front until midnight. Let's go out on the town and have some fun."

"Fun? In Petrograd?"

"There must be some, somewhere."

George put out his cigar. "I shall have to think about that one."

They strolled along the Nevskiy Prospekt. At least the harbor bustled with activity—there was still trade to be had with Sweden, for those captains prepared to risk the German submarines—and at least the soldiers guarding the Winter Palace and the Admiralty were willing to salute an army officer. The crowds here, if cynical, were not bad-humored. They read the bulletins pinned to the palace gate, and commented to each other with neither belief nor enthusiasm about the invariable list of "victories" or "strategic" and "planned" withdrawals. George could not help remembering that August day, two years ago, when all Petrograd had been here, cheering and weeping in their fervor, when the tsar and his family had stood on the balcony and waved, and Preobraschenski Guards had marched off to war.

Two years. As he had prophesied, it had been a bitter period. But not for him. For him it had been the experience of a lifetime. He had not realized how much he missed the life of a correspondent, how much he disliked being merely an executive. But for two years he had been able to play to the hilt the role of the correspondent, with Ilona and the children always within reach of a telephone call or even an occasional weekend. He could ask for nothing more, especially since she, able after so long to live with her mother and experience the pleasure of her own home, was happy too. Even Father had understood, had brought no pressure for him to go home, but had willingly resumed the active presidency of the paper—for the duration, as he put it. He glanced at Peter. What did *he* think of those two years?

But Peter was preoccupied, watching the bridge from Petrograd Island, the people walking towards it, among them a dark-haired girl in a nurse's uniform. "My God," he muttered.

"Rachel Stein," George commented.

"Do you see a lot of them?"

"I see nothing of them at all. The girls are both working as nurses, and nurses are pretty busy."

"Ah . . . would you excuse me?"

"I'll excuse you," George said. "But will she?"

Peter flushed. "She is Tigger's fiancée. Even if unofficially. It would be discourteous of me not to speak with her. You do understand, George."

"Sure. Should I expect you for lunch?"

Peter hesitated, then smiled. "Who can say? I will come if I can."

"Today is Saturday," George pointed out. "You won't get much at the Steins'. But have fun."

He watched Peter hurry across the street, watched the girl stop as she heard her name shouted. Rachel Stein. He had called at the Stein house himself, only a month before. He would have been hard put to tell himself why; he had never considered doing so while Ilona had remained in Petrograd. It had been a depressing experience. The drinks he had been offered had come from half-empty bottles that clearly had not been opened for some time. The house was shabby and their clothes were shabby: that was not altogether surprising in wartime, but the Steins themselves had seemed depressed, Rachel perhaps most of all. But there had been more than depression about her. Her eyes had been haunted, and she had made little conversation, even though he had imagined they had established a certain rapport at Starogan. Was it what she daily saw and heard and felt in the hospital? Or was it a growing certainty that her marriage to Tigran was an unattainable dream, her engagement only a sham, an expression of his sudden determination to be his own man, to separate himself from the cloying confines of his family, but not really to saddle himself with a wife?

Rachel lacked the sterner fiber of her sister. But then, she had not yet suffered to the extent that Judith had. The one was as fascinating as the other. Which was of course why he went to see them. Dangerous thoughts for a happily married man, especially when his wife belonged to the family that had inflicted most of the damage. And was about to inflict even more? Certainly Peter, just returned from an obviously unsatisfactory vacation in Starogan, where he would have been nagged by his wife and tormented by his sister, was on the look-out for some fun, as he put it. And was therefore using Rachel as an excuse to get into the Stein home, and renew his acquaintance with Judith.

The truly tragic aspect of the situation was that Peter of course did not understand that he was harming anyone. He was the Prince of Starogan. All his life he had been brought up to suppose that for him to bestow even a smile, much less a passing caress, upon any inferior species was an act of utter kindness. And George did not suppose the war was going to alter that state of affairs.

"Good morning, Mr. Hayman."

He turned in utter surprise, and gazed at Judith Stein. "But . . . I was just thinking of you."

She was not in uniform, and from the look of her clothes, which were quiet and neat, and her relaxed, unhurried air, he guessed she had come from the synagogue. She smiled. "You are very gallant."

"I'm telling the truth. Look—" He turned, but Peter and Rachel had disappeared into the crowd on the bridge.

"I know," she said. "I saw them."

"Well, then . . ."

"I would rather walk with you, and let them get away from us."

"Um. Hell hath no fury . . ."

"I am not angry with Prince Peter, Mr. Hayman. I have never been angry with him. A man is what he is."

"And a woman, mademoiselle. How is life treating you?"

"About the same as it is treating anyone else."

"And Rachel?"

A quick glance. "What about Rachel, Mr. Hayman?"

"Well . . ." He flushed. He hadn't meant to ask the question. "She didn't look very well, last time I saw her."

Judith nodded. "She has become very depressed, this past year." She sighed. "I suppose it is the war. But for the war, she would be Tigran's wife. As it is, she has to wait while things go from bad to worse. If I am not depressed, it is only because things have not yet become as bad as Siberia."

"But you don't want to see Prince Peter again?"

"I would prefer not to."

"Well, then, come and have lunch with me, Judith. I think he's going to be around your house all day."

"Another day, another death," the Grand Duchess Xenia Romanova said cheerfully, as she washed her hands. "Do you realize, my dear Mademoiselle Stein, that by the time this war ends, if it *ever* ends, I shall probably have seen men die more often than I will have slept with my husband? Is that not a droll thought?"

Judith made no reply. It was, fortunately, a rare occurrence for her to finish a shift at the same time as the grand duchess, and even rarer for her to finish at the same time as her sister. She glanced at Rachel, also scrubbing away. But Rachel, as usual, seemed preoccupied with some inner problem. For this past week it had been simple enough to decide what that problem was; the Brusilov offensive had officially been successful. It had rocked the Austrian empire to its foundation, and had only been halted, a few weeks before, by a hasty transfer of German troops from the French front. In a purely military sense this had been the most successful summer the Russians had yet had. But the cost had been frightful, and the hospitals had been filled to bursting throughout August and September. There had been enough horror to make anyone introspective.

"Well." Xenia put on her fur coat, which she wore although the weather had not yet turned cold, and even though it was inclined to rain every day. "At least we can relax for a while. I am sorry I cannot offer you a ride home, Mademoiselle Stein, but Rachel and I have somewhere to go."

"Oh, but . . ." Rachel turned, and gazed at Judith with enormous, anxious eyes.

"We are expected," Xenia said firmly. "Good night, Mademoiselle Stein."

"Good night, your highness," Judith said.

Rachel, half into her coat, hesitated, and had her arm seized by the grand duchess. "Good night, Judith," she muttered, as she was marched down the corridor.

Judith followed them more slowly. Perhaps Rachel was fortunate in that the grand duchess, alone of her family, had decided to make a friend of her. Judith did not altogether approve, though. The Grand Duchess Xenia had a reputation for wild living, which she had accumulated before her rather late marriage. She smoked cigarettes, for example, and some of her parties had made the gossip columns. On the other hand, she was supposed to be Rachel's future sister-in-law, and Rachel would surely grow closer to her as time went by, even at the expense of her own family. And if she was learning to drink too much and to smoke at Xenia's house, she had brought neither of those bad habits home yet.

Anyway, Judith reflected as she went down the steps, feet splashing in the puddles left by the drizzling rain, Rachel was twenty-three years old and a woman. And Judith had enough to think about, without worrying over her sister. Had she been a fool, last May? According to Rachel, Prince Peter had wanted only to talk about her, had waited at the house all day in the certainty that she would eventually come home. Instead she had spent the entire afternoon in the company of George Hayman. It was amazing to realize that although she had met Mr. Hayman for the first time down at Starogan two years ago, and on only two occasions since, she felt she had known him for a very long time. That must be because of Ilona.

But George Hayman, happily married to a beautiful woman, surrounded by the confidence of success, and protected by the aura of neutrality, could have nothing to do with her future. Did Prince Peter? A soldier, home on a brief leave before returning to the front? Such occasions were not intended for words, but rather for deeds. Well, they had shared their deed. And even if there had been time for words, they had nothing left to say. Time could not be turned back, even for a Prince of Starogan.

Even supposing he wanted that.

So what did the future hold for her? Wasn't she content, despite all the misery surrounding her, despite the fact of the war, which kept her from making any decisions, which kept her from looking ahead? She was twenty-seven years of age, and nothing more than a shell. The rest of her had been abandoned, in Siberia.

She wrapped her coat tightly about her, and plodded through the rain towards the tram stop. The tram was crowded, as usual. Faces were pinched. Damp, and the threat of the coming cold, made people appear smaller than they really were—cold and hunger, for most of these people were hungry. Not Judith Stein, as yet. Even if Poppa was digging into his savings to keep the family in the style to which he had made it accustomed. And not any Borodin, as yet. Never any Borodin.

"Mademoiselle Stein?"

She turned her head, and when she discovered the man who had spoken, she was surprised. He was a doctor named Purishkevich, and since his clients included most of the Petrograd aristocracy, he did not usually travel by tram. But she knew him; he served as a replacement surgeon at the hospital when Dr. Alapin was resting. He gave her a reassuring smile. "I wonder if I might have a word with you."

"Of course, doctor." I must have been doing something wrong, she thought. I am going to get a reprimand. But what a strange way to go about it, when he could merely have summoned her to his office.

"Not here," he said. "Shall we get off at the next stop, and walk for a while?"

Judith hesitated. But he was an extraordinarily well-mannered little man. And he was her superior. "Of course, Dr. Purishkevich."

The tram stopped, and he assisted her down, held her elbow as they made their way carefully between the puddles. "There are two gentlemen who would like to meet you," he said.

Judith tried to stop; it was difficult on the slippery surface. "Two gentlemen?"

"Two very great gentlemen, who wish to meet you and talk with you, Mademoiselle Stein. Here we are."

They had arrived at a door that was set in a wall between two shops and which obviously led to an interior staircase. Brass nameplates suggested that the upper floor of the building was used as offices. And two men were waiting for her. Shades of Rasputin, from what she had heard. According to Poppa, all of Petrograd was immoral.

"I really don't think—" she began.

Purishkevich had unlocked the door. "It is a very important matter, mademoiselle. An affair of state. You are a loyal servant of Russia, are you not?"

"I hope I am, doctor."

"Well, then, you will listen to these gentlemen." He was holding her elbow, and gently but firmly urging her into the doorway. And he was, after all, Dr. Purishkevich. Why, there could be no more respected doctor in the entire city. She found herself climbing the stairs, the doctor still holding her elbow. The corridor at the top was gloomy, but a door was already open, and beyond there was electric light and a glowing fire. She stepped inside cautiously, was reassured by the scent of rich cigars and better brandy, the sight of carefully drawn heavy draperies, the comfortably upholstered armchairs. Then she saw a curtained alcove, and beyond, a bed. She hesitated. Someone's pied-à-terre. Oh, Lord, she thought.

She tried to turn, but Purishkevich had closed the door, and now one of the two men in the room came forward to kiss her hand. "Mademoiselle Stein. We have never met, but I have heard much of you. I am the Grand Duke Dimitri Pavlovich."

Judith could only goggle at him.

"And this is Prince Felix Yusupov."

Judith stared. The grand duke was a cousin of the tsar, and of Xenia's husband, and Prince Yusupov was married to another royal cousin.

"Let me take your coat, mademoiselle." The prince assisted her, then guided her to a seat. Her head was in a spin. Though she had never met either of these men, she knew them well enough by reputation. And if any Petrograd reputations were secure, theirs were. Then what could they want with her?

"Mademoiselle is cold," the grand duke said. "Pour her some brandy, doctor."

"No," Judith said. "No, really, thank you."

"As you wish." But a glass was placed at her elbow. The grand duke sat opposite her. The prince stood to one side, Purishkevich to the other. "What did you tell her?" the grand duke asked.

"That it was an affair of state."

"And it is that." He leaned forward. "Your sister is engaged to be married into a famous family, mademoiselle."

Oh, Lord, Judith thought again. She had not thought the Borodins would still be pursuing the matter, after all this time. But she could do nothing but wait, and listen to what they had to say; Purishkevich had locked the door.

"Yes, your highness," she said.

"A family which, in many ways, is not all it should be."

"Your highness?"

"I am speaking of my cousin-in-law, the Grand Duchess Xenia."

Judith stared at him.

"Did you not know that the grand duchess is a disciple of the beast, Rasputin?"

"I . . ." There had been rumors. But that was before Xenia's marriage.

"And do you not know that she has made your sister, the future Countess Borodina, into a disciple as well?"

Judith realized her mouth was open, and hastily closed it. It could not be true. Rachel? But of course it was true. She had known all along that there was something unnatural in Xenia's friendship.

"Do you not know, Mademoiselle Stein, that the grand duchess and your sister lie naked with that monster? Bathe him? Fondle his private parts?"

Judith drank some brandy. She could not think.

"And are fondled by him in return," the grand duke went on. "Nor are they the only ones. The list of his conquests would fill a book. It stretches even farther within the royal family than Xenia Romanova. We all know that he influences the tsarina, who *is* the government. Mademoiselle Stein, these gentlemen and I have determined that Russia must be saved, and it can be saved only if Rasputin is removed."

Judith's head jerked.

"Arrested," Purishkevich hastened to add.

"But it is difficult," Yusupov said. "He never leaves his house without guards and attendants, and of course it would be impossible to break into his house without a large force of men."

"And as the tsarina is completely under his spell," the doctor said, "we cannot go to the police. We should have to recruit such a force ourselves. And once we enlarge our circle, why, the empress would soon know of it, and we would be the ones arrested."

"Will you help us, mademoiselle?" asked the grand duke. "For Russia?"

"And for your sister," Yusupov added.

Judith discovered her glass was empty. "But, your highnesses, how can *I* help? I have never met this Rasputin. I know nothing of him."

"The holy father adores your sister," Yusupov pointed out. "We have that on the best authority. From Xenia Romanova herself. Now then, suppose he discovers that Rachel Stein has a sister, a sister who is even more beautiful than herself, more voluptuous, more attractive."

"But—"

"You are those things, mademoiselle."

"You . . . you wish me to . . ."

"We should never ask such a sacrifice of you, mademoiselle. No, no. But you see, our only hope of carrying out a successful arrest of the monster is to discover him alone. How can this be done? There is only one way. Rasputin will occasionally attend a private party, if it sounds interesting enough."

"He suspects nothing of our intentions," the grand duke said. "On the other hand, we are not friends of his. There is no reason for him to accept any invitation he might receive from us, unless we make our guest list unusually attractive."

What they were proposing was impossible, inconceivable. She could not avoid seeing Rasputin from time to time; he still visited the hospital. She had never in her life seen anyone more repulsive. But Rachel . . . and undoubtedly he looked at her with utter possessiveness. What a fool she was not to have realized that before. Rachel! Rachel could not be allowed to go on seeing him. But how could she be stopped? By telling Momma and Poppa? She could not imagine what would happen then. Besides, as these men had just told her, Rasputin, secure in the tsarina's support, was omnipotent. He could have *them* arrested, as Jews and possible enemies of the state, if he even guessed they opposed his desires.

"Are you not eager to see the end of the beast?" asked Prince Yusupov.

"It is the only way to save Russia from disaster," the grand duke said. "Once the beast has been arrested, we can have access to his private papers. Witnesses will come forward, and the tsarina will have to accept the truth. Certainly the tsar will do so."

Judith looked from one to the other. The three most honest, most honorable men in Petrograd. Perhaps in all Russia.

"Now listen very carefully," Dr. Purishkevich said. "This is what we plan to do."

Once again she was a conspirator. An incredible thought. And once again against the state, or against the tsarina's confessor, which amounted to the same thing. Her last venture into such a conspiracy had earned her a life sentence in Siberia. Was she not being a fool?

But this time she was working for the good of the state. Had she not thought that the last time, too?

And there could be no doubt that one reason they had approached her was that they knew her record, her past. She was someone they could trust, because her accusation against them, should she decide to betray them, would be worthless; on the other hand, if they decided to abandon her, she would have no defense at all. So she *was* being a fool. But the other reason they had approached her was Rachel. She sat up that night, in her bed, long after the rest of the family had gone to sleep. It was not unusual for Rachel to come home very late; she could come to no harm, because of course she was with the Grand Duchess Xenia, was delivered home in the grand duchess's Rolls-Royce. Why, to have that car come to the house so often, Poppa might even acquiesce in her going to visit Rasputin.

At the sound of the door she was out of her own room, and waiting on the landing. "Where have you been?" she demanded.

"With Xenia Romanova," Rachel said. "Where do you suppose I've been?"

"At Rasputin's salon?"

Rachel's head turned, but in the same instant her face closed. "Is that any business of yours?"

"It is if what they say of him is true."

"I don't suppose anything they say of him is true," Rachel said. "And I would not expect you to understand about him."

"Then it is true," Judith said. "He is a vicious beast. You must be mad. Suppose Tigran finds out?"

"Tigger will never find out," Rachel said. "What will you tell him? Will you accuse the grand duchess? And several other grand duchesses as well, I can tell you that. They'd send you back to Siberia. And you'd deserve to go."

She brushed past and went to her room.

"Rachel," Judith begged.

"Leave me alone," Rachel snapped. "I told you, you wouldn't understand. And who are you to stand in judgment on me? You tried to be Peter Borodin's mistress, and he wouldn't have you. Because you don't belong with them, at Starogan or in their homes. Well, I do. I'm going to see that I do. I'm going to marry Tigger, and I'm going to belong. And that means I must be like Xenia. Like an aristocrat. Because I'm going to be an aristocrat. You work out your salvation, and leave me to work out mine." She opened her door. "And if you try to make trouble, I'll have you sent to Siberia myself."

The door closed behind her, and Judith discovered she was weeping. But why? Rachel *had* worked things out for herself, and was going about implementing them. She *would* be an aristocrat, just like any of the others, just as corrupt and insincere and vicious as Xenia or Irina Borodina, or perhaps even Tattie. After all, Tattie had also been a disciple of Rasputin's, when she had been under Irina's wing. And come to think of it, she was again under Irina's wing, down on Starogan. Did Peter, who had risked his entire career to oppose the beast, not realize that?

Oh, Peter, Peter. There was where she had made her mistake, in not seeing him last spring. Peter, for all his stuffiness and his carelessness and his arrogance, was at least a good man. There was no corruption there. If only she could see him now, discuss the matter with him . . . but Peter was hundreds of miles away, fighting a war. If he was still alive.

Whom did that leave? George Hayman? Ilona was not a typical Russian aristocrat, and that was because of Hayman's influence. But Hayman was nearly as helpless as Judith herself, when it came to controlling events. He could only report, and comment. But there had to be other decent, incorruptible people in Russia, in Petrograd. Of course there were. And she had just met three of them. Three men who had come up against as many brick walls as herself, and had resolved to seek their own salvation. And who had invited her to help them.

But how to survive the days until they could arrange their party, and obtain Rasputin's acceptance? Suppose they overdid it, and he told Rachel that he had been invited to a party to meet her sister? Rachel might well give the whole thing away by declaring that it had to be impossible.

How to survive in other ways? How to avoid Xenia's smile every day, when she wanted to stare at her, to convey to her that her starets' days were numbered? How to greet and bow to the Grand Duchess Tatiana? She, under the influence of her mother, regarded Father Gregory as a saint. But she is a sensible girl, Judith reminded herself, and will understand when it is over, when we can make the truth about him public. We. A grand duke, a prince, an eminent doctor, and Judith Stein. She was reminded of Mordka Bogrov and Michael Nej.

But there was the hardest part of all—not to conceal her guilt at being involved in a conspiracy, but to conceal her excitement at being part of such a group, men who wanted her because she was important to their plans. She supposed at heart she was a born conspirator, and was only now realizing how empty her life had been since her return from Irkutsk.

How to keep from revealing herself to the family? But that was not difficult, because they were no longer a family. Poppa's business had dwindled to nothing; no one was buying or selling property, no one was going to lawyers any longer in Petrograd. Poppa spent much of each day sitting at his desk with his head in his hands, worrying about his dwindling savings. Momma worried equally, about her inability to produce a full meal for every luncheon, about the fact that she had had to let all her maids go, save only Hilda. Joseph worked as a laborer, since there were no other jobs available, and spent his time talking about the inevitability of a German victory. Joseph might well find himself under arrest after Rasputin was put into prison. But as one of those who had contributed to his downfall, she might be able to help her brother. She might be able to help them all.

Even Rachel, who belonged to this family least of all.

Rachel had her own life to live, and she was not about to share any of it.

In time the waiting, the concealment of her thoughts and her hopes and her fears, the withdrawal of herself into herself, much as Rachel had done, became a way of life, just as the arrest of Rasputin became an impossible illusion. When the note arrived from Purishkevich, saying simply, "My car will call for you at midnight on December 16," she read it over several times before she could properly understand what it meant. Then her heart slowed before leaping ahead with tremendous speed. It was happening. At last, it was happening. She might have waited her entire life just for this moment, to accomplish this one deed, for Russia. And for the decent things in life.

Judith dressed with great care. There was no choice but to wear the evening gown Poppa had bought for her visit to Starogan, a dark blue satin; there was no money for new clothes, even if there had been material available. It fitted her rather snugly now; despite the food shortages she had put on weight since her return from Siberia. But she supposed that was to the good. The gown bulged at the bodice and exposed more of her breasts than she would normally have liked. Rasputin would be pleased.

Rachel was not at home, thank God. But Momma was amazed. She had not seen her eldest daughter in evening dress for more than two years.

"I have been invited to a small soiree at Prince Yusupov's salon," she explained.

"Prince Yusupov? Such a nice man. Such a charming wife. Oh, I am so glad that you are going out to have a good time," Ruth Stein said, and then frowned. "But . . . the princess is in the country. I read that in the newspaper."

Judith poured herself a glass from her father's dwindling stock of brandy. Determined as she was, she could not stop her hands from trembling. "I am going with Dr. Purishkevich." She sipped, and felt better. She smiled at her mother. "One does not refuse an invitation from one's superior."

"Dr. Purishkevich? Such a nice man. Will you be too late? It is after eleven already."

"Dr. Purishkevich does not finish duty until ten. I may not be home until about two. It is just a small supper party. There is the car." She pulled on her coat and hurried out of the door, leaving Ruth Stein staring after her in disappointment. No doubt she had been looking forward to a chat with Dr. Purishkevich. But tonight was no time for decorum.

He opened the door for her, and she collapsed beside him. "Are you nervous?"

"I am terrified."

"Well, you look delightful. The beast will not be able to keep his hands off you." He squeezed her hand. "You do understand that he must be made to feel at home?"

"You promised me—"

"And we shall keep our promise, be sure of that. But you also must play your part. He assumes he is coming to meet you, that you are anxious to meet him. We have suggested that you are jealous of your sister's position, but not being friends with the grand duchess, you have no means of obtaining an entree to his salon. I swear you will not be alone for more than a few minutes. Quite insufficient time for him to . . . well, to do more than touch you."

I don't want him to touch me, she thought. I don't even want to see him.

"For Russia," Dr. Purishkevich said, apparently able to read her mind.

For Russia. The car had stopped outside Prince Yusupov's house on the Moika Quay. Purishkevich helped her down and escorted her into the hall, where the grand duke was waiting.

"Thank God you are here. Mademoiselle, you look enchanting. And brave. Russia salutes you."

"Where is the prince?" Purishkevich inquired.

"He has gone for the beast."

They were so excited that Judith had to take off her own coat. The hall was empty, the house silent.

The grand duke smiled at her nervously, and suddenly remembered to help her. "We have sent all the servants home. There will be no questions asked. They think there is going to be an orgy."

My God, Judith thought, suppose something goes wrong? Suppose . . . The grand duke had taken her arm and was escorting her, not upstairs to the drawing room, as she had expected, but down a flight of stairs at the back of the hall into a comfortably furnished servants' sitting room. Here there were bottles of Rasputin's favorite Madeira already opened on the table, as well as plates of cakes and biscuits. A fire roared in the grate, and before it a sleepy black retriever stretched himself.

"We thought we'd use the servants' quarters, eh?" the grand duke said.

"Just in case there is a struggle," Purishkevich explained.

"A struggle?" Judith cried.

"Nothing for you to worry your pretty head about, my dear. Now listen to me very carefully. Under no circumstances must you drink any of the wine, or eat any of the cakes. They are . . . drugged, yes, they are drugged, to make him sleepy. He is literally as strong as an ox, you know, and we must avoid violence if we can. Do you understand?"

"Yes," she said. "But I would like a glass of brandy."

"And you shall have one. Now, the beast believes that the prince has persuaded you to, ah, accommodate him, but that you prefer to meet him here privately rather than go publicly to his house. Therefore he does not expect to see us. We shall remove ourselves upstairs. Have no fear, we shall be watching you through a peephole, and we shall be with you in moments if he tries to assault you. But you understand that it would be better if you could persuade him to drink some of the wine and eat some of the cakes. And in addition, you must try to make him move about, once he has eaten or drunk. That will enable the drug to reach his brain faster."

"Remember," said the grand duke, "we are with you at all times."

The door closed, and she was alone. Judith Stein, *femme fatale*. Oh, my God, she thought, what am I doing here? What is going to happen to me, in just a few minutes? She sipped some brandy, sat down, but felt too restless to remain still. She got up again and stroked the dog, who raised his head obligingly but was obviously not about to leave the warmth of the fire. She wondered if he would just lie there if Rasputin attacked her. But why should the dog defend her?

She had a sudden desperate urge to go to the bathroom, made herself sit down again, crossed and uncrossed her legs, and wished that she smoked, like Xenia. Or Rachel. My God, would Rachel ever forgive her for this night's work?

Feet sounded on the stairs outside, and the distinctive guttural tone. She got up and found herself backing across the room to stand against the far wall; she watched the door swing in. Prince Felix came first, Rasputin just behind him. "Mademoiselle Stein," said the prince. But he was very nervous; his mouth trembled.

"Good evening, your excellency," she said, hardly believing it was her voice she heard. "Father Gregory."

"You are Rachel's sister?" The priest came farther into the room. "Come here and let me look at you."

She gave Yusupov a despairing glance, and he attempted to help her. "You'll take a glass of Madeira, Father Gregory?"

"Not now," Rasputin said. "I wish to look at the girl."

Judith sucked in her breath. She stepped away from the wall and went towards him. He seized her hands, drew her closer yet; his breath played on her face, so foul she almost stopped breathing.

"Some wine," the prince insisted. "We'll all have some wine." He thrust the glass at the priest, and Rasputin took it and tossed off its contents without even looking at it.

"Leave us," he growled, and Judith was drawn even closer, afraid to resist him, afraid to move. A great dirty hand rested on her shoulder, and then thrust its way into the bodice of her gown. She gave a little shiver of distaste, even as she felt her nipple hardening; despite herself she was just as excited as the men. "Leave us," he said again, and she heard the door close. She was alone with the monster. How long would it take the drug to work?

He kissed her ear, suddenly swept her into his arms and kissed her lips—a savage kiss, spreading her mouth to fill it with his tongue, so huge and questing it touched the back of her throat. She gasped for breath and pushed him away. He frowned at her. "You do not like me, little Judith?"

Judith got her breathing back under control. "If I did not like you, Father Gregory, I would not be here. But I . . ." She bit her lip.

"You are shy. Wine. You shall have some wine."

She opened her mouth and closed it again. Why not drug herself, and pass out with him? But if she passed out while he was still awake, he might rape her. And he was showing no effects at all from the first glass.

"For you," she said, and held out another glass.

"And you."

She hesitated and took one. Rasputin once again threw his head back and drained his glass at a gulp. Judith was able to pour three-quarters of her glass into the one he had just emptied. But she would hardly have the opportunity to do that again.

Rasputin wiped his mouth on the back of his hand, and sat down. "Come here."

Two glasses, and he had not even blinked. She moved towards him, and he seized her hand and sat her on his lap. He started to feel her as if he were searching for something—squeezing her breasts, fingering her ribs through the satin, sliding his hand up and down her leg and then suddenly going lower, to her ankles, to get his fingers under her skirt and drag them up her stockings.

"No," she gasped, and managed to get up.

"You must not be shy with me," he said.

"I am not. I . . ."

"You are not a virgin?" He threw back his head and gave a bellow of laughter. "You are Peter Borodin's woman." He leaned forward. "Undress. Slowly."

Judith took a deep breath and looked around the room. What to do? Things were not going as the conspirators had planned. Or had they meant all along to sacrifice her? "Slowly," she agreed. She went to the table and placed the bottle at his elbow, together with the plate of little cakes. "And you must eat and drink, while you watch me."

"I will watch you," he agreed. "You are beautiful. You are even more beautiful than your sister—there is more of you." He picked up the bottle by the neck, and then put it down again. "I'll undo those buttons."

She hesitated, then went towards him, turned her back to him, and felt his fingers on her gown; it began to slip from her shoulders. "Haha!" he shouted, and drove his hands inside the material to give her another going over, this time sliding his hand down the front of her petticoat to squeeze her groin, a movement so hard and distasteful she fell forward and lost her balance, landing on her hands and knees. He gave another bellow of laughter, put his boot on her hip, and pushed, to send her rolling across the floor. "Oh, you are a lovely child," he said.

Judith regained her knees. Her hair had started to come down and was drifting across her face. She blew it away, now as aware of her anger as of her fear and embarrassment. But he had picked up the bottle again, and even held one of the cakes in his free hand. She got back to her feet, allowed the gown to slide down to her ankles, and watched him chewing the cake, then washing it down with a gulp of wine. Surely, now . . . but he was waving his hand for her to continue, spilling wine as he did so.

She gathered her petticoat in both hands and lifted it over her head. In the winter she wore a woolen chemise beneath, and thus still felt reasonably protected. She held the petticoat before her and saw that he was drinking again. Only a few seconds now. It had to be. Had he slipped a little in his chair? She was sure of it.

"The chemise," he said, and his voice was definitely slurred. "The chemise."

She hesitated, biting her lip. Make him move, the grand duke had said. She threw the petticoat to the floor and ran for the door. Rasputin gave a roar and got up; she ducked away from him, reached the door, and dragged it open. "Felix," she screamed, forgetting rank and manners and plan.

He was standing outside, waiting for her. To her horror she saw that he was carrying a revolver, and at the same moment a gramophone started playing, very loudly, in the room above. She gasped, and turned, and saw that Rasputin had sat down again, and was struggling for breath, his eyes constantly opening and closing.

"Leave," Yusupov snapped. "Quickly." He pushed her behind him, went inside, and closed the door. Judith looked around in desperation, wondering what they had done with her coat, discovered that the hallway was freezing—she had left gown and petticoat behind her—and heard the sound of a shot. She turned, and the door burst open. Yusupov did not seem to notice her, and ran up the stairs. She looked through the door and saw that the dog was rolling over by the fireplace with blood pouring from its neck. The dog?

Rasputin was on his hands and knees, holding onto his own neck, but not bleeding. She took a step towards him, then hesitated. But if she could just reach her clothes . . .

Feet pounded behind her, and all three of the men came down. "I'm sorry," the prince was saying. "My hand was shaking. I . . . I could not."

They stood in the doorway, watching the starets. He had fallen over now, but his eyes were still open, glaring at them.

"Give me the gun," Purishkevich said.

"You can't," Judith shouted. "You can't shoot him. You told me—"

The grand duke caught her round the waist when she started

to run forward. Suddenly she felt exhausted, quite unable to move. She watched Purishkevich step away from the door, closed her eyes as the revolver exploded twice, and opened them again to see blood streaming across the floor.

"He is dead," Purishkevich said.

"Oh, my God." Released by the grand duke, Judith sank to her knees. Purishkevich stepped past Rasputin, picked up her gown and petticoat, and brought them to her.

"You did magnificently, Judith. Without you it could not have been accomplished."

"You said he was to be arrested," she whispered. She could not take her gaze from the body. She had seen men die before, in the hospital, in Siberia. But Rasputin . . .

"There was no other way," Yusupov said. "I am sorry you saw it. We did not intend that. It should not have been necessary to shoot him. The poison should have killed him."

"The poison?" she shrieked.

"There was no other way," the grand duke repeated.

The poison. And she had nearly drunk some of it herself. "You lied to me. An imperial prince. You lied to me."

"For the good of Russia. Now dress yourself, and we shall send you home. No one will ever know of your part in this, unless you tell them."

Unless I tell them, she thought, pushing herself to her feet. Oh, my God, unless I tell them. She dropped the petticoat over her head. But she could not keep her gaze from returning to Rasputin; it was as though she expected him to move, to get up, to give that unforgettable laugh of contempt for all mankind. And then she saw one eye open, and stare at her in turn.

She screamed, and pointed. The men turned in horror. "He's alive," Yusupov shouted, "Oh, my God, he's still alive!" He turned as if to retreat, was stopped by the grand duke.

"We must finish it," he said. "We *must*." But he made no move.

Purishkevich gave what might have been a groan, and ran forward. From his jacket pocket he took a long-bladed knife, and with a howl of misery he threw himself upon the body of the dying starets and began stabbing Rasputin in the chest.

"Comrades." Lenin stood, his glass in his hand, and the other seven people seated around the table rose with him. "Let us drink to 1917, with all the success that it will bring."

"1917," they said obediently. It was impossible not to agree with Lenin, even when they all doubted there was any longer any substance to his words. But in his very appearance—the chunky face, the aggressive red-brown beard, the sparkling eyes—and even more in the power and *anger* with which he debated, he was not a man to be opposed. Not, at least, by these members of the faithful. Not even by me, Ivan Nej thought. But then he was still basking in the glow of being in Switzerland at all. Sometimes he could not believe it, thought back over those days spent huddled beneath trees and in hollows, those nights spent crawling across mist-shrouded hills in the teeming rain, expecting every moment to hear a challenge and feel the dull thud of a bullet crashing into his body, as a long, endless nightmare. But that had been months ago. He was here, and he had been made welcome; the mere fact that he was Michael's brother had insured that. Lenin needed all the people, the reliable people, he could find, if his plans were ever going to come to fruition. And they would bear fruit, someday. Ivan certainly believed that. He was even contemplating taking a false name. Michael still called himself Nej, but Michael was nothing. Lenin had once been known as Ulyanov. But to the world at large he was only known as Lenin, a shadowy pseudonym at the bottom of inflammatory articles. As Lenin he was famous. As Ulyanov he could live in obscurity wherever he chose, whenever he chose.

With Krupskaya. She sat on his right hand, gazing at him with complete absorption. They were married, and yet she worshipped his every word. They were *married*. There was an incredible thought for a revolutionary, a permanent clue to Lenin's bourgeois background. But how marvelous it must be to have a worshipful woman always at your side. That was something that would never happen to Ivan Nej, unless the woman were a peasant like Zoe Feodorovna. He was a dreamer, not a doer, and like most dreams, his did not stand the light of day.

Lenin had remained standing, where his company had seated itself. "Why so gloomy?" His voice boomed over them. "Do you not believe that 1917 will be a good year?"

They exchanged glances.

"Why, comrades..." His voice lowered in that winning fashion of his. "In Russia they will just be celebrating Christmas. Is that not an accusation against the entire commonwealth of nations, that our Christmas should be fourteen days behind everyone else's? Is it not?"

This time they could murmur their agreement.

"And this Christmas they will have something to celebrate," he said, his voice still low and caressing.

"We have won another victory?" Kamenov asked. A simple fellow, Kamenov, Ivan had concluded.

Lenin snorted. "Another victory? There are no such things as victories when capitalist-fed armies engage, comrade. And do Russian armies ever win victories, betrayed as they are by their leaders? No. But the Russian people *have* won a victory. It has been delivered to them by the very taskmasters we are sworn to overthrow. Did I not always tell you that when the princes and the dukes and the priests fell out, then would be our time?"

Another murmur of agreement.

"But when will it happen?" Michael Nej asked. "When could it possibly happen?"

Lenin gave a roar of laughter. "It has happened, comrade. It has happened. The news came in today, and I saved it for this evening. Rasputin is dead. The great beast is dead, my friends, struck down by members of the imperial family itself. Petrograd is in a furor. That furor will grow, comrades. It will grow and grow until it bursts. Yes, 1917 is our year, comrades. I feel it. I know it: 1917 is our year."

Chapter 7

"NURSE STEIN." SISTER STOOD IN THE DOORWAY, VERY STRAIGHT, her uniform neatly pressed, as always. "Report to Dr. Alapin."

Oh Lord, Judith thought. For two months she had lived in terror of this summons. No matter how faithfully the Grand Duke Dimitri, or Prince Felix, or Dr. Purishkevich, had kept their promises, she knew her secret could not be maintained forever.

She dried her hands on her apron, gave her charge a hasty smile, and walked along the corridor. The other nurses stared at her. Xenia was not among them. There had been no sign of Xenia since Christmas. She had been taken ill, it was said. But rumor had it she had slashed her wrists on learning that the holy father was dead. She had been found in time, but her mother had taken her down to Starogan to recover.

And no Rachel either. Rachel was also ill. With grief? It was impossible to be sure. At least she had not tried suicide. She had merely become more withdrawn than ever, hardly answered when spoken to, and went about her duties with an air of abstraction. Then she had suddenly developed a high temperature. Logically it was a result of the cold. It had been the coldest January anyone could remember, an added burden to those of hunger and uncertainty and fear that the population of Petrograd already carried. But now it was February, and surely the end of winter was in sight. Rachel would be well again soon. For Judith, having to leave the hospital in the evening and sit at her bedside was the hardest thing of all—how she wanted to confess to someone. But surely Rachel, once she was well again, would understand what a lucky escape she had had.

The cold had thinned the numbers of the nurses by a good fifth. Today there was not even the Grand Duchess Tatiana. Another casualty of that terrible night? But the grand duchess had not seemed very much affected, had come to the hospital up until three days ago, for all that she had lost much of her gaiety, and had worn black for her mother's friend. More likely she was being kept at home because of the riots.

For that was the most terrible thing of all. Judith had become an accessory before the fact of a murder, as Poppa had put it, to no avail. What had they accomplished? The grand duke and Prince Felix had both been banished to their estates; they were too close to the royal family to be tried for murder, even if they had attempted to deny their guilt. Purishkevich had been sent to the front as a field surgeon. That there might have been a fourth person involved, a woman who had lured Rasputin to his fate, remained only a rumor. And nothing had changed, except that the tsar had relinquished command of the army to General Alexeiev and returned to Petrograd, but more, it seemed, to be at the side of his wife in her hour of grief than to pick up the reins of government. The tsarina might have lost her confessor, but it was still her creatures, Protopopov and Sturmer, who ruled the country, whose incompetence, or worse, kept everyone in a half-starved condition. In the two months since the starets' death—the two months of darkest winter—agitation and discontent had grown. Not a day passed without news of a clash between police and striking radicals. However bravely the soldiers at the front might still be fighting, the country behind them was utterly disenchanted with the war. And over the past week the disturbances seemed to have grown.

She walked along the corridor to the superintendent's office. And now she was to be sent . . . where? They could hardly bring her to trial, for fear of what she might say, whom she might accuse. But they could send her all the way back to Siberia. And yet she was almost glad it had happened, at last. For two months she had not slept without a nightmare, without a vision of that single eye open and staring at her, without remembering how they had dragged that huge body out of the house, out through the yard, and broken the ice on the Neva to push it beneath—and how, horribly, inconceivably, when it had been recovered, several days later, it had been established that the priest had died by drowning. Two bullets, heaven knew how much poison, and repeated stabbings by a knife had all failed to quench that gargantuan spirit. And so, for two months, she had been almost unable to eat, aware all the while that Momma and Poppa were watching her; they knew, even if they had tacitly agreed to keep the secret from Rachel and Joseph. Momma knew where she had been that night, and she had told Poppa. Perhaps, as people were saying, it had been no murder, but rather the justified execution of a ferocious and traitorous beast; they still had to live with the fact that their daughter had taken part in the death of a man.

As she also had to live with that fact. She had been falsely accused of being a partner in the assassination of Stolypin. But there could be no falsehood about the coming accusation. There could be no plea of innocence.

She knocked.

"Enter."

She closed the door behind her and stood before the desk. Dr. Alapin was the hospital's senior doctor. He was a short, plump man who had seen much service; he had been in Port Arthur during the siege by the Japanese. Why, Judith realized for the first time, he must know Ilona Borodina, because she had served with the nurses during that war. Should she try telling him that she was a friend of Ilona's?

He did not even raise his head; his bald spot gleamed at her. "Nurse Stein, I have a change of scenery for you. You will be glad of that after two years in this place, eh?"

Was he trying to be funny? "Yes, doctor."

"There is a car waiting for you. You are to report to Tsarkoe Selo, immediately."

"To—" Her heart seemed to do a complete somersault. Tsarkoe Selo was the tsar's private palace, outside the city. Oh, my God, she thought; the tsarina wishes to question me herself. But why were there no policemen?

"Yes," the doctor went on. "It seems the tsarevnas have contracted measles. I suspected it several days ago, and now it has been confirmed. The Grand Duchess Tatiana has requested your sister, but since she is also ill, I am sending you instead." At last his head raised, and a brief smile flitted across his features. "One Stein will do as well as another, eh? There's not much nursing to be done, but someone must be there. You will stay until they are entirely recovered. Understood?"

Judith inhaled slowly. No one knew, after all.

But how could she go to Tsarkoe Selo, live in the tsarina's own house? Whether anyone knew or not, she *was* guilty. Even if she had had no idea of what was going to happen, she *had* lured Rasputin to his death. Surely the tsarina would know that, just by looking at her? Or surely she would betray herself?

But to escape the horror that was the hospital, the seething antheap that was Petrograd, the constant reminder that was Rachel—at Tsarkoe Selo all would be peace and quiet. The tsarina would see to that.

Dr. Alapin was frowning. "Do you understand, Nurse Stein?"

Judith nodded. "Yes, doctor."

"Have you ever had measles?"

"Yes, doctor. When I was eleven."

"Good. Good. Well then, you will leave immediately. The car will take you to your home to pick up some changes of clothing, and then out to the palace. But do not delay."

"Yes, doctor."

She went downstairs in a daze. No arrest. No, nothing save the honor of nursing the tsarevnas. And at Tsarkoe Selo. She pulled her cape around her shoulders, stepped into the chill of the courtyard, and smiled at the uniformed chauffeur who stood at attention beside the gleaming car. He held the door for her, she got in, sat down, and the door was closed. Judith Stein, riding in one of the tsarina's own cars.

But how *could* she face her? The tsarina had not visited the hospital since Rasputin's death. Would she not know, the moment she looked into Judith's eyes, how guilty she was? *She* could see it every time she looked into the mirror. She twisted her fingers together so tightly that one glove came off. What to do? But not to go . . . her head jerked at a sharp sound, and the car screeched to a halt.

"What was that?"

The chauffeur did not turn his head. "That was a shot, nurse. And listen."

There were more sharp sounds, and now she could hear shouts and screams, and the ugly growl of an agitated mob.

"It is a riot, nurse," the chauffeur said. "And it is coming from the Nevskiy Prospekt. I do not think we will be able to cross the bridge."

"But—my house . . . my clothes . . . my parents—"

"It will not be safe," the chauffeur said. "Especially with the imperial crest on the car. Your parents are in no danger, mademoiselle, and neither is your house. But you may be." He backed into a side street and turned the car. "I will take you out to Tsarkoe Selo, and we shall explain the situation to her majesty. She will let you come in for your clothes when the rioters have been dispersed."

Judith supposed he was talking sense. There were riots nearly every day, and shots nearly every day as the police and the garrison dispersed them. Even as they drove away from the noise, a fresh outbreak of shooting started to their left, and then to their right, and the noise of shouting people seemed to block out the sound of the engine. She peered out the back window, and saw several soldiers run round the corner. They were not going to allow the riot to spread any further, thank God. She watched in fascination as the men lined up, knelt, and started shooting. But they were shooting at her. Or at the car, at least.

Soldiers?

George Hayman ran up the steps outside the foreign ministry, ducked into the doorway, and paused for breath. Behind him the sound of shots, overlaid by the far more sinister rattle of machine-gun fire, continued to distort the morning. He knew that no one had actually been shooting at him, and besides, he was fairly used to being under fire, both as a combatant, with the Rough Riders in Cuba in 1898, and as a war correspondent, in South Africa with the Boers and in Port Arthur with the Russians. But civil strife of this nature was new to him. It was so uncertain. A crowd of people would gather, apparently good-humored and unarmed, something would spark them off, and the next minute shots would be exchanged and bodies would be lying on the snow. While if the rumors were to be believed . . .

He realized that he was alone in the downstairs hall of the ministry. While he had been running across the street he had seen the female secretaries gathered at the upstairs windows, watching him. But where was the major-domo normally on guard here? Why, the mob, if it chose, could rush in here at will.

But supposing it did choose, would one major-domo be able to keep it out?

He ran up the stairs, passed a young woman in the white blouse and black skirt of the staff, her arms filled with files. She gave him a brief smile. Not a hair was out of place, and she continued on her way without a second glance. The fact that half the city was fighting, while the other half went about its daily round without apparent concern, was the most absurd aspect of this situation. And when the halves were as closely intertwined as they now were, the absurdity became almost farcical.

He hurried along the corridor and opened the door to Tigran's outer office. The secretary peered at him through spectacles. She was a good-looking girl in a tight-faced fashion, and had a full figure.

"I'd like to see Monsieur Borodin," he explained.

"Have you an appointment?"

George shook his head. "Give him my card."

She looked at the card, raised her head again to look at George, and then got up and went into the inner office. George barely had time to light a cigar when Tigran hurried out.

"George, my dear fellow. I haven't seen you for over a week."

"Yes, well, I've been busy. Tigger, what are your people doing about this situation?"

"What situation?" Tigran held his elbow and escorted him into the huge inner office.

"You wouldn't say there's a situation?"

"Sit down, my dear fellow." Tigran poured two glasses of brandy, then cocked his head. "You mean the shooting?"

"That for a start."

"It's the police dispersing mobs. You know that."

George took his brandy and sipped. "I don't know that anymore. What of this rumor that the men of the Pavlovsky Regiment have shot their colonel?"

"Only a rumor." Tigran sat behind his desk.

"May I quote you?"

"Of course you may. There is a great deal of unrest. That

was true last February as well, you may remember. Hungry people behave very oddly. I'm afraid it may be necessary to shoot quite a few of them. But it is nothing serious."

"May I quote that as well?"

"Certainly. Shall I tell you how I know it cannot be serious? Two days ago the tsar left Tsarkoe Selo to return to the army."

George stared at him openmouthed.

"It is a fact," Tigran said. "Now, surely you can see that he must be satisfied the situation here is well in hand. He knows a great deal more about what is going on than we do."

"Does he?"

Tigran raised his eyebrows. "Of course he does. Were you in Petrograd in 1905? Or in Moscow? I was here. Ilona was in Moscow. You should ask her. There were pitched battles between the Cossacks and the strikers in Moscow. Cannon were used. And in the end they were dispersed by your old friend Roditchev. Since he is in Petrograd now, and in charge of the police, I can promise you the same thing will happen here."

"It's actually Ilona I came to talk to you about," George said. "I can't get through to Starogan. All the lines are busy, I'm told, time and again."

"That is nonsense," Tigran said.

"Exactly how I feel. Do you suppose you could get through for me?"

"Well, of course I can. Dora," Tigran called.

The door to the outer office had been left open. "Yes, your worship?"

"I'd like to place a call to Starogan. To the Dowager Princess Borodina. Tell them it's urgent state business and is to be put through without delay."

"Yes, your worship." Dora withdrew, leaving the door open.

"It will not take long," Tigran said. "But she will be perfectly all right, you know. These disturbances are local affairs, and confined to cities, where people have something to grumble about. Besides, my mother and Xenia are down there, as you know. They would certainly have been in touch had anything happened. Nothing ever happens in Starogan." He drank some more brandy. "Now, you tell me about these far more interesting rumors that your people are coming in on our side."

"It certainly sounds like it," George agreed. "We've broken

off diplomatic relations with the Central Powers. It had to happen, I guess. And not a moment too soon."

"I'll say amen to that," Tigran agreed. "It's the best news I've heard in years. And once it reaches the streets, you'll see a change of attitude, believe me."

"It might take a little while," George pointed out. "The president can't declare war. He has to persuade Congress to do that."

"But you believe he will persuade them?"

"I believe so, yes. That's why I want to get in touch with Ilona. I'd like her and the kids to go home."

"Home? To America, you mean? Are *you* going home?"

"Not immediately. I'd like to stay and see what happens here. I'm a shade too old to do any more fighting as a front-line soldier, I guess. But I'd be a lot happier if Ilona and the kids were out of the way."

"You suppose they'll be safe, crossing the Atlantic? Anyway, they'll never be able to pass the Dardanelles."

"I've got a different idea." He paused as Tigran's secretary once more appeared in the doorway. "All the lines are busy, as far as Moscow, your worship."

"Damnation," Tigran said. "I shall try again later, George, and let you know."

"I'd be grateful." George got up, and Tigran frowned at him.

"You really think there's going to be a revolution, don't you?"

"I think there *is* a revolution, at this moment. That business in 1905 came at the end of a war. Your government had the men and the resources to cope with it. This time the war is still going on, and going badly. And it's been going on too long."

"What about your people?"

"I told you, it's going to take time for a declaration of war to be made at all, and then for mobilization, and then to transport our men across the ocean. I don't think the tsar *has* any time. I don't think any of you have any time. If I were you I'd start thinking about that."

Tigran got up and refilled their glasses. "Are you asking me to desert my post, George? You're not deserting yours, and you're merely an observer. Besides, Rachel is ill."

"Rachel?" George frowned.

"She seems to have caught some kind of a chill. She's running a high fever and has to stay in bed."

"She really means that much to you?"

"For heaven's sake, we're engaged to be married."

"You've been engaged for three years. How often have you seen her in that time?"

"There's the war, George."

"Do you love the girl, Tigger?"

"What a question. I'm going to marry her."

"Not the same thing."

Tigran walked to the window, looked down at the yard behind the building. "She is the best and most honorable woman I have ever known. She is also one of the most beautiful women I have ever known. And the sweetest, most innocent woman I have ever known."

"That sounds more like admiration than love. Don't take offense, Tigger. But if you're marrying her because you think she'll be good for you, or if you're trying to make some sort of point to your family—"

"I am marrying her," Tigran said, turning back from the window and smiling. "And I hope you will be here for the wedding, George. Now I really must do some work, I suppose. What are you going to do now?"

"I think I may just pay a call on Sergei Roditchev," George said. "I should have done so before, don't you think, since I've been in Petrograd for three years? I'd like to find out just what *he* intends to do about what's happening."

"I've just been talking with George Hayman. Do you know he—" Tigran opened the door to his brother-in-law's office, and hesitated in embarrassment. The grand duke had his secretary on his knees; her stenographer's pad lay conveniently nearby on the desk. Now she stood up; she had not been able to move so quickly that Tigran had not seen her skirt falling back into place—Philip had had his hand underneath. She did not look the least embarrassed, though. She was a pretty girl who liked to smile, and liked to enjoy life.

"That will be all, thank you, mademoiselle." Philip did not seem embarrassed either. The lucky dog.

"Thank you, your highness." The girl gave Tigran a smile,

and closed the door behind her.

"I say, I'm most terribly sorry," Tigran said. "Bursting in here like that."

Philip waved his hand. "I should prefer it if Xenia did not know."

"Of course."

"Natasha is only a child. But a delightful child. You were saying something."

Tigran wondered if he would ever have such aplomb, such confidence. It was not a question he would have considered asking himself during the early part of his engagement. But in an inexplicable way Rachel had grown apart from him over the past few months, and the distance she had placed between them had somehow reduced him in his own eyes. He blamed Xenia. He had been happy when Xenia, alone of the entire family, had befriended his fiancée. That Xenia would draw Rachel into Rasputin's circle had been inevitable, and not, to his mind, something to be concerned about. Women, young and old, seemed to need these priestly advisers, and that Rachel, a Jew, was attending the salon of an orthodox priest seemed to promise a less controversial future than he had feared. The rumors, spread mainly by German sympathizers, that the female Russian aristocracy did more than worship the starets, he could dismiss as enemy propaganda.

But this business since Rasputin's death—Xenia's attempted suicide, and Rachel's mental collapse, conveniently camouflaged by her fever—had made him think, and thought had developed into doubt. Now he was reviving notions he had supposed were behind him forever. He wondered if Dora Ulyanova would ever sit on *his* lap?

"Tigger?"

"Ah . . . George Hayman thinks the situation is more serious than it appears."

"Hayman?"

"Well, I sometimes wonder if these newspaper people don't actually know more of what is going on than we do."

"I am quite sure the situation is serious, Tigger. I'm very much afraid the police are going to have to make an example of someone, rather soon."

"I'm wondering if there shouldn't be more troops in the city. Listen." There was an outbreak of firing from very close at hand, and once again accompanied by the rattle of a machine gun.

"Oh, nonsense. There are a hundred and sixty thousand men in the garrison already. You must keep calm. It is the duty of people like us to give the lead, in troubled times." He glared at the door as once again it burst open. "Have you no manners?"

The girl Natasha panted. "Forgive me, your highness. But there is fighting in the street. The guards have joined the rioters, and they are attacking the police."

"What?"

"Oh, my God," Tigran said. "Oh, my God. If the garrison—"

Philip snapped his fingers. "Obviously things *are* serious. Tigger, close up your office. We'd better get along to the Duma and see what's happening. And Tigger, do you have a pistol?"

"I have a revolver."

"Then bring it with you, and make sure it's loaded."

Tigger nodded. He turned toward the door and gazed at the girl. She was no flirt now, just a very frightened young woman. "You had better get on home," he said.

"Yes," Philip said. "You get on home, Natasha. I'll send a messenger to you when it's safe for you to come back."

"But . . ." Natasha looked from one to the other. "Couldn't I have a car?"

"A car would be far more dangerous," Philip said. "A girl on foot will attract no attention. Hurry now. Let yourself out the back door, and go home." He got up to look down from his window, and hastily stepped back as the glass shattered. "There are men down there with guns," he complained. "Shooting at me."

"Hurry." Tigran pushed Natasha out the door, turned her towards the stairs, and gave her another push. "I'll get my gun." He ran along the corridor and into his own office. Dora Ulyanova stood at the window, looking out. "For God's sake," he shouted. "They're shooting at us. Get away from that window." He sat at the desk, pulled open the drawer, and paused in bewilderment; the revolver was gone. He looked at Dora Ulyanova. She had stepped away from the window, and he saw that she held the gun in both hands. "In the name of God—"

"The American was right," she said. "The revolution *has* started."

"*A* revolution, to be sure. Now you get on home. Give me

the gun. His excellency and I are going to the Duma to discover what measures are being taken." He stepped round the desk, and stopped as the gun was raised.

"The first duty of the revolution," she said, "is to destroy all traitors."

He could not see her eyes behind the glasses. Was this some idea of a joke? At a time like this? "What are you talking about, Dora?"

"You gave the cipher file to a German agent," she said. Her voice was quiet and utterly composed.

"Of course I didn't. I've never heard such nonsense. I—" His mouth sagged open as he saw her knuckles tightening. My God, he thought, I am about to die. But I cannot die. I am Tigran Borodin, heir to Count Igor Borodin. I am a future foreign minister of the empire. I am only thirty-five years old. I have been saving the second half of my life to build a career, to love Rachel Stein. I . . .

"What's happening here?" Philip hurried into the room and paused in surprise. Tigran turned to warn him at the same moment as the revolver exploded. He had never seen anyone die before. The entire front of Philip's suit seemed to dissolve into a red mess, and he fell over backwards without a sound, his body striking the floor with a thump that shook the room.

"My God." Tigran turned back to face the girl, saw the red flash as the gun exploded again.

Shots, behind him and to the left. And he had heard more shots to his right, a moment ago. George Hayman hesitated, stepped into the shelter of a convenient doorway. This door, like all the others he had passed, was closed and bolted, and there were shutters over the windows. It was impossible to decide if there was anyone inside. Certainly there were enough people on the streets. As he watched, a gang of youths ran by, a few armed with rifles and revolvers, mostly carrying wooden beams and uptorn paving stones. They paid no attention to the well-dressed man in the doorway. For the moment, at least, the hatred of the mob was directed against men in uniform rather than the obviously well-to-do.

Some men in uniform, however, had already stuck red cockades in their hats to denote that they too were for the revolution. There were too many of those for comfort. George left the doorway and went to the corner, from where he could see the

Okhrana headquarters. The square before it was entirely filled by a mob, the biggest of all the mobs he had seen this week, swaying and chanting outside the iron gateway. It reminded him of the mobs that had stoned German-owned shops and houses in the first days of the war. Those mobs had been dispersed by the Cossacks and Okhrana. Who would disperse this mob?

The Cossacks, of course. He listened to the dreaded bugle call, to the clip-clop of hooves. The crowd heard them too. The swaying stopped, and became a continuous movement, a retreat. But not yet a rout. This crowd had weapons in their hands. A few of the bolder spirits were even prepared to oppose the Cossacks.

The cavalry trotted into the square, drew rein at a command from their captain, and formed rough lines; the horses shuffled and stamped the cobbles. George had seen it all before. His only thought was that they should have been called out sooner. Now, if the mob was prepared to stand and fight, there was going to be bloodshed on a scale Petrograd had not yet witnessed.

The captain raised his sword and gave another command. The horsemen trotted forward, and George was struck by how young they were. They wore Cossack uniforms, but they were no more than recruits, whose fathers and elder brothers were engaged in fighting the Germans. These boys had seen no service, had developed no sense of superiority over the poor souls they were intended to terrify. He watched in fascinated horror as they advanced, but never above a walk. He watched the people form up to receive them, wooden clubs and rifles thrust forward, and he watched one of the young men suddenly hurl away his whip and leap from the saddle, to throw his arms around the first of the mob he could find.

The officer gave another command, tried to strike the deserting Cossack with his sword, and was prevented as another horse jostled his and threw him off balance. Now more men were dismounting, mingling with the crowd while their horses waited patiently. The officer pulled his mount to one side, gazed at the scene in disgust for a moment, then wheeled his horse and rode down a side street. Someone fired after him—George was not sure whether it was one of his own men—but the shot went wide. Then the entire Cossack force had dismounted to join the mob.

This, then, was the end. Throughout history the Cossacks had been the ultimate bastion of the Russian crown, ever since Peter the Great had won their allegiance during the campaign against Charles XII of Sweden. This day, just two hundred years later, the Romanov dynasty had lost control of its principal weapon.

The Okhrana were about to find that out. For they could exist, could carry out their dreadful work, only with the nation sufficiently cowed to accept them. Now the nation was being led by the young men with the fur hats and the glittering lances. Once again the mob surged against the railings outside the Okhrana headquarters, and shook them as a huge man might shake a small dog. Men climbed the steel bars, and others thrust their shoulders against them. With a mighty creak the whole structure caved inwards, and with an even louder shriek the mob surged across it.

From the front porch of the building came the chatter of machine guns, and the leaders of the mob fell, tumbling over each other in bloody heaps. George felt his breath constrict. There could be no more compassion now, no more humanity. For the crowd had gathered itself after its momentary pause, and surged forward once again. Even the machine gun could kill only so many. Men appeared at the upper windows, and rifles and revolvers cracked. Then the machine gun was overrun and the front doors caved in like matchwood. Women screamed from within the building, others cheered as they joined the menfolk in the assault. George could only stand and watch as people appeared at windows, wailing and shouting; as men and women were thrown from the upper levels, to come crashing to the lawns below and lie in still and lifeless mounds; as, through the shattered glass, papers, the files of a century's tyranny, were scattered to the February wind; and as, inevitably, a wisp of smoke suddenly appeared behind the paper, to be joined immediately by billowing clouds.

Cheering and yelling, the mob flowed back out of the doomed building. But it did not leave empty-handed. It carried its victims with it, other men and women, dragged like toys, screaming their pleas for mercy, being kicked in the faces and the stomach as they were hurled on the grass, some being shot out of hand, others being marched along streets to the nearest lamppost, there to be hung, sometimes by the neck, sometimes by the ankles, all the while accompanied by a dreadful jeering and laughing, as trousers were torn off, eyes were poked out, genitals cut away, female secretaries held down and raped before being hoisted.

It was the most dreadful scene he had ever witnessed, but still the mob was not satisfied. "Roditchev," they shrieked. "We want Roditchev!" They filled the trampled, bloodstained lawns before the burning building, and shouted their hatred and their lust at the flames.

"Roditchev," gasped someone close to George. "Is he dead?"

He turned his head in surprise, saw the young woman, Dora Ulyanova, from the Foreign Ministry. Tigran's secretary. Did Tigran know this side of her? For her clothes were disheveled, and she had lost or thrown away her glasses, and in her hand she carried a revolver. "Is he dead?" she shouted. "Have you killed him?"

The young man she was addressing shook his head. "He was not there. The beast has escaped."

The girl's shoulders seemed to slump, then she shrugged, turned away, and faced George. Instinctively her hand went back to the pistol she had just thrust into the waistband of her skirt, and he wished he had brought his own weapon; with everyone else so trigger-happy, he had thought it safer to leave it at home.

For a moment they gazed at each other, then the girl showed her teeth in a smile. "You are the American correspondent, Hayman," she said.

George raised his hat. He wished she'd lower the gun. Finally she did so.

"Why should I kill you, American?" Dora Ulyanova asked. "You must tell the world that we are free, at last. Tell them that, Mr. American Hayman. Tell them we are free."

A bell tinkled, its clear tones ringing along the corridors, up and down stairs. There was no other sound throughout the palace.

The quiet was the most delightful thing about Tsarkoe Selo. It was surely possible to be happy here on a scale impossible anywhere else. It *should* be possible—if only it were possible to stop worrying. To stop thinking what might be happening in Petrograd, or in other places as well. But it was Petrograd that concerned Judith. Momma and Poppa were in Petrograd, as well as Rachel and Joseph, and Petrograd, from all accounts, was in the hands of a mob. The chauffeur who had gone back in to get her clothes—was it really only a week ago—had said her family were all right, but who could tell how the situation might have changed?

And yet in Tsarkoe Selo, all was peace, and it was time to rise. Claudette, her French maid, was already in the room, holding open the door to the shower stall. Incredible that Judith Stein should rise at dawn and take a cold shower. She had risen at dawn in Irkutsk, but there had been no showers there. But the empress had taken it for granted that the nurse's habits would be the same as their own, and it would not do to offend the empress. Judith gave Claudette a hasty smile, gritted her teeth as the rubber cap was fitted over her head and the maid carefully tucked away every last strand of hair, and braced herself for the sudden shock, the icy cold water that battered her flesh like a million needles, driving her breath away, leaving her gasping and panting and then suddenly filled with an enormous sense of well-being as she stepped back onto the carpet and was enveloped in a towel.

The tsarina. She was probably the most hated woman in all Russia, Judith reflected. Yet there could have been no kinder employer. Judith was treated as a friend, brought into all the family amusements and entertainments, and they were very much a family who entertained themselves. And how *she* must be worrying. Apart from her responsibilities as head of the state now that the tsar had once again returned to the front, and her fear for him, and her own ill health—for she was given to heart spasms that would leave her quite prostrate—there was the tsarevich's health; it was only this last week that Judith had realized just how seriously ill the tsarevich was. Ill, and yet not ill. He was a typical excitable, happy, and boisterous teenager, with the millstone of death hung around his neck in that the slightest bruise could develop into internal bleeding that left him writhing in pain. It had been his ability to soothe the pain and even stop the bleeding that had apparently brought Rasputin to the tsarina's notice and later made her worship his powers. In her newly gained knowledge, Judith could almost understand that. For now that the starets was gone it was quite pitiable to watch the most powerful woman in Russia gazing at her son, willing him to sit quietly, waiting for disaster whenever he mounted a horse or even went for a ramble in the woods behind the palace. She must know, Judith thought, that such a potential invalid could never be tsar. But what was she to do? There were no other sons, and she was past forty.

And her daughters' nurse had helped to destroy the one man in all Russia able to bring the boy relief. If she knew *that*...

Judith was dressed in her uniform. Claudette was very efficient. Now her hair was pinned up and the cap set in place. "There we are, mademoiselle. Not even her majesty will be able to criticize."

For all her gentle courtesy, Alexandra Feodorovna was possessed of an eagle eye, and everything had to be just so. Judith might be a friend of Tatiana's, but she was also a nurse, and must fill that role every moment of the day.

"I thank you, Claudette. Is there any news from Petrograd?"

"News, bah! There were some men, this morning. Members of the Duma—would you believe it, mademoiselle?—wishing to see her majesty, and she still in bed."

"Have they gone back?"

"No, no, mademoiselle. Her majesty graciously consented to see them after breakfast. They are waiting downstairs."

Judith hurried along the silent corridors. Would it be possible to have a word with them? Members of the Duma. Very possibly friends of Poppa. They would know what was happening. In fact, they must have come to Tsarkoe Selo to inform the Tsarina of what was happening. But first, breakfast. She paused in the doorway to the sun-filled room, and curtseyed, and was immediately surrounded by bubbling sound. In many ways these young women—both Olga and Tatiana were not much younger than herself—were strangely childish for their ages, given to silly jokes and absurd conversations.

"Me first," the Grand Duchess Marie shouted, and Judith produced her thermometer.

"You'll line up," their mother said. "Are they not looking well today, Mademoiselle Stein? I do think the worst is behind us."

"I am sure it is, your majesty," Judith agreed, carefully writing down the temperature and rinsing the thermometer before popping it into the next dainty royal mouth. "Will the doctor be coming out today?" He was a fairly reliable source of information.

"I imagine so. There are some *gentlemen* from the Duma to see me." Alexandra herself poured coffee. "So the roads must be clear."

"I think Papa should call out all the soldiers," the tsarevich, Alexis, said. "And imprison everyone found rioting."

"I'm sure the Germans would like that," Tatiana said. "The soldiers are supposed to be fighting *them*."

"Anyway, didn't Sedlov say that the garrison has joined in with the rioters?" Olga said. "And the Cossacks."

There was a short silence as every head turned to stare at her. She had just uttered the unutterable.

"I am sure that is nothing but a rumor, my dear," her mother said. "But I will discover the truth from the people downstairs."

"What *is* going to happen, Mama?" Anastasia asked. She was the youngest of the sisters, and her voice was high.

Once again the exchange of glances between the eldest sisters. Judith sipped coffee.

"Nothing is going to happen, my dear," the tsarina said. "There is a shortage of bread, and that makes people unhappy." She glanced at the neat rows of toast waiting in their racks. "But the winter will soon be over, and then there will be lots of bread for everyone. Then the people will be happy again. Besides, your father will soon be home. I have telegraphed him, and he will be coming back to attend to things." She got up. "Now I must go and see these people. Be sure you finish your breakfast."

They stood, and she swept from the room. The footmen closed the door behind her.

"Poor Mama," Olga said. "There's so much to worry about. And now us being ill . . . When will we be able to go out, Judith?"

"I want to go out today," the tsarevich said, staring out the window. "Look at all the snow, just lying there going to waste. As Mama says, winter will be over in a few weeks, and the snow will all be gone. And I won't have played in it."

Tatiana sat beside Judith. "What do *you* think is going to happen, Judith?"

"Why, I'm sure her majesty is correct in her judgment. She knows a great deal more about what is really happening than any of us."

"She has sent for Papa to come back," Tatiana said, "even though he has only just left. She would not have done that if things weren't serious. Do *you* believe the garrison has gone over to the rioters?"

"I can't believe that," Judith said. But she remembered the day she had been driven to Tsarkoe Selo when men in uniform had fired at the car with the imperial crest. If only there had been a few regular battalions of the Guard, perhaps with Prince Peter at their head, stationed in Petrograd! These men were all recruits, unsure where their loyalties lay, far too prone to being swayed by agitators.

"But you do believe it," Tatiana said.

Judith flushed. "I'm too easily frightened, your highness."

"Aren't we all!" Olga had been standing behind them. "Do you know what Karlovsky said, yesterday?" Karlovsky was one of the royal tutors. "He said this is very like 1789, in France," Olga pronounced.

"Then we'd all be going to have our heads cut off," Anastasia said, and gave a high-pitched giggle.

The two older girls, Tatiana and Olga, looked at each other.

"They didn't cut off the heads of any princesses," Marie objected. "It was only . . ." She stopped, her mouth open. Her sisters were all looking at the window.

The tsarevich turned round. "Well, no one is going to cut off my head," he declared. "I'll kill them all. I'll have the army at my back, and I'll . . ." It was his turn to pause, as the door opened again. Once again they hastily rose to their feet as they saw their mother standing there. She was not alone; there were men immediately behind her. In the private apartments of the palace?

The tsarina entered the room and waited. The two men came in behind her. They looked horribly embarrassed; their faces, thrusting out of their high white collars, were pink and shiny with perspiration. They gazed at the five young women, and the tsarevich, as if mesmerized.

"These *gentlemen* have something to say to you," Alexandra Feodorovna said. Her voice was quiet, but Judith could tell that she was controlling herself with a great effort.

They waited, and the elder of the two men stepped forward. "Your highnesses . . ." He hesitated, and looked at Judith uncertainly.

"Mademoiselle Stein has been nursing my children through their illnesses," the tsarina said.

"Ah, Mademoiselle Stein . . ." Once again there was a hesitation, as her name registered. "Well, your highnesses, it is my, ah, painful duty to inform you that you are under arrest."

There was a moment of absolute silence. Then Olga opened her mouth, gazed at her mother, and closed it again. Judith realized that her mouth was also open. This could not be happening. Nothing like this had ever happened in Russia before. Tsars had been arrested, perhaps, by members of their own family, but never by their people. The tsar was the tsar, and his family was beyond any laws, any comment, any restriction he did not himself impose. She must be witnessing the end of the world.

The man licked his lips. "It is mainly for your protection, of course. The mob . . . well, mobs are unpredictable. Now, I want you to know that we shall make things as easy for you as we can. You will remain here at Tsarkoe Selo for the time being . . ." He glanced at Judith.

"Mademoiselle Stein will also remain," the tsarina said.

"Of course. And you will be permitted to use the grounds, when the weather improves. There will be guards . . ." He looked at the tsarina.

"We already have guards," she pointed out.

"I meant, ah, within the palace. And when you are walking."

"For our own protection," the tsarina suggested with heavy sarcasm.

"Of course."

"Papa will never permit it," the tsarevich shouted. "He will have you sent to Siberia."

The man gazed at him for a moment. "Your father has abdicated," he said. "For himself and for you as well, Tsarevich Alexei." He clicked his heels. "Your majesty. Your highnesses. Mademoiselle Stein."

They left the room.

"You sent for me, your excellency?" Captain Alexei Gorchakov entered the tent and stood to attention.

"Ah, Alexei." Colonel Peter Borodin gave his future brother-in-law a quick smile. "Yes. They want the regiment back in the line. It doesn't sound too good." He prodded the map spread before him on the trestle table. "It looks like a very big gap to me. But apparently there are no other troops available. We must do what we can. Are the company commanders outside?"

Alexei nodded. "There'll be grumbling, your excellency. We've only been out of the line for three days. The men were promised a week."

"They'll have to put up with it. And I would like you to get through to brigade headquarters and tell them that I simply do not have enough men to plug that gap. If the Germans do manage a breakthrough, they'll overrun our rear. Perhaps we should send a messenger rather than use the field telephone. Yes. Have a man brought here, and I will write out the situation."

"If I may have a word, your excellency," Alexei said. "In private."

"What's that?" Peter Borodin straightened; his cap touched the top of the tent.

"Leave us," Alexei said, and Peter's orderly saluted and stepped outside.

"What is the matter, Alexei?"

"Have you received any news from Petrograd, your excellency?"

"Of course I haven't. I receive my information from brigade, whenever they remember that we exist. Why are you so interested in Petrograd?"

"A rumor is going through the regiment that there's a serious revolt there."

Peter raised his eyebrows. "There are always revolts in Petrograd. It's nothing more than a bread riot. There were bread riots the last time I was there."

"The rumor says that this is more than a riot, your excellency. It says that the garrison has joined the rioters."

"Do you believe such rubbish, Alexei?"

"The men believe it, your excellency. And now this morning they are saying that the tsar . . ." he hesitated.

"Out with it."

"That the tsar has abdicated, your excellency."

"And the men believe *that*?"

"Well, your excellency . . ."

"I don't know what this army is coming to, Alexei. How did this rumor reach us?"

"By this morning's munitions wagon, your excellency.

There were fellows on board—well, they claim to represent the Duma."

Peter's brows drew together in a frown. "And why was I not told?"

"I am telling you now, your excellency."

"But you have not arrested these people?"

"Well, your excellency . . ."

Peter stepped outside, and his orderly came to attention. His horse was ready for him, together with Alexei's, and those of the company commanders who had been waiting patiently in the drizzle. "You'll mount, gentlemen."

Peter swung into the saddle. He was aware of being angry. Agitators from the Duma. Once he had supposed that the Duma might be a good thing, a safety valve for the feelings of the nation. In recent years he had changed his mind. Summoning the Duma had been an act of weakness. But then, so many of Tsar Nicholas's actions had been the result of weakness; it was impossible to imagine his father, that huge mountain of a man, Alexander III, ever having a moment of weakness. Russia had been a great country when he was on the throne. And it would be a great country again, when next it had a strong ruler. Perhaps it would be a good thing for Nicholas to abdicate, together with that German woman and his weak-kneed son, and give the throne to the Grand Duke Nicholas.

He found himself flushing at the temerity of his own thoughts, and kicked his horse forward, his officers following at his heels. The regiment lay in its encampment only a hundred yards away. As he approached he saw that although it was well past dawn, campfires continued to burn, and men sat or reclined around them as they sipped their soup; except for the distant rumble of gunfire, there was no suggestion that this army was at war, and that the Germans were breaking through only twenty miles away. Well, he would soon have them on their feet.

He reined. "Where are these people from the Duma?"

Alexei Gorchakov pointed, and Peter saw a larger-than-usual group of soldiers gathered around an improvised platform, where two men were standing.

He kicked his horse forward once again.

"Your excellency." Alexei urged his horse alongside. "If you propose to arrest them, it would be best to turn out the guard."

"To deal with two agitators? You surprise me, captain." Mud flew from his horse's hooves as he rode through the encampment. Men were scattered to either side, but their curses died as they recognized their commander. "Out of the way," Peter shouted, riding into the crowd of listeners. They also moved to left and right, and he was immediately before the platform. The two men wore uniforms of a sort, but they carried no equipment. And they were remarkably young. Peter found his anger growing. "Get down from there," he snapped. "Get down. You are under arrest. You and you," he said, pointing at the soldiers nearest to him. "Place these men under guard."

No one moved.

"We can only be arrested by agreement of the soldiers, colonel," said one of the young men.

Peter stared at him with his mouth open. He had never been so surprised in his life.

"You can also be arrested by decision of the men," said the other young man. "How now, comrades?" he shouted. "Do you wish this colonel to command you, in the future? Would you not prefer to elect your own colonel?"

"Why, you—" Alexei shouted, and drew his revolver. But before he could level it there was a surge against his horse, and he tumbled from the saddle; the gun went off harmlessly. Peter saw one of his company commanders being dragged from the saddle, and another beating men away with his drawn sword. He looked down to where Alexei was half-buried in the mud, being trampled on by his own soldiers. He saw them surging about his own horse, freed one leg from the stirrup to kick at a man who would have seized his foot, and drew his revolver to shoot another at pointblank range. Their faces were no longer those of disciplined soldiers, but angry and twisted and vicious, and he knew that he would be dead in a matter of seconds.

He slapped his horse and gave a shout of defiance. The stallion rose on his hind legs, his flailing forefeet catching two men and sending them spiraling away with shattered jawbones. Peter fired again, and brought down another man. Then he was bounding forward, and people were falling to either side of him. A moment later he was clear, and momentarily drawing rein. There were a great number of soldiers in the camp. It should be possible to rally them and arrest the mutineers. It should be. But as he turned his head he saw them all surging towards him, and his entire staff had disappeared, presumably trampled to death in the mud.

Peter kicked his horse again and sent it racing between the tents. Behind him he heard a single shot, and then several others, but the men were too excited to hit him. He bent low over his horse's neck and sent it careering across the mud and the snow. His heart was pounding, and sweat was pouring out of his face to join the tears that trickled down his cheeks. It was only when he was out of range, and could rein in his horse, that he realized he was riding west, towards the German lines.

Chapter 8

"NEVER," DECLARED THE DOWAGER PRINCESS OLGA BORODINA. "Leave Starogan? That is preposterous. Whatever would Peter say?"

George Hayman sighed. He looked up and down the table at the rows of female faces. But had he expected anything different? Perhaps he had, because he had come from the anger and the turmoil of Petrograd, and he had been the bearer of tragic news. But even before he had arrived, as the train had puffed its way through the endless sweep of open countryside, leaving the dust and the grime and the passions of the cities behind, he himself had begun to wonder if it had not all been a bad dream, from which he was just awakening. Starogan was eternal. It had been, it was, and it would be. He had known then that his journey was unnecessary, even to satisfy himself that Ilona and the children were safe. As for persuading this family to take any action, that was out of the question.

There had been grief, but far less than he had expected, because Count Igor had already telegraphed the terrible news. George's arrival and the fact that he had seen Tigran on the day of his death, had merely sparked off some remaining tears. But there was no sign even of tears this morning. The family had suffered a serious loss, but it had closed up, almost like a company of soldiers, to present a united front. Closed up, and turned in. No one had even asked about Rachel Stein, and how she had taken her fiancé's death. Rachel was excluded forever from Borodin affairs, along with her grief and her illness, which was more serious than had been supposed. They had asked only a few questions even about the royal family, sent from Tsarkoe Selo to the east—for their own protection, the government claimed, but in reality so that their imprisonment could be guaranteed, he was sure. And with them was Judith Stein. There was a strange sequence of events, that a convicted anarchist should find herself sharing a prison with the tsarina. But none of that was significant to the Borodins, compared with the necessity of preserving Starogan.

"It may be some time before Peter comes home," he said. "The provisional government is pledged to continue the war against Germany to the bitter end. Even with my people on your side, that may take months. Even years."

"But it will happen," Olga said triumphantly. "And Peter will come home. What would he say if we were not here?"

"Anyway, where could we go?" Princess Irina asked. "The Turks would not let us pass through the Dardanelles. We are entirely surrounded by enemies."

"Not entirely," George said. "I have thought it out—"

"But why *should* we go?" Peter's mother insisted. "There has been a terrible revolution, but it is over. There have been revolutions in Russia before," Olga said.

"Not like this one," George said.

"Stuff and nonsense, George. You are a pessimist. Believe me, I am as shocked as anyone that his majesty has been deposed, that there will be no more tsar. But I cannot help but reflect that he brought it on himself, by weakness and by profligacy. So you tell me I will no longer be known as the dowager princess, but instead as plain Madame Borodina. Well, what's in a title? As long as we have Starogan—"

"That's just the point," George said. "There's no guarantee that you will still have Starogan, this time next year."

The family stared at him coldly.

"They *will* find that girl?" Countess Anna Borodina asked. It was about the seventh time she had asked it. She did not seem to be thinking of anything else. "They will catch her, and hang her?"

George glanced at Ilona. How could he explain to these people what Petrograd was really like? How to explain that they could scarcely hang Dora Ulyanova for murdering two Foreign Office officials without hanging half of Petrograd for murdering God knew how many policemen?

"Not have Starogan?" Olga boomed. "What absurdity. My dear George, I have known Prince Lvov for years. I cannot pretend to approve of what he is doing, but I can assure you—"

"And I can assure you, madame, that Prince Lvov is nothing more than a figurehead. The government is in the hands of the socialists. Now, they seem level-headed, moderate-thinking fellows. Their decision to launch an offensive this summer proves that. They're basically on our side. But they *are* socialists. It is a part of their program that land will be redistributed. It will happen, madame."

"So we may lose a little of our land," Olga declared. "There will always be enough for us. Believe me, George, it has happened before. Tsar Alexander II insisted on a redistribution of land. He was a socialist, if you like. But we survived."

George felt like tearing his hair out by the roots. But he drank some coffee instead. "You may be right, madame, if the socialists retain control. But they are also pledged to holding elections, in a couple of months. Absolutely free and open elections. And there are many groups in Russia today who are far, far to the left even of the socialists. If they gain power—"

"Oh, really, George. You are now dreaming up catastrophes. How can they gain power? One thing I can tell you, for it is in all the newspapers: Monsieur Kerensky, whatever his faults, has the backing of the army. Otherwise he would not have been able to overthrow the tsar. He will not allow any riffraff to take over Russia." She looked up, and Nickolai Nej, listening with as rapt attention as he had always shown to his mistress's pronouncements, hastily pulled back her chair. Olga Borodina stood up. "I must go down to supervise the work in the fields," she said. "Come along, Irina."

The princess stood up dutifully. It was remarkable what nearly three years of confinement on Starogan had done to her. Or *for* her, would be a better word, George thought. She dressed simply, wore a bandanna over her hair, and seemed almost content to be a farmer's wife. Perhaps Olga is right after all, he thought, and they *will* survive. The family must have faced crises as severe in the past.

Or at least, some of them would survive. He gazed at Xenia Romanova, slowly buttering bread. The others ignored her most of the time, treated her with easy patience whenever they had to notice her. Presumably nervous breakdowns were not an acceptable part of Borodin behavior. Presumably they found nothing tragic in the way she never brushed her magnificent auburn hair, let it drift over her shoulders, and did not appear to wash very often. He wondered how many of the glittering butterflies of Petrograd society were reduced to this level by now.

Tatiana got up, held Xenia's chair, and murmured in her ear to make her rise. Tattie alone cared for her cousin. That was because they shared. Xenia had lost her husband, and a brother of whom she had been fond, and Tattie had lost her husband-to-be, and a cousin of whom she had been fond. And both of them had lost their guiding light, Rasputin. But Tattie was much stronger, much more able to bear the shock. A strange word, strength, to use about Tattie Borodina. But George was realizing that it was there, because after all, what is strength, but depths, reserves of self on which to call in times of adversity? Xenia had always lived on the surface, loudly and extravagantly and entirely physically. Tattie had begun to do that, six years ago, when she had first been sucked into Xenia's orbit. By all accounts she had been crushed by Peter's decision that she should return to Starogan and live there. But Tattie had always had her music on which to fall back, and her inner thoughts and feelings, which she had never revealed to anyone, and which George supposed only he even suspected she possessed. Now she spent much of her time by herself. No longer did anyone object to her playing ragtime on the piano, or dancing by herself in the privacy of her room; often she could be heard thumping about up there. Tattie had withdrawn from the real world of tragedy and disaster into a private world that might be even more real. Possibly she too was having a long nervous breakdown, George supposed; if so, hers was still under control.

"I can't help feeling that Mama is right," Ilona said. They were alone at the table now; Alice, the nursemaid, had taken the children for their morning walk. Now she got up and came round to stand by his chair. "I know it's easy to say, There has been a catastrophe, we must get away from here. But surely that is the worst thing we can do. It is up to people like us to remain, and steady the country, offer the leadership that it will require in the months ahead."

He squeezed her hand. "You are sounding like a politician."

"And you think I'm being absurd."

He got up and put his arm round her shoulders, as they walked down the hall, past the bowing footmen and the curtseying housemaids, towards the veranda. Starogan had never changed. Pray God that it never would.

But it would. "I think you are being very sensible. Very brave, and very determined. I always knew you would be. But that is in the light of what you know, what you have seen."

She rested her head on his shoulder. "I know Petrograd must have been horrible during the revolt, George. But I have been in a revolt, you know. I was in Moscow in 1905."

"Things are a little different this time, my love. This revolt has succeeded. Sergei wasn't there with his cannon. He wasn't there at all."

"Where is he, do you suppose?"

"I have no idea. Maybe he saw the writing on the wall. He's done a good job of disappearing. But that's the point. Other people are *re*appearing. I didn't want to tell you in front of your family, but that fellow Lenin—you remember him?"

"I spoke with him once," she said. "On the Moscow barricade."

"Well, he's back in Russia. With all his cohorts. Do you know who's among them?"

She lifted her head to look at him, eyes wide.

He nodded. "Michael Nej."

"Oh, my God. Have you seen him?"

"No. The names were listed in the papers."

"But . . . we have nothing to fear from Michael Nej now, George. That was a long time ago. And you saved his life."

"Johnnie is his son, Illie. What do you think he would do if he knew his son was in Russia? And if he also had power?"

Ilona freed herself. She walked away from him and stood at the veranda rail to look out at the fields of early wheat. Closer at hand were the river and the apple orchard. And in the orchard the children were playing under Alice's watchful eye.

"Can he ever have power, George?"

"I don't know. I do know it would be a mistake to suppose this revolution is over yet. Everything depends on the success of Kerensky's military offensive, and on the elections this autumn. And I can tell you that the offensive isn't going too well. Would you like to see Michael again?"

She turned quickly. "No. Of course not." She flushed. "It was utter madness. Because I couldn't have you. Because I could see nothing in the future but Sergei. Because—"

"Easy, my love. Easy. I wouldn't like him to see you again, either."

"But I can't leave Mama. Not right now, George. When Peter is home, well then—"

"And if things take a turn for the worse before Peter gets home?"

She sighed. "Anyway, where could I go? With America at war, I'm no longer a neutral. The Turks wouldn't let *me* through either."

"There's another way."

"How?"

"Across Siberia. Listen, I've worked it out, even arranged it, as much as I can. You could take the train from here to Kharkov, thence to Moscow and the Trans-Siberian railway. Remember coming back across with me, in January 1905? Even after everything that had happened, it was a wonderful trip."

"I remember," she said. "We were a lot younger then."

"We're not all that old now. You'd get off at Vladivostock. There are boats between Vladivostock and Japan all the time. Once in Japan, you'd go to our agents, Murgatroyds in Yokohama. They'll put you on a ship for San Francisco. I've even taken out enough money to cover your journey."

"My journey?"

"You and the children."

"And you?"

"I'm going to have to stay on in Petrograd for a while."

"Now, George . . ."

"It's not just for the paper, my love. In the circumstances, Dave Francis, our ambassador, feels that I may be useful, because of my knowledge of the country and the people. I've promised to help him any way I can. Russia is officially an ally now, you know, and asking for all kinds of aid. It's very important to see that they get the right things, and that the right things go to the right people."

"I see," Ilona said. "You want me to run away, while you and my family stay here."

"Ilona, don't you think you have a responsibility to *your* family?"

"It's yours as well. And what about the newspaper back home? Russia is only a part of the news. Don't you have a responsibility to the *People*?"

"Now, love, you know I squared that with Dad. What's happening now in Russia is one of the fundamental events of our times. It's important that I be here. Dad agrees with me. I just don't want to have to worry about you as well."

He held her shoulders. "Listen, it may be that, as your mother says, I'm being a pessimist. It may be that the provisional government will keep the situation fairly stable. In that case, no problem. But just supposing the Lvov government doesn't make it, and is succeeded by—well, I have no idea what it could be succeeded by, but I can tell you the result will be sheer anarchy—will you promise me that if I send you a cable, you'll take the kids and leave at once for Japan?"

She gazed at him for some seconds. "If that is what you really want me to do."

"It is."

"But you'll wait until there's no doubt that there's going to be a collapse."

"I'll wait as long as I can. Until I'm sure."

She gave him another long look. Then she nodded. "All right, George. I'll run, when you tell me I have to."

"When you tell me I have to." She had placed the burden of the decision squarely on his shoulders—not to take it too soon, not to separate her from her family until it was absolutely necessary, or at least until after Peter came home. If only Peter could come home. But there was no hope of that, even after the disastrous failure of the summer offensive. "We shall fight on," had been the declaration of Monsieur Kerensky, now Prime Minister as well as Minister of War. "We shall not desert our allies."

And we shall pay little heed to what is happening in the country. In the beginning, George had even recovered some optimism. As he had suspected would be the case, Lenin and his followers had overplayed their hands, presumed they had more support than was actually the case, and tried to force issues. When warrants were issued for their arrest, they had again fled the country. George had hoped the crisis was over. But as autumn arrived, and the news of the enormous defeat suffered by the Russian armies in Poland began to filter home, and as the time for the election of the Duma came closer, he began to worry all over again. The Bolsheviks were back, wearing absurd disguises and yet recognized by everyone, including the government and the reorganized police. But no one dared arrest them this time. Now they *did* have the support of the people, and in their meetings openly preached the overthrow of the provisional government and the establishment of a Bolshevik society.

"It could never happen, of course," George wrote in his despatch. "Russia—old, traditional, loyal, and deeply religious Russia—would never accept the rule of a handful of doctrinaire atheists who wish only to overturn. No doubt it is the weather that encourages depressing thoughts. There has not been an autumn like this in years. It rains every day, there is a freezing wind coming in from the Baltic, and the situation seems much worse because the city is so decrepit. There is mud everywhere—no one cleans the streets anymore. Electricity is available only from six to midnight, and only at low voltage. There are hardly any streetlamps. And as may be imagined, the petty crime rate has just about tripled. Everywhere there are lines, but even in a line one has to pay quite ridiculous prices for such items as fruit, sugar, or bread. And all the while the leaders do nothing more than argue, and orate, and shout and scream.

"And now Lenin is back. He returned just over a week ago, wearing a wig and with his beard shaved, and accompanied by his Praetorian Guard, men like Kalinin and Nej, and with his faithful Krupskaya ever at his side. His return was prepared for by his bolder supporters, men such as Trotsky, who has been haranguing mobs hour after hour. Now Lenin himself calls daily for revolution and Bolshevik control. Thank God he is not even supported entirely by his own party. But as each day passes and Kerensky does not act—decisively and even brutally, if need be—the possibility of another revolution daily comes closer."

He laid down his pen, stood at the window. It was already nearly six in the evening, and dark. But the city seethed. It had been humming for the previous few days, as the Bolsheviks had become bolder, had moved into the streets to talk with the people. The atmosphere was heavy, as if a thunderstorm were about to strike. But he could not stay indoors. He went for a walk most evenings about dusk, listening and watching, accumulating the information that he wrote in his journal or despatches the next day. Now he pulled on his overcoat, put on his hat, and left the apartment. He stood outside the apartment building and watched the people surging by. Tonight there seemed even more of them than usual, and they were all wearing red cockades in their hats, or red arm bands. But this was the way of it. The anti-Bolsheviks were the stay-at-homes, the ordinary people who wanted only to get on with the business of living. These Red Guards, as they called themselves, were a tiny minority. But they were the people who made themselves obvious.

George stuck his hands in his pockets and walked along the street towards the Nevskiy Prospekt. This was another nightly promenade, to visit the building where the government was in almost perpetual session; they were guarded—absurdly, George thought, but in accordance with their high-flown notions of total equality between sex as well as class—by a regiment of women soldiers. Which at least made romantic reading for the folks back home, he thought.

Tonight progress was slow. He pushed through the mass of bodies, found himself in the midst of an enormous number of Red Guards, men as well as women, boys as well as girls, and suddenly faced Viktor Borodin.

For a moment he couldn't believe his eyes. Viktor Borodin wore a fur hat on which was placed an enormous red star, and an overcoat on which there was an equally large armband.

"Viktor?" he asked in disbelief.

"George Hayman." Viktor slapped him on the shoulder. "I was told you had left the city."

"I went down to Starogan for a visit," George explained. He held Viktor's arm, pulled him away from the crowd. "What in the name of God are you doing?"

Viktor frowned at him. "I'm a Bolshevik."

"You? But—"

"I haven't told Mama, and I'd be obliged if you don't either, for the moment. But it is the future of Russia. Tonight it will become the future of Russia."

George could only stare at the flush of excitement, the near-hysterical gleam in his eye.

"Tonight?"

"Kerensky has sent for troops," Viktor said. "General Dukhonin is marching on Petrograd now, at his command."

"Well then—"

Viktor smiled. "We are not going to wait for Kerensky's troops, George. We are going to smash the government now, before they can stop us. Wait and see."

But these people murdered your brother and your brother-in-law, George wanted to say. At least, everyone approximated anarchists like Dora Ulyanova with the Bolsheviks. Perhaps that was unfair. But whatever the truth of that matter, for a Borodin to ally himself with these gutter politicians . . .

"There," Viktor shouted.

The sound of a gun rumbled across the harbor and the street, rattled windows in the house behind them.

"Where?" George demanded, as other heads turned as well.

"The cruiser *Aurora*," Viktor shouted. "That is the signal we have been waiting for. The navy is with us."

The navy, George recalled, had always been in the forefront of revolt; in 1905 the battleship *Potemkin* had led the bombardment of Sevastopol.

"Come on," people were shouting. "To the Winter Palace. To the Winter Palace!"

Where they would meet the regiment of women. Truly, he thought, this world has gone mad.

"Come on," a man was shouting, leaping onto a lamppost stand, the better to be seen and heard. "Come on."

"But that—" George said.

"That is our leader," Viktor said. "Michael Nej. Come on, George. Come with us to storm the Palace."

George let Viktor run on ahead. Slowly he approached the lamppost, the arm-waving figure. "Michael Nej," he said. He had carefully avoided Michael during his previous visit to Petrograd. And he had had no reason to see him since his return. He was surprised at how little the man had changed.

Michael Nej jumped down from his perch. "George Hayman!" he said. "In Petrograd?"

"Doing my job, Michael," George said. "But you seem to have changed jobs."

"Often enough." Michael looked to left and right, as if expecting to see Ilona.

"She's safe, Michael. I wouldn't want her in a mess like this."

"And the boy?"

"Is a fine boy."

"Does he know of me?"

George shook his head. "Best, don't you think?"

Michael Nej frowned. "I thought so once. Then I thought there was no future for me. But now . . . after tonight I shall be part of the government."

"After tonight," George said, "you are very likely to be hanging from a gallows. Don't you know Dukhonin is marching on the city with a brigade of regular troops?"

Michael smiled. "Dukhonin is nothing. Our agents have already infiltrated his brigade. There will be no trouble from them. This city is ours tonight, Hayman. This nation is ours, after tonight. It will be ours, to do with what we will. And believe me, my friend, we have much to do. Come with me. Come and see the fall of the Winter Palace."

In the distance George could hear the screams and the shouts, the rifle shots and the rattle of the machine guns. It was February all over again. And this time the result would be something far worse than the socialists taking power.

"You go ahead," George said. "There's something I must do." He turned away and ran towards the telegraph office.

The train was slowing. Ivan Nej took his feet off the cushions in front of him and stood up. His throat was dry, and his heart began to pound.

The other passengers stared at him, as they had stared at him for most of the journey. They had entered the first-class carriage instinctively, as they were accustomed to doing, and they had not expected to see a commonly dressed soldier sitting on the plush upholstery, his muddy boots on the seat opposite him. They had expected him to raise his cap, perhaps, and scurry away. When he had not, one of them had gone to find the guard. But the guard belonged to the Party. Ivan could imagine what he had told the fop who confronted him. Things were changed in Russia today; the dirty-looking soldier wore the badge of a political commissar.

The badge had been pinned on his sleeve by Comrade Lenin himself. The day after the Winter Palace had fallen, Lenin had lined them all up. "You are my spearheads," he had said. "You, I am going to hurl into the darkness. Be sure you find your targets."

He had expected Michael to be given Starogan. But Michael had not wanted Starogan, and besides, Ivan had not fully realized how close Michael had become to the leadership itself. All because he had been one of Stolypin's assassins. That was ridiculous, really, but a stroke of fortune for himself. Michael had been needed for a greater task, that of going to Siberia to see about the tsar and his family. It was Ivan who had been given the task of returning to Starogan, along with all those other young men, and even some young women, who were being sent to their homes to ensure that the revolution encompassed all Russia.

His fortune. He stood up, peered out the window at the snow-covered fields, at the wisps of smoke rising into the air from the first house, and discovered that his stomach was turning over and his throat was dry. Suppose he failed? Suppose he just could not do it? Suppose the people were not as willing to support him as Lenin assumed? The headman of the village would be there, and Father Gregory the priest, and Feodor Geller, the schoolmaster, his father-in-law. But Feodor Geller, at least, had always had socialist leanings; Michael had said so.

But suppose he could not find the words?

The brakes squealed as the train pulled to a halt. The door was swinging open. He tilted his cap at an angle, slung his rifle—all Lenin's idea, that he should appear to them as a hero, a soldier returned from the wars—and stepped down. The old wooden boards of the platform creaked beneath his weight, and the drizzle immediately settled on his glasses. And he could remember none of the people on the platform; nor did they seem to remember him.

He was the only passenger disembarking at Starogan. The train halted for only a moment, then it puffed, and drew away into the rain and the snow and the distance. He was alone with the people of Starogan. But they were his people, if only they would recognize it.

He crossed the platform, stood in the shelter of the roof, paused to clean his glasses. Three or four people stood around.

"Where are you from?" they asked him.

They looked cold, and poor, and miserable. Ivan's spirits started to rise. "I am from Starogan," he said. "I am Ivan Nikolaievich Nej."

"Ivan Nikolaievich," they murmured, and clustered forward to take his hand.

He pushed them aside and strode to the steps. From these steps the Borodins had addressed their people when something important happened. "Listen to me," Ivan shouted at the village square. Heads turned, doors and windows opened to see what the noise was about. "I am Ivan Nej," he shouted. "Home from the war. Ivan Nej. I have come from Petrograd."

People ran into the streets, hurried to the foot of the steps. "Ivan Nej," they said. The news spread.

"We heard you were dead," someone shouted.

"Do I look dead to you, comrade?" Ivan shouted back. "I am back from the war. I have come to you from Petrograd. I have things to say to you."

"Ivan?" Feodor Geller pushed his way through the crowd, his wife waddling at his heels. "Oh, Ivan. We are so happy. Zoe will be so happy. We must go up to the house. The princess will be so happy."

"Princess?" Ivan bawled. "There is no more princess. Princesses are a thing of the past, schoolmaster. I have come to set you free." He looked around them, at the gawking faces, and saw one he recognized. "You," he shouted. "Stefan Gromek. Is that you?"

The big man limped forward. His crutch fitted neatly into his right shoulder, his right trouser leg was neatly pinned back against his thigh. He looked thin, and hungry. "Ivan Nej?"

"It is I, Gromek. They took away your leg. Why did they do that, Stefan?"

"I . . ." Gromek looked from left to right. He had explained it all so often. "They said it could not be saved."

"They could not bother to save it, you mean," Ivan shouted. "Listen to me. How many of us marched away to war? Was it twenty or thirty? And how many of us have come back? Stefan Gromek, with only one leg. And me. Why did we fight, comrades? For the tsar. For the man who betrayed us. For his German wife. For the little German whores that are his children. Ask Gromek. Gromek has seen them. I have seen them," he lied. "I know the evil that lies in their hearts. But no more, comrades. No more Romanovs, and no more Borodins. *We* own Russia now." He reached into his pocket, pulled out the sheet of paper given him by Lenin. "I have here a warrant for the arrest of Xenia Romanova. By order of the government."

"The government?" Father Gregory pushed his way through the crowd and blinked at Ivan through his misting spectacles. "You claim to represent the government, Ivan Nikolaievich?"

"I *am* the government, in Starogan," Ivan shouted. "I am commissar for this whole district. I have been appointed to the task of freeing you all, comrades. Freeing you from the Borodin yoke, from the Romanov yoke. I am here to set you free. Why, I am here—" He drew a long breath. "—to give you the right to live in the big house, if you so choose. Ask yourself, comrades: why should the Borodins live up there, in splendor, and we live down here, in the dirt?"

"But my friend . . ." The priest climbed the steps to stand beside him. "Where is the church's place in all this?"

"The church belongs to the state, Father. It will take its place as the state decrees. We have no quarrel with the church, only with those who oppose the will of the state, the will of the people. You will not oppose the will of the people, Father? Your people?"

Father Gregory pulled his beard. "My duty is to obey Prince Peter," he said. "And in his absence, to obey the Princess Irina and the Dowager Princess Olga."

"No more," Ivan shouted. "They are deposed, stripped of their titles and their privileges by order of the Soviet in Petrograd. I have a warrant to serve on Xenia Romanova. Will you accompany me, comrades?"

They hesitated, and Ivan felt his stomach beginning to roll again. Suppose they rejected him? What would they do to him? Where would he go? It had all seemed so simple, in Petrograd, listening to Lenin. But now . . .

Stefan Gromek heaved his bulk onto the bottom step. "It is the will of the government," he shouted. "Our government, my friends. Ivan Nej is right. They cut off my leg because I was not worth saving. They did not cut off any princes' legs. The time has come for us to be men. It is the will of—" He glanced at Ivan. "Who did you say?"

"Comrade Lenin," Ivan said. "But there is also—"

But one name was enough for Gromek to remember at a

time. "It is the will of Comrade Lenin," he shouted.

"Our new leader," Ivan added.

"The Grand Duchess Xenia Romanova is Prince Peter's cousin," Father Gregory said. "And besides, she is not well. I could not permit you to arrest her in her own home, when she is ill."

"Father, you are opposing the will of the people," Ivan said. "There is no such thing as a grand duchess any more. You heard Comrade Gromek. She is citizen Romanova, and I have a warrant for her arrest. If we do not arrest her, we are traitors to our country."

"Come down from there," shouted Feodor Geller. "Come down, you wretched boy. Our loyalty is to the prince and his family."

Ivan drew a long breath. But Lenin had told him what to say. "Loyalty?" he shouted. "Loyalty to our prince? Gromek and I 'volunteered,' comrades, because our prince told us to. Do you know what they gave me, comrades? They gave me a wooden rifle, and they told me to attack a German trench. That is the weapon they gave me, gave all of us, my comrades. That is loyalty? They care nothing for us. Why should we care anything for them?"

"And they have taken away our vodka," someone muttered.

"And now they are sending our wheat away," said another.

"Wait," Feodor Geller shouted, climbing onto the lower steps. "Do not listen to these men. My God, that a son-in-law of mine should utter such dreadful words! The prince is kind to us. He and his family have always been kind to us. True, they sent Michael Nej into exile. But had it not been for the prince's friendship, he would have been hanged. He is our prince, and we must—"

One word more, Ivan realized, and the revolution in Starogan would be lost. These people had too much respect for age, for authority; all their lives had been governed by authority. They had never seen authority sprawling in the dust. Before he could give himself time to think he raised his foot and thrust it into Feodor Geller's back. The schoolmaster gave a gasp and fell forward into the mud.

"He would oppose the will of the people," Ivan shouted. "No one can oppose the will of the people. Follow me. To freedom!" He ran down the steps, trod on his father-in-law's back as he attempted to rise, and hurried for the road to the house. He did not have to look over his shoulder to know they were following.

And at the end of the road there would be the Borodin sisters.

Tatiana Borodin sat at her desk and wrote to her sister. Ilona and her children had been gone only a month; she probably had not even reached Vladivostock yet, much less America. The letter would be waiting for her when she got home.

Tattie had always been an enthusiastic letter-writer, but over the past year she had had little writing to do. All her normal correspondents had accumulated in Starogan, and in the oddest fashion, as they had arrived, her loneliness had grown. She had supposed life would be easier with Irina living here with her. They had had such fun when she had been at school in St. Petersburg and Irina had taken her out occasionally. It was Irina who had introduced her to Rasputin, to all that was important in life. But Irina had changed since her return and the start of the war. Perhaps she was growing old. She was four years older than Peter, and that meant she must be approaching forty. A dreadful age for a woman to have to contemplate, especially a woman like Irina, who had spent her life dominating men and women by her aggressive beauty, her flawless femininity. The Irina of Starogan was a tired and impatient woman, who grumbled all the time and snapped at the servants.

Thus Tattie had hoped for much when, just a year ago, it had been announced that Xenia was coming to stay. During those frenetic days in St. Petersburg she had been even closer to Xenia than to Irina, for Irina had not remained a disciple of the holy father's for very long; she was too easily bored, and she was capable of being bored even by Father Gregory. Xenia had never been bored, just as she had never been boring, in her beauty, her gaiety, her brilliance. But now Xenia was here, and this was a Xenia Tattie neither knew nor liked, hair loose, clothes untidy, eyes great dark pools of misery. Although it was a year ago that she had attempted suicide, the scars on her wrists remained livid. Tattie could not imagine anyone cutting her own wrists. It seemed such a futile thing to do. And over a priest? Even a priest like Father Gregory. He had been kind to her, he had let her play whatever music she wished and had even obtained sheets of some of the latest

American music for her: he had also encouraged her to dance; in return he had liked her to sit on his lap while he stroked her, almost as if she were a cat. She had liked the stroking, but like Irina, she was becoming bored by it even before Peter descended like the wrath of God and brought her back to Starogan. Anyway, that was a long time ago. But surely she had enough to grieve about, as much as Xenia did. If Xenia had lost a husband whom she had obviously found boring, Tattie had lost a fiancé she had only just been getting to know. That Alexei *would* have been boring was certain. But still, he had been her fiancé, and he was dead. She had every right to be desolated.

Instead of which she had been sensible, and resumed laying plans. Her fiancé was dead. The country was in a state of revolution. Mama and Irina seemed prepared to accept that theirs would be a life of farming and genteel good living here in Starogan, forever. Well, they had already lived. She hadn't even started yet, and she was twenty-four years old. They really couldn't expect her to sit around here waiting for some man who might never turn up. Her future clearly lay in America. She had said as much to Illie, had even begged Illie to take her with her to Vladivostock. And Illie, predictably, had refused. She herself had been reluctant to leave, had done so only because she had promised George she would, when he decided the time was right. Tattie would have to wait for Peter's return, for things to settle down.

But they would settle down, and no doubt soon. If the army kept on losing battles, the new government would *have* to make peace before too long, and then Peter would be home. And then all things might be possible. So it was undoubtedly a good idea to keep in touch with Illie. And when she was finished with this letter she thought she would write George, because he was an even better bet, and he was still in Russia. When he left...

The clock chimed one. It would soon be time for luncheon, and Mama liked them all to come down at least half an hour early, to enjoy an aperitif. Tattie peered at herself in the mirror, straightened her tie, smoothed her skirt, and brushed her hair. She frowned as she heard a noise coming from the road to the village. She went to the window, looked down the drive, and could see nothing for a moment through the steady freezing drizzle that curtained the landscape. Nowhere on earth could look more desolate than Starogan in a wet winter. The flowing wheatfields that provided so much of the summer beauty were just acres of glutinous mud; the trees in the orchard were bare of leaves and fruit; the lawns were green as ever, but strangely attenuated; and the river looked even more brown than usual, somehow dully angry. But worst of all, the unending blue sky and the brilliant sun and the gentle summer breeze were all gone, and in their places there was unending gray sky and drizzling rain and when it blew, the wind was more often than not a gale.

There was definitely a lot of shouting beyond the orchard. And now she could see people, men and women, and even children, flowing up the drive towards the house. What on earth could they be doing? Certainly Mama was going to be very angry.

She ran down the stairs and saw that Mama was already in the hall, with Irina. Nikolai Nej was there as well, as was Alexei Alexandrovich, the butler.

"What is the meaning of these people, Alexei Alexandrovich?" Mama was asking.

The butler looked nervous. "I cannot say, madame."

"There has been some disaster," Irina said. "I know it. There was a train this morning. There has been a disaster."

"Well, smile," her mother-in-law commanded. "You must not let them see that you are worried."

"Do you think we have surrendered?" Tattie asked from the stairs. "That the Germans have won?"

Their heads turned together to stare at her.

"Don't be absurd, Tatiana," Olga Borodina said, her voice harsh. "How could the Germans have won?"

The crowd was now surging across the lawn before the house; Tattie estimated there might be two hundred of them. That was nearly the entire village.

"You had better speak with them, Nikolai Ivanovich," the dowager princess commanded.

Alexei Alexandrovich hastily opened the doors, and the steward stepped through. The crowd paused at the sight of their senior citizen, but some still continued to shout, and now that the door was open the women could hear what they were saying.

"Death to the tsar!"

"Death to the German woman!"

"Death to all Romanovs!"

"Bread and liberty!"

"Down with the imperialists!"

"Oh, my God," Olga Borodina said. "Oh, my God."

"Go to your room, Mama," the Princess Irina said, as if she were speaking to a child. "Tattie, take your mother upstairs. And then go to your own room."

Nikolai Nej was staring at the crowd's leader, now at the foot of the steps. "Ivan?" he asked, his voice quivering. "Ivan, is that you?"

"It is I, Papa," Ivan said. "Home from the war."

"Ivan." Nikolai took a step forward, arms outstretched, and then checked himself. "But what is the meaning of this noise? What do all these people want?"

"I have a warrant here for the arrest of Xenia Romanova," Ivan said.

"You will hand her over to us," said Stefan Gromek.

"And then we are going to live in the house," said someone else.

"It is our house now," said another. "Why should they live in it?"

Olga Borodina, halfway up the stairs, stared at her daughter-in-law in consternation. Tattie's attention was caught by four of the footmen, standing just inside the corridor to the servant's pantry, watching and listening.

"Go to your rooms," Irina said again, without looking at them, as she started to walk to the door to stand beside Nikolai Nej. He had recovered his breath.

"Why, you scoundrels," Nikolai shouted. "You, Ivan Nikolaievich. You are a traitorous dog. May God forgive me, for having two such sons. Why you—" His voice ended in a curious choking sound, and Tattie abandoned her mother and ran back down the stairs to watch the old man fall to his knees, fingers tugging at his collar.

"His heart," Irina cried. "Alexei Alexandrovich, help him." How strange, Tattie thought, that Irina should be taking command while Mama is so obviously terrified. She had never supposed Irina had so much courage. All she needed was a little support, and she'd send these people running back to the village.

But the butler remained standing in the doorway in indecision, while the crowd also hesitated for a moment at the sight of the steward on his knees. Then Ivan ran forward. "A judgment of God," he shouted. "A judgment of God. Seize the Romanov bitch. Seize her."

Tattie turned and ran for the stairs. Her shoulder brushed against her mother's, and the dowager princess almost fell over. She looked over her shoulder to catch a glimpse of Irina, standing motionless in the doorway, staring at the mass of people about to engulf her. Now her mother was running through the double doors into the drawing room. Tattie had lost sight of the crowd as she raced upwards. But not the sound. The house filled with a baying roar, and then there was the crack of a pistol, and the sound momentarily died, before rising again. Oh God, Tattie thought as she reached the landing. Oh God. Somehow she knew that that pistol shot was the end. But who had fired it?

Her feet skittered along the corridor. She threw open Xenia's door. "Xenia! Xenia, are you there?" Her cousin lay on the bed, fully dressed, staring at the ceiling. It was Xenia's favorite pastime, since coming down to Starogan. "Get up. Get *up*." As Tattie tugged at her cousin's hand, her ears filled with the screams and shouts coming from downstairs, to which was added the sound of breaking glass and shattering furniture. A mob, loose in their house. This must be a nightmare.

"Go away," Xenia said. "You *are* a beastly nuisance, Tattie. Go away."

Tattie released her and turned to face the door, where three men stood. One was Ivan Nej, the second was Gromek, walking with the aid of his crutch, and the third was one of the boys from the village. She backed against the wall as they crowded in, and Xenia sat up.

"Get out of my room," Xenia said. "Get out."

"She nursed me," Gromek said. "That one. She nursed me when they cut off my leg."

"Then you have her," Ivan said, and went towards Tattie. She stared at him, truly seeing him for the first time in her life. His face was hungry. She had never seen a face quite like it.

"Don't hurt me," she said. "I have never hurt you."

He reached out and seized the bodice of her gown. Nothing so brutal had ever happened to her before. She could only stare at him as he pulled her towards him, and when she instinctively started to lean away the material ripped.

"Xenia," she screamed, and heard her own name being screamed in turn; the village boy had grasped Xenia's ankles and dragged her off the bed. Xenia made an effort to check herself, and then her head hit the ground with a terrible thump, while her skirt rode up to her knees. She attempted to sit up and straighten herself, but the man Gromek placed his crutch in the center of her stomach and pushed. Xenia fell flat again with a terrible wheezing sound.

"Oh, God," Tattie begged. She was outside in the corridor now, and there were more people up here, opening doors, entering bedrooms and bathrooms, and pulling out the contents of cupboards and drawers. To her horror she saw that some of the servants were with them. She recognized Zoe Nej and several other women in Mama's room, and Zoe looked through the door and saw her husband.

"Ivan," she screamed, and ran towards them, while the other women cheered.

"Go away," Ivan snarled.

"But Ivan," she clung to his shoulder. "You are back. They said you were back, and I did not believe them. Ivan . . ."

Ivan gave her a push with his free hand that sent her staggering across the passage to hit the wall and slide down it. "Go away," he said again. "I divorce you. Go away."

Other women had come out of the room, and some pulled at Tattie's clothes, ripping her shirt right off so that only the collar remained, with her tie hanging down, and then kicking and slapping at her back and shoulders and legs. "Please," she said. "Please . . ."

She was thrust through a half-open door. It banged her head and for a moment she was quite dizzy. She fell across a bed and realized it was her own bed, and the door was being closed and locked. By Ivan Nej. She rolled over and sat up, looked through the window at the great tree that grew only thirty feet away, and nearly retched in horror as she saw another crowd, mostly men, holding Alexei Alexandrovich beneath the tree while other men climbed into the branches with a rope, and dropped it down to have it placed around the butler's neck. Alexei Alexandrovich was also begging, she could tell by his expression and the movements of his lips, although she could not hear him through the closed window and above the roar of the crowd.

She threw herself back onto the bed, tried to roll over on

her stomach and had her shoulder seized to turn her on her back. She stared at the hungry face above her. "Please," she said. "Don't hurt me. *Please*." She was sure that if she could just survive for the next hour, unhurt, she could survive forever.

"Then lie still, little girl," Ivan said. "Lie still, and I won't hurt you." He took off his spectacles and dropped them on the floor.

She licked her lips and stared at him. Only at him. Nothing else. Only that way lay safety. She felt his hands on her chest, tearing her chemise, touching her breasts. Then they slipped down to her waist, and once again there was the sound of ripping material. I would take them off, she thought, if you asked me. And now she could no longer stare at his face, because his face was gone, and her drawers were being ripped, and his face was in there, taking the whole of her groin into his mouth so that she thought he was going to bite it off. Nothing in her experience, not even Rasputin, had prepared her for anything like that. Her knees came up in alarm, and he thrust them flat again.

"Lie still," he growled.

Tattie lay still, even when she felt him parting her legs. Oh, God, she thought. Lie still. Just lie still. And now she could see his face again, surging down to hers, seeking her lips with his own, even as she felt something pressing into her where his teeth had been moments before, thrusting, sending her arms and legs flying wide with a sudden surge of unwanted, terrifying passion.

Peter Borodin stood at the gateway to the Stein house. But could this be the Stein house? The wrought-iron gates were gone—even the hinges were torn from the stone pillars—while the stone itself was pitted with bullet holes. Beyond, the flowerbeds were trampled, the lawn a mass of scarred footprints. This house was too much like all the others he had seen in Petrograd. Too much like his own.

And then there were the people. They came and went constantly, casting him careless glances. He wore the uniform of a colonel, but that was no reason for respect or salutation. He was used to this by now. Discipline in the army, respect for rank, had ended with the earlier revolution, before he had even been taken prisoner. It had been Kerensky who had decreed that all men should be equal, except when actually marching into battle, that soldiers need no longer salute, need no longer address their officers as your worship, or those of field or noble rank as your excellency, that they need no longer even give up a seat on a tram or a train to an officer. That decree had certainly cost them last summer's offensive. Lenin was merely carrying things to a logical conclusion, just as it had been a logical conclusion for the Bolsheviks to conclude an ignominious peace.

Besides, he reflected, this sudden contempt for officers was to his advantage. Nowadays one hid more easily as an officer than as a private soldier. Poor Smyslov. No one was going to miss the man whose name Peter had taken, just as no one was going to miss Peter Borodin.

His heart was pounding. He had got here, and in a few minutes she would be in his arms. If she had survived. But she had to have survived, where poor Tigger and Philip had not. If all the world had collapsed, if rank and family no longer counted for anything at all, then surely he could choose the girl he would love for herself alone.

Besides, since he was in the mood for complete honesty—and he had been in such a mood ever since leaving the German prison camp—he knew that he wanted her strength, the strength of experience, of suffering, to help him through the unimaginable problems that lay ahead.

And Judith? He had not seen her since that terrible night in 1914. But of course she would have forgiven him for his weakness then. He was the Prince of Starogan, and he was going to offer her the life of which she had only been able to dream, the life that would have been hers had Irina not come back so unexpectedly.

The life that would be hers now, regardless of Irina. All he had to do was convince her of that.

He walked across the ravaged lawn, trying not to look anxious. He went up the stairs, where Vasili Mikhailovich had used to take his hat and coat. Whatever had happened to Vasili Mikhailovich? Here were three grubby children, playing in the center of the hall, while their mothers labored at great washtubs behind them. Here was a stench of unwashed bodies and untreated sewage basking in the summer heat. Here was destroyed furniture and peeled wallpaper. Through an open door he could see the settee on which he had sat with Rachel in the summer of 1916 as they waited for Judith to come home; now a man slept on it, open-necked, sweat-stained shirt and great workman's boots resting against the upholstery.

Peter hesitated, and one of the women raised her head to look at him. "I am seeking Comrade Stein," he explained.

"Upstairs," she said. "What regiment, comrade?"

"The Preobraschenski."

She tossed her head and gave a brief laugh. "Name?"

"Smyslov, comrade. Colonel Peter Smyslov."

It meant nothing to her. "Upstairs."

Peter climbed the stairs and reached the landing. He had never been up here before. This was a place of bedrooms, of Judith's bedroom, of all the hundred-and-one things that should have been theirs by now. That would have been theirs, had he possessed the courage to defy the weight of his ancestors. That *would* be theirs now, and in better surroundings than these had ever been. He stepped round a puddle of urine, knocked on the first door, and gazed at Rachel. She gazed back, her mouth forming a large O. How like her sister she was. Like and yet unlike. Where Judith's gaze would never have left his, Rachel's drifted down his body, his uniform.

"Don't you remember me?"

"Prince Peter. Oh, my lord. Prince . . ." She threw the door wide. "Momma, Prince Peter is here."

Peter stepped inside and closed the door; he did not want his real name heard all over the house. He stared around himself in dismay. The room was cluttered with what bric-a-brac the Steins had been able to rescue from downstairs, precious family photographs in tarnished silver frames, including a very large one of Judith, head and shoulders, carefully and lovingly colored by the photographer. But there was still a bed in here, and clearly the entire family slept in this one bed, just as they cooked on the tiny gas ring occupying what had once been a fireplace, as they dressed and undressed together.

They had apparently collapsed together, under the strain. He took off his cap, wondered whether he should hold out his hand. Ruth Stein looked no different from the washerwomen downstairs. Her hair was loose, and was gray. He had never noticed the gray before. Her gown was dirty and shapeless, and she wore no jewelry. But she had never worn jewelry, only rings; today even the rings were absent. Her fingernails were dirty. But she had fared better than her husband, collarless and unshaven, whose hand trembled as he held it out.

"Prince Peter. Oh, Prince Peter."

"Prince Peter." Ruth Stein clung to his arm, and great tears rolled down her cheeks. "We thought you were dead. We had not heard—"

"How long have you lived like this?"

They stared at him. Rachel came to their rescue. "Six months."

Peter supposed her clothes were no cleaner than her parents', yet she looked fresher, less frightened. But he had already observed a simple fact, in himself as much as in others: only youth could adequately cope with revolution.

"You have enough to eat?"

They exchanged glances. "We manage," Rachel said. "Momma has sold—"

"Be quiet, Rachel," Ruth Stein said. She twisted her ringless fingers together.

He could delay no longer. "Where is Judith?"

The Steins exchanged glances.

"I have come to take her away," he said. "I am going south to—" but he decided against telling them that he sought General Denikin's army. "I have false papers, in the name of Colonel Smyslov. I am appointed to a position in Odessa. With my wife. I have train tickets." He paused, looking from one to the other. "For Judith and myself."

"Judith is with the royal family."

"What?"

Ruth Stein had recovered some of her poise. "She has been with them for more than a year. The girls had measles when the tsar was made to abdicate. The tsarina had sent for her to come to nurse the princesses, and then the whole family was placed under arrest. Judith as well."

"Under arrest?" Peter cried. "But—"

"When the royal family was taken from Tsarkoe Selo and sent to Siberia," Ruth went on, "Judith went with them. We have not heard from her in a year."

"She is well," Jacob Stein said. "I am sure she is well, since the royal family are well treated. I have heard this from my . . . friends."

"She is better off than any of us," Rachel said. "They still have servants. And food to eat."

Peter walked to the grimy window and looked out at the croquet lawn, where children played and their mothers chatted in the sun as they hung out the washing. Fate, he thought, ever conspiring to keep us apart, to leave her only an image at the back of my mind. Was he relieved? He wanted her. Oh, there was no doubt that he wanted her. And yet, every time he could not have her, he was aware of the problems he had thereby avoided.

"Will you still go south to Starogan?" Jacob asked.

"I cannot stay here. I—" He turned, and his hand dropped to his holster as the door opened and he stared at the two young men who stood there. Neither of *them* was the least pinched or starved, and their khaki uniforms were neatly pressed. And one was his own cousin. "Viktor? My God, Viktor—" He stepped forward, then halted at the expression on Viktor's face.

"I heard that a colonel had been asking for news of the Borodins," he said. "You? My God."

Peter frowned at him. "What is that uniform?"

"It is the uniform of the Special Police," Joseph Stein said. "And you are under arrest, Borodin."

"Arrest?"

"You are masquerading under a false name, with false papers. You are a tsarist, an enemy of the people. You will come with us."

"You can't do this!" Rachel screamed, seizing her brother's arm. Desperately she clutched Viktor's arm as well. "You can't arrest your own cousin."

Viktor looked down at her for a moment. Then he closed the door. "What are you doing in Petrograd?"

"Looking for anyone from my family. Looking for Judith."

"This man is a deserter in time of war," Joseph said. "We have had your name on our list for a long time, Borodin. It was expected you would come back to Petrograd. Hand over that revolver."

"Only when it's empty," Peter said, backing against the wall.

"You cannot permit this, Comrade Borodin," Ruth begged.

"If he were to give himself up, swear allegiance to the new government, as I have done," Viktor said, "there would only be a short sentence for desertion."

"The sentence is death." Joseph's voice was harsh.

"Let him go, I beg you," Jacob Stein said. "He has harmed no one. Once he saved your sister's life. And he only came here to find out about her. Now he knows she is safe, let him go."

"Where?" Viktor demanded.

"I had planned to go down to Starogan," Peter said.

"Starogan?" Joseph sneered. "Do you suppose Starogan still stands? There is civil war in the south. It is a battlefield."

"My mother and sisters are there," Peter said. "Your sister as well, Viktor."

"I have renounced them," Viktor said. "Starogan is in the hands of the Whites. I renounce them."

"A counterrevolutionary army has formed in the Crimea," Joseph said. "*That* is where you wish to go."

"I wish to go to Starogan," Peter said. "To be with my mother, and my wife, and my sister. If you prevent that, Viktor, you are more of a criminal than I had supposed."

Rachel squeezed Viktor's arm. "Please, Viktor. Please."

Viktor looked at Joseph. "He can harm no one, Joseph. He will never even get to Starogan. You know that. Someone else will see him and arrest him."

"You'd let him go?"

"Well . . . Father has disappeared, and as for me, I have my own way to make. You understand that, Peter, my own way?" His voice was again strident.

Peter shrugged. "Every man has his own way to make, Viktor."

"You will take care of the women?"

"Of course I will."

"Well . . ." He chewed his lip nervously. "We need not have come yet, Joseph. Listen. We shall leave, and we shall return in an hour. One hour, Peter. If you are here, if you can be found anywhere in Petrograd, you will be arrested and shot. Do you understand me?"

Peter gazed at his cousin for some seconds. Then he nodded. "I thank you."

"You will tell no one my cousin has been here," Viktor told Jacob Stein. "Do you understand? No one at all. If you do you will be shot for having harbored a tsarist."

"I will tell no one," Jacob Stein promised.

"Come along, Joseph," Viktor said, and shrugged himself free of Rachel.

Joseph hesitated, then he too shrugged. "One hour, comrade. One hour."

The door closed behind them.

"He is a good boy," Ruth Stein said. "They are both good boys."

"But they have their way to make," Peter said.

Jacob Stein sighed. "They think it is for the good of the country."

"Yes," Peter said. "Well, I do no good standing here. If you can manage to get a message to Judith, tell her I will find her, and come to her, wherever she may be, as soon as I can. Tell her—"

"We will tell her," Jacob said.

"Thank you." He hesitated, saluted, and turned for the door.

"Peter," Ruth Stein said. It was the first time she had ever called him by his name.

He turned back to them. Ruth was looking anxiously at her husband.

"Do you think you will reach Starogan? The Crimea?"

"I shall try."

"Peter . . . take Rachel with you."

"What?"

"Me?" Rachel cried.

"Yes," Ruth said fiercely. "She cannot remain here. There is not enough to eat, and she . . . there are no morals anymore, in Petrograd. Girls will sell themselves for a piece of bread, a glass of vodka."

Peter gazed at the girl. She flushed, and turned away from him.

"I cannot take a woman with me on such a journey," he said.

"You were prepared to take Judith."

"That is different. We were . . . well . . ."

"It does not *matter*," Ruth cried. "It does not matter anymore. Rachel was betrothed to your cousin. She is almost your cousin, by marriage. I am begging you, Prince Peter. If she stays here I do not know what will become of her."

Peter gazed at Rachel. She met his eyes for a moment, then lowered her own; her cheeks flared into a sudden flush. "Do you wish to come with me, Rachel?"

Her head came up. "Oh, yes. But only if you want me to."

"It will be hard. It is more than a thousand miles to Starogan. And if we are found out we will be shot. Madame, do you really suppose—"

"I wish her to get out of Petrograd," Ruth said fiercely. "She will die here, and even more quickly. She will die of hunger and disease. She will die of despair. We will all die of despair."

"Then why do you not all come with me?"

"Your train pass is for two people. We would only be a hindrance. Do this for us, your excellency, I beg of you. Look after both my girls for me. I can no longer do so myself."

Peter looked at Rachel. This time she did not flush. Her teeth showed as she smiled. "I'll get my things together," she said.

With a clanking and a groaning the train came to a halt. "Everybody out," shouted the conductor. "Poltava. Everybody out."

Peter sat up. He wanted to stretch, to relieve some of the pressure on his cramped limbs, but there was no room for stretching. They were lucky to have secured a seat for the journey from Moscow; all the first day from Petrograd they had been forced to stand. Now Rachel was wedged in his arms, while on his other side was wedged a stout lady. The stout lady had not washed in a very long time. But then, he realized, neither Rachel nor he had washed in a very long time either.

But they were at Poltava, and the end was in sight. Starogan was only a few hours away. He wondered what he would find there. He wondered what his family would think, what Irina would say. This girl had come here four years ago, with her sister, when the world must have seemed especially created for Borodins. Now she came with a Peter Borodin who had neither rank nor title, and she came masquerading as his wife. But Irina would understand that it was, after all, only a masquerade. The exigencies of war.

And yet... Rachel stretched slightly and sat up, pushing herself away from him with that still-nervous reaction at finding herself in his arms, but at the same time giving him that shy smile. It could have been Judith. A Judith who smiled, and who seemed prepared to endure any hardship without complaint, a Judith who never argued, who was content to obey his every command. A Judith who was only as good as she had to be? He did not know about that, about the real Judith. War made many strange things happen; many people behaved differently from their norm. Why, in war, he had killed, and he really had no desire ever to kill anyone. Who was he to criticize what a hungry girl might have to do to keep alive? He had never criticized Judith.

"Everybody out." The guard had reached the crowded compartment, and people were getting up, gathering their scanty belongings together. "You too, comrade colonel," said the guard.

"I have tickets to Odessa," Peter said.

"That is canceled. This train is to go no farther."

"Why not?"

The guard shrugged. "Orders, comrade colonel. Who can say? Perhaps the Whites have won a victory. You should report to headquarters here." He passed along the corridor.

The compartment was empty now, except for them. "What are we to do?" Rachel said, but she did not look anxious. She trusted him, as she had trusted him for three days; after all, he had got her this far.

"We'll walk the rest of the way. It is only fifty-odd miles."

"Walk? To Starogan?" Her eyes were enormous.

"Why not?" He held the door for her, and she stepped onto the platform, straightening her gown. She had chosen her very best for this trip, a brown serge costume with a matching felt hat and a red feather. It was far too hot for June, and was by now sadly crushed, but she was still far better dressed than any other woman on the crowded, confused platform, and as always she was attracting glances.

"Will they let us?" She was watching the armed soldiers by the exit.

"They won't know. It'll be dark in an hour. Come along." He held her hand, took her little suitcase in the other—his own change of linen was packed with hers—and walked her towards the guards. "I am Colonel Smyslov. I wish directions to army headquarters."

"Turn left at the gate and then two blocks straight ahead," said the first soldier, inspecting Rachel.

"Thank you, comrade." They went through the door, and mingled with the crowds outside, cast adrift by the ending of the line, trying to make up their minds what to do.

"They're so rude," Rachel hissed. "I don't know how you put up with it."

"Sssh," Peter suggested. "I put up with it because I have to. Come on." They walked through the gate, turned left as directed, just in case the men were watching, and made their way down the street. The revolution had reached Poltava as well. Several shops had been looted, and every so often they saw a burned-out house. The streets had not been cleaned this year, and there was the usual smell of garbage and sewage and unwashed bodies hanging on the still air. He wondered if he would always associate revolution with dirt. It was dirtier even than war.

"Down here." They turned left at the first block instead of the second, and then left again at the next corner, and found themselves in what must once have been a residential street. The setting sun was on their right. "We'll just follow this street for a while."

"I'm terribly hungry," she said. "Do we have any of that bread left from Kharkov?"

"Yes. But we'll find somewhere to rest first," he said. "Away from the crowd. There." He pointed to another burned-out house, timbers jutting gauntly into the sky. And the street was momentarily deserted. "Come on." They ran across the road and clambered over the rubble-filled front garden.

"It stinks," Rachel remarked.

"The whole town stinks. Sometimes I think the whole country stinks. But it won't stink at Starogan, I promise you that."

She squeezed his hand, and grunted as her shoe came off. She was wearing high-heeled shoes, quite unsuitable for a journey like this. But they were the best she had.

"I'll carry you." Peter swept her into his arms and stepped over fallen timbers and dislodged pieces of masonry. He found himself with the remains of a wall separating them from the street, with sprouting grass for them to sit on, with the sky above as a roof, and in front of them the original wall of the house, cracked open by the heat of the fire that had destroyed it to reveal the darkness of a cellar. "This is perfect." He set her down and sat beside her, and opened the suitcase to take out the half loaf of bread; there was another loaf left, but that had to see them to Starogan.

Rachel knelt beside him, tore at her portion. "God, what would I give for a steak. Will there be steaks at Starogan?"

"There'll be steaks at Starogan. There'll be everything you want at Starogan."

"A hot bath?"

"Of course."

She rocked on her heels, smiling in anticipation.

He returned her smile, then frowned. "Listen."

She turned her head. "Water." They had not heard it before, with the exertion of getting here. But now the steady trickle was amazingly loud. "Oh, water." She scrambled to her feet, kicked off her other shoe, and made her way into the cellar.

"Be careful." He hurried after her, blinked to accustom his eyes to the gloom, and made out the stream of water running across the floor and disappearing into a gutter beyond. "It's been flowing there all summer," he said. "Think of the waste."

"Can we drink it? Oh please, can I have a drink?"

"Not too much," he said. "It's probably contaminated." But he knelt beside her and scooped the liquid up to his mouth. It tasted better than nectar. "There'll be champagne at Starogan."

"Just so long as I can have a bath. Colonel . . ." She still would not call him Peter, and she could no longer risk, "your excellency." "Do you think I could wash?"

"I don't see why not. I'll leave you to it." He went back outside, leaned against the wall, and gazed at the sky. He wished he had a cigar, because suddenly he knew that he had succeeded. If the railway was blocked, it could only be because of Denikin's army. That meant he was going to reach them, and if they were this far north, then they must still have possession of Starogan. The estate, and the family, were safe. He would get there and he would take this girl with him, to safety. If only she could have been Judith, no matter what Irina might say. Circumstances were different now. Circumstances could never be the same again.

Besides, he thought wryly, since he presumably was now penniless, at least until the White Army, the counterrevolutionaries, won this war, Irina would no longer be interested in him.

If only it could have been Judith. But Judith too was safe. No one was going to trouble the royal family; they were too valuable as assets to whoever controlled them. And he and Judith would find each other eventually. They were young enough to survive things like revolutions, as Judith had survived Siberia and he had survived the war. That was the privilege of youth, while people like the older Steins were crumbling beneath the strain.

He was sitting up, gazing into the gloom, when he suddenly realized he was watching white flesh. Rachel had taken everything off, was carefully scooping water over her shoulders, allowing it to run down her back. Oh, Lord, he thought, because suddenly he was harder than he had ever been in his life, a hardness composed not merely of lust, but of everything of which he had been deprived for so long. Judith's sister. Was she a virgin? Not if he had known anything about Tigger. And a girl who had slept in his own arms for three nights . . .

He was on his knees, and she had heard him move. She turned, still on her knees, and he gazed at the upturned breasts with their water-hardened nipples, the pout of her belly, the silky brown hair at her groin. Then she stood up and he could see her legs. Did Judith have legs like those? Could any woman have legs so magnificently long and straight?

"How . . . how will you dry yourself?" he asked.

Her shoulders rose and fell; it was the most entrancing gesture he had ever seen in his life. "You said we had time to spare," she said. "Until it gets dark."

The call of a lone crane had Peter awake in an instant, rubbing the back of his head to banish the last drowsiness, and gazing above him at the sky. Gently he squeezed Rachel's arm. "Dusk. Time to move."

She nestled her head into the hair on his chest. "Must we? Could we not just stay here forever?" She sighed. "I'm so tired."

He was sure she had never walked so far in her life. They had left Poltava in the darkness, made their way out of the town, and walked all night and into the dawn, following the river that crept south to Starogan. When he had decided it might be unsafe for them to continue, they had fallen together, feet blistered, mouths parched. But the river had been there, for them to drink and then to bathe in, exhaustion suddenly forgotten beneath the cool caress of the water, and banished entirely, for an hour, as they once again fell to exploring the mutual delight that was their bodies.

In Poltava, as he remembered it, there had been no enjoyment. There had been desire, tremendous swelling desire. When he had knelt before her to take her in his arms he had had no will of his own. For three days before she had slept in his arms, and for three days, although he had not been prepared even to consider it, his awareness of her as a woman had been growing. But it had been the knowledge that she was Judith's sister, a second edition of Judith, that had kept him from enjoying her body as he had wanted to, had left him miserable at the end of it.

But she had continued to kiss him and run her hands through

his hair, to finger his penis with all the wonder of a child, to tickle and suck at his nipples with the abandonment of a woman who wanted. Her innate honesty had been uncontainable. "I want you to *know*," she had said, and he had shut her up. But as they had walked through the night it had not been possible to shut her up. And besides, her talking had kept them both awake. But Rasputin? He remembered how furious he had been when he had discovered that Tattie had been a disciple, how he had assaulted the starets' house with righteous anger, how he had been absolutely crushed when the tsar had banished *him*. And how relieved he had been when it had been apparent that Tattie had not really suffered, or been changed in any way, by her corruption.

Neither had this girl. Amazingly, for someone who had been engaged to Tigran Borodin, and who had had to survive in Petrograd after the revolution, she had been a virgin. And yet this too had not disturbed him, because she had wanted so badly, and because she had been so experienced in the art of love even if she had never known the ultimate.

Had she wanted him? Or had she simply been insuring her own survival, since that could be accomplished only through him? It would not have been necessary; he had made no bargain, demanded no price, for taking her to safety. But if she had simply wanted, was it him that she wanted? Or any man? It was not a question to be answered at this moment, except in his favor. When they had stopped on the bank of the river, when they had undressed together, when she had jerked against him in a series of climaxes he had not known it was possible for a woman to experience, and even more afterwards, when they had again returned to the water and floated together, touching each other from time to time as if to reassure each other that it was no dream, it had been possible to forget everything except the beauty and the passion and the eagerness of this woman. Rachel Stein. Judith's sister. But to allow himself to suppose that this might be Judith, that Judith might be able to know such passion, that Judith might be able to give herself so completely, would be to drive himself mad. Judith was a thousand miles away, and Rachel was in his arms, wishing to stay in his arms forever.

And did he not wish to stay in her arms forever? If it could be done. He kissed her ear. "We have eaten the last of the bread. We will starve."

"We will build a house," she said dreamily. "And set a fish trap. And snare birds. That is how our ancestors lived, thousands of years ago."

He got up. "They did not have Starogan just a few miles ahead. Hot baths. Steaks. Champagne."

She caught his hand as he stooped to pick up his pants. "And us?"

He looked into her eyes and she flushed, and would have pulled her hand away, had he not held it tightly. "If that would content you."

The flush deepened, and then faded. "That would content me, Peter. I swear that would content me."

They walked through the night, slowly now. But the ground was soft by the river, and Rachel could take off her shoes, and become a barefoot urchin. From time to time he carried her, over stony patches, and from time to time they stopped and sat by the river, with their arms round each other. Neither mentioned Judith. Judith was to be considered when the war was over, when the revolution was over, when civilization had returned to Russia. Neither of them knew when that would be, if ever.

And neither of them mentioned Irina. Irina was close at hand, soon to be faced. But somehow, walking along the banks of the river, holding hands, they saw Irina as no more serious a problem than any of the others they had faced during the previous week. Peter had no idea whether or not they loved, but they *were*, together. Suddenly it was no longer possible to contemplate a life without Rachel walking at his side, without Rachel sleeping in his arms.

It was dawn when they came to Starogan. For twenty-four hours they had seen not a living soul, not an animal except for the birds. And as they climbed across the railway track they knew that they were not about to see any living creatures now, either, except for mangy dogs fighting each other over some unspeakable piece of carrion. They saw burned-out houses, the remnants of a village. Empty fields, covered with tangled grass rather than ripening wheat. There was not even a smell, anymore. Whatever had happened to Starogan had happened several weeks ago, and since then it had been deserted.

Peter found himself running up the long, straight road. Rachel panted as she tried to keep up with him, gave up when her bare toes stumbled on a stone. He ran through the orchard, its trees heavy with unpicked fruit, across the lawn, scuffed by hundreds of feet and hooves, and paused at the steps, to gaze at the house. Amazingly, it had not been burned; it still stood foursquare to the wind and the world. But there were bullet holes in the walls. Slowly he climbed, and stood on the veranda. The front door had been torn from its hinges, and beyond there was nothing but wrecked furniture. He hesitated, afraid to step inside for dread of what he might find there, but knowing there was nothing to be found there, except more wreckage.

"Peter," Rachel screamed.

He turned, and heard the sound of hooves at the same time. A cavalry patrol. With their lances, the rifles in holsters at their sides, their swords and revolvers, they were the most heavily armed cavalry he had ever seen. They wore khaki uniforms and peaked caps and were as Russian as he could imagine. And they had surrounded the limping Rachel, one of them sweeping her from the ground to lay her across the saddle, before continuing towards Peter.

Slowly he went back down the stairs, and the horsemen came to a halt on the lawn.

"Regular army," said the commanding officer. "Hang him."

"And the girl?" asked one of the troopers.

"Oh, you may have her for a while. But hang her afterwards."

"Good morning, Mark Ivanovich," Peter said.

The officer, already wheeling his horse while three of his men dismounted to surround their victim, pulled on his rein. The soldiers hesitated, six feet from Peter. Rachel had stopped screaming and was gasping for breath.

"Peter? Peter Dimitrievich?" Slowly Mark Liselle dismounted. "But . . . wearing that uniform?"

"How else would I have got here? And you? Would you have had me shot without trial? And raped Mademoiselle Stein?"

Liselle took off his cap and wiped sweat from his forehead. "I fight for General Denikin."

"As I would hope to. But does that give you the right to behave like a savage?"

"Put the girl—put Mademoiselle Stein down," Liselle said, and saluted as Rachel was set on her feet. "My apologies, mademoiselle. I did not recognize you."

"I doubt you have ever met her," Peter pointed out.

"Oh." Liselle considered the matter briefly. But it was not important. "You have not asked what happened here."

"Tell me."

"The village went for the Bolsheviks. They were led by an ex-soldier named Gromek."

"One of my footmen, by God."

"Well, he is dead. We hanged him. We hanged all of them we could find. One or two escaped. But we got most of them."

"For joining the Bolsheviks?"

Liselle looked at him for some seconds. "You'd best come with me," he said at last, and walked round the house towards the rear. Peter and Rachel followed. Peter's brain seemed to be suspended in space. He had thought of Petrograd as the threshold of hell, and he had been right. But now he had stumbled into hell itself, with Rachel on his arm.

Liselle stood before a large mound in the earth. "We buried your family here," he said.

Peter fell to his kness and stared at the neatly packed earth.

"The dowager princess, your mother, had a bullet wound, but we think she was trampled to death. The Dowager Princess Marie was certainly trampled to death. The Princess Irina . . ."

"Go on," Peter said.

Liselle sighed. "She died of suffocation."

"She was strangled?"

Another sigh. "I think she was dragged through the dust until she choked."

"She was not . . ."

Liselle licked his lips. "The . . . cuts might have been inflicted after death. She *died* of suffocation."

The cuts, Peter thought. My God, the cuts, on that swelling, voluptuous body.

"Go on," he said.

Liselle seemed to be having trouble with his breathing. "Xenia . . . the grand duchess also died."

The last time he had seen Xenia had been in the summer of 1916, a glowing red-haired goddess. "How?"

"She . . . she had also been mutilated, but she was left to bleed to death. So far as we know."

Rachel gave a great wail of horror, and dropped to her knees beside him.

"Go on," Peter said.

"That was all the family we found. Some of your servants had also died, trying to defend the house, I suppose. One was hanged from that tree over there, another had almost been torn to pieces."

"That cannot have been all," Peter said, speaking quietly. "Both my sisters were here. And my three nephews and nieces. They were here." For the first time his voice threatened to rise.

"We did not find them."

Peter got back to his feet, slowly. He looked from left to right, as if expecting Tattie and Ilona to emerge from the long grass. "You hanged the murderers," he said. "Every one?"

"Every man, every woman, and every child we could find," Liselle said.

"But there must have been others," Peter said. "Why are we standing here?"

Chapter 9

"THE TRAIN IS STOPPING," SAID THE GRAND DUCHESS OLGA.

"Are we there?" cried the tsarevich. "Are we there? Is Papa there to meet us?"

Very carefully Judith Stein moved the edge of the heavy curtain that was draped across the window of the third-class compartment, and looked out at the track. But there was nothing but track. Nothing except for the mountains. They rose in every direction, warm in the sunshine. But she could imagine what they might be like in the winter.

And then suddenly, houses. Hastily Judith put the curtain back. It would not do to let the guards know they had attempted to see out.

"Well?" the tsarevich demanded. "Where are we, Judith? Is Papa there?"

"I don't know, your highness," Judith said. "But we are in the mountains."

"The Urals," said the Grand Duchess Tatiana. "They said we were going to the Urals."

The sisters looked at each other, then at their brother. They depended on each other now, as they depended upon Judith; they had had no one else to depend on, since their parents had been taken away three weeks earlier. Three weeks, Judith thought. It might have been a lifetime. Every day was a lifetime, had been a lifetime this past year.

While they had remained at Tsarkoe Selo, there had been hope. The tsar had come home full of optimism. What he said to her majesty in the privacy of their bedchamber, whether or not he wept, no one knew. To the girls, to his son, to his servants, he was still the tsar, and if his duties consisted of nothing more than digging in his garden, he had not despaired, nor allowed them to despair. Besides, Monsieur Kerensky had come to visit often enough. There were things Monsieur Kerensky had to know, which only the tsar could tell him. And there were things that only Monsieur Kerensky could tell the tsar.

"He is not at all a bad fellow, Kerensky," the tsar had said.

"A socialist," the tsarina had said bitterly.

"Nonetheless, a good fellow. And it seems all the world is socialist nowadays. He means us no harm, you may be sure of that. He'd exchange us, if he could, or send us to England. But there are difficulties.

The difficulties had apparently grown. Soon they were leaving Tsarkoe Selo, for Tobolsk in Siberia. "You will not need me, your majesty," Judith had said. The girls were well again, and she had no desire to return to Siberia, even Tobolsk.

"Of course we need you, Judith," the tsarina had said. "What would my girls do without you? Of course you must stay with us."

Like so many Russian aristocrats, Judith thought, it simply never occurred to the tsarina that other people, lesser people, might have lives of their own to live. At the least she had been able to exchange messages with her parents, learn that they were still well, in the collapsing chaos of Petrograd. She had not heard from them since she had left Tsarkoe Selo.

But she was reconciled, now, to accompanying this family wherever it went, whatever its fortunes. There was even a grim irony in her returning to Siberia after all, and as an exile—and in the company of the man and woman who had originally sent her there. Not that their exile in Tobolsk could be compared with hers in Irkutsk. In Tobolsk they had lived in the governor's house, had been treated deferentially by the guards, had still been kept informed of what was happening in Petrograd and in the world at large. Until last October. Then a sudden silence had descended on them, and with it, a slow but perceptible diminution of respect by the guards, accompanied by an even more perceptible tightening of security. It was from the guards that they had learned the cause: the Bolsheviks had seized power, Kerensky himself was an exile, and Lenin was the ruler of Russia.

Lenin! I fought beside him on the barricades in Moscow, she wanted to say. But that was twelve years ago. Would he remember her? Should she declare herself? She had not wanted to. She had not wanted to incur the hatred of this strange family she was slowly growing to respect and even to love, for their courage, for their family closeness, indeed their simplicity, which left them perfectly content with each other even when all their power and their glory had been taken away. Besides, she had known, in her bones, that there were harder times coming. As Lenin's friend, she might be able to help them.

And three weeks ago the moment had arrived. There was a sudden awakening in the early dawn, a command to gather their belongings together for a train that was waiting. Near-hysterics from the tsarina, who for all her exterior presentation of stoic reserve was the nearest to collapse. And this time with cause. The tsarevich was in the course of one of his periodic, horrifying bouts of illness. He had grazed his knee, and the bruise had turned purple with unreleased blood beneath the skin, while the boy had writhed and moaned in his agony. He could not travel. And his mother could not leave him. The guards had had to drag her away; their only concession to the majesty that had once been was to permit three of his sisters, and the Jewish nurse, to remain with him in Tobolsk until he recovered.

There followed three of the longest weeks of Judith's life. But now they were ended. And what would they find? She stood up and faced the door as it opened, to reveal an officer flanked by two guards.

"You will disembark here," the officer said. He gave a brief smile. "Your parents are waiting for you."

"Papa," Alexei Nikolaievich cried, and tried to run forward. Judith hastily caught his hand to prevent his being pushed by the officer, for even a push could trigger his hemophilia.

"Dignity, Alexei," Olga said. "One must always be dignified. Especially . . ." She bit her lip. She could no longer say the heir to the throne. "Especially growing boys."

They filed down the corridor and stepped onto the platform. Ekaterinburg. Catherine's town. Named after the greatest of the tsars, the woman tsar, who had faced plenty of revolutions and revolts and triumphed over them all. Judith wondered what she would make of this situation.

"Do you know it?" Tatiana whispered.

Judith nodded. "I passed through here in 1911. It is on the main railway line to the east."

"Do you think we are going farther east?"

Judith looked over her shoulder. The train was still standing by the platform.

"This way." The guards were waiting to escort them from the station. They went down a short flight of steps, past railway officials, one of whom started to salute, then hastily tucked his hands behind his back, while the others stared at them in stony silence.

Then they were on the street, dusty, dirty, leading between two rows of uninspiring houses. Ekaterinburg. It was a small manufacturing town, as Judith recalled. Today the population was looking, not working. They had to walk along the street, the guards behind them and in front of them and to either side, between people who stared and pointed and whispered.

"The tsarevnas."

"The Romanov women, you mean."

"Look how they walk, chins in the air."

"We'll soon bring them down."

"I'd rather bring something else down, comrade." This earned a roar of coarse laughter, and Judith, walking behind with their tiny bundles of spare linen, saw the girls' ears reddening. She wondered if they realized that more than their lives were at stake. She had no doubt at all that if they were presented to a firing squad, or even an executioner's block, these girls would meet death unflinchingly. But suppose they were handed over to a rape-minded mob? How would their sheltered sensibilities react to that?

For that matter, how would she? Would it do her any good to remember Roditchev and his cane, and his minions? Was not every time just as bad as the time before, however often it happened?

They came to a wall surrounding a brief garden, and then a three-storied house—almost the only three-storied house they had seen. And the gate was opening to allow them in. There was still some small piece of comfort to be offered them, another governor's house. They walked into the yard, and the gate closed behind them, to shut out the curious and the vicious and the amused and the obscene. And standing before them were the tsar and the tsarina and Anastasia, running forward to greet her sisters.

"My darlings." Alexandra swept them into her arms, one after the other. She held the tsarevich close. "My darlings."

Tears showed in the tsar's eyes, and he turned away to keep the guards from seeing them. Or even to keep me from seeing them, Judith thought. She stood by herself, waiting for the greetings to be completed, waiting to be given some instructions, and heard her name.

"Judith? Judith Stein?"

She looked to her right, where the ladies-in-waiting and the other attendants were standing, and gazed at Ilona Hayman.

"Ilona?" Judith took a step forward, stopped to look again. But it was definitely Ilona, if not an Ilona she had ever seen before. The sublime, abstracted confidence, together with the perfect hairstyle and the Paris gown, were all gone. This woman's magnificent hair was loose, her dress was made of cotton, and she wore no jewelry other than her wedding ring. There were anxiety lines on her forehead. But the absence of the true Ilona must be only temporary. Unlike the Romanovs, who knew that life could never be the same for them again, Ilona Hayman knew her present circumstances had to be but an irritating mishap, an inconvenience in the even flow of her life towards happiness.

But how had it happened?

"Judith," Ilona took both of her hands. "Thank God you are here. You know these people . . . no, no, not the tsar," she said as Judith's gaze strayed. "I mean these guards. Don't you?"

Judith shook her head.

"They don't seem able to understand," Ilona explained. "They have placed me under arrest. They think I am Russian. But I am an American citizen."

"How long have you been here?" Judith asked.

"Since Christmas."

"Since . . . my God. By yourself?"

"My children are with me. All we were trying to do was get to Vladivostock. These commissars or whatever they call themselves made us get off the train here and wait—for instructions from Petrograd, they said. But they don't ever seem to get instructions from Petrograd. I was so happy to see his majesty and her majesty the other day. And now you! Are they to be kept here too?"

"I think so," Judith said.

"But—"

"Prisoners will stand at attention," came the command. They turned and saw the Romanovs also cease their greetings and face the gate, through which there came a tall thin man, wearing a uniform. His face was as thin as his body, and was twisted with a mixture of embarrassment and determination. Judith realized that she had seen him before, briefly; he had been on the train with them, had in fact already been on the train when it had called at Tobolsk, and he had been on the platform to inspect the girls and the tsarevich as they had embarked. Now he stood in the center of the little yard and faced the tsar.

"I am Comrade Beloborodov," he said. "I am the new commandant of this Soviet. You will take your orders from me, as of this moment." He paused and looked at each of the prisoners in turn; it took some time as there were about thirty of them. "This house," he said at last, "is reserved for Comrade Romanov and his family. You may retain two assistants, Comrade Romanov, one male and one female."

"But we cannot manage with only two," the tsar said, his voice drowned in the babble of protest that arose from the ladies-in-waiting and the valets.

"Be quiet, all of you," shouted Beloborodov. "I am here to instruct you, not listen to complaints. The doctor may also remain here. The other prisoners will go with their guards."

"Where are you taking us?" Ilona demanded.

Beloborodov turned his head. "To a house, comrade. To a house."

"I demand to be released," Ilona said. "I am an American citizen. My children are American citizens. You may ask this young lady, Mademoiselle Stein. She is one of you. She has been exiled to Siberia for her beliefs. She will not lie to you."

Beloborodov gazed at her for some seconds, then at Judith, who found herself flushing as the royal family also looked at her, although they had of course known of her background. Then he consulted the list in his hand, slowly turning over pages. "Your name?"

"Ilona Hayman. Mrs. George Hayman."

"Ilona Borodina," Beloborodov said. "Latterly the Princess Roditcheva." He raised his head. "Where is your husband?"

"My husband? My husband is Mr. George Hayman, vice-president of the *American People*. He is in Petrograd now, doing what he can to help Russia."

"I meant, where is Sergei Roditchev?"

"How should I know?" Ilona cried. "I have not seen him for six years. He is not my husband anymore. We were divorced years ago. Ask Mademoiselle Stein."

Beloborodov looked at Judith and once again consulted his list. "Judith Stein," he said. "Your father was a member of the Duma."

"Yes," Judith said.

"But not a member of the Party," Beloborodov said. "Nor of any party, apparently. I remember you, Comrade Stein. You were implicated in the Stolypin plot."

Judith hesitated. Then she nodded. "Yes."

"And exiled to Irkutsk." Beloborodov glanced at the royal family. "And have apparently changed your coat. We don't like people who change their coats, Comrade Stein." He flipped the list closed. "Remove the prisoners."

"But you can't take Judith," the Grand Duchess Tatiana protested. "She is our friend."

Beloborodov smiled briefly. "You will have to make friends with each other," he suggested. "And nurse each other. Remove the prisoners." He turned his gaze back to Ilona. "It would do you some good to tell me where your husband is," he said. "There may come a time when we will compel you to speak."

"It is utterly incredible," Ilona declared. "It is like a nightmare. And now is not the worst. If we have to spend another winter here I shall go stark raving mad. As for the children . . ." She considered them, playing at the other end of the room with Alice, the maid. "This was all George's idea, you know. He thought we would not be safe at Starogan. He wanted us back home. My God! One of the guards told me that Starogan is now in the hands of General Denikin's White Army. If only we'd stayed there." She sighed and lay back on the cot, her hands beneath her head. "If only I could get a message to George."

Judith realized that Ilona's prevailing emotion was anger.

That was all to the good; at least she had not yet succumbed to the despair that had overtaken most of the other prisoners. But suppose she did have to spend another winter here?

"Surely," she said, sitting beside her, "if Mr. Hayman is expecting you to return to America, he will know by now that you have not got there. He will be trying to find you."

"Of course," Ilona said. "George will most certainly find me. I only wish to God he'd hurry."

She sat up as the door was opened, without a knock. The guards were always doing this, looking in on the women. It was part of their job, to make sure no one was up to anything, but the duty also carried its possible bonuses, since they often caught someone in dishabille, or even performing an act of nature on the single pot they were forced to share.

But for Ilona the interruptions were especially disturbing, because of Beloborodov's threat. It really was not imaginable Judith thought, that so much proud beauty could be exposed to "interrogation," as it had been practiced by Ilona's first husband, and was no doubt practiced by the Bolsheviks. And Ilona, although she refused to appear afraid, was well aware of what might be involved.

The door closed, and Ilona lay down again with another sigh. She wiped sweat from her forehead. It was early July, and stiflingly hot, but they were not allowed to open the window and were taken for only the briefest of walks in the garden every day. Bathing was not permitted, and even washing was limited to a single bucket of water; the air was heavy with the odor of sweat.

"Was your exile in Irkutsk like this?" Ilona asked.

"No," Judith said. "We had to work. But that was better, I think, than just sitting here."

"Yes," Ilona said.

"And we were not segregated," Judith said. "We were allowed to live with whomever we chose."

"Ah," Ilona said. "Was that when you had your baby? Peter told me."

"Yes," Judith said. "That was when I had my baby. But it did not survive the next winter." She got up, walked to the window, and peered out. They were more fortunate than most in that the window overlooked the street beyond the fence. She could not see the street itself, but she could see the trees and the heads of the people walking along it. In the past few weeks she spent a lot of time standing here, trying to discover what was going on.

Fingers tugged at her skirt. She looked down at the little boy. "When are they going to let us out?" John Hayman asked.

He was nine years old, and had probably had as remarkable a life as any nine-year-old in Russia, she thought. Whisked away when he was three, brought up for three years as an American boy, enjoying the perquisites of being a Russian noble for the next three years, and now a prisoner, with his mother, for six months. What sort of a man would he be when he grew up? she wondered. But then, what sort of a boy was he at all? Ilona's son. But by which father? Even in the intimacy they had shared these last few weeks, Ilona had not offered to confide that vital piece of information, and Judith had never felt she could ask.

"Soon," she said.

"When Daddy gets here?"

"Of course. He is coming, you can be sure of that." She rumpled his hair and looked over his head to Ilona, still lying on the bed. She worried more about Johnnie than about the other two, because they were so young they did not really understand what was happening; amazingly, despite their poor living conditions and their unappetizing food, they were all perfectly healthy. So far. But next winter . . . "He'll soon be here," she said, and turned back to the window again. Suddenly there was a great deal of activity out there; soldiers were marching down the street. "More prisoners," she said.

Ilona got off the bed and hurried to stand beside her. "Are they Reds? The soldiers, I mean. They could be Whites. I have heard a rumor that Admiral Kolchak is not far from here. The Reds are being defeated everywhere."

"Is Daddy with Admiral Kolchak, Mummy?" Johnnie asked.

Ilona gave him a squeeze. "No, love. He will be coming from the other side, I think."

"Those are Reds," Judith said. "If they were Whites, we would have heard firing."

Ilona straightened, and looked through the grimy glass. "As you say, more prisoners. But at least they should have some news."

"If we can get to them." They seldom saw even the other inmates of this house, since the guards treated each roomful as a separate cell. They did not even know for certain that the royal family were still across the road. But surely if they had left, Judith thought, I would have seen them from the window. Unless they had been spirited away in the dead of night.

The soldiers had disappeared. Ilona walked back to her bed and threw herself on it. She spent all day and all night on that bed, except when eating or walking in the yard or hugging her children. There was nothing else to do. And they had exhausted most of their conversation.

Doors opened and banged. Judith leaned against the wall to watch their own door. It was possible that someone else might be put in here; there were only six beds, but the guards insisted that the two younger children share one; thus there was a vacant cot for someone else. Who had not yet arrived.

Feet sounded on the stairs. Ilona sat up again.

"Hush, children," Alice admonished as Felicity and George junior continued their prattle; she could recognize that a fresh crisis might be approaching.

A key turned in the lock. Judith found she was holding her breath, and holding Johnnie's hand, as well.

The door swung inwards, and she gazed at Michael Nej.

"Judith Stein," he said. "I could not believe my ears, when they told me you were here."

She had not seen him since they had stood together in the dock in St. Petersburg, as it had been called then, listening to the sentence of death being pronounced on them. Now, seven years later, they were both alive, she again a prisoner and he . . . he wore khaki uniform and a peaked cap, carried a revolver holstered at his waist, and displayed red stars on his collars. She thought he might have put on a little weight, but he was obviously in the best of condition. Michael Nej. He had been taken from Russia by George Hayman, to escape the hangman. Thus he had to be their savior.

Ilona's savior, certainly, for his gaze was already drifting across the room. "Princess."

Ilona slowly dropped her legs over the side of the cot, slowly pressed down on the wooden floor with her feet, slowly stood up. Judith had never seen anyone look quite so thunderstruck.

But again Michael Nej's gaze was wandering, this time to the children, who had stopped playing and were kneeling, staring at him, and then to the boy holding Judith's hand.

"Ivan?" he asked.

Ilona crossed the room in long, anxious strides; she had not waited to put on her shoes. "John," she said. "John Hayman." She held her son's other hand.

Michael Nej gazed at her for some seconds, then he snapped his fingers. "Outside," he said. "All of you."

Judith hesitated; Alice gathered the two younger children close to her.

"Yes," Michael said. "You four. Mrs. Hayman will stay here. And the boy."

Judith glanced at Ilona. But Ilona was staring at Michael Nej. Judith went through the door, where three guards were waiting. Alice and the two children followed, and the door closed.

"You will stay here," the guards said. "Until the commissar is finished."

With Ilona Hayman, wife of his rescuer. And the nine-year-old boy. Judith leaned against the wall, trying to think.

Michael squatted before John Hayman and stared at him.

"He is a Borodin," Ilona said.

Michael nodded and held out his hand.

The boy glanced up at his mother, who released him. "Michael—"

"Be quiet," Michael said. He grasped the boy's hand, held him close. "I knew your father," he said. "I knew him very well." He stretched out his other hand to run it through the boy's hair. "Love your father," he said. He released Johnnie, stood up, and opened the door. "Go to your brother and sister."

Johnnie glanced at his mother, and Ilona gave a brief nod. He went through the door, and Michael closed it again.

"Thank you," Ilona said.

"Was it not very foolish of you to come back?"

"There was no war, no revolution when I came back."

"Well, then, to have stayed?"

"George wished to stay. He loves Russia as much as I do. Or you, Michael." She frowned. "*Do* you love Russia?"

He ignored the question, reached for her hand, then released it again. He stood close to her, stroking her cheek with his finger, running it up the line of her temple to touch her hair. He had always been an extraordinarily gentle man, she remembered. "I have seen George. In Petrograd."

She grasped his hands. "Is he well?"

"I think George Hayman will always be well. But he is worried about you. You were supposed to have been back in America by now. I promised him I would find you. It is not easy for foreigners to travel in Russia today. He should leave, in fact. When you get home, write him and tell him to leave, Ilona Dimitrievna."

"When I get home?"

He gave a brief smile. "You are an American citizen. We have no right to keep you here."

A slow flush filled her cheek . "I told them that. I told Beloborodov that. But he only threatened to interrogate me about Sergei."

Michael nodded. "Roditchev is still missing. I suspect he has joined the Whites in the south. But we will get him, eventually."

"Have you news of my family?"

He sighed, released her, and sat down on the bed. "They are dead."

She slowly sank to her knees in front of him.

"What did you expect?" he asked. "Revolutions throw up creatures like this Beloborodov. Like my own brother. He was sent to Starogan to spread the revolution. I do not know what happened. But I do know there was a massacre, with no survivors."

Ilona clasped her cheeks between her hands. "Peter . . . ?"

Michael shrugged. "I'm afraid we must suspect the worst there too. When we made peace in March, the Germans sent our prisoners home. But there is no record of Peter Borodin among them."

"My God," she said. "My God."

He gave a wry smile. "So my son out there could be the Borodin heir. Is that not a remarkable thing?"

She blinked back her tears. "Yes," she said. "It is a remarkable thing. Michael—"

"Do you ever think of Moscow, of Starogan, when we loved?"

"Yes," she said. "I think of them."

"And Hayman knows, I suppose. Did he know when he exchanged himself for me, in prison?"

She nodded.

"He said he did," Michael mused. "But I wondered how much he knew."

"Everything."

"And I must be grateful to him forever," Michael remarked. "Well, I *am* grateful to him. I am even more grateful to him for bringing you back to Russia, for keeping you here long enough for us to meet again."

She licked her lips. "Michael—"

"Oh, I am not going to make love to you, Ilona. I could. If you fought me I could have my men come in here and hold you down. Those are the perquisites of being a commissar, you know." He stretched out his hand and touched her cheek again. "I should very much like to make love to you again, Ilona Dimitrievna."

"Michael—"

"But your husband saved my life." He stood up. "I am grateful to have seen you again, and to have seen my son. There will be a train leaving for the east tomorrow morning, and you will be on it. It cannot go very far, since Admiral Kolchak is not very far. The train will stop when it reaches the limits of our control, and there you and your children will get off. We are in contact with the Whites, and you will be handed over under a flag of truce. Identify yourself to Kolchak, and he will be happy to help you."

"But . . . what of the other prisoners? What of the tsar?"

Michael shook his head. "They never saved my life, Ilona Dimitrievna. They must stay here."

"Then how can I go?"

"Because you are not one of them. You have a husband who is anxious about you. You have a son, whom you must care for, and make into a good . . ." Another wry smile. "A good American."

"And you?" she asked.

Michael gazed at her for some seconds, then he took her face between his hands and kissed her on the lips. "I have many things to do," he said. "And many of those things are dreadful, by your standards. Do not think of me any more, Ilona Dimitrievna. And never tell Ivan the truth."

Miraculously, their baggage, which had been taken away when their train had been halted, reappeared. Ilona and Alice were able to dress the children properly; Ilona was able to put on a clean traveling suit. "I don't know what to say." She brushed her hair, adjusted her hat. "I feel somehow guilty."

"What ever for?" Judith asked. "You always said you would not stay very long." She smiled. "You will be home for winter."

"Home." Ilona's face twisted. "I asked him if . . . if he would not let some of the other prisoners go. If he would not let you go. And he refused."

"He is a commissar," Judith pointed out. "He is probably exceeding his authority as it is. Besides, I came with the tsarevnas, remember?"

"Oh, Judith . . ." Tears sprang to Ilona's eyes. "We said we would help you."

"If you could," Judith said. "When you can."

Ilona squeezed her hands. "Promise me? If I ever can help, if George ever can, promise me you will let us know."

"If either of you ever can. I promise." Judith kissed her on the cheek. "You have the hardest part. You do not know what lies ahead of you." She smiled again. "I have only to sit here and wait. I am used to doing that." She kissed her again and gave each of the children a hug. "I shall think of you."

They were all crying now. But the door was open, and the guards were waiting. In the distance Judith even thought she could hear the hissing of the train. And how she wished they would go, before she broke down and wept. How she wished she were going with them.

They filed from the room, and the guard followed. Remarkably, the door was left open. Judith went to it, but a guard had remained at the top of the stairs. So she stood at the window instead and looked at the road. In a few minutes they emerged, accompanied by the guards. Ilona turned her head to look up at the house, and Judith waved, but she did not think Ilona saw her through the dirty glass. She watched them walk down the street towards the station, and disappear from her sight. She used her sleeve to dry her eyes.

The door closed softly. "Of course, you were friends even in Moscow," Michael Nej said. "I had forgotten."

She turned, embarrassed.

"She sent me to spy on you," Michael said. "To find out where you were holding your meetings. Not with any intention of betraying you. She only wanted to come."

"I know," Judith said.

"It is strange how people meet, and become friends, and are parted, and then meet again, in entirely different circumstances."

"You were her lover," Judith said. "That boy is yours. I never realized. It never occurred to me."

"That a princess could have a love affair with her brother's valet?" Michael said. "It never occurred to anyone."

"And you love her still," Judith said. "It is very gallant of you to let her go, when you could keep her here. And your son."

Michael sat on her bed. "Even a Bolshevik valet can possess a certain code of honor, Comrade Stein. Besides, I could not keep her here. There is going to be no joy for those who are forced to stay here."

Her head came up. "The tsar . . ."

"Has become an embarrassment. As well as a rallying point for all the counterrevolutionary forces, and there are enough of those."

"You could not."

"It is my duty. At least to give the necessary orders, sign the necessary papers."

"But . . . the girls . . . her majesty . . ."

"I am not a murderer of women, Judith."

She gave a sigh of relief.

"Yet must they be imprisoned so securely that the world never hears of them again."

"Oh, my God," she said. "And the boy . . ."

"He is the tsarevich."

"He can live only a few more years, at the most," she cried.

"A great deal can happen in a few years. All male Romanovs must be executed. All female Romanovs must be reduced to less than nothing. It is a fact of life. And do not suppose we are being unnecessarily cruel. What is so sacred about a Romanov? It is only life that is sacred, and you should know the number of lives they took, with a careless stroke of a pen—the even greater number of lives they would take, if they were ever returned to power. The fact that they once gave you *your* life, with equal carelessness, because of the plea of your lover, does not excuse any of their other crimes."

Judith's shoulders slumped. "And their servants?"

"Some of them too. Certainly the men."

"And us?"

He shrugged. "Prison. Do you wish to spend the rest of your life in prison, Judith?"

"Does it matter what I wish, comrade commissar? You have

at least promised me my life."

"I might promise you a great deal more than that."

She frowned at him. His cheeks were slightly flushed. "I have had an odd life," he said. "I spent the first twenty years of it as a servant, dreaming. Then I spent two or three remarkable years when all my dreams came true. Then my world exploded, and I spent six years in exile, dreaming all over again. Now, quite remarkably, I am in a position to make all my dreams come true once more."

"And now you have sent your dream away," she said. "You will never find another."

"Perhaps not quite like her," he agreed. "But a man needs a dream, and a woman. He needs a woman of importance to him. You are that, to me, Judith. Not so much as Ilona, perhaps, but more than any other woman. You were my master's mistress—"

"I was never Peter's mistress," she said.

"A technical matter. He wanted you. He was in love with you. That made you attractive to me, from the beginning. Besides, you are an attractive woman in your own rights. And then there is the fact that I listened to you screaming, in the cell next to mine, when Roditchev was torturing you. I could only imagine what he was doing to a lovely girl like you. I would like you to tell me what he did to you."

"I'd see you damned first," Judith said.

Michael's face never changed expression. "So you see, I also dreamed of you, after that. I felt I *knew* you. We had shared pain and humiliation and despair, separated only by the wall of a cell. I have thought of you often since that time. But there is more. Not long after we came to power, I met a returned prisoner-of-war, a doctor by the name of Purishkevich. By then I had learned you had worked in his hospital, and I asked about you. He told me. Well, he is a broken man. But you—you should be treated as a heroine of the Soviet. You led Rasputin to his doom. Of course you did not do it for us. There are those who would say that you had no wish to bring down the tsar. But I think, in time, I will be able to make them see it my way. I might find myself possessing the most famous woman in Russia."

"For a moment," Judith said, "just a moment, I thought you were a decent man."

"All men are decent in certain circumstances, and indecent

in others. I have done my honorable deed. Now I want to have a woman to call my own. A woman of importance. And in what way am I being indecent? I am offering you an apartment in Petrograd, all the food you can eat, all the vodka you can drink, all the clothes you can wear, all the money you can spend. You would be a fool to refuse me, Judith. I am far more powerful now than Prince Peter ever was. And what is the alternative? To remain here, dying of starvation and disease, or to be sent to some mine to work out the rest of your days? Is that a sensible attitude?"

"It might be preferable to being the whore of a Bolshevik murderer," she said.

Michael Nej smiled, and got up. "I am also offering you the chance to save your parents' lives," he said. "They are starving, in one room, in Petrograd. But more than that, your father made the mistake of dabbling in politics, of being elected to the Duma as a moderate socialist. My dear Judith, there is no more room for moderation in Russia. And as a moderate, even an ex-moderate, socialist deputy, he is generally regarded as an enemy of the state. Why, we have shot more than fifty of those moderate deputies in the past six months. Jacob Stein has escaped, so far, only because I have insisted on it. If you come back with me, Judith, he will live and perhaps even prosper. So will your mother. If I go back to Petrograd alone, I will have no more interest in keeping him alive." He was close to her now, and he put out his hand to tuck one finger under her chin and raise her head. "I am leaving this afternoon," he said. "Collect your belongings. I will send a man for you."

Judith Stein slowly descended the stairs from her parents' bedroom. It was necessary to walk slowly because the steps were covered in dirt and litter, in the midst of which screaming children played their games. It was also necessary to smile at the perspiring women in the front hall, doing their washing and cooking on portable stoves, side by side, and staring at her with hostile eyes. They might not like her, but she was about to become one of them.

Fortunately, she supposed, she had never actually regarded this house as home. The family had moved here after her arrest, and although she had lived in the house during the four years since her return from exile, she had never thought of it as permanent. So, was she not moving into something permanent?

There was the suggestion of that, with none of the form. But perhaps Bolsheviks did not believe in the accepted forms of permanency in sexual relationships. Assuming Michael even intended them to have a sexual relationship. She could not be sure. She could not be sure of anything. He had not touched her on the train, had not attempted to hold her hand or kiss her; to do more than that would have been impossible anyway, with even the commissar's compartment crowded with aides and soldiers. She had slept one night with her head on his shoulder, but then, she had slept the second night with her head on the shoulder of the man sitting on her other side. That was what Communism was all about.

And on their arrival this morning, he had brought her straight here. He was, she was realizing, an entirely honest man—and thus, far more dangerous than any of the hypocritical or self-deceiving men she had previously known, or those, like Prince Peter, who saw the world from only a small, private angle. So he was playing straight with her. She wondered what he would say if she now claimed that her parents were as well off as ever in their lives, and had no need of his protection. Would he send her back to Ekaterinburg?

She reached the porch, and inhaled the relatively clean air of the harbor. Only relatively clean, however; Petrograd smelled like a sewer.

Michael Nej was seated on the bottom step, watching some of the older children at play in Poppa's rhododendron bushes, or what was left of them. He wore his commissar's uniform and the children kept a respectful distance; in only six months the red stars had become symbols of unquestioned authority.

He stood up when he saw her. "Well?"

Judith inhaled. "They have asked me to thank you for the hamper."

"The hamper was from you."

"They knew I had no means of finding food like that."

"Ah." He began walking towards the gate, and she fell into step beside him.

"My sister has disappeared," she said. "Do you know of her?"

"No. Lots of people have disappeared this last year. Do your parents know nothing of her?"

"I think they know something," Judith said. "But they would not tell me. They say she just left."

"Then that is the truth. She has left, with some man able to protect her. Some man able to feed her. It is a revolutionary pattern. Did you tell them of our arrangement?"

"They would not have understood."

"Do you understand?"

"Not entirely."

They were on the street, and walking towards the bridge. The Fortress of St. Peter and St. Paul loomed on their right.

"You will understand in time," Michael Nej said. "There is a great deal to be done. The entire country needs reconstructing. But first, of course, it is necessary to defeat all the counterrevolutionary forces. We hope this will not take very long. It is our first and greatest task."

"And to execute the tsar," she said. "Or has that already been done?"

He glanced at her. "It would be very foolish of you to be bitter about the fate of one man, one man for whom you can surely have no love."

"I have lived with his family for over a year," she said. "I grew to know them, even to love them, perhaps."

"You were still a servant to them. And if they had regained power, or even safety, they would have forgotten all about you. You are a sentimentalist, Judith. There is no room for sentiment in this modern world. As for the tsar's life, it is in danger exactly in proportion to the success of Kolchak's army. We shall have to wait and see." They were across the bridge now, and he pointed. "There will be your new home."

She could only goggle. "On Nevskiy Prospekt?"

"Why not? That one used to belong to a prince. I have forgotten his name. Was it perhaps Borodin?"

Judith closed her mouth with a snap. But her head was spinning.

Michael led her across the street. "I asked for this apartment, especially. It is only an apartment, you understand, but it contains three rooms. And our own bathroom. There is no finer apartment in Petrograd."

He led her into the front garden, a mass of broken statuary and trampled shrubs. Here the Princess Irina had entertained her friends for tea. For a brief time, Judith had dreamed of coming here with Prince Peter. This was the first time she had even entered the gates.

They climbed the great staircase, past the inevitable children and women, but these were better dressed than the urchins who haunted the Stein house, and more disciplined too. Nor were they quite as much in awe of the red stars as most people were. Judith realized that this entire house was reserved for commissars and their wives or women.

Next they climbed the small, upper staircase, and reached the upper landing. "The Princess Irina's apartment," Michael explained. "Once upon a time. I think you will be happy here."

He fumbled at the lock, while Judith looked around her, down the well of the stairs at the gallery below, up above her to the next landing, where the servants' quarters would begin, and whence there came the sound of banging. Not even six months of Bolshevik occupation could diminish the grandeur of the place, the expense of the wallpaper, the gilt banisters; only the blank patches on the walls where the paintings had been removed, the absence of furniture, and the trampled garden outside indicated that this house had been sacked like all the others.

The door was open, and he was waiting for her to step inside. Princess Irina's sitting room. Why, in here there was even a piece of the original furniture, a settee upholstered in cloth of gold, strangely incongruous with the two straight chairs arranged in front of it, and the lack of carpets on the parquet floor. Judith went to the french windows opening onto the balcony. She stepped outside and looked down at the Prospekt, at the harbor and the bridge to the island, at the fortress. The breeze ruffled her hair, and she turned. Michael Nej had opened the inner door.

There was the bed. A large double, with hanging draperies. There was not another stick of furniture in the room.

"I will arrange for a stove," Michael said. "But as I said, there is a bathroom." He opened the door on the left, and Judith gazed at the gold-plated taps; even after so long there was a faint tang of perfume in the air.

"Watch." Michael turned on the taps, and after a moment's gurgling a thin stream of somewhat rusty water flowed. "There is no hot, yet. But it is summer. You may have a bath."

"I should like that," she said.

"Well, then," he said. "Have a bath. I must go."

"Where?" she demanded. She had been bracing herself for this moment when they would be here together, yet was suddenly alarmed at the thought of being left alone.

"I must report to the Soviet. They will know I am back by now. I shall not be very long, I hope. I will bring food with me when I come. Have your bath."

"May I lock the door?"

"There is only one key. I will lock the door, when I leave."

She gazed at him. Don't you want me? she wondered. Don't you want to throw me on that bed and rip the clothes from my body? Isn't that what our bargain entails? Her heart began to pound and her breathing grew labored. If it had to happen, then why not now?

Michael smiled at her. "Have your bath. I shall not be long." He left the room.

The water was tepid, and yet felt cold. But it was the most luxurious feeling she had known in several weeks, since leaving Tobolsk. Judith soaked, and scrubbed, and then let out the water and drew another bath, standing beside it and dripping while she waited, her body goose-pimpling in the breeze drifting through the opened windows. All around her was sound, the sound of Petrograd, but a Petrograd that had never before existed. It was the sound of voices, the shouts of children at play, rather than the growl of traffic and the ringing of bicycle bells. Nor were there any trams. Like the cars, like bicycles, the trams had vanished. Temporarily, Michael had said. But for the moment, people walked in Petrograd.

And in the midst of this enormous babble, of an entire city of people for whom the lid had been taken off, for whom society had been turned upside-down—so that the lowest became the highest, and the highest disappeared, no doubt forever, into the underworld of prison and gutter—Judith Stein lay in her bathtub, washing her hair. It was an incredible feeling; she wanted to laugh and to weep at the same time. What was she paying for this privilege? What would she *have* to pay? Instinctively she had defied him, had been prepared to oppose him, in Ekaterinburg. What foolishness. Had she not resolved, when she returned from Irkutsk with Dora Ulyanova, that she would accept whatever offer came along?

What on earth had happened to Dora Ulyanova? Surely, as Lenin's niece, if that story were true, she would now be one of those on top of the heap.

What would she make of me now, Judith wondered? Dora had condemned her for accepting Peter's invitation to Starogan;

she had never told Dora what a disaster that visit had been, had let her suppose they had had an affair that was interrupted by the war. Well, she supposed they had had an affair. One night, lying in a wheatfield, as if they were children. But she had brought it on herself.

And now she sat in the Princess Irina's bathtub. How Irina, wherever *she* might be, would hate to know that! And here she prepared to prostitute herself. For there was no other word to describe what she was about to do. And did it matter? With the entire world collapsing about her, did it matter? With her own sister apparently embarked on a parallel life? Did it matter, since this obviously had been her fate, preordained for at least eleven years, but perhaps from birth? Almost the first time Peter Borodin had met her he had suggested she become his mistress, and she had refused. Again and again and again, until, when she had accepted, it had been too late. So now she was to become the mistress of Peter Borodin's valet. But it did not matter, because Michael Nej was on top of the heap, and Peter Borodin was probably dead. Dead, dead, dead. All dead. And those of us who pretend to live are doing no more than pretending. The entire world is dead.

The sound of a key in the lock made her start. For a moment she thought that she was about to be molested by some stranger with access to the apartment, then she heard Michael's voice, and realized that she had sat in this tub for well over an hour.

She leapt out of the bath, scattering water, and realized too late that there was no towel. Her hair lay like a wet mane down her back, and water rolled down her arms and legs. She was naked, and there was a man in the apartment with her. Desperately she reached for the door, and then stopped. Of all the absurdities. The man in here was to be *her* man. Would he think any less of her for being naked when he came home? Did it matter? He was a valet become assassin become, by a quirk of fate, revolutionary leader. He could know nothing of love, of gentleness and manners. She was about to be raped, whether she submitted or not, an assault no doubt as crude in its own way as that of Roditchev's cane. Did it matter what he thought, or what she thought?

But he had once loved Ilona Borodina. All that beauty, all that femininity, had been his. Would he expect her to be like Ilona? If only she knew what Ilona was really like.

She started to pull the door open, stopped again. Michael was giving instructions.

"Put it down over there," he said. "Yes, that will be fine. Thank you, comrades."

She heard the outer door close, and waited. A moment later the bedroom door opened, and he stood there, looking at her, framed in the bathroom door.

"I . . . there was no towel."

He came closer, still looking at her, pulled the bedspread off the bed and held it out. "I would not have you catching cold."

Slowly she approached him, took the heavy cloth, and wrapped it round herself.

"I have brought you a stove," he said, and went to the sitting-room door.

She stood beside him, water forming little puddles at her feet. The kerosene stove had been placed in the corner, and there was a tin of kerosene beside it.

"It will smell," she said.

"We will get used to it. And here . . ." There was a large paper bag on the settee. Michael opened it and took out a bottle of champagne. "There is caviar, as well, and some crackers."

"A feast for a princess," she said.

He smiled, and then as quickly frowned. "Not a princess. Never a princess. A feast for a beautiful woman." The cork popped, and champagne bubbled over his hands. "There are no glasses."

He held out the bottle, and she took it, held it to her lips. She had not drunk champagne in some while. The liquid burned her throat and bubbles got up her nose.

"And no plates either." Michael regained the bottle, drank in turn.

"And no table to put them on," she said, and found herself smiling.

He stood the bottle on the floor. "That is the first time I have ever seen you smile. When you smile, you *are* beautiful. Will you smile more often, for me?"

"I can only smile when there is something to smile about."

"Then I must make sure that you have a great deal to smile about, Judith Stein." He sat down. "Will you not eat?" He felt in his pocket. "I do have a knife."

She sat beside him, the paper bag between them. He spread caviar on a cracker and handed it to her, took one for himself. She chewed, slowly and luxuriously; she was very hungry, having had only a piece of bread at the station. Another cracker, more champagne. She was almost dry now, save for her hair, and felt splendidly cool, just as her body was feeling splendidly relaxed. He was a valet, but he was seducing her far more skillfully than Peter Borodin had ever done. Than Peter Borodin had ever thought necessary, she supposed.

A last swig. "The bottle is empty," she said. The room was swaying very gently to and fro.

He smiled. "There is another. But not now, or we will fall asleep."

"Yes," she said.

He gazed at her, then he stretched across the paper bag to touch her hair, allowed his hand to slip onto her cheek and then down to her neck. Below her neck, tucked under her arms, was the damp bedspread. His finger touched it, and she inhaled, and shrugged her shoulders. The bedspread fell to her waist.

"Do you fear me?" he asked.

She shook her head.

Gently his fingers slid down her shoulder, touched her breast, and moved across it to hold the heavy flesh from underneath. "Well, then," he said. "Do you hate me?"

"I do not know," she said. "I hate what you stand for."

"You would rather the old times were back? Sergei Roditchev in charge of the city? You would prefer it if Prince Peter were sitting here, instead of me?"

She caught her breath. There was no answer to that.

His smile faded. "You must learn to make do with what you have, Judith Stein. We must all learn that." He stood up, waiting.

She got up in turn, and allowed the bedspread to slide down her thighs and slump to the floor. She had angered him, and must now suffer that anger, just as she must now honor her part of their bargain; her parents were alive, and had received their hamper of food. At least, she thought, I have half a bottle of champagne inside me.

He was waiting by the door, determined to be the gentleman. She brushed his arm as she passed him, and hesitated, waiting for him to grab her; he must want to. It was the cold-blooded impersonality of his approach that disturbed her most. Had he seized her, thrown her to the floor and leapt on top of her, she could have understood. But just to stand there, when a naked woman brushed against him . . .

She reached the bed, and sat on it, watching him undress.

She guessed he must be in his early thirties; there was no way of knowing. And he was in superb condition, of medium height, and stockily built, but revealing strength in every ripple of his muscles. Strength and indifference; his penis continued to droop between his legs. My God, she thought; suppose I do not arouse him sufficiently for him to enter me? What will happen then, to our bargain?

He sat beside her. "Do I disappoint you?"

"Of course not. You are a handsome man."

"A handsome man, and a handsome woman. We should make a handsome pair. Will we make a handsome pair, Judith Stein?"

"I do not know that." She could not prevent her gaze from dropping.

He smiled. "Perhaps I have not had a woman for too long. Perhaps I have spent too much time in dreaming, after all. Or perhaps I cannot make love to a woman who hates me."

She gazed at him. A valet, but a gentleman. A revolutionary, a murderer, but a *gentle* man. Her gentleman, if she wished. If she could achieve nothing better. But could she ever achieve anything better?

She held his face and kissed him on the mouth. His hands closed on her shoulders and slipped under her armpits to hold her breasts. He did not squeeze and he did not caress; he merely held them, and it was the most delicious feeling she had ever known. Still kissing, she slid her hand down his body in turn, to find his penis and hold it, and feel it harden, and know that they were, after all, going to make a handsome pair.

"So then?" asked Michael Nej. "Do you hate me, still?"

"Hate you," Judith murmured. "Hate you." She nestled her body against his, moved her legs so that her thighs in turn moved over his hand. He was the first man who had ever made love to her with his hands. She had not known that was a masculine accomplishment, had presumed, having shared so much with Dora, that heterosexual love must always be the least satisfactory of the possibilities. And now knew that it was immeasurably the best, when the man knew his art. Hands first—gentle fingers, arousing her to a pitch of passion she had not supposed possible, thrusting penis to complete her cascade into flowing orgasm, and then hands again, more gentle than before, sliding between her legs to hold her buttocks, so that she could just lie there, knowing his presence, moving her body when she chose to reawake sensation. To reawake love.

But she could not love. She dared not love. Not Michael Nej. She had seen too much of him already. She knew his sense of duty to the revolution, to the Bolshevik Party. He had behaved like the most gallant of gentlemen to his erstwhile mistress—had Ilona been the one who had taught him to use his hands like that?—and he was behaving once again like the most perfect gentleman to his present mistress; but he had also condemned an equally gentle man and a dying boy to execution, and four lovely girls and their ailing mother to a living death. She dared not love a man cast in so grim a mold.

She could only enjoy him. And that meant, once again, precluding the future. She could not anticipate her situation, their situation, a year hence, a month hence, or even tomorrow. There could only be today. And today, this afternoon at least, she was happy.

His hand slid away and he got out of bed. She sat up in alarm but he only went as far as his uniform jacket to find a packet of cigarettes.

"Do you smoke?"

"I never have."

He lit two and gave her one. "Do not inhale."

She puffed, and coughed, and put the cigarette out. "I can see no point in it."

He got back into bed, leaned against the headboard, and put his arm round her so that she could rest her head on his chest. "It soothes the nerves. Would you like to have a child? Another child?"

"Do you think this is a good world for children?"

"You are talking like a bourgeoise. This is going to be the best world ever known, when we complete our task."

"When," she said.

"It will happen. I have not told you my news. There are two items."

Sometimes, when he spoke even in private, it was as if he were making a speech, she thought drowsily.

"Item one," he said. "I saw George Hayman today."

"Oh?"

"I went to see him, to tell him that I have found Ilona and the children, and that they are safe."

"He must have been very relieved."

"He was. I suppose it will never affect him, but when I see a man like that, I think how crazy it is for anyone to give such hostages to fortune as to have a wife and children."

"But you just suggested I should have your child."

"Perhaps I am hoping to achieve such a position of invulnerability as George Hayman." He smiled into her hair. "I did not tell him that I had also found you. Would you have liked me to do that?"

"No," she said. "No, I would not like that. I do not wish to see him."

"I did not know you were a friend of his."

"A friend? Never a friend, Michael. An acquaintance. But . . . he represents memories, of Starogan, of the Borodins. I do not wish to have such memories."

"Not while you are in bed with me, eh? Well, the second item of news. The war in the south goes badly. Denikin appears to be quite a good general, and he has accumulated under his standard a great number of the old aristocracy, men who have been trained as soldiers since birth. You will never guess who is among them. Sergei Roditchev."

"Then he did escape."

"There is talk that the Whites may even take Kiev. That would be a disaster. So we are going to mount our principal effort against them this winter, when they will expect to cease campaigning. To accomplish that, Comrade Lenin has decided that we need a completely new military setup. Comrade Trotsky is to take overall command of the army. He has studied a great deal of military history and methods. And you will not guess who is to be commissar of the army in the south, opposing Denikin."

Judith sat up. "Commissar?"

"My task will be to keep the generals up to scratch. Soldiers tend to see things purely in technical terms. Strategy should be dictated by political necessities, not tactical difficulties."

"And you and Trotsky will teach the soldiers how to fight? You have never even been to war, either of you."

"We have both studied the business. Besides, these generals were only junior officers a few months ago, sometimes only sergeants. The real generals are with Denikin. Our people *want* to be told when to fight and when to run. And more important, when to die." He was smiling at her. "It is the greatest opportunity of my life. If I succeed, I will be more than just a friend of Lenin's. I will be one of the great men in the party."

"And if you fail?"

"I won't fail. But you could say, if I fail, if Denikin can take Kiev and hold it as a base for future operations, then the entire revolution has failed."

She gazed at him. He looked confident enough. An ex-valet who had once shot a policeman, and who claimed to have read a few military manuals, was intending to take on an army commanded by a professional general officer, supported by an entire officer caste, including the man who had put down the Moscow uprising of 1905. That was the true measure of this chaotic revolution.

"When do you go?"

"Next week."

"Take me with you."

"What?"

"You cannot leave me here, Michael Nikolaievich."

"It may be dangerous. It *will* be dangerous. If you were to be taken by the Whites . . . Michael Nej's woman . . . This is a filthy war. All civil wars are filthy, but this is the filthiest I have ever heard of. They hate us, and we hate them. Prisoners are not recognized, and execution is never quick."

"I cannot stay in Petrograd without you," she pointed out. "Besides, if you are going to win, how can we be taken by the Whites? Take me with you. And until you go, make love to me. Every minute of every day."

Chapter 10

"JUDITH STEIN." LENIN HELD BOTH JUDITH'S HANDS AND KISSED her on each cheek. "It is too many years since last we met."

Thirteen years. But he had changed in more than just the process of time. There were strain lines on his forehead, and trailing away from his lips. And he moved with a curious hesitancy, every so often seeming to check the gesture or the step he was about to make, before resuming a more normal flow.

Yet there could be no doubting his success. It showed in the deference paid him by all those surrounding him, in the way the soldiers on the station platform stood at attention, and even more in his own aura of omnipotence.

"Years in which you have prospered, Comrade Lenin," she said.

He smiled. "Latterly, Judith. Latterly. And have you not also prospered? At least, latterly?"

She glanced at Michael, standing beside her, and also smiled. "Latterly, comrade."

Now he laughed. "And are you still writing?"

She shook her head. "I have not written a word in seven years."

The smile changed to a frown. "But you must. Any revolution, this revolution most of all, needs a literature. You are one of our most experienced and by all accounts"—it was his turn to glance at Michael—"ablest in that field. I would have you write, Judith Stein. Now come, you have never met my wife."

Krupskaya had been waiting patiently with her husband's aides at the back of the platform. Now she came forward to embrace Judith and Michael in turn.

"And Comrade Trotsky, my commissar for the army."

Judith saw intense eyes, only partially hidden by the spectacles, and a militarily neat mustache; or did the mustache only appear military because of his uniform?

"And Comrade Stalin, our party secretary."

Stalin had an enormous mustache that gave him a curiously innocent appearance. Indeed, his entire face was cherubic, and his smile was wide and friendly. But his eyes, unprotected by glass, sent out a gaze like twin beams of light, so penetrating it left Judith feeling slightly breathless. Bolsheviks! Men who would kill whenever they had to, take whatever they needed. But Michael was one of them. Did that mean they could also be kind and loving when they wanted to? Krupskaya looked contented enough.

"I have some news for you, Michael Nikolaievich," Lenin was saying. "Which you may use as you see fit." He held out a piece of paper.

Michael glanced at it, then read it again before raising his head. "Do you mean to make it public?"

"Oh, indeed. It has happened."

Michael gave the paper to Judith without a word. She read it, and her heart seemed to stop.

"By order of the Ural Soviet, the ex-tsar Romanov, his wife, and family, were today executed in the town of Ekaterinburg. This measure became necessary owing to the imminent evacuation of the town by our forces in the face of the advance of the traitor Kolchak."

She raised her head and stared at Lenin. "You ordered this?"

"Michael Nikolaievich ordered it, on my authority."

She turned to Michael. "You said only the men."

"Those were my instructions," he agreed.

"But—"

"Who can say what happened? Perhaps Kolchak's advance

was faster than had been supposed. I also said that under no circumstances were *any* of the Romanovs to fall into White hands."

"But . . . those girls . . ."

"Potential tsarinas," Trotsky pointed out. "Rallying flags for every enemy we have in the entire world."

"And you think you will diminish your enemies by this act of murder?" she cried.

"I know you were acquainted with the Romanovs, Judith," Lenin said. "But you must understand that we are at war. We are fighting for our very survival. And you are showing your bourgeois background, you know. Half a dozen lives, maybe one or two more. Hundreds of our people are being killed every day, fighting for the right to have the Russia they want and need. You do not know their names, so they do not interest you. But they are human beings, just like Nicholas Romanov, or his wife, or his daughters. There was a time, only a few hundred years ago, when the Romanovs were anonymous members of society. They had no God-given right, whatever their pretensions, to fame and wealth and power. They seized those things. Well, we are seizing them back. Now you are going with Commissar Ncj, to fight against the White army. It is an army that would turn back the clock, stand in the way of inevitable progress, reduce Russia once again to a medieval tyranny. But it is not going to succeed, because we are going to defeat it. Remember that, Judith Stein. We are going to smash it. We must smash anything and anyone who would stand in our way. Times are going to be hard, Judith, for us no less than for our enemies. But we are going to triumph. Because we must. History demands it. But more important, Russia demands it."

As soon as the great hissing train came to a halt, faces appeared at the windows of the first-class carriage, staring in, breaths misting the glass. Judith left her seat and walked to the other side, where at least the width of a track separated her from the next, crowded platform.

"Kharkov." Michael raised his head from the map over which he was poring. The entire carriage had been converted into a military headquarters, only a single washbasin and one pair of bunks remaining of the original furniture. "You have been here before?"

"Yes," Judith said. "In happier circumstances." Once, she thought. And once in unhappier circumstances, on her way back from Starogan. But could any circumstances be unhappier than these?

Michael merely sighed. During the three-day journey from Petrograd he had not attempted to touch her, was content that she should be there; he was counting on the certainty that she would get over her initial reaction to the news of the execution of the royal family. And she would get over it, Judith had told herself because she had no choice. They had made a bargain, and it was her own family she must protect.

Doors opened, and the local commanders came in, followed by orderlies.

"Good afternoon, comrade commissar."

Michael nodded. He wore the aura of authority as if born to it. But then, Judith thought, he had had years to study Peter Borodin.

"I do not like being stared at," Michael said. "Clear the platform."

"Of course, comrade commissar." The colonel gave the necessary orders.

"I want information." Michael gestured at the map spread in front of him.

The officers clustered round, one or two giving Judith a curious glance before concentrating on the task in hand. "The Whites hold here, and here, and here, and here," the colonel said, prodding with his finger.

"And they are still advancing," Michael suggested.

"No, comrade commissar. The front is for the moment stable."

"You mean they have outrun their supply train. Then why are we not counterattacking?"

"We are short of ammunition, comrade commissar, and men. Besides, we have learned that General Denikin is preparing an offensive, to be launched this autumn."

"Learned?" Michael demanded. "How have you learned this?"

The colonel gave a brief smile. "We take prisoners from time to time, comrade commissar."

"We have heard nothing of this, in Petrograd."

Another brief smile. "We do not keep them, comrade commissar. But before we shoot them, we usually manage to obtain information. I have set up a special department to deal with this."

"Have you," Michael remarked.

"Yes, comrade commissar. As a matter of fact—"

"Where is our most advanced post?" Michael asked.

"There." Another prod.

"On the line. Is the railway intact?"

"Yes, comrade commissar."

"Good. I will proceed to Tsaritsyn, then. You will provide a mounted regiment as escort."

"To Tsaritsyn, comrade commissar? But . . . we have a headquarters prepared for you here. Tsaritsyn is too close to the White lines."

"Which is why I should be there, comrade colonel, and not here. I will leave within the hour."

"Yes, comrade commissar." The colonel exchanged glances with his staff. They had not expected an anarchist playing at soldier to be quite so decisive.

"Is there any other report you wish to make?"

"Merely to ask for ammunition, comrade commissar. And men. Men who know how to fight."

"They will be available in due course," Michael said.

"Yes, comrade commissar. I would also have you meet my captain of intelligence. He is the man who obtains our information from the prisoners."

"Before he shoots them," Michael said.

"The Whites treat us in the same way, comrade commissar."

"I am sure they do," Michael said. "I am sure it is all very necessary, comrade colonel. But I am here to command an army to victory. I cannot meet every subordinate with an unpleasant job to do, especially if he enjoys doing it, as I am sure your man does."

"He performs his duty conscientiously, comrade commissar, as I would have expected. The captain has especially requested to be allowed to see you. He is your brother, Ivan Nej."

Judith turned back from her window, while Michael raised his head. Ivan stood in the doorway. He wore a uniform, and with his glasses he reminded her of Trotsky.

"Michael Nikolaievich," he said, stepping into the room, and then remembering and coming to attention. "Comrade commissar."

Michael got up. "We had heard you were dead."

"Not me," Ivan said.

"But..." Michael snapped his fingers. "Leave us."

"Of course, comrade commissar." The colonel and his staff left, followed by the orderlies.

"You were sent to Starogan," Michael said. "Several months ago."

Ivan nodded. "It was a bad business." His gaze drifted. "Mademoiselle Stein."

"What happened at Starogan?" Judith asked.

"A long story."

"Well, sit down." Michael filled three glasses with vodka. "It is good to see you again, Ivan Nikolaievich. I want to know about Papa and Mama. And Nona. Where are Zoe and the children?"

"A bad business." Ivan sat down and drank some vodka. "I was told to arrest Xenia Romanova. You know that, Michael."

"I know that," Michael said.

"That is all I intended to do," Ivan said. "It was all I was commanded to do. But they resisted, Michael. They fired on me."

"Fired on you? Who?"

"The servants, but they were commanded by Irina Borodina."

"My God," Michael said. "Then what happened?"

"The village was with me," Ivan explained. "All the village. They became angry. I tried to speak with them, and was knocked down. Then they charged the house. It was terrible."

"What happened?" Michael shouted. "What happened to Papa and Mama? What happened to Nona?"

"It was terrible," Ivan said again. "Papa died of a heart attack. Mama... I think she was killed. Nona..."

"You *think*?" Michael shouted.

Ivan licked his lips. "While they were still... still sacking the house, while I was still trying to get them under control, the Whites came. Thousands of soldiers, mounted. They seized everyone they could, and they hanged them. Men and women and children, Michael." He glanced at Judith. "They hanged them. Even poor one-legged old Gromek. They hanged him."

Michael's face was the grimmest Judith had ever seen. "But they did not hang you."

Again the tongue darted over his lips. "I got away. I could

see no point in staying to be hanged. I escaped into the wheat-fields."

"Those people were your responsibility," Michael said. "And some of them were your own family. You simply abandoned them?"

"I . . . there was nothing I could *do*," Ivan insisted. "And besides, I—I had someone with me."

"Who?"

"Well . . ." Ivan took off his spectacles and polished them. "Tatiana Borodina."

"*What* did you say?"

"I . . . I tried to do what I could, Michael. I did not believe Mama and Nona were in any danger. Not from their own people. I do not think they were. So I went to save Tattie. I did save Tattie, Michael. I would have saved them both, but Ilona was not there. So I saved Tattie."

"My God," Judith said.

Michael continued to gaze in astonishment at his brother, but he knew Ivan had always worshipped the two girls. "So," he said at last. "Dreams do come true. And you do not know what happened to Nona or Mama? What about Zoe? What about the boys?"

"I don't know," Ivan said miserably. "I don't know."

"But they may have been hanged." Michael got up and walked to the window. He stared out at the platform.

"And Tattie?" Judith asked. "What happened to her, eventually?"

"Ah—nothing. She's outside." Ivan began to speak very quickly. "I brought her here, when I joined the army. I identified myself, and they gave me a commission. This job. And Tattie, well, she is with me. We . . . well, I thought, now that you are here, Michael, that perhaps Tattie could stay with Mademoiselle Stein." He paused for breath.

Michael turned back from the window. "You mean she wants to remain here, with us? With the Red army? With *you*?"

"Well . . . I am very fond of her," Ivan said. "I love her, Michael. I have always loved her. You know that."

"And she is very fond of you? After her family was murdered?"

"She . . . why should she not be fond of me?" Ivan demanded.

Judith ran to the door and opened it. Standing beyond the

guard was a young woman dressed in a somewhat shabby gown, but whose flowing yellow hair drifted in the wind. With an air of complete disinterest she leaned against the other door and inspected her fingernails, occasionally removing a speck of dirt.

"Tattie?" she whispered. "Tattie Borodina?"

Tatiana raised her head, glanced to left and right, and saw Judith. For a moment she frowned, then she smiled. "I know you," she said. "You're Judith Stein. You were Peter's friend. He's dead, you know. They're all dead. Every one of them. Except me."

Judith seized her hand and dragged her inside. There was no suggestion of fear or tragedy in Tattie's face; even her eyes were flat. And now she smiled carelessly at Michael. "You're Michael Nej," she said. "I remember you. Oooh, is that vodka?" She went to the table, picked up Ivan's half-empty glass, drank it, and refilled it from the jug.

"She's been under a great strain," Ivan said.

Michael and Judith gazed at each other.

"Won't you sit down?" Michael invited.

Tattie sat down, crossed her knees, and drank some more vodka. "You're the new general," she said.

"I'm the commissar for this army." Michael also sat down, opposite her. "Tell me what happened at Starogan."

A peculiar look came over Tattie's face; although the mouth and eyes continued to smile, her face seemed to close up.

"It is very important," Michael said.

Tattie shrugged. "They are all dead. The mob killed them. I think so, anyway. The mob trampled Irina. But then I ran away. I don't know what happened to her, really."

"But my brother rescued you?"

"Oh, yes," Tattie said. "He took me to my bedroom, and made me lie there, quietly, until they had finished killing people. But then the soldiers came, and we had to run away." She smiled at Judith. "We had to walk for days, through the wheatfield." She held out her glass.

Judith glanced at Michael, who nodded. She refilled the glass and gave it to the girl.

Tattie giggled. "We only had a bottle of vodka. For two whole days."

Michael picked up his pen, looked at it, then put it down

again. "Are you grateful to Ivan for rescuing you?"

"Oh, yes." Tattie glanced at Ivan, and there could be no doubting that she liked what she saw. "Oh, yes. Otherwise I'd be dead, wouldn't I? And besides, he is very nice to me."

Ivan actually blushed.

"Yes," Michael said. "Well, Ivan would like you to stay in this train, with Judith, while he and I fight the war. We should be happy for you to do that."

Tattie pouted. "I want to go to St. Petersburg. Ivan said you might let him go to St. Petersburg. He said you might give him a letter, to Monsieur Lenin, to say that he had done well here, and asking him to give Ivan a post in St. Petersburg." She leaned forward, resting her hands on the desk. "I do so want to go to St. Petersburg."

"Well, I will have to see what can be done," Michael said. "Ivan, you'd better show me exactly what you do here. Judith, you'll look after Mademoiselle Borodina." He got up, gazing at her. She went to the door with him. "Try to find out what she really feels," he muttered.

"Yes, but . . . I think she's having some kind of a breakdown."

"Then get through it. It may be important. Come along, Ivan."

The door closed behind them, and Judith turned round to discover that Tattie had also turned, and was watching her. Now she held out the empty glass.

"Too much vodka will give you a headache," Judith said.

"It never gives me a headache," Tattie pointed out. "As soon as I feel a headache coming on, I have another glass of vodka, and it goes away again. You should try it."

Judith refilled the glass and took one for herself. "Does Ivan give you a lot of vodka to drink?"

"Oh, yes. Ivan gives me anything I want. Ivan sleeps with me." She giggled. "Well, I suppose it would be right to say he sleeps *on* me. Have you ever had a man sleep on you?"

"Yes," Judith said.

"Isn't it just marvelous? Do you know, nobody ever slept on me before Ivan. Father Gregory used to touch me, and it was fun. But not like a man sleeping on you. I love it." A thoughtful look crossed her face. "I was afraid the first time he did it. I didn't know what to expect. But it was such *fun*."

"When was the first time?" Judith asked.

"In my bedroom. When we were hiding from those dreadful people."

"But you didn't want him to," Judith said. "You tried to fight him."

"Oh, no," Tattie said. "Not when I realized what he was trying to do. Well, I thought it must be better than dying, like Irina. I didn't know how much fun it was going to be, though."

Judith put down her glass and sat down behind the table. She leaned forward. "Tattie, whatever Ivan did to you, whether or not you liked it, he led the people who murdered your family and destroyed your home. And now he is fighting against the men who would give Starogan back to your family. Don't you hate him for that?"

"Well . . ." Tattie drank some more vodka. The liquor didn't seem to be having any effect. "It wasn't his fault. He told me it wasn't his fault."

"And you believe him?"

"Of course I do. He saved my life. And he lies on me and makes me feel so good. And he lets me dance. He *makes* me dance for him. Every night. I take off my clothes, and I dance for him, and that makes him want to sleep on me." She pouted. "*They* never let me dance. Peter locked me up on Starogan for six years because I used to dance for Father Gregory."

"But . . . don't you want to go back to your own people? There'll be friends of yours, with General Denikin. Don't you want to go to them, rather than stay here with us?"

Tattie frowned at her. "Why should I want to go to General Denikin? I want to go to St. Petersburg. I want to dance. Ivan says he is going to make me into a great dancer, when I get to St. Petersburg. That's what I want to do."

Endless wheatfields. A few had been harvested, but in most the grain was rotting on the stalks—thousands of acres of decay and waste. Burned-out villages, scattered corpses with only the crows for company. And at one station living corpses, half-starved children who begged for food in the most pitiful fashion. But the train never stopped.

"Can't you do something for them?" Judith asked.

"I am fighting a war," Michael pointed out. "Not conducting a charitable exercise."

"But those are the people you are fighting for," Judith cried.

"They are Russian, like you." Even more than you, she thought, since they have not spent years in exile.

"We can only do so much," he said. "We can only feed our armies, and try to win this war as rapidly as possible. When that is done, all will prosper. Until that is done, none will prosper, and some will die. Better these peasants than the workers, or any of our Bolsheviks."

"You are a heartless monster," she said.

"I am a man with many difficult decisions to make," Michael told her. "And I am commissar of this army because I am capable of making those decisions. Go and sit with Tattie."

Tattie occupied the settee at the far end of the compartment. She did not seem the least concerned by starving children, so long as she had vodka to drink. And Ivan to look at. She had provided herself with a pair of binoculars, and with these she watched the horsemen who rode to either side of the train. During the day Ivan rode with them, on the lookout for White deserters or stragglers.

Ivan Nej and Tatiana Borodina. How odd, Judith thought, that each brother should have secured one of the sisters, if only temporarily. But Ilona and Michael, and the circumstances in Moscow, as she remembered them, could be understood. That Tattie did not understand she had attached herself to a monster, that she even seemed fond of him, that she wanted only to have sex and vodka, was frightening. Judith found her attitude symptomatic of the country as a whole. Russia had collapsed. And it was still impossible to be sure what, if anything, would rise from the debris.

At least, she thought, if Michael is right about this being the decisive conflict, then I will be present at the moment of decision. That moment might be closer at hand than she had supposed. For suddenly the wheatfields ended, and in their place there were tents and horses and men, waving at the train. Now the train itself was stopping. Tsaritsyn was behind them, and they had reached the field army.

The escort pulled their horses to a halt, leaving dust clouding into the August air, and Ivan Nej waved his cap. "The new commissar has arrived, comrades," he shouted. "Now we will drive back the Whites."

Men got up, left their tents and their horses and their campfires, and ran to surround the train.

"How does it feel to be popular?" Judith asked.

"It is better than being hated." Michael opened the door, stepped onto the platform, waved his hands, and made a quick impromptu speech, repeating all the party clichés Lenin had told him so often. He did not imagine the soldiers, many of whom were merely peasants, understood much of what he had to say, but they seemed pleased to see him, and cheered him loudly. A large number of them, he estimated, were drunk. "I will see all officers in my compartment immediately," he told Ivan, and came back inside.

Judith was peering through the window. "There are women out there."

"Of course. There are many women in our army. This is a people's war, not a man's war, specifically."

"Should not I be in uniform then? And Tattie?"

Michael put his arm round her waist and kissed her on the cheek. "Some women have more important duties than merely fighting. Besides, could you fight? Could you kill a man, or another woman?"

She met his gaze. "If I hated enough."

"There is the point. You do not hate the Whites enough. I think you hate us more than you hate the Whites."

"I wonder you do not have me shot."

"I intend to convert you. Ah, comrades, come in."

The officers filed into the room—a general, several colonels, and a host of lesser ranks. And among even these, Judith observed, positioning herself in a corner with Tattie, there were several women.

"Well, comrades." Michael stood behind his desk, hands thrust into the side pockets of his jacket, right thumb hooked over the top of his revolver holster. "As you will have gathered, I am your new commissar. I seem to have arrived at a quiet time."

"The enemy is assembling men, comrade commissar," said the general.

"Where?"

"About ten miles from here. There are some guard units on the move, but nothing more."

"We can do nothing about this concentration?"

The general shrugged. "Not without another ten thousand men, comrade commissar, and the necessary supplies of ammunition. My artillery cannot fire more than ten rounds a day."

"They are coming," Michael said. "But they will take time.

When do you suppose the Whites will launch their offensive?"

"It must be soon, comrade commissar. Even down here the roads become impassable after November. It must be soon."

"Well then, we shall have to accept their attack," Michael said. "But we must be prepared. Why are there no fortifications, no positions ready to receive the Whites?"

The general gave a contemptuous smile. "Because there is nothing to fortify, comrade commissar. This country is completely flat, and at this time of the year even the rivers are no more than streams. There is no position we can propose to hold with any hope of success."

"Then we must create such a position, Comrade General Malutin."

"Create a position?" Malutin looked to right and left for support.

"We cannot create hills, forests, ravines, comrade commissar," said one of the colonels.

"We can dig trenches," Michael said.

They stared at him.

"Yes," he said. "I want us to dig, and dig, and dig. I want us to prepare to meet this onslaught that is coming, to meet it and to hurl it back. I want to see your men working, comrades. Working for victory."

"Our men will never dig trenches," the general said. "They deserted from the regular army just so they would not have to dig trenches anymore."

"Well, they will have to start again."

"They will not do it, comrade commissar," the general said. "They will desert all over again."

"Have you no reliable troops?"

"Well, there's the cavalry. We can count on them."

"Very good then," Michael said. "I wish you to place the cavalry so that any deserters can be prevented from leaving. Then I wish you to assemble your men and give them my orders. Should they refuse, I wish you to take every tenth man and shoot him."

There was a moment of absolute silence.

"But . . . suppose—" Malutin began at last.

"It is my task to do the supposing, comrade general. Yours is to carry out my orders. You were going to ask what would happen if the cavalry also did not support us? Well, then, we should all die. But I can promise you that we are going to die, in any event, unless we stop General Denikin. So get to it. Ivan Nikolaievich, I want intelligence. I want you to take a company of cavalry and scour this country, get me a prisoner or a deserter. That is important."

"Of course, comrade commissar. I would have you meet my aide. She is my principal interrogator. Believe me, comrade commissar, whoever I bring in, she will obtain the truth from him. Comrade commissar, Captain Ulyanova."

Dora Ulyanova saluted.

"Dora?" Judith could hardly believe her eyes.

"Good morning, Comrade Stein." Dora's voice was cold.

"But . . . we had heard you were dead."

"As from time to time I heard that you were dead, comrade. But we are both alive, and seem to be prospering."

Michael was looking from one to the other in bewilderment.

"Dora and I knew each other in Siberia," Judith explained. "And after our return in 1914 she lived with us for a while."

"It was thanks to you that I was given a post in the foreign ministry," Dora said. "I am grateful for that, comrade."

"A gratitude you showed by murdering your superiors," Judith said.

Dora smiled at her. "It is the duty of all good Bolsheviks to kill traitors wherever they are found," she said. "It is a duty you should perhaps have practiced."

"So you are the woman who killed the Grand Duke Philip," Michael said. "And Tigran Borodin. Well, well. But . . . Ulyanova?"

"That is my name, comrade commissar."

"Then why are you not in Petrograd?"

"Seeking favors from my uncle? I prefer to be here, comrade, fighting for our cause. I have no interest in politics. I am a revolutionary."

Not for the first time Judith wondered if Lenin really was Dora's uncle, or if she had just laid claim to the name. She had thought it odd from the beginning that no member of the Ulyanov family had ever tried to make contact with her after their return from Siberia.

"And as your brother has said, comrade commissar," Dora continued, "I am fulfilling a valuable role here, where we are face to face with the Whites." She smiled again. "There is no man who can resist my interrogation. The Whites go in terror of being captured and given to me. They call me Red Dora, and frighten themselves awake at night when they dream of me. Why, Comrade Stein, do you know what I have recently discovered?"

"How should I know that, Comrade Ulyanova," Judith said, "unless you tell me?"

"I have discovered that Colonel Peter Borodin serves in the White Army. That indeed he is chief-of-staff to General Denikin."

"Peter Borodin?" Michael snapped.

"Peter?" Tattie had been listening after all. Now she jumped off the settee and ran forward.

"That cannot be true," Michael said. "He never returned from Germany."

Judith could only stare at them, her heart pounding.

"It is true, comrade commissar," Dora said. "He seems to have made his way the entire length of Russia, disguised as a Colonel Smyslov. And he did not make the journey alone. He was accompanied by a young woman. Your sister Rachel, Comrade Stein."

"My—" Judith's jaw slipped.

"You have not reported this before," Ivan said. "Why have you not reported this before?"

"I did not think it necessary. I wished to keep the information until it could be used to best advantage. Do you not find it sinister, comrade commissar, that this woman's sister should have joined the Whites? Do you not suppose it possible that Comrade Stein here may also be contemplating deserting to them, to be with her lover who now is the lover of her sister? Perhaps she intends to buy back his affection by telling him our dispositions and our plans?"

Judith stared at Michael.

"Rachel Stein," Ivan said, apparently to himself. "He went to Petrograd to find Rachel?" He turned now to Judith.

"He was looking for me, I imagine," Judith said. And I wasn't there, she thought. I wasn't there.

"You won't send me back to him?" Tattie begged, clutching Ivan's arm. "Please don't send me back to him. He'll lock me up again. I know he'll lock me up again. And he won't ever let me dance."

Ivan shrugged himself free. "Go and sit down, you stupid cow. You won't see him again until he is brought here a captive." He continued to look at Judith. "But if he went to Petrograd and found Rachel there, and persuaded her to go away with him, then he must have gone to your house, Judith."

"Why, I—" She bit her lip, suddenly realizing the trap into which she had nearly fallen, on behalf of her parents.

"Oh, indeed, comrade," Dora said. "Comrade Stein's family would certainly have known who he was. A traitor. A man with a price on his head. They are all the same, comrade commissar. Why do you not give Comrade Stein to me, comrade commissar? I will soon have her begging to tell you all about her family."

"You are insane," Judith said. "You have always been insane." But she could not stop herself from looking at Michael. Too often she had told him how much she hated the Bolsheviks.

"The man who gave you this information, Comrade Ulyanova," Michael said. "Is he still alive?"

Dora smiled. "Oh, yes, comrade commissar. I do not let them die so easily."

"I would like to speak with him," Michael said.

"Of course, comrade commissar."

"You had better come with me," Michael said to Judith.

"I? But—"

"I think you would enjoy it," Dora said. "It will make you think."

Michael had already put on his cap and was walking to the door of the compartment. Tattie had resumed her seat and was staring moodily out of the window. Ivan and Dora fell in beside the commissar. Judith sighed, and followed. She had no doubt at all that she was going to see something terrible.

They climbed down from the train and walked along the track, beside the tents where the soldiers were already grumbling as they were issued picks and shovels by their commanders; beyond the train the cavalry sat their horses with menacing patience. In the center of the encampment the tents gave way to huts, so comfortable had this army made itself. Outside one of the huts a sentry stood at attention, and Dora opened the door.

Judith caught her breath. The atmosphere inside was fetid, redolent of sweat and excrement, and above all fear. There were no windows, and even with the sun high the room was gloomy, but not so gloomy that they could not make out the single occupant, a man who was tied to an upright chair against the far wall. He was naked, and his body was a mass of cuts and bruises, but he was conscious, and his head jerked as the door opened. But he did not look directly at the door. His face moved in various directions, almost as if he were listening rather than seeing.

Almost? Judith felt deathly sick.

"That man is blind," Michael said.

"Of course," Dora agreed. "I always take out their eyes first. It makes them more frightened. He is frightened now, simply from hearing my voice."

"What else have you done to him?" Michael's voice was thick.

"Very little, as yet."

"My God." Michael glanced at his brother. "You authorized this?"

"He is a White," Ivan pointed out. "It is his kind, perhaps it was this very man, who hanged our people in Starogan. They hanged Mama and Nona, Michael Nikolaievich. He is going to be shot anyway. What happens to him before that is irrelevant, as long as he is able to give us information. You have just asked for information, comrade commissar. Do you suppose that prisoners, men who know they are going to die anyway, will tell us anything if they are not forced?"

Michael stared at the man for a few minutes more, then turned and left the hut. Judith ran after him and clutched his arm.

"You must stop it. Stop her."

He looked down at her, then walked on, more slowly. He did not shrug his arm free.

"You must, Michael," Judith begged. "She is mad, you know. Hatred has turned her mind. Just like Tattie, though that from sheer shock, I suppose. You cannot give her power of life and death over innocent men."

"Innocent men?"

"Well . . . men who are only obeying orders."

"So if we happen to capture Peter Borodin you would agree to handing *him* over. If he is chief-of-staff to Denikin; he gives the orders."

"Michael, you can't be serious."

"I am an inhuman monster, remember. You said so."

"Michael . . ." She pulled so hard he had to stop. The soldiers, already started on their digging, leaned on their spades to gaze at them. "Whatever I said, I never believed it. I do not think you are a monster. I do not think you enjoy any of the things you have to do. I think you are forcing yourself, just as you forced yourself to go with Bogrov after Stolypin. But Michael, surely there comes a time when duty must give way to common humanity and decency."

"No," he said. "One can only afford to be decent and humane when one has the time and the circumstances. The Swiss are decent and humane. But they did not take part in the war, did they? And I can tell you that when they *were* fighting wars they didn't find much time for decency and humanity. And this is more than a war. This is a conflict of ideologies. The Whites must be destroyed, not merely defeated. They must be stamped out of existence like vermin. And they think the same about us. So the mob sacked the Borodin estate. Can you really equate the murder of a few aristocratic ladies and a few of their servants with the hanging of an entire village—men and women and children? I told you that this war is filthy and vicious. You wanted to come. Well, do not complain now."

"Then why *don't* you hand me over to her?" Judith shouted.

"You are hysterical," he said. "She is doing a job. I do not like what she is doing, but she is obtaining information and she is undermining the morale of the Whites, by the very fear of capture. And Ivan was quite right when he said that it does not matter. That man is going to die. Whether he dies after a few hours or even days of agony, or whether he stops a bullet in the chest in the heat of battle, is neither here nor there. He is going to die so that we may triumph, and you and I may live."

"You and I," she muttered. "Don't you believe what she said of me?"

He smiled, put out his hand to thrust it beneath her hair and cup the back of her head. "It does not matter, what she says or what I believe. I love you, Judith."

Chapter 11

A BUGLE CALL DRIFTED ACROSS THE MORNING, AND THE ENcampment began to stir. Peter Borodin was awake in an instant. He rolled onto his back and stared at the thatched roof above him.

A thatched roof, and wooden walls to keep out the gazes of the curious. There was an air of the permanence into which this war, like so many wars, had settled. Most of his fellow officers believed the season for campaigning was already over, and that he had delayed until it was too late to execute his plans before next spring. Did they really suppose huts like this would keep out the winter winds? Or that they would *have* an army, come next spring, if they remained in the center of this vast wheatfield, where there was no wheat?

"Then why did we not attack sooner, in the height of summer?" they had asked. And he had had to explain that they lacked the matériel to fight a long campaign. Their offensive must be perfectly timed to sweep them forward at least as far as Tsaritsyn in one great burst, thus giving them a railhead and a solid town in which to spend the winter and to replenish their stocks of ammunition. From there they would spread the word of their invincibility; there they would recruit and train and arm in preparation for next year—the decisive year, he was sure, the year in which they would seize Kiev and knock the first prop out from beneath the crumbling edifice of Bolshevism.

At least Denikin appeared to have faith in his new chief-of-staff. Denikin and Roditchev. He had never expected support from Sergei Roditchev. But they fought on the same side now, in a deeper sense than they had ever fought on the same side for the tsar. They might never be friends, but for the moment, they were comrades with but a single goal.

The girl beside him stirred, and turned on her side. Her eyes did not open, but she half-smiled in her sleep. For all the hardship and discomfort she had to endure, she was happy. To be with him. In her shy, whispered confessions she had told him how she had always idolized him, almost from the first moment he had entered her parents' house in Moscow, back in 1907. He could hardly recall what she had looked like then; he could only remember that there had always seemed to be a younger sister underfoot. But now she was happy, because she spent every night in the same bed as Prince Peter Borodin.

And was he happy? He sat up, dropped his legs out of the cot, and reached for his clothes. Could anyone in this army be happy? Was not their driving force the emotion of hatred, of a burning desire for revenge? The tsar was dead, put up against a wall and shot. With him had died his son, and by all accounts his wife and his four lovely daughters. Any many of his servants. How many? If that had been Judith Stein's fate, after all she had endured, all she had suffered by the decree of that very tsar, then truly was she the most unfortunate woman ever born. And having been responsible for at least some of that misfortune, having known her and loved her and then abandoned her to her fate, could he ever be happy again?

He looked down at the sleeping face on the pillow, and her eyes opened. They possessed that much telepathy now, the telepathy of two people who had shared everything there was to share. And suppose, he thought, with that facility of conscience which came easily to him, suppose he had refused to take Irina back, had instead set up Judith Stein at Starogan, certainly to the disruption of his family and his hopes of a career? Had he done that, Judith Stein would have been raped and murdered by a mob, instead of being shot by a mob. Would she have gained anything more than a very few weeks of happiness? Assuming they would have been happy at all.

Weeping over Judith, even remembering her, was a waste of time, useful only as long as it inspired his determination to avenge her probable death. The woman herself had been doomed from birth.

But not her sister. Rachel smiled at him, and seemed about to say something, then realized that he was fully dressed and changed her mind.

"I will be back for breakfast," he said, bent to kiss her on the forehead, and had his hand seized tightly for a moment. She knew, as well as anyone, that the offensive was close, and she feared for him. Without him she had nothing; she would degenerate into one of the common herd of camp followers that haunted this army, eager to accept any man who would give her warmth and food, and the hope of survival when winter came.

He stepped outside, saluted the double-eagle flag, and headed towards the staff house, outside of which the general and his other officers were already gathered, a safe distance from the squalor of the main encampment. Here too was Roditchev, uniform spattered with mud, chin stubbled with beard, eyes heavy with exhaustion. But Roditchev preferred to patrol at night. With him were two of his Cossacks, who appeared to be guarding a small, frightened man in a disheveled khaki uniform.

"News, Peter," Sergei boomed at him. "A good night's work."

"Indeed?" Peter saluted Denikin, a stocky man who wore a beard and mustache like the tsar's.

"It appears that the Reds have received a new commander-in-chief," Denikin said.

"Worse than that, for *them*, your excellency," Roditchev said. "They have received a new commissar, as they call it. He is not the commanding general. His duty is to tell the commanding general what is best for him to do, for the good of the Bolsheviks. A sure recipe for disaster, eh? But you will never guess, Peter Dimitrievich, who this commissar is. Oh, a terrible fellow, a man steeped in military experience, a veteran of years of warfare."

"As you say, Sergei Pavlovich, I shall never guess," Peter agreed, dryly.

"His name is Michael Nej," Roditchev said, and gave a

bellow of laughter. "Michael Nej! Prince Peter's valet, my friends. Michael Nej, commanding the army that would oppose us. Has he ever fired a shot in anger? Oh, yes, I forgot. He once murdered a policeman, in a back street of Kiev. But he did not fire that shot in anger, my friends. He fired it in terror. I know, because he told me so when I had him stretched out in front of me begging for mercy. There is the measure of the man who would stop us. He shoots only in terror."

The other officers shuffled their feet in discomfort. They did not really appreciate Roditchev's outbursts of ferocious humor any more than they enjoyed being reminded that he had once commanded the tsar's secret police. They wanted to avenge the fall of the monarchy, and even more they wanted to regain their lands and their bank accounts but few of them really wanted a return to Russia as it had been in 1914.

"Nonetheless," General Denikin remarked mildly, "If what you say is true, Prince Roditchev, this fellow Nej has at the least inspired the Reds with some energy."

"They are digging trenches," Roditchev said contemptuously. "Would you believe it? Trenches, here in the basin of the Don. Where do they think they are, Flanders? I suppose that is the only war these Bolsheviks have heard of, since they spent so much time in Switzerland."

"Still," objected one of the other staff officers, "a fortified camp may be a difficult nut to crack. We lack artillery."

"Bah," Roditchev said.

"Prince Borodin?" Denikin inquired, still speaking quietly. "How does this news affect your plans?"

Michael Nej, Peter thought. After all these years, Michael Nej. But it was logical. The man had always been an anarchist at heart. He should have been hanged years ago. He would have been hanged, but for George Hayman. He wondered what Hayman thought, now that the man he had saved had become a warlord. But perhaps Hayman approved; he had always been a bit of a radical himself.

And surely Sergei had to be right. Michael Nej might have read books and newspapers, but he had never fought in a battle. He could have none of the iron mental discipline that could command an entire regiment of men to march to their deaths just to insure victory for the army as a whole. Only the experience of continuous command created such determination. That and the right upbringing, and even more, the right birth.

It was not a characteristic a muzhik could ever hope to attain.

"Prince Peter?" Denikin asked again.

"I think we should attack, as planned," he said.

"They will know we are coming," someone objected.

"They already know that," Peter pointed out. "But we will regain the element of surprise because, like so many of you, they will expect us to try to outflank their fortifications. They have no more artillery, no more machine guns than we do, and even less ammunition. Now is the moment for us to risk all. We shall bombard for no more than five minutes—" He smiled. "—we lack the shells for a longer attack, anyway—being careful to leave the railway line undamaged, and then we shall attack them in their front, where they will not expect it. And if anyone is doubtful as to our success, I am perfectly willing to lead the assault myself."

"We shall all lead the assault," Denikin said. "Is there any more information to be obtained from that man, Prince Roditchev?"

"No, general." Roditchev snapped his fingers. "Hang him," he said.

The man gave a wail of terror. "You promised, general," he shrieked. "You said you would exchange my life for information. You—"

"Oh, take him away," Roditchev said impatiently. "Hang him."

The officers waited while the screaming man was dragged away; none of them was disposed to interfere. They had no capacity for holding prisoners, even if they had had any desire to.

"Well, gentlemen," Denikin said. "Will you fix the hour of the advance, General Borodin?"

"At dawn tomorrow morning, sir," Peter said. "We will never be more ready than we are now."

Peter stood by the fire outside the hut, watching Rachel fry eggs, aided by his orderly. At least the army was well-supplied with food, because they held the Crimea and the granary of the South. But only with food. For as long as the war in Europe continued, there was no hope of obtaining additional arms and ammunition. But now that the Americans were pouring men and matériel into France there was every prospect that Germany would collapse within a year. All they had to do was maintain themselves that long, as Kolchak was maintaining himself in Siberia, and then surely, with Allied support, it would be possible to trounce these makeshift armies with their makeshift commanders, and restore the Russia he remembered and loved.

But maintaining a position could never be a matter of standing still.

"Do you know that I had never cooked in my life before coming here with you?" Rachel asked. She was unusually bright and cheerful this morning—too bright and cheerful. She knew the offensive was imminent, but she did not yet know it was to begin tomorrow morning.

"Then it must always have been one of your secret talents," he said, sitting on the camp chair before the folding table and sipping the cup of scalding coffee held by Boris Ivanovich.

"Perhaps I shall be able to make a living as a cook," she said, and caught her breath as Peter frowned. She flushed. In the six months they had been together they had never once discussed the future, just as they had never discussed the past. Their world had begun the day he had visited the Steins' house in Petrograd, searching for Judith. No doubt she supposed it would end when the war ended, and he would be able to resume his proper place in society. Like him, she assumed that Judith had to be dead.

Or it might end when he stopped a bullet. He had survived too many years of war not to imagine his luck might be running out.

"I have no doubt you could," he said, and finished his coffee. But she had to be told. "We move out at dawn tomorrow."

"At—" Her mouth opened, and for a moment he thought she was going to cry. But then she controlled herself, as she had always managed to control herself.

"We intend to crush them," Peter said. "It is then our intention to continue the advance and seize Tsaritsyn. We shall make the town our headquarters for the winter. It has a railhead and will be ideal for our purposes."

"When will you get there?" she asked.

"If we win tomorrow? Within a week. But it would be best for you to remain with the commissariat until we are sure of victory. I will send for you then."

"But you are going with the attack?"

"Of course."

"You are on the staff," she insisted. "You *are* the staff. Without you they will have no plans at all. You should not risk your life."

"War is a matter of risking lives," he reminded her. "And tomorrow's attack is riskier than most. But we must strike before the enemy has completed its preparations, and I must be there to see that the attack is carried out in accordance with my ideas." He smiled at her. "I have never been hit yet. Even when my own men were firing at me, I was not hit. There is no reason why I should be hit now."

She glanced at Boris Ivanovich. "I think, Boris, that you should go and have your own breakfast," she said.

Boris stood at attention and looked at his superior. Peter turned to Rachel and read the message in her eyes.

"Yes, Boris Ivanovich," he said. "Go and have your breakfast. You may come back for the dishes afterwards."

"Yes, your excellency." Boris saluted and marched off.

"Now you will have to do the serving yourself," Peter said.

"I do not mind." She ladled eggs and cornbread onto his plate, and placed it before him.

"You knew that I came here to fight a war," he said. "I am fighting for you and your family, as much as for anything else."

"I know that," she said.

"So it is unreasonable of you to be so upset about an offensive. We will need many such offensives before we cleanse Russia of Bolshevism."

"I know that too," she said.

"Well, then . . ."

"It is just that we have our lives to live, as well as your fighting to do. I have lived here with you for six months. I have been happy. I have not cared about anything that might be happening, because I have been with you. But life is going on despite the war, Peter." She sat down with a sigh and stared at the table. "I have not menstruated in four months."

Peter put down his laden fork just before it reached his mouth. "Four months?"

She raised her head slowly. "At first I thought it was the constant traveling, the fact we didn't eat properly, all sorts of things. But it can't be, anymore. We have been here for nearly a month, and we have eaten well."

"My God," he said.

"Are you very angry with me?"

"Angry with you?" He reached for her hands. "I have never had a son. Never, never, never. I had supposed I would be the very last Borodin."

She smiled through her tears. "You have not yet got a son. It may be a girl."

"It will be a son," he said. "What, conceived on the march? It will be a son."

"Then you *are* pleased?"

"Pleased?" He pulled her round the table to sit on his lap. "My darling, darling child, I am delighted."

"But you will still lead the advance tomorrow morning."

"It is my duty. I shall come back, I promise you that. Anyway, it will not matter."

"Not matter? she cried.

"Not to you. You are the mother of my son. Then you should bear my name. This afternoon we shall be married."

"Your excellencies, ladies, mesdames and messieurs, fellow officers, I give you the Princess Borodina." General Denikin beamed.

They clustered round to kiss the bride and shake Peter's hand. The Princess Borodina. The position of which Judith had always dreamed. No, no, Judith had never dreamed so high. *Rachel* had dreamed that it might be possible through Tigran. But now the position was hers. Mistress of Starogan. All that wheat, all those cattle and sheep. All that wealth and splendor, the Rolls-Royces, the house in Petrograd . . . but most of all, all that power. When she thought of the way Irina Borodina had swept into the drawing room that terrible night in 1914, she felt almost faint; now she possessed that omnipotence. She smiled at the ladies who surrounded her. Let them think what they liked. Let them even *know*, for those few ladies who had elected to be with their husbands here in camp rather than remain safely in Sevastopol had nothing to do but gossip. In one step she had risen above them all.

"Now that we are about to campaign, princess, the ladies will of course be returning to the Crimea," General Denikin said, taking her hand. "I have reserved a first-class compartment for you."

"Oh, but . . ." She gazed at Peter. It had never occurred to her that she would not be staying with the army. Was it impossible to be both a princess and a camp follower?

"It would be best, my dear," Peter said. "For every possible reason. In Sevastopol you will be safe, and there will be people to care for you." He smiled at the look of alarm on her face. "Believe me, as soon as the campaign is over and we have gone into winter quarters, I will come to visit you."

She bit her lip to keep back the tears. But was this not just another mark of her new-found rank? She was too precious to risk, or rather, her baby was too precious to risk. She carried the future Prince of Starogan. Why, she realized, but for me, if Peter were to die, the princedom would pass to Ilona Hayman, and through her to John Hayman. Roditchev's son. Her head jerked as she found herself facing the man himself.

"Princess Borodina." He bent over her hand. "May I suppose this is the happiest moment of your life?"

She threw back her head to look at him. "By no means, Prince Roditchev." How marvelous it was to be able to call him Prince Roditchev, and smile, where always in the past she had had to call him your excellency, and tremble. "The happiest moment of my life will be when the Prince and I can begin the reconstruction of Starogan."

"Of course. I do not think it will be very long now. But still I congratulate you, Princess Rachel. You have come a long way. But then, I suppose all Russia has come a long way, in the past few years. If only it were possible to decide whether the route were up or down."

"I hate him," she told Peter that night. "Oh, how I hate him." She clung to him in the intimacy of the narrow bed, willing time to stand still, the moments to cease their senseless ticking away. Willing the night never to end.

"You are beyond his reach now, my dear," Peter said. He spoke drowsily. He was very tired. And tomorrow he would need all his faculties. Yet she could not let even his consciousness go.

"But for him, Judith—" She stopped herself. Her wedding night was not the time to talk of her sister.

Peter knew that too. He held her close. "I have not yet given you your wedding present," he said. "Starogan. And I cannot give you that until the Bolsheviks have been destroyed—until Michael Nej has been destroyed. You will have to be patient just a while longer."

Until Michael Nej has been destroyed. That was his goal. Did he, then, hate the man so much? There was no reason. As boys they had been friends together, first at Starogan and then in Port Arthur, before the responsibilities of manhood and the looming threat of the Japanese war had put an end to their games. When he had succeeded to the princedom it had been natural for his boyhood friend to become his valet. Thus the shock of Michael's sudden departure from Starogan had been the greater; for more than three hundred years the Nejs had been servants of the Borodins.

Yet at the time he had felt only irritation toward the silly fellow, and pity when he learned that Michael had become involved in an anarchist plot, had actually shot a policeman. It had not occurred to him to intercede for his former servant's life—he had had enough to do to save Judith from the gallows—but the pity had remained, that a life so full of promise—why, in the course of time, he might have followed his father and become steward of Starogan—was going to be ended so abruptly and so senselessly. There had been no hate, then.

He had no evidence that Michael Nej had harmed him or his family in the intervening years. He had rarely thought of the man until yesterday. But now he hated him. It was the hatred that a soldier must feel for the enemy in order to be able to kill him, but it was also something far deeper. Michael Nej was a Bolshevik. A participant in the Red disaster that had spread across Russia. A friend of Lenin. And an instigator, even if by proxy, of the events at Starogan. Michael Nej was a symbol of everything that had to be rooted out of Russian life, Russian culture, Russian history.

Today would see the matter concluded. In the semidarkness of early morning he rode ahead of the tramping columns of men, stood his horse on a low knoll, a rare feature on this endless plain, and looked out at the encampment in the distance, at the railhead, where there were still a couple of engines and a good deal of rolling stock, at the earthworks and trenches that surrounded it, at the track stretching from beside him, through the Red lines, and away into the distance. The Bolsheviks undoubtedly knew they were coming, but they were unable to do anything about it. Like the Whites, they lacked the ammunition to set up a true artillery barrage, and even their small arms had to be kept for the assault itself. They could only wait, and watch. If I had even one squadron of tanks, Peter thought, I would hardly have to sacrifice a single life. But he had no tanks. And no gasoline to make them move. In many ways, this war in the south of Russia had stepped backwards in time by forty years, to the conflict between France and Prussia, or to that earlier struggle between Prussia and Austria. To men and horses and trains. Bullets and cold steel. To discipline over mere misguided enthusiasm. On that was he pinning his faith.

"A strong position." General Denikin had been inspecting the Bolshevik entrenchments through his glasses. "I still wonder if it might not be a better plan to turn their flanks."

Peter pointed to the crowd of horsemen in the distance, hovering beside the railway track. "If we could maneuver under cover of some high ground, then perhaps it would be, general. But they'd smell us out in a moment. Indeed, they're anticipating some such plan. And do you see that rolling stock down there? They could withdraw their army before we could ever get round behind them, on foot."

"A frontal assault is going to be costly," Mark Liselle observed. He also had been using his glasses.

"We must balance men's lives against the gain in time and morale that a victory here would bring us." Peter looked over his shoulder at the mass of khaki-clad infantry plodding across the plain, at the Cossacks ranging to either side, at the train on which they had ridden, silent now, but the key to his strategy. "We must believe that we are the stronger force, morally as well as physically. Do you doubt that, Mark? We fight for all that is good in Russia. The enemy are representative of everything that is hideous. Do you doubt that?"

"No," Liselle said. "No, I do not doubt that, Peter Dimitrievich. I will go to see to the ordering of the men."

"What did you feel like, the night before a battle?" Michael Nej smoked a cigarette, and listened to the whisper of sounds that seeped through the night that was actually early morning.

Ivan shrugged. "We never knew when it was going to happen. Or if it was going to happen. We do not know now that it is going to happen."

"They are there," Michael pointed out. "Prince Peter is there, with his army."

"Prince Peter," Ivan said contemptuously. "Comrade Borodin, the traitor, you mean."

"I would like to have him, if you take him prisoner." Dora Ulyanova had, as usual, approached them silently. "I should like that very much."

Michael glanced at Judith, her face lost in the semidarkness.

She turned away and walked back to the train.

"If we take him prisoner," Michael said, "I want him brought to me, and no one else. Remember that."

"If, comrade commissar?"

It was Michael's turn to shrug. "I do not know how tomorrow will turn out," he said. "As Ivan Nikolaievich has said, I do not even know if the Whites will attack us. We have created a strong position here. I imagine their best course would be to attempt to outflank us, and then seize the railway line behind us."

"Which is why I have said we should pull back," the general complained.

"And back, and back, and back?" Michael demanded. "Is that the sum of your military knowledge, how to retreat? We are here to defeat the White army. We cannot do so unless we stand and fight. If they attempt to outflank us, then we will have our best opportunity." According to his books. He had no other experience on which to call. My God, he thought, do these people realize that? Do they know that I have never been under fire? That I have no concept of what will happen tomorrow, of how I will react, of whether I will even be able to think? But they did not know that, and they must never suspect the churning terror that seemed to have gripped his stomach.

"If they retreat, then we will shatter them," Dora said. "When we have repulsed their attack, and they attempt to pull back, then we will destroy them."

"Then," Michael agreed. "When they have been repulsed. I suggest now you attempt to get some sleep. Be sure your sentries are alert, comrade general."

"They are alert, comrade commissar. But the Whites will not attack before dawn." Malutin smiled contemptuously. "You will have time to sleep, if you can."

If I can. If I wish to, Michael thought. But what a waste of time it is, to sleep the night before I may well die. Time enough to sleep when the battle is over. If I am still alive.

He climbed the steps and entered the darkened compartment. Tattie Borodina slept with her face turned to the wall, making little snoring whimpers. Tattie Borodina. Ivan's dream woman, now his sole possession. A shell.

Or a very deep, very composed young woman, seeking her own salvation in the only way she knew? But that was nonsense. Tonight he was questioning even his own sanity, because of his doubts about being here at all.

And about having Judith here. He lay down beside her, and her hand closed over his.

"Are you afraid?"

Was he afraid? Was he a coward? How could he know? He had not been a coward when the judge pronounced sentence of death upon him, but then he did not care. Having suffered so much in Roditchev's cell, he had wished only to die. Now he wished only to live.

"How can I be afraid?" he asked. "I am the commissar. Are you afraid?"

"I have nothing to fear," she said. "You know that."

"Of course. Even if you are captured, you will be captured by Peter Borodin. But tell me this, Judith Stein: Do you wish us to lose?"

"Yes," she said. "I wish you to lose."

He raised himself on his elbow to peer at her in the darkness, and listened to the sound of Ivan getting into bed beside Tattie. How odd, he thought, that we two brothers, who have never been close, as brothers should be, who have been separated for half of our lives, should be together at the end, sleeping in the same compartment, waiting to triumph or to die, together.

Judith neither moved her head nor shut her eyes. But he knew her now. Hating him, or rather what he stood for, and making her hatred plain, was her only defense against what he had made happen to her.

He lowered his head and kissed her on the lips. "After we have won," he promised, "you will be happy that we have won. I will make you happy." He wanted to love her now. But he knew he was not going to. The seething hell in his belly made an erection impossible. "After we have won," he said, and lay down beside her.

He awoke to a blaring bugle, and an unimaginable high-pitched screaming, which ended in a thudding explosion that made the train tremble on its tracks.

He rolled out of bed and sat on the floor with a bump. Above him Judith sat up, pushing hair from her eyes. On the far side of the compartment Tattie started to scream, a continuous high-pitched sound almost as disturbing as the wail of the shell; the scream ended when Ivan slapped her face.

Michael scrambled to his feet and reached for his clothes, his cap with its star, his symbol of authority. "What in the name of God is happening?" He spoke without intending to.

"Bombardment," Ivan said, also dressing hastily. "An attack always begins with a bombardment."

Michael realized they were both shouting; the noise was now continuous, and was augmented by the other shouts and screams from outside the carriage. Could men and women stand up to such noise, much less the death on the end of it?

"Michael." Judith reached for him, but he shrugged her off, ran across the compartment, wrenched open the door, tripped, and plummeted across the steps to land on his hands and knees. He was staring at boots. The general.

He stood up and straightened his hat.

"There is no danger here, comrade commissar." Malutin, as usual, filled his voice with contempt. "They are deliberately not aiming at the railway line. It is the railway line they want to preserve, comrade. May I suggest that we detach a company to tear up the tracks?"

Tear up the tracks? Michael wanted to scream. Are you mad? The tracks are our only means of escape.

He swallowed. "We are here to fight for those tracks, comrade general. See to your men."

The general hesitated, then saluted. "As you wish, comrade commissar."

He hurried into the darkness so punctuated by bursts of light. But they were not aiming at the railway line. The general had said so. A gallant man, the general. Courage began to flow back into Michael's veins. "When will they attack?" he asked Ivan. Above them Tattie was screaming again, but he could hear Judith attempting to soothe her.

"When the barrage stops," Ivan said.

"Then let us get into the line."

"The line?" Ivan demanded. "I do not belong in the line. My job is interrogating prisoners."

Michael realized that Ivan was as terrified as he was. "Then wait for them," he said. "My job is to win this battle."

He hurried away from the safety of the train. What am I doing? he asked himself. How can men withstand such a barrage? Should I not order the retreat? If we retreated now, with the railway intact, we would all get away—the commanders would, anyway. But why else was he here? What had Lenin said, on the platform? There was no other reason for his existence. No other reason, by God.

But Lenin had said there was no God.

The barrage ceased. The suddenness of the silence was terrifying. Michael staggered and almost fell beneath the weight of it. All around his men were crawling out of ditches and from behind hastily improvised shelters, shouting at each other. Women wailed and children cried; there was the measure of how long this army had remained immobile. But at least the barrage had ceased. He could think again.

"Comrade general," he shouted. "Comrade general."

"Look there, comrade commissar." A junior officer seized his arm and pointed. Michael stared at the railway track, at the engine, only just visible in the darkness, hurtling towards him. And behind the engine there were half a dozen carriages, each one spurting red flame from every aperture.

"Fire," he shouted. "Fire."

Men threw themselves down and began to shoot their rifles. Machine guns chattered. Red flame distorted the night, and turned it into hell. Michael found himself on his knees. He had drawn his revolver and only knew what he was doing when the hammer clicked on an empty chamber. As if revolver bullets could possibly check a runaway locomotive. The engine smashed into the barricades, threw them left and right, derailed itself and threatened to fall over, but then remained upright. The doors of the carriages behind burst open, and the White soldiers leapt out, shooting as they did so, while the first glimmer of dawn picked out the points of their gleaming bayonets.

And his revolver was empty. Michael stood up, and the men around him looked at him. He realized that the lieutenant to whom he had been talking was dead. Then where was the general?

From left and right came the yells of advancing infantry. The Whites were all over the plain, and charging his entrenchments. But entrenched infantry can always repel attacking infantry. His books had said that.

"Run," someone shouted.

"There are too many," another screamed.

"Run," came the general cry.

Michael ran. He threw away his revolver and ran for the

train. "Leave," he yelled at the bewildered driver. "Leave."

Judith pushed her head out the window of the first-class compartment. "What is happening?" she shouted.

"Leave," Michael screamed. He leapt onto the step as the train gave a jerk and emitted steam. "Full throttle."

The train started to move. A bullet whanged into the woodwork beside Michael's head, and he threw himself inside the door and landed, panting on his hands and knees. But the firing was dying away as the train gathered speed.

It was almost light now. As he regained his breath he could look up at Judith and Tattie, standing above him. Judith's face was the picture of concern. Tattie's lip curled.

"Where are your men, comrade commissar?" she asked.

"You are to be congratulated, General Borodin." General Denikin reined his horse and looked around him. Peter wondered if he had ever before seen such a scene of destruction. Certainly *he* had never witnessed such a complete victory before. The Reds had fled, almost at the first shot. All around him were discarded rifles and ammunition pouches, discarded caps, discarded haversacks and water bottles. And in the midst of the debris of a defeated army were the discarded bodies, women and children, as well as men. The majority had been destroyed by the brief artillery barrage, and were horrible to look at, for it was difficult to tell where one human being ended and another began. Only a few had been hit by bullets, and lay in their trenches or behind their earthworks, legs and arms scattered in the ballet of death.

"Was it not the Duke of Wellington," Denikin remarked, "who said, 'Next to a battle lost, the most horrifying experience is a battle won'?"

"I think so," Peter said.

"But we have the railway intact. We even have some rolling stock to put with our own. Should we not advance?"

"Indeed we should, General. To Tsaritsyn. Sooner or later it will occur to Nej that the only way he can halt us is to destroy the line."

Nej, he thought. Nej had run away, as he might have been expected to do. He had fled in his command train, with his staff, no doubt with his women as well. It had not really been a battle at all, merely a rout of an undisciplined horde of guerrillas. Well, had he expected anything different?

But Rachel would be pleased. The Princess Borodina. A Princess Borodina who would at last be worthy of the name.

"I wonder if you will be as successful when you are opposed by real soldiers." Sergei Roditchev had cantered across the dead bodies, the shattered tents and huts, and now drew rein beside Peter.

"Will I ever be opposed by a real army, Sergei?" Peter asked. There was no need for him to take offense now, or ever again.

"Probably not," Roditchev agreed. "What are we to do with those fellows?" He pointed at the men being herded into a giant ring by the Cossacks.

Denikin glanced at Peter. "They will have to be shot."

"There seem to be a great number of them," Peter remarked.

"I would estimate about four hundred," Roditchev said. "But certainly my men will pick up a lot more as we advance. They must be scattered all over the steppe."

"We certainly cannot cope with several thousand prisoners," Denikin pointed out.

"Yet some of them are surely just muzhiks, dragooned into fighting by the Bolsheviks," Peter said. "They would probably be just as happy fighting for us. And even happier being allowed to go home and grow wheat for us."

"Once a Bolshevik, always a Bolshevik," Roditchev said.

"But Prince Borodin has a point, Prince Roditchev," Denikin said. "We must be on our way. We must pursue the Reds while their morale is crushed by their defeat. And we shall need the Cossacks, both for scouting and for hanging. You will remain here, Prince Roditchev, with one infantry regiment. Talk with the prisoners. Find out which of them would be prepared to fight with us. I leave that in your charge, Prince Roditchev."

Roditchev saluted, and smiled at Peter.

"In your charge, the general said, Sergei," Peter reminded him. "Colonel Liselle, have our people form up to continue the advance. We'll camp for the midday meal when we've advanced a few miles further." Away from this growing stench of death, he thought. Away from Roditchev and his victims. "No doubt you will join us with your men as soon as you have attended to matters here, Sergei Pavlovich."

"Of course, Prince Peter. I will not be long. It will not take me long to interview these people."

He pulled his horse back, saluted again, and General Denikin and his staff clattered off, riding beside the railway track. Behind them the locomotive abandoned by the Bolsheviks was slowly shunted onto the main line, and its carriages attached; there was no hope of getting the engine used in the assault back on the track without a crane. And behind the train the infantry fell into line, while the Cossacks already began to range the open country to either side, to chase and destroy the defeated enemy.

The men were happy. Their own casualties had been remarkably light, and there is no greater boost to morale than to advance and keep on advancing.

"To Tsaritsyn," they shouted. "You'll join us in Tsaritsyn, your excellency."

It was a mood to be encouraged. Roditchev took off his cap to wave it at them, and they cheered him as they tramped by. At last, he thought. At last we are striking back. And winning. Perhaps Peter Borodin, poor confused Peter Borodin, has some talent after all. More likely he was just lucky.

But he had a job before him, an important and enjoyable one. He wheeled his horse and walked it across the charnel house that had been the Red encampment, towards the prisoners. The colonel in command of the infantry regiment saluted him.

"I have made a count, your excellency. There are three hundred and forty-seven men, twenty-four women, and five children."

Roditchev nodded. "Shoot the men and the children. Your people may have the women, for a while. Then they had better be shot as well. Use machine guns on the men, it is quicker. And then I want this place cleaned up. Burial squads, and burn all this rubbish. I want this encampment to be nothing more than a scar. Understood?"

The colonel saluted. "And you, your excellency?"

Roditchev smiled. "I will have a look at these Red women."

The colonel nodded, and turned away.

Did he really want any of these women, Roditchev wondered? Perhaps, to hurt them. He had always enjoyed hurting women, ever since his first wife, Anastasia, had died in childbirth, screaming his name, cursing him and hating him. Anastasia Roditchevna had not even been beautiful, merely female; the marriage had been arranged by his father. And he had been so very young. After her death he had turned inwards, concentrated on his career, used only card-bearing prostitutes when he needed sex. Until Ilona Borodina.

The marriage had actually been proposed by the new prince, young Peter. Roditchev had not been able to believe his ears. Later, of course, the truth had been explained to him. Ilona had had an affair with the American newspaperman, Hayman. He had hardly been able to believe his ears about that either, that a Russian princess would share herself with some common businessman. But of course, Ilona had always had the mentality of a slut. He had been overjoyed at the thought of possessing all that haughty beauty. And he had enjoyed the possession. But only to hurt, since he could never truly dominate. Beating Ilona had been one of the great pleasures of his life, until Peter had so stupidly interfered. But by then, by her own confession, Ilona had accepted not only a businessman, but her brother's valet, as a lover. She had not, of course, revealed that to him until she had already left Russia; she had known he would have killed her. But he had never doubted it was true. She had only confirmed what his eyes, his ears, his senses, had suggested ever since the birth of the boy. Ivan Sergeievich was not his. He had been able to discern no spark of Roditchev in the little boy. But Michael Nej's . . .

His fingers curled into fists. That was the only disappointment of today, that Nej and his cohorts had got away. But they would not get away forever. They would be caught, and they would be delivered into his hands. And then . . .

Hatred, the wish to inflict suffering and pain, had been all that he had salvaged from the wreckage of his life with Ilona. And it was a craving he had been able to indulge. The tsar had recognized that Sergei Roditchev was the ideal man to command the Okhrana. And there had been enough people brought to his office to satisfy even his craving to see others suffer. Some were even memorable. Judith Stein, for instance, because every time he had laid his cane across her shuddering flesh he had thought of Ilona. It was a pity her sister had got away. Although . . . the world was in such a state of flux that it was even possible to suppose that the Princess Borodina might one day find herself in the hands of the police. His police.

But there were others. And once he had actually had Michael Nej at his feet. If only one could foresee the future.

"A ragged bunch," the colonel remarked, pointing with his cane.

Roditchev looked at the women. They huddled together as

if for mutual support, stared less at him than at their menfolk and their children, being marshaled into lines, and at the soldiers who watched them like wolves, eagerly awaiting the orders they knew were coming, which would leave these poor creatures at their mercy.

"As you say, colonel," he said. Nothing for him there. No one of interest, no one of beauty; merely a collection of dirty frightened females. He wheeled his horse, still looking at them, and a shot rang out. The bullet must have passed very close to his head. Had he really felt its wind? He turned back, drawing his own revolver as he did so, an example followed by the colonel beside him. But already the soldiers had dashed forward, knocking women left and right with their rifle butts, arriving at the culprit just as she was leveling the revolver again, throwing her to the ground and threatening her with their bayonets.

"Stop there," Roditchev shouted. He glanced at the colonel. "Were they not searched?"

"I gave the orders, your excellency," the colonel said. "A thousand apologies. My God, if she had hit—"

"She didn't hit." Roditchev walked his horse forward until it stood almost above the woman. She was spread-eagled on the ground, a booted foot on each of her wrists, another man holding her hair, and two more holding her feet. She panted, and stared at him, pure hatred emanating from her eyes. She was better dressed than the other women around her, with her khaki uniform bearing a red star on its shoulder. A woman of authority, with a vaguely familiar face. A face he had studied often enough, in a tired photograph, but suddenly recognizable. The day was not wasted after all.

"Well, gentlemen," he said. "We have made a capture of importance. Help the young lady to her feet. She wishes only to sit on my chest and pick out my eyes. Is that not true, Mademoiselle Ulyanova?"

"Ulyanova?" The colonel peered at Dora. "Not the fiend known as Red Dora?"

"The very one," Roditchev said.

"Let me have her," the colonel said. "I found some of my men after she had finished with them, not a week ago."

"I understand how you feel, my dear colonel," Roditchev agreed. "But I am afraid you must leave her in my care. After all rank does have its privileges. I do promise you, however, that her execution will be public. Tomorrow morning, I think."

"As you wish, your excellency."

Roditchev looked to left and right. Most of the huts had been destroyed, and all the tents. But there remained the derailed train, with its sad tail of carriages. He pointed. "Take her over there," he commanded.

The soldiers dragged Dora to her feet. She was still gasping for breath, but she had not spoken. Her spectacles had slipped down her nose and she attempted to toss her head to move them back up. And still she stared at Roditchev.

The men pulled her forward, past the waiting officers. One of her feet slipped, and she lurched against the man holding her right arm. He promptly swung his free arm to hit her in the stomach. She gave a terrible retch and fell to her knees, to be kicked in the buttocks.

"Don't hurt her," Roditchev said, wheeling his horse to walk behind her. "I do not want her hurt."

They dragged her to her feet, and across the shattered ground towards the railway line.

"That one will do," Roditchev said, pointing to the first of the carriages.

The soldiers dragged the girl up the steps, her knees bumping, and opened the door. They held her in the center of the compartment while they waited for Roditchev to dismount. He lifted down his haversack, draped it over his arm, and climbed the steps.

"Now let me see," he said thoughtfully. There was a chandelier in the center of the ceiling, and Dora was a short girl. "That ought to do. I want you to hang her by her wrists from that bracket. Make sure the cord is good and strong. Oh, and you may undress her first. We want to be sure she does not carry any other concealed weapons."

The men fell to work with a will. They reminded Roditchev of midgets peeling an oversized banana. Dora's clothes were ripped and torn, but she wore little in the way of underclothes; in only a few seconds she was naked and held up by two of the men, while two others attached her wrists to the swaying chandelier. When they were finished, her toes hung about three inches from the floor, as he had estimated, and her body turned slowly, round and round. It was a peculiarly pale body, he realized, and heavier than he had expected. In a few years Dora Ulyanova would have become fat.

"Thank you," he said. "You may leave us now. I want no man to approach within fifty yards of this carriage. Understood?"

"Yes, your excellency." They saluted, and took their leave, closing the door behind them. Roditchev went round the compartment, pulling the draperies over the windows. Some of them had bullet holes, and a good deal of the glass in the windows was shattered, but there was enough to turn the interior of the carriage into a gloomy cavern.

The girl watched him. "Are you ashamed, Roditchev," she asked, "of what you are going to do to me?"

He turned his head. It was the first time he had heard her voice. "Do you know," he said, "I think I probably am. It would not be good for the enlisted men to see that I am capable of extreme passion. They think that officers have no feelings at all."

He stood in front of her. Suspended as she was, her eyes were on a level with his own. He reached out his hand, took the spectacles from her nose, dropped them on the floor, and trod on them. "I understand it is your sport first to make your victims blind," he said.

Dora inhaled. The heavy breasts swelled away from her chest. "It makes them frightened," she said.

"But it would not make you frightened, eh? I am inclined to agree with you. Besides, I want you to see everything that I am doing to you. I want you to watch it happening. Do you know, there is so much I want to do to you, I hardly know where to begin. But there is no hurry. We have all day."

He took off his belt, laid it and his revolver on a table, took off his cap and jacket, and turned up his sleeves. Then he opened his haversack, took out a bottle of wine and some bread and cheese.

"A soldier's life is not a happy one, as regards food," he said. He sat down and crossed his legs, watched her swinging very gently to and fro. "But a man must make the best of it, I suppose." He used his pocketknife to cut the cheese, then ate, chewing slowly, and drank some wine. "And of course, once this war is over, I will again enjoy the good things of life."

"You will never win," she said. "Never, never, never,"

"I'm afraid I cannot share your point of view," he said. "And recent events have supported my viewpoint." He replaced the cork in the wine bottle, and wiped his hands on a napkin. "You'll forgive me for not offering you any lunch, mademoiselle, but it would be rather a waste, don't you agree? And food—even more, wine—is not that plentiful." He stood up. "Now then, what shall we do first?"

"You are insane," she said. "When I question people, it is for information."

"I don't imagine you have any information worth giving me," he pointed out. "We obtain most of ours from deserters. It is not even necessary to interrogate them. We merely promise them their lives, and they tell us everything they can think of."

"And then you shoot them anyway."

He shrugged. "Bolshevism is a foul disease, Mademoiselle Ulyanova. Once a human being is so contaminated, there is no further hope for him. Or her. He or she must be destroyed, like a rabid dog. Now, let me see . . ." He reached into his pocket, found a box of matches, and struck one. "I don't suppose whipping you would have much effect. I think a woman like you might even enjoy that. I think what I must aim at is a slow destruction of you *as* a woman, a destruction you can see and appreciate. A destruction that you will know is irreversible. I think *that* would be the best way to make you scream, to reduce you to what you really are, a crawling thing from the gutter. Ow!" The match had burned down, and the flame had reached his fingers. He dropped it on the floor and stepped on it. "Yes. I think that would be best."

He struck another match, held it immediately beneath her left nipple, and watched the flesh turn black. For a moment Dora made no sound, then she gasped and kicked at the same moment. Her legs came up wildly, desperately, but Roditchev merely stepped to one side.

The match went out, and tears rolled down Dora's cheeks. But she had not screamed.

"As I supposed," Roditchev said. "You have a high resistance to pain. Still, you know, that only makes my task more interesting. Let's try somewhere else."

He struck another match and held it to the shaggy fringe of her pubic hair. After a moment the hair began to smolder. Once again she gasped, and writhed, and kicked. Roditchev had put his free arm round her thighs, to hold them together and prevent them from moving. But the vehemence of her reaction took him by surprise. He jerked away and stood up, and she kicked again, with deadly accuracy, her bare foot catching him in the groin. His turn to gasp as he fell to his knees. Dora kicked again, aiming at his face. She missed, but the third violent movement in succession was too much for the chandelier; it tore away from the ceiling of the carriage and crashed to the floor, carrying the girl with it.

Roditchev knelt against a chair, reaching for breath. "By God," he said. "By God, I am going to *skin* you."

Dora rolled over and over, taking the clattering chandelier with her. She arrived against the table where Roditchev had thrown his tunic and belts, and sat up, hefting the chandelier in her arms. Too late Roditchev realized what she was after. He pushed himself away from the chair, reached his feet, and watched, helplessly, as Dora, hands still secured and still weighted by the trailing chandelier, managed to open the holster and take out the revolver, holding it between her hands.

"You fool," he shouted. "What do you think . . ." He ran forward. But Dora was already squeezing the trigger, again and again and again. The revolver exploded six times. The first bullet took Roditchev in the chest, and checked his advance. The second hit him in the stomach, and he began to fall. The third hit him in the chest again. The other three slashed aimlessly into the wall behind him. But they were not needed. General Prince Sergei Roditchev was dead before he hit the floor.

Slowly Dora Ulyanova lowered the revolver. From outside the carriage she could hear shouting. But it would be a few moments before they came in. Long enough.

Still carrying the chandelier she got to her feet and reached the table where Roditchev had left his knife. By the time the soldiers threw open the door she had been sitting on his bleeding chest for several seconds.

The soldiers stood at attention—or as close to attention as these men could ever stand, Michael Nej thought bitterly. But they could hardly be blamed when their leadership had proved inept and cowardly.

And besides, it was cold. The snow was ankle-deep in the station yard, and in places threatened to clog the tracks themselves. It was difficult to keep still in such cold. And the train was late.

He half-turned his head and glanced over his shoulder at

the people behind him. His officers avoided his gaze. They knew that his career had come to an end, that he would be lucky to escape with his life. That none of them had been able to check the series of disasters that had overtaken the Red army in the autumn was neither here nor there. The commissar had given the orders. The commissar must take the blame.

Ivan would not meet his gaze either. But Ivan was undoubtedly wondering how he could escape the punishment that was about to overtake the name of Nej. Beside him Tatiana as usual looked indifferent to her surroundings. She no longer smiled; her swelling belly precluded that. Tatiana's child would be his own Ivan's cousin, on both mother and father's side. There was a thought full of implications for the future, assuming there was any way the pair could meet.

Obviously *he* was not going to have another child. He looked now at Judith, who not only returned his gaze, but even attempted a brief smile of encouragement. She was a strange woman. She swore that she hated everything he stood for, that she welcomed every defeat his army had suffered since that first disaster. And he believed her. But through her hate and her anger had come something very close to love. She would never admit it, of course. He did not suppose she would ever admit it even to herself. Yet it was there. She was revealing it now. Perhaps it was impossible to live with someone, to share everything with him, and not eventually grow to love him. Or perhaps, as he hoped, it was impossible for a woman to be loved, as he loved her, and not reciprocate. He would need a psychologist to explain it to him. It was enough to know that in this whole, dismal, catastrophic world in which he found himself, only in the strong arms of Judith Stein was it possible for him to feel happy.

A whistle blared, and the train rolled slowly round the bend, throwing spumes of snow to either side as it crunched to a halt. Behind him someone gave an order, and the honor guard came to attention. No doubt they were as sloppy as usual. He did not turn his head to look at them.

The train hissed its way to a halt, and Red Guards jumped from the doors, their rifles and revolvers at the ready, their eyes scouring the assembly on the platform. Michael stood at attention, watched the center door open, watched Trotsky step down. The manner was as fussily crisp as ever, the spectacles glinted as ever, the chin jutted as aggressively as ever. But

Trotsky had not taken the field and faced defeat. He remained in Moscow, like a gigantic spider, moving pieces and issuing decrees. Giving commands and taking them away.

"Comrade Trotsky." Michael embraced him and was kissed on each cheek.

"Comrade Nej."

Michael stepped back, saluted, and began to introduce the officers. "Comrade General Malutin."

"Ah, comrade general. You were a captain in the seventy-fourth infantry regiment in Galicia."

Malutin beamed. "That is so, comrade commissar."

"A fine regiment," Trotsky said. "A fine regiment. Do you have any of your men here with you?"

"Half a dozen, perhaps, comrade commissar."

"And the going has been hard, I understand."

Malutin's gaze moved to Michael, before returning to the tront. "It has been difficult, Comrade Trotsky."

"I know," Trotsky said. "It has been difficult for all of us."

"And now that the war in Europe is over—" Malutin began.

"The Whites will be reinforced? We must anticipate that. But we are also being reinforced, comrade general. I can promise you that. You have only to exist until the spring. Do not fear for the future. The future belongs to Russia, and we are Russia. I confirm you in your rank, and in your command here in Tula, and to the south."

Tears sprang into the general's eyes; presumably he had expected to be involved in his superior's disgrace. "I thank you, comrade commissar."

"You can thank me by defeating Denikin," Trotsky said, and passed on to the next man. For each officer his remarkable memory could evoke some recollection of past service, and for each he had one or two searching questions. Some he transferred immediately to other duties; the majority he confirmed in their rank and appointments. If only I had the power to inspire men like that, Michael thought. Or perhaps all one needs is the authority.

Ivan was at the very end of the line. "Comrade Captain Nej," Michael said. "In command of my military police."

"Comrade captain." Trotsky saluted, shook hands. "We have heard of you."

"Me, comrade commissar?" Ivan was clearly terrified.

"Indeed. Your efficiency has become a byword. And your

assistant." He looked at Tattie. "Is this she?"

"No, comrade commissar. This is my woman."

Trotsky looked at Tattie's belly. "Yours is a successful, and therefore a happy relationship. What of the other woman?"

"Her name was Ulyanova, comrade commissar. She was taken by the Whites, some months ago. We understand she was executed."

Trotsky nodded, and Michael wondered if he had already known that. "But no doubt you have chosen other able subordinates, Comrade Nej. No doubt you are good at choosing able subordinates."

Ivan's turn to glance at Michael; was this all a trap?

"Well?" Trotsky demanded.

"I . . . I think so, comrade commissar."

"Good. Good. I am relieving you of your post here."

"Comrade commissar?" Ivan's voice trembled.

"There has been an attempt on the life of Comrade Lenin. The whole country, but especially Petrograd, is riddled with anarchists and Whites and tsarists, who seek nothing more than the disruption of the Bolshevik state, the death of our leader. They must be weeded out and destroyed. I wish that to be your task, Comrade Nej. I think you are the man for it. I am sending you to Petrograd to head the police there."

"Petrograd? The police? Me?" Ivan looked like a little boy.

Trotsky rested his hand on his shoulder. "You will not fail me, Comrade Nej. Remember. They must be destroyed." He looked at Tattie. "It will be good for your woman to have her baby in Petrograd. There are better facilities there than here."

"Petrograd?" Tattie cried. "We're going to Petrograd?"

Trotsky smiled. "You like Petrograd, Comrade Borodina? That is good. I like for my people to be pleased with where they are posted. I will see you in Petrograd."

He continued down the line. Comrade Borodina. My God, Michael thought, there is no end to this man's knowledge.

"Comrade Stein, comrade commissar. My woman."

Trotsky kissed Judith on each cheek. "I wish I could also be sending you to Petrograd, Comrade Stein. But no doubt you would not wish to go, alone."

Judith glanced at Michael. Pink spots appeared in her cheeks. "No, comrade commissar. I would prefer to go where Comrade Nej is sent."

"Then you will be staying here," Trotsky said.

"Here?" they asked together.

Trotsky turned away, walked to the edge of the platform, and looked out at the troops assembled in the courtyard. Michael hurried along just behind.

"Those men need discipline," Trotsky remarked.

"It is difficult, comrade commissar. They have been defeated too often."

"They will go on being defeated, Michael Nikolaievich, until they are disciplined. That is your first task. Make them into soldiers. Shoot as many as you have to. You will receive replacements by the spring. But make yourself an army."

Michael stood at attention. He could not believe his ears. But he could not continue under false pretenses, either.

"Comrade commissar," he said. "The defeats we have suffered are not the fault of the men."

"I know," Trotsky said. "You ran away from the first battle. Did you also run away from the second?"

Michael bit his lip. "No, comrade commissar. But by then it was too late. The Whites knew they were going to win, we knew we were going to lose. That too is my fault. I have let down my command. I have let down the Bolshevik Party. I have to let down Russia. I deserve to be shot."

"Do you suppose," Trotsky said, "that it is *easy* to command? Or to command victory? These men you are fighting, these Denikins and Borodins and Roditchevs, they have commanded all their lives. They went to schools that taught them how to command. They know no other way of life. You have had no such advantages, Michael Nikolaievich. But you have learned the problems of command in the field. Do you not think it would be a waste to shoot you, now that you have learned so bitter and so costly a lesson?"

Michael sucked air into his lungs. He must be dreaming. But he could not lie.

"I will still be unable to stop the Whites next spring, comrade commissar. Especially with new recruits. They will continue the advance. I do not even think we will hold Kiev."

"Then give them Kiev, comrade commissar. You have two advantages Denikin can never have. You have all of Russia at your back. Territory is meaningless to us. Let him have Kiev, on loan. And you also have a world that is fed up with war, even civil war. The world will do anything to bring peace. Denikin will receive no physical support from the democracies.

He may receive a little matériel, but even that will not last forever, whereas we are creating armies, creating tanks, creating guns and bullets, every day. Because *we* are not tired of war, Comrade Nej. War is our watchword. War and revolution are our sole reason for being. We have declared war on the entire world, and we shall win that war. But first, we must win the war here in Russia. I want those men out there to be disciplined. I want you to take this army by the scruff of its neck and make it into the best fighting force in the world. I give you *carte blanche*, Michael Nikolaievich. Do what you have to, and be sure the Supreme Soviet will endorse your decisions. Retreat for as long as you have to. But retreat with the intention of advancing again. Wait until Denikin, like a coiled spring, has reached the limit of his stamina and his lines of communication, and then hit him, Michael Nikolaievich. I know you can do it. I know you *will* do it." He smiled, and threw his arm round Michael's shoulders as the assembled officers watched in wonderment.

"Every man is entitled to be a coward once in his life. And every man is expected to be a hero once in his life, too. You have been the one. Now I am counting upon you to be the other, comrade commissar."

Chapter 12

THE SUN SPARKLED FROM THE WATERS OF THE BLACK SEA, RIPpled over the rooftops of Sevastopol, outlined the grim shapes of the battleships lying at anchor beyond the port. Those ships flew the White Ensign, and were symbols that whatever was happening on the land, Britannia still ruled the waves.

But only, Peter Borodin thought sadly, in her own interests. And he wondered if even the great ships would be there in a few weeks, when this dying sun grew cold, and the wintry winds came blasting out of the east. Bringing what? He wrapped his dressing gown closer about his shoulders, and restrained an involuntary shudder.

"My darling, I did not know you were up." Rachel Borodina came out on to the terrace, carrying two cups of coffee. "Isn't it a marvelous view? You have no idea how happy I have been here, this last year. Happier than at any time in my life, I think. And now to have you back . . ."

He put his arm round her shoulders and held her close. Even after a year of marriage and almost a year of motherhood, she looked like a young girl, and she talked like a young girl. Don't ever grow up, my Rachel, he thought; don't ever grow up. Yet he could not control the sombreness of his own thoughts. "Only for a week."

"Still, a week . . ." She turned her head to nuzzle his cheek with her nose. "You have not said good morning to baby Ruth."

"I did not wish to awaken her." But he allowed himself to be drawn back inside, to stand at the cot and take the girl from Rachel's arms, give her a hug and a kiss. Ruth Borodina. A strange name. But no more so than Rachel Borodina. Unless they had a son, or his cousin Viktor had a son—and no one knew what had happened to Viktor—the famous name would die with his generation.

But of course they would have a son. One day.

"She's wet," Rachel complained. "Nurse," she called. "Nurse. Come and change the baby." She laid the child back in the cot, and squeezed Peter's arm as she steered him towards the bedroom. "You hardly had a chance to look at her, last night. Isn't she adorable?"

"The most adorable thing in all the world, after her mother." He sat on the bed, his arm once again round her shoulders. "I am terribly sorry I could not be here for her birth."

"What nonsense. You were better off away. It really was a very simple matter." How she had blossomed, as the Princess Borodina. She sparkled, where always before he had thought her rather withdrawn. Not as withdrawn as Judith, but certainly never vivacious.

Oh, Judith, Judith. What a Princess Borodina *you* would have made.

"But I'm glad you like her," Rachel confided. "It would be terrible if you didn't." She freed herself and lay down, allowing her dressing gown and nightdress to ride up to her knees. She knew how irresistible he found her legs, and it had been a long and lonely year, even in the almost frantic gaiety of Sevastopol society, with the British officers dancing attendance upon every good-looking Russian girl. "I wish you could come back more often, and for longer." She smiled at his frown. "Or better yet, I wish I could come to you. I shall come to you, when you reach Moscow. When will you reach Moscow? I suppose it'll have to wait until next spring, now."

"Next spring," he said. "Do you realize that next spring it will have been very nearly six continuous years of war, for us?"

"But it'll end next year," she said, raising herself on her elbow as he showed no signs of lying beside her. "Everyone is agreed on that. I mean, now that you have Kiev, half of

Russia is in our hands. And the Reds are in a terrible state. Everyone says so."

Peter got up and walked to the window, to resume looking at the sea.

Rachel frowned at his back. "Don't they?"

Peter sighed. He had not meant to discuss the situation with her. He had wanted to use every moment of this leave to hold her in his arms. But if he didn't talk, he'd go mad. And she was his wife.

"You know that Kolchak is dead? His armies have dispersed?"

"Yes," she said. "But that's only Siberia. No one cares what happens to Siberia. It is here, in the south, that Russia matters."

"And you know that the British and the French, and the Americans have definitely refused to come in on our side, or even to give us military aid?"

"Well, I suppose they're as tired of fighting as we are," she said. "Anyway, at least they're not helping the Reds."

"No," he agreed, "they're not helping the Reds."

"So next spring you'll march on Moscow," she said. "And then Petrograd. There's not so much left to be done. And then we'll be able to see Momma and Poppa again. And they'll be able to see Ruth. They'll adore Ruth."

He returned to the bed, sat down, and held her in his arms. "We won't be taking Moscow next spring, my sweet."

Her head jerked. "What? But—"

"Not unless there is a complete collapse by the Reds. We have run out of almost everything we need to fight this war. We haven't got enough bullets, enough shells, enough rifles, enough guns, or enough trucks, to fight a battle. And the soldiers know this. They are beginning to desert."

"But . . . all summer you've been winning."

"All summer we have been *advancing*, because the Reds have retreated. But slowly they have been stiffening their resistance. Michael Nikolaievich is no fool. He is practicing what Peter the Great and Alexander the First practiced. He is using the country as his main weapon."

"But he *has* been retreating," she insisted. "And you have not lost a battle."

"That's true. But even I can't win battles without munitions, without men and horses."

"Peter." She clung to him. "You are tired. If you are in bad way, the Reds must be worse off. You yourself said they might collapse."

"I said *if* they collapsed. There's no immediate sign of it happening."

"But it could happen."

"Of course it could."

"It will," she insisted. "This winter. You watch. They're up there starving in the cold, and we're down here, basking in the sun. It will happen, Peter, and then next spring you'll be in Moscow. It must happen."

He kissed her, pressed her head back against his shoulder, and looked out once again at the sea. It must happen, he thought. Or God help us all.

George Hayman walked along the Nevskiy Prospekt. His hands, deep inside fur lined gloves, were shoved inside the fur-lined pockets of his fur-lined topcoat. It was his sixth consecutive Petrograd winter, and this was the worst of them all. Not merely in the near-zero temperatures; that seldom varied in February. But in February 1920 the city had had another year to decline into ruin.

Presumably there had been some progress. The trams were back, but they ran slowly and with total irregularity. The current joke was that it was quicker to freeze to death by standing at a tram halt than by taking a swim in the Neva. Not that it was possible to swim in the Neva anyway, in February, without first breaking the ice. The only cars to be seen were the few for which gasoline could be found. They belonged to the military and the commissars, and they too had to travel slowly to avoid the gaping potholes in the street, and even in the Nevskiy Prospekt. But then, walking along the sidewalk, he had to step round innumerable potholes as well.

There were no dead bodies in the street anymore. There were many scarcely living bodies, however, making their slow and unsteady way from shop to shop in search of food. It was hard to say which was the more disturbing.

And the city still stank, even in winter. But it was less the odor of decaying garbage, decaying sewage, than of fear. People were afraid. Of the starvation that seemed inescapable. Of the counterrevolution that would take place when the Whites won the civil war—if the Whites won the civil war. Of the increased repression that would follow a Red victory, if the

Reds gained a victory. Of the GPU, as Lenin's Secret Police were called. And of the force's diabolical second commissar, Ivan Nej. Presumably Petrograd was but a microcosm of all Russia. And presumably, in all Russia, only one man, Lenin, was not afraid.

But since Lenin was a human being, it was probable that he too was afraid. And that was the most terrifying thought of all.

So, would he be sorry to leave? The first thaw was expected any day now, and his passage was booked on a Swedish ship trapped here for the winter, and leaving for Stockholm the moment it was possible to sail. From Stockholm he would take the train to Göteborg, and in Göteborg he would find a passage to New York. After six years George presumed he would board the ship with the usual mixed feelings he had always experienced toward Russia. Despite all that he had witnessed, and every nightmare that would come back to haunt him for the rest of his life, despite his two-year separation from Ilona and the children, he did not really regret a moment of it. He had not changed his opinion from the very beginning, when he had decided that there was a fundamental force at work here, the greatest primeval human explosion since Tamerlane had burst out of these same steppes half a millennium ago. Every instinct he possessed, as journalist, author, historian, and thinking man, had called upon him to witness this cataclysm at first hand, to record it for posterity—a doubly fascinating prospect since he had no idea whether that posterity would be a projection of the world he knew and loved, or whether its prevailing color would be Red, its prevailing philosophy the brand of Marxism that Lenin preached, and was apparently prepared to practice with devastating results.

But he now knew that he had fallen into the trap common to all human beings, that of supposing the pace of history could be accommodated to a single lifetime, or worse, in this case, to a single episode in a lifetime. He has estimated that this revolution would be as short-lived as Kerensky's. Watching the ferocity with which the rival armies attacked each other and anyone else who got in their way, watching the rapidity with which even the greatest city in the land had crumbled into decay, watching the growing agony of a people who had already spent the last four years in agony, it had been impossible to suppose anything different. While the European War had continued, he had been able to rationalize. But he had always imagined, like everyone else, that once that war was over the western democracies would either throw all their weight behind Denikin and Kolchak, and crush the Red peril out of existence before it could send its roots far into the human consciousness, or else the democracies would come to the conclusion that whether or not Bolshevism was a good thing, it was what the Russian people had chosen, and therefore should be recognized, and Denikin and Kolchak be dismissed as aimless counterrevolutionaries.

Neither of these developments, which would have ended the war and the misery in rapid order, had occurred. The Reds were certainly regarded as a peril to civilized life. But the western democracies, like people everywhere, were weary of fighting and bloodshed. If the Russians wanted to go on killing each other and starving each other to death for the rest of the century, the world seemed to be saying, then let them get on with it. The British and American forces that had occupied Archangel had been withdrawn. The French no longer occupied the Crimea. There was a British naval force in the Black Sea, but it was evidently there to prevent the civil war from spreading down to an already war-torn Turkey and Greece rather than to assist the Whites.

But neither had the country simply come to a standstill from sheer exhaustion. Yet. The Reds had concentrated their effort in the east, while endeavoring to hold the south. And now they had triumphed in the east. Kolchak was shot, his armies dispersed. Siberia was saved for Bolshevism. But at what cost? Denikin's armies lay from Kiev to just south of Tula, itself only just over a hundred miles south of Moscow. In exchange for the frozen wastes of Siberia, Lenin had conceded a break-up of Peter the Great's empire, with the Ukraine and the homelands of the Cossacks reverting to their age-old separate kingdoms. But since he would never accept such a situation permanently, the war would go on and on and on, and people would die and die and die.

And George Hayman would at last watch from afar. It was not merely the fact that he had been here too long. It was not merely the fact that he had seen enough misery to last him a lifetime. It was not merely that he yearned to hold Ilona once again in his arms. And it was not merely his father's illness, calling him back to his proper responsibilities.

It was, more than any of those things, a feeling of despair. He could see nothing ahead but destruction, a collapse of this tremendous force, whether good or evil, that had dominated European politics for three hundred years. And he could see nothing to take its place, until a new Tamerlane emerged from the steppe to spread destruction the length and breadth of Europe and Asia.

Would he regret nothing he would leave behind? Of course he would. He had many friends in Russia, and there were many loose ends. There was Peter Borodin down in the south, fighting with the Whites, and apparently proving himself a most able general. And with him there was that young girl, Rachel Stein. How had she got there? No one knew for sure. But she was there, and she was the new Princess Borodina. Ilona had been scandalized. But then Illie, for all her determination to carve her own destiny, was a Borodin to the core.

And opposing Peter was Michael Nej. There was a strange quirk of fate, especially since with Michael there was Judith Stein. Perhaps George regretted leaving Judith behind, unseen for a last time, more than any of the others. He wanted to know how she had prospered. Because she had, at last, prospered, the mistress of a commissar, of Lenin's friend. And when the Whites won she would be hanged beside her lover. She had at least emerged into the fresh air for one brief period in her life. And if the Reds were to win . . .

Then what about Tattie? Poor, strange, confused, beautiful Tattie, living with possibly the greatest monster in all Russia, a man who seemed to be determined to outdo even Sergei Roditchev in the ferocious enthusiasm with which he went about his business of destroying humanity in the name of the state. Strangely, he felt less pity for Tattie. It was impossible to decide what went on inside that magnificent head, to be sure whether she was mad, or just entirely selfish, or merely nothing, a human animal who wanted only a crust of bread, a glass of wine, or in her case vodka, the caress of man's hand, and the right to dance when she chose and to play what music she liked. But that determination alone, and it was a determination, would have separated Tattie from the animals, even as it made her unique among her fellow humans. Somehow he never doubted that Tattie would prosper.

Or of them all, would he most miss the people he was on his way to see now? He had turned onto the bridge to Petrograd

Island, was already under the shadow of the Peter and Paul Fortress where Ivan Nej carried out his dreadful work. It was a street he knew well; he had traversed it often enough. Over the past year he had come almost every week to sit with the Steins, to talk and listen. Was it because their daughters had fascinated him, and continued to do so? Oh, certainly. But there were other factors involved. Those at the bottom of the slag heap can only rise. Those at the top, when the ground begins to tremble, can look back on centuries of sunshine, and fight with absolute dedication to hold their place. But those in the middle, who have spent countless generations slowly improving their lot, who wish only to be left in peace to live their lives, to pass on their insignificant treasures to their children, to enjoy the weddings, the births and even the deaths, the anniversaries and the memorable holidays that should be the lot of every human being—in an upheaval such as this they had nowhere to climb, because they had never anticipated having to climb so hard or so frantically, and every slip downwards was the more painful because recovery would take so long.

The Steins were somewhat better off than most. He supposed Judith had the most to do with that. Rachel had run away with a White, Joseph was an out-and-out Bolshevik who despised his mother and father. But Judith was the mistress of a senior commissar, and it was due to her, as they freely admitted, that the senior Steins lived in a little comfort.

George turned in at the gate and surveyed the wreckage of the garden. No garden flourishes in March, but this one would be in an even more desparate state come June. He walked along the cracking pavement of the drive, up the cracking stone of the front steps, while above him the paint peeled from the walls and a loose slate rattled into a gutter. The elder Steins ate well, and they had two rooms to themselves, and they were unmolested by the spasms that from time to time shook the Red Guards and, through them, the entire city. But they were forced, day by day, to watch the gradual disintegration of their house and their garden, of all they held sacred. Were they truly better off than anyone else?

He climbed the stairs and pushed open the front door.

"Shut that damned door," a woman bawled, and he hastily closed it behind him. From the cot in the center of the hall a baby began to wail.

Its mother glared at Hayman. "Are you trying to give him

pneumonia? American swine."

George raised his hat. "My apologies. But one can only get in through the door, comrade."

"Bah." The woman resumed hanging out her washing. "You're wasting your time, anyway, comrade."

"What do you mean?" George, already started up the creaking, carpetless stairs, paused to look down at her.

"The Steins are gone, comrade."

"Gone? Gone where?"

She shrugged. "The Peter and Paul, I suppose. The GPU took them. About time, too, bourgeois scum."

George Hayman ran, panting, up the second flight of stairs. He seemed to have been running up and down stairs for the entire afternoon. And if this final flight proved unproductive, he would not know where to go.

The Borodin town house. He had never been here in the great days of the Russian aristocracy. Those days had coincided with his own eclipse in Russian society. And indeed, however forgiving the Borodins themselves might have been, he had never been reinstated.

Since the revolution he had come here several times. As an American he was popular with the Bolsheviks, and besides, he was Tattie's brother-in-law, and even if she had had a dozen brothers-in-law, he would have been her favorite. So now . . .

He reached the top landing and paused for breath. From beyond the end door there came the rippling notes of a piano. It was no tune he had ever heard in his life before, except from this landing. It had been created within Tattie's head, contained all the wild Circassian ancestry which had made the Borodins what they were, and, too, Tattie's own peculiar outlook on life. Perhaps in a hundred years—even sooner, if Lenin succeeded in overturning the world—it might be recognized as a work of genius. For the moment it was a burst of rhythmic barbarism cutting through the afternoon; he often wondered what the other commissars' wives thought of it.

He knocked on the door, urgently. But it still took several other bangs to make the music stop. And immediately the sound was replaced by that of a baby crying. But Tattie was a surprisingly sympathetic mother. There was no slap, no admonishment. Merely a soft cooing noise, and the baby cooed in return.

The door opened, and she pushed hair out of her eyes. "George!" All the warmth of the coming spring was in that simple greeting. She held his arm and pulled him into the room, smothered his mouth in a huge kiss. "I have heard the most dreadful rumor."

"Yes," he said. "Listen—"

"That you are going back to America."

He pulled his head away. "Now how do you know that?"

She squeezed his arm, then released it. "Ivan knows everything. Did you know that? Everything. Why are you going, George?"

"Well, I have got a wife and children, you know, Tattie. Listen—"

"Friends," she said darkly, and went to the table to pour two glasses of vodka. Presumably, as an alcoholic, she would eventually sink into a fattened mass of degenerate tissue, George supposed. But it was equally likely, since she was Tatiana Borodina, that she would give the entire medical profession the lie. Certainly the amount of liquor she consumed, most of it hardly better than the bathtub variety, seemed to have no effect upon her at all. "I do not have any friends except for you."

"Oh, come now." He sipped the vodka. "Aren't Michael and Judith your friends?" When Tattie was in an introspective mood it was necessary to tread carefully.

She shrugged, and suddenly gave one of her tremendous whirls. Her skirt rose to her thighs and settled again. Incongruously, for one as instinctively sexual as Tattie, she wore woolen stockings and enormous woolen bloomers. And yet she managed to make him wish the skirt had taken a second longer to settle.

"Say hello to the baby."

He bent over the cot and tickled Svetlana Ivanova's chin.

"There's to be another." She gave another whirl.

"Tattie? You?"

"Well, nobody else," she said. "I'd scratch out his eyes."

It was a remarkable fact that Ivan Nej, second commissar of Lenin's secret police, was like putty in the hands of his wife. But that, George reminded himself, was why he was here.

He caught her in the midst of a third pirouette and kissed her on both cheeks. "Are you happy about it?"

"Of course. I adore children. I'm going to teach them to dance."

"What a splendid idea. Tattie—"

"I'm going to have twelve children," she said. "My own dance troupe. I'll bring them to America, George. Will you advertise us in your newspaper?"

"Promise." He held her hands. "Tattie, I've just come from the Steins'."

"Oh?" Her eyes flickered, but it was impossible to decide whether she knew something or was just uninterested. She freed herself to refill their glasses; his was only half empty, but hers was dry.

"Tattie, do listen to me. They've been arrested by the GPU, and taken to the Peter and Paul. Now, what can they possibly have done? They never leave that room."

She shrugged again and took another long swallow of vodka. "You'll have to ask Ivan."

"That's just it. I can't get to Ivan. I've been to the Peter and Paul, and been told he's too busy. I've tried to find Joseph, but he's not even in the city. Judith is down in Tula with Michael. Tattie, you've got to get hold of Ivan and ask him what's happening. There must be some mistake."

"Sit down," she said. "Have another drink." She took the glass from his hand, saw that it was untouched, drank it herself, and refilled them both. "You'll see him yourself. He'll soon be home."

George sat down. He supposed he had no alternative. And at least she was right; Ivan would certainly come here when he left his office.

"They're Jews, you know," she said conversationally, handing him his glass.

"What's that got to do with it?"

Tattie cranked her gramophone. "Well, they're hardly important, are they? Just Jews. Listen to this. Ivan found it in some store."

The music blared forth. Here again was a strange sound, but the rhythm was unmistakable.

"It's called Dixieland," Tattie explained condescendingly. "It's all the rage in America. Haven't you heard of it?"

"It's a few months since I've been home," he said.

"I think it's wonderful. I'm going to write something like that." She cascaded across the living room, skirts flying, heavy yellow hair tossing, sheer joy in living bubbling from every movement. The amazing thing was that when he had first met her, nearly sixteen years ago, when she had been not quite eleven, she had been exactly like this.

"Good for you," he said. "Tattie . . ." Footsteps sounded on the landing, and a key turned in the lock.

Ivan Nej dressed very correctly, his khaki cap set exactly square on his head, every button of his uniform done up, his belts highly polished. He had been in charge of boots at Starogan, George recalled; presumably he polished his own belts now. "Hayman." He gave a brief nod. His dislike was never concealed.

"Ivan Nikolaievich." Tattie flowed over him—she was distinctly taller and broader—hugged him and kissed him. His hat fell off and his glasses became disarranged. He had to push her away.

"Vodka, woman. When do you leave, Hayman?"

"Whenever the ice melts," George said. "Comrade Nej—"

"George is here about the Steins," Tattie said, watching with a happy smile as the liquid flowed into the glass. "He says you've locked them up."

"I'm sure there must be a mistake," George said. "I mean, they can't have done anything recently. They've spent the last year in that room."

"A man or a woman," Ivan said, "is not necessarily always condemned for what he has done recently. A crime is a crime."

"Oh, come now," George said. "What crime did Jacob Stein ever commit? His daughter is one of you. So is his son."

"What of the other daughter? The Steins gave assistance to a wanted man, a dangerous counterrevolutionary, who has proved even more dangerous since his escape. Peter Borodin."

"For God's sake . . ." George glanced at Tattie.

"Well," she said. "My Vanichka is right, George. Peter wouldn't let me come to Petrograd. He never would. He wanted to keep me locked up down on Starogan. He wouldn't let me drink and he wouldn't let me dance. He *deserves* to be locked up."

"I sometimes think I'm going mad," George said. "So they helped your wife's brother to escape. And Rachel. She's Judith's sister. What do you suppose Michael would say to their being locked up?"

"Michael is a soldier," Ivan said. "I am a policeman. I am

willing to admit I understand very little of his problems. He understands none of mine. The Steins are enemies of the state. This has been proved. And there is an end to the matter."

"Does Michael know?" George asked. "Does Judith know?"

"It is not my business to inform every army commander whom I have arrested. Even less their women. And I can tell you, comrade, that there is more than enough evidence in my archives to hang Judith Stein. If she were not Michael's doxy . . . but her parents are also guilty of crimes against the state."

Again George looked at Tattie, but she was still dancing, now with her baby in her arms, and still holding a glass of vodka. "Okay," he said. "So they broke the rules. But surely you can make an exception. Just once."

"There can be no exceptions," Ivan said. "We are engaged in a life-and-death struggle. There can be no exceptions. Comrade Lenin himself has said so."

"Well," George said, "if that's your attitude, I might just take the matter to Comrade Lenin himself. He's promised me an interview before I leave."

Ivan shrugged. "It would do you no good, Comrade Hayman. The Steins were shot this morning."

"This—" George put down his glass.

"It was necessary," Ivan said. "Now come, let me fill your glass. Have you not heard? Tattie is again to be a mother."

The train slowed to a halt, and it was possible to open the doors. A blast of freezing air immediately rushed into the compartment, which became a place of coughing mist. But it smelt like the sweetest perfume ever invented, after two days aboard.

It had actually been no less cold inside the train, but that was a strange cold, composed of odors and sighs; even sitting shoulder to shoulder with two other men, with three other men opposite, equally crowded and cramped and miserable, George had been unable to create any warmth, any rapport. But he supposed he was lucky to have got a seat at all, much less a travel permit. And for what? Whatever tragedies were taking place in Russia, there was nothing he could do about them. The ice in the Baltic was already beginning to crack, and within another week or less, ships should be able to leave. He had already turned his back upon Russia in his mind, was prepared to regard it only as an experience to be written about with feeling and, he hoped, insight, since he had witnessed so much of it at first hand; he had no doubt that the years here would govern attitudes for the rest of his life. But why become involved again? Because he could not bear to consider one more catastrophe crushing Judith Stein? It was not as though he could alleviate the catastrophe of her parents' death. But he feared for her, after Ivan's veiled threat.

On the other hand, perhaps he had never had any intention of leaving Russia without seeing her once more. The first time he had ever seen her, she had been lying naked on Roditchev's floor, with the marks of the cane on her legs and buttocks and shoulders. From that moment, although she had not even known he was there, he had felt somehow linked to her, in his determination to oppose the grim reality of tsarism. And on the moonswept railway station at Starogan he had pledged his help, if she ever needed it.

"Your pass, comrade."

He was in the line shuffling across the platform, and realized that he should be paying more attention to his surroundings. Tula had been a hubbub of military comings and goings. But this place made Tula look like nothing more than a recruiting center. It had probably once been a farming village. So much of Russia had once been a farming village. Now the snow-covered earth was itself covered in tents and huts. But these soldiers were regulars now. After two years of savage and unsuccessful fighting they had had to learn that in order to survive, some discipline, some military behavior, was essential. Thus the huts and the tents were in orderly lines, the horses were picketed and guarded by sentries, the trucks, waiting for the first thaw that would enable them to take the road again, were in pools, also guarded. He had visited this army once before, last summer, when it had been in its usual headlong retreat, and had known at a glance that it was not going to stop retreating, that it was beaten before it began any battle. This morning he realized that its days of instinctive flight might well be over. There was a new air of purpose around him, and the soldier who had just been inspecting his pass and his travel permit came to attention almost like a Guardsman.

"The commissar's house is in the square, comrade," he said.

"Thank you, comrade."

George stepped through the gate, following the rest of the

officials and journalists and replacement officers who had shared the first-class compartment with him, and found himself already on the main street of the village. He could see the square and the Zemstvo house in the distance, and in front of it . . . his heartbeat quickened. Six tanks, British Mark IV's, he estimated, waited like enormous predatory frogs, while the snow was lovingly cleaned from their upper works and guns by leather-helmeted crews.

He quickened his step. Perhaps this army had not merely stopped retreating. Perhaps this army was about to advance.

"George Hayman." Michael Nej rose and came round his desk, arms outstretched. "You could not have come at a better time." He embraced his friend, kissed him on each cheek, then stepped back to shake hands in a more American fashion. "You are here for the offensive?"

"Well . . . where'd you get those tanks?"

Michael smiled and snapped his fingers. "Vodka, comrade."

Michael's aide, who had been sitting at the desk in the corner, rose immediately and opened a cupboard.

"From the British."

"The *British*?"

The girl poured, and handed a glass to George. Michael raised his own. "The British did not *mean* to give them to us, George. But the fools took them to Archangel, when they were still intending to fight us, in the name of tsar and God. When their own people repudiated the scheme, they found that they lacked the ships to evacuate all the matériel they had landed. These tanks are only part of what they—and your people, George—abandoned. They could not have been kinder to us. And now that the thaw is here—"

"Denikin will know you are coming."

"Of course he knows we are coming. I've made no secret of it. I've made no secret of the tanks, either. And several batteries of new guns, with all the ammunition we can use. He doesn't have things like that. They know we are coming, George, and their men know we are coming, and there's not a damn thing they can do about it. Do you know?" His eyes danced as he finished his vodka. "The snow has been so thick they have not even been able to pull back, as they should, and leave us to bite on air. They are preparing to retreat now. But now is too late. You'll have another drink?"

"Not right this minute, thank you. How's Judith?"

"Well. No man could ask for a better companion. Do you know, in all the hardships we have endured these last couple of years, she has never complained? But you have come from Petrograd, have you not? How are things there?"

"Grim."

"Ah, but they will change, once this war is over. Once it is won, we can get to work reconstructing the country. And it will not be long now, George. Have you seen Ivan? Tattie?"

"They are well," George said. "Tattie is pregnant."

"Again? How splendid. Two children—" He hesitated, and a brief shadow crossed his face. "When are you going home?"

"When the ice melts."

"You are not staying for the offensive?"

"I have a family. Besides, I think I've seen enough offensives these last few years."

"Yes. Well, you'll . . ." He held out his empty vodka glass to be refilled.

"I'll give Johnnie a hug for you," George promised. "You know how grateful I am for what you did for Ilona and the children."

"You have told me so, George. You do not have to repeat it."

"Yes." He glanced at Michael's aide. "May I have a word in private?"

Michael raised his eyebrows, then waved his hand. The girl saluted and left the room.

"Ruth and Jacob Stein are dead," George said.

Michael's brow creased in a frown. "Both of them? But how? I left instructions that they were to be supplied with food."

"They were shot," George said. "By order of the GPU. By order of Ivan."

Michael had been raising his glass to his lips. Now he slowly lowered it again.

"Apparently," George said, "they helped Peter Borodin and Rachel to escape, back in 1918. Did you know that?"

Michael walked round his desk and sat down. "Of course."

"Well, then, maybe you'd better think of your own position."

"I have nothing to fear," Michael said. "And once I have defeated Denikin, I shall never have anything to fear again.

But Ivan . . . I suppose he was only doing his duty. They *were* traitors. I neglected my duty in . . . in not reporting the situation."

"Your *duty*?" George demanded. "His duty? To shoot helpless old people who wished only to save the life of their daughter?"

"I understand how you feel, old friend. War is a hideous business, and civil war is the most hideous of all. But—"

"Michael," George said. "Let's skip the claptrap. The Steins were murdered. As thousands, maybe millions of other Russians have been murdered, are being murdered every day by the thugs your Comrade Lenin has turned loose. You have to face the truth."

Michael's head came up. "And what of the thugs the tsar loosed on the country? Every tsar since time began?"

"I had thought it was your intention to improve on the tsars."

Michael sighed. "We will do so. I can give you my word on that. But it is not possible while we are fighting a war. So sometimes the innocent are killed along with the guilty. It can happen in a bomb blast too." He leaned forward. "And the Steins were not even innocent. They *were* guilty of crimes against the state. You are only interested because they happen to be friends of yours."

"And aren't they friends of yours?" George asked. "What are you going to say to Judith?"

George Hayman awoke with a start. The room was utterly dark, as was the night outside. But the darkness was alive with the stealthy rustle of an army preparing for battle.

He sat up and watched the door open. "Michael?"

The door closed again. "Yes." The light came on. Michael Nej was fully dressed, down to equipment and holstered revolver, worn on the outside of his fur-lined greatcoat.

"Where are you off to?"

Michael smiled. "We are moving out. In half an hour my artillery barrage will begin."

"Today? But—"

"I could not tell you, old friend. An army commander must keep his secrets, eh? Especially from newspapermen."

"But . . . in the snow?"

"It is thawing fast. Besides, the enemy must be surprised if possible. Listen."

From outside the window there came the growl of the tank motors being started.

"My men have had fires lit beneath those tanks all night," Michael said. "To make sure they start."

"But won't the ground be impassable, even for tanks, in a day or two?" George asked.

"We will have won this victory by then," Michael said. "The enemy will be in retreat through melting snow. Then it will be time for my cavalry to harrass them, and turn them into a rabble. But they must have been defeated first. Are you sure you will not accompany the army? It will be a famous day."

George shook his head. "I must get back to Petrograd. I've booked a passage." He hesitated. There was so much he wanted to ask.

Michael knew that. "Then I'm sorry. That you are going at all, and that it should be in such circumstances. That you should have come so far to see us before you leave, and that you should have eaten alone last night. Things will be different next time we meet. I give you my word."

"How did she take it?" George asked.

Michael sighed. "Who knows how Judith takes anything? But she would not eat with me, either. She retired to her bed." He gave a brief smile. "Our bed. But I slept in a chair. No matter. I would hardly have slept anyway. Today is the greatest of my life. It had better be. George . . . see her before you go."

"Will she wish to see me?"

"Of course. Whether or not she wishes to at this moment, she will wish she had, in a few days. Tell her . . . tell her that when I send for her to join the army, it will all have been worth it. We will have won. Russia will have been saved for Bolshevism."

"You're sure that's what she'll want to hear? Right this minute?"

"It is the truth. It is what matters. It is a fact of life. Her life as much as mine, as much as any of ours. I must go." He held out his hand. "Will you wish me luck?"

George shook hands. "I'll wish *you* luck, Michael Nikolaievich, but not necessarily your army. Or your Bolsheviks."

Michael gazed at him for some seconds, still holding hands. "One day," he said at last, "you and I will have the time really to be friends, George. One day I may be able to visit America, and take my son to a movie, eh? Would you let me do that?"

"Of course I will."

"And when that day comes, you will agree with me, George, that it was all worthwhile. That it was all inevitable, if you like."

"One day," George said.

Michael released him, saluted, and left the room. George lay back, and almost immediately got up again. To get up was to dress, for it was too cold for pajamas. He dragged on his clothes, stood at the window and watched the men assembling, watched the tanks rolling ponderously onto the street in column, watched the cavalry mounting and loosening sword and rifle and lance . . . and wished he were going with them. However unpalatable their philosophy, they were going to fight for it. And this time, he knew, they were going to win. It would not merely be a matter of superior equipment, more shells and more bullets, and those tanks, although those factors would probably be decisive in the end. But the reason they possessed such a superiority in matériel was simply that they had stood up to everything the Whites, with *their* superior equipment in the beginning, and their superiority in training and above all in military leadership, had been able to throw at them. They had taken it and they had not disintegrated as the Whites had hoped. And that was the reason they were now going to gain a victory.

Again the door opened. He turned and watched Judith Stein step inside, and quickly close the door behind herself.

"Judith." He crossed the room and took her hands. Had she spent the night weeping? It was impossible to be sure; if her eyes were swollen it could have been from lack of sleep.

"Has Michael gone?" she asked.

"Several minutes ago. They are moving out to attack the Whites."

"He told me." She freed herself, and sat down on the bed.

"Judith, if you knew how sorry I am . . ."

"I do know," she said. "If you had not cared, you would not have come all this way to tell me. Besides, Momma and Poppa . . ." She sighed. "They had written me often, to say how kind you've been, going to see them." She raised her head. "Was it really Ivan who gave the order?"

"I'm afraid so."

She continued to gaze at him for some seconds, and he almost felt the hair on his neck begin to prickle.

"These people," he said. "This philosophy, this revolution—like all revolutions, it throws up tragedy along with triumph. It throws up people like Ivan into positions of authority, because decent people won't do what Lenin wants him to do. But it also throws up people like Michael. A valet, the son of a serf, and now proving himself to be a great general."

"Where are you going now?" she asked.

"Back to Petrograd. The ice is melting, and I've booked my return to America. I'd like to see the end of this business, but my father isn't very well, and there's the paper."

"And Ilona," she said.

"Well, of course. And the children. I've been away a long time."

"Take me with you," she said.

"What?"

"Take me to America with you, George."

"But . . . what about Michael? He's not responsible for what happened, you know."

"Only by being what he is." She got up. "I don't blame him, personally. But he is what he is, just as Ivan is what *he* is. I don't hate him. I don't even hate Ivan. Sometimes, this last year, I have even thought I was falling in love with Michael. He . . ." She flushed. "He is very kind. Very gentle. But I could never love him now. I cannot even stay with him." Her face broke into a twisted smile. "We made a bargain, he and I. Well, the bargain is now broken." She lifted her head. "You promised me once that I could call on you, George Hayman, for help. I am asking you for that help now."

The noise was continuous. It was like nothing Michael Nej had ever heard before. He thought of Ivan, who had heard it during the war with Germany, and wondered what Ivan would think.

He watched the brilliant flashes of light from the explosions behind the White lines, listened to the whining and roaring of the shells passing overhead. His officers, gathered on the observation platform of the train, were restless. Well, so were his men, and he could hear horses neighing. He looked at his watch; only a few minutes more.

Ivan. Had he only been doing his duty, as he saw it, or had it been something personal? Certainly Ivan had always seemed to hate the very name of Stein.

But it *had* been his duty, there was the point. Of course Judith could never understand that. But it need not affect them personally. They had lived together for nearly two years, and in that time he had made her happy. He had taught her how to love, and he had shown her how she should *be* loved. He had a very simple theory, that when a woman was happy in bed she found it very difficult to be unhappy anywhere else. And he certainly made Judith happy in bed. However much she might hate Ivan, her emotions must still be built around that simple fact.

The barrage stopped, and immediately the earsplitting crashing of the artillery was replaced by the rumble of the tanks. There was no time left to think of Judith.

The train started to move. It was crowded with soldiers. He had never forgotten how Peter Borodin had smashed through his lines down in the south, the autumn before last. Well, this time the tables would be turned.

He stood at the window and watched the snow rushing by, watched, too, the cavalry keeping pace with him. He listened to the growling of the tanks and was suddenly alerted by the screaming of tortured metal as the brakes were applied. Sparks flew and the entire train shuddered, and he knew they were about to leave the track.

"Hold on," he shouted, but already bodies were being hurled to and fro as the carriage shook itself like a wet dog and then plunged over onto its side, into the hardpacked snow, but still sliding down the embankment, almost seeming to stand on its head.

Michael found himself sitting on what had been the ceiling. The lights had gone out and the carriage was utterly dark. All around him men were shouting, and someone was screaming. But above him there was a patch of lighter darkness, an open window.

He fumbled at his belt, drew his revolver, and squeezed the trigger. The shot sounded like a cannon in the confined space, and it had the desired effect of silencing the shouts.

"I must get out," Michael said. "Through that window. Help me."

Hands scrabbled at his legs and arms to raise him up.

"The line was intact yesterday morning," someone said. Modlov, the captain in charge of the scouts, quickly tried to defend himself.

"Then it was torn up this very night," said someone else.

"So they knew we were coming. How?"

"A spy," someone said, and the word was taken up. "When we get back to camp—"

Michael got his gloved fingers over the sill of the window, and dragged himself up. There were men all around him now; the infantry were scrambling from the rest of the train, which still clung precariously to the track, the cavalry had gathered in groups, and even the sound of the tanks had stopped.

"We are not going back to camp," Michael said. "We are continuing the advance. Get out of that carriage. Haste, now. Haste." He scrambled to his feet. "You and you and you," he shouted. "Mount up and ride to the brigade commanders. Tell them the train has crashed, but that the advance continues. Tell them their objectives are unchanged, and must be seized by noon. Haste. You, give me that horse."

The trooper obligingly dismounted, and Michael took his place. He had been forced to do enough riding over the past two years to regain the skill he had possessed as a boy on Starogan. Now he kicked the animal through the snow, sending the white powder flurrying away from its hooves. He drew his sword and waved it above his head. "Advance," he shouted. "Follow me."

The men gave a cheer and came pouring out of the carriages, bayonets fixed as they hurried forward. Michael suddenly realized that this was no place for the commanding general to be. But he was not turning back now. Today he would win. Today he *must* win, and not only for Russia. Today he was fighting for himself and for Judith, as well. For a justification of everything he had attempted in his life. Even to justify Ivan's crime.

The midday sun sent sheets of brilliant, reflected light from the snow, stabbed pain and tears into any eyes unprotected by goggles, brought the steady drip of melting icicles from the shattered huts.

But it was still too cold for a smell. Michael was glad of that. For all around him were twisted bodies, lying beside their discarded guns and rifles and their empty revolvers. Caps lay half-embedded in the snow, booted feet thrust out of drifts, and as he watched, one of his staff crouched beside the shattered flagstaff and carefully drew out the torn flag, its double-headed eagles seeming to snap at his fingers as it slowly unfolded.

"A victory!" General Malutin's face was flushed, and he kept kicking his horse with his heels, even though the exhausted animal refused to move. "A victory!"

"My congratulations, comrade general," Michael said.

"Ah, but you shared in it, comrade commissar." Today even Malutin could afford to be generous. Besides, over the past year he had learned to respect the commissar. Now he wagged his finger. "But it is no place for a commissar, at the head of an assault force."

"As you say, it brought us a tactical victory," Michael said. "What news of the enemy?"

"They are retreating along the railway line."

"In good order?"

"It would appear so, comrade commissar. No doubt they had long laid plans for such a retreat. If they had anticipated being able to advance further they would hardly have torn up the railway track. But they also knew that we possessed the tanks, of course, and the artillery."

Michael nodded. "Now we must pursue."

"Comrade commissar? The men are exhausted."

"Use the tanks."

Malutin made a deprecatory gesture. "They are out of action."

"All of them?"

"I'm afraid so, comrade commissar. They have lost their tracks, they have suffered mechanical failure . . . it will take days to repair them. Perhaps weeks."

"Well, then, use the cavalry."

"Comrade commissar, the cavalry is exhausted. We are all exhausted. And we have suffered heavy casualties. Besides, the enemy is undoubtedly beaten. Now is the time for us to consolidate and regroup, before advancing again."

Michael was suddenly distracted by one of his aides galloping up from the direction of the broken railway line.

"Captain Gonarov," he said. "He will bring the news we seek. Did you get through to Moscow, Captain?"

Gonarov drew his horse to a halt; despite the cold it was in a lather of quickly drying sweat, as was the captain. Now he saluted. "Yes, comrade commissar."

"You reported our initial success? You demanded reinforcements?"

"Yes, comrade commissar."

"Good. Now, comrade general . . ."

"There are none to be had, comrade commissar," Gonarov said, his face scarlet.

"What do you mean?"

"That is the reply from Moscow, comrade commissar. The army is mobilizing against Poland. You must do the best with what you have."

"You would suppose they would wish to finish one war before starting another," Malutin commented.

But Michael was still studying the young man's face. "There is something else, Gonarov."

"Yes, sir." Gonarov started to lick his lips, and hastily changed his mind as the chill burned his tongue. He swallowed.

"From Moscow?"

"No, comrade commissar. I went to see Comrade Stein, as you commanded, to tell her of our victory."

"Yes?" Michael demanded.

"She is not there, comrade commissar. She left two days ago, on the very morning of the assault. With the American."

"Left?" For a moment Michael could not think.

"For Petrograd, comrade commissar."

"I never trusted that American," Malutin said. "Have you telegraphed to have them arrested?"

"I came to report to Comrade Nej first, comrade general."

"Well, it can easily be done," Malutin said. "The train will hardly have reached Petrograd Central yet. Telegraph at once, and have it met."

"No," Michael said.

Both officers looked at him in surprise.

"She is more upset than I had thought," Michael said, "over the death of her parents. They were executed, you know, by the GPU. By my brother."

"I did not know," Malutin said. "Well, then, comrade commissar, perhaps she has gone to visit their graves."

"They will have no graves," Michael said. "And she knows that. She has left me. I am sure of it. She will leave Russia with the American." His face twisted. "He is good at getting people out of Russia. He got me out once. And the other woman I loved."

"Then he *must* be stopped," Malutin said. "The telegraph—"

"No," Michael repeated.

Malutin hesitated, then snapped his gloved fingers. "Of course. You would not have Comrade Stein hurt. Then go yourself, comrade."

"What?"

"The thaw has just begun. They can hardly leave Petrograd for another couple of days. You can get there in two. See to their arrest yourself, and then you can see to Comrade Stein's safety as well. As for the American—"

"Go to Petrograd?" Michael said, half to himself. "But what of my command?"

"You have won a great victory, comrade commissar. Now there will have to be a breathing space, in order for us to regroup and replan. Besides, there are the tanks to be repaired. I estimate that it will be at least a week before we are ready to proceed. In that time you can easily get to Petrograd, arrest the American, regain Comrade Stein, and be back here. I promise you that headquarters will not even know you have left at all."

"In a week the Whites will have built new defenses," Michael said.

Malutin shrugged. "That is a fact of life. A fact of war, comrade commissar."

"There is only one fact of life or of war, comrade general," Michael said. "To win. We are winning now. We must not stop, or we might not win again. This army will advance tomorrow morning. I give you until then to regroup, comrade general."

"But—the tanks . . . ?"

"We will have to manage without the tanks, comrade general."

"But—" Malutin looked at Gonarov in amazement. "Our people are exhausted."

"So are the enemy, comrade general. War is not merely a test of physical strength. It is a test of will, as well, We shall advance."

"And Comrade Stein? If you do not go after her you will lose her. Perhaps forever."

Michael looked at him for some seconds, then he wheeled his horse. "This army will advance," he said. "Make your preparations."

The train scraped to a stop beneath the roof of Petrograd Central, releasing its excess steam in a vast hiss that clouded up to the roof and brought the frozen snow slithering down But the snow was melting anyway, the thaw was real.

The platform was crowded; all platforms in Russia were always crowded. It occurred to George that an entire civilization was being rebuilt around the railway system, inadequate as it was, simply because there was no other even remotely reliable system of travel in this vast country. And as usual most of the travelers were soldiers, entraining for the Polish front or for the southern front, he presumed. Those getting off the train were the wounded, and government officials returning to the capital from their probing, fact-finding, tsarist-eliminating missions to the ends of the empire.

He glanced at Judith as they took their places in the line before the ticket barrier. They had spent two days on the train, huddled into a seat intended for one, buying what food and drink could be had from the vendors who thronged every country platform trying to earn a little money. She had slept with her head on his shoulder, as he had rested his head on top of hers. They had spoken little. There was very little to talk about. They knew too much, about Russia, about Bolshevism, about horror, about war, even about each other. And if he knew more of her than she knew of him, that was not something for discussion at this moment, because they also knew the risk they were sharing. If Michael Nej had had the time to telegraph . . . but a general in the middle of a battle could never have the time to telegraph. Their entire escape was based on that simple fact.

Was it the coward's way out, to steal a man's woman and take her away while the man's back was turned? But George could not even condemn himself. There was no other way to save Judith Stein. From what? From an inevitable descent through the grades of kept woman. Or from eventually becoming Michael Nej's wife because she had nowhere else to turn, and thus from having to accept Bolshevism and a brother-in-law who had murdered her parents. And what could he offer her in place? Not a damned thing, save the freedom to think as she chose, and hate as she chose. And love, as she chose?

Their passes were inspected and stamped, and they were on the street.

"We'll go to my apartment first," he said. "And collect my things."

Judith looked down at the small valise in which were all her worldly possessions.

He put his arm round her and gave her a squeeze. "I haven't

got that much either. It pays to travel light."

And when we get to Stockholm, he thought, I'm going to buy you a cabin-trunk full of clothes, Judith Stein. Full of everything you have ever wanted. Just because of that day in Roditchev's cell.

If only he could be sure what else he wanted to do for her, give to her, for that day in Roditchev's cell. And that night on Starogan station. And then that night, two days ago, in the camp south of Tula.

They walked through darkening streets. He was afraid to make himself conspicuous by summoning a cab.

They climbed the empty stairs, and he unlocked the door and turned on the light. The place was as he had left it, his suitcases still standing neatly, side by side, in the hall.

"Hungry?"

She put down her valise. "Do we have the time?"

"She won't sail before dawn. I have some caviar over here. With crackers."

Judith sat down. "And champagne?"

"Ah . . ." He opened his drinks cupboard. "There's a bottle. I'm afraid it's not cold." He lifted it out. "On the other hand, it's not exactly warm, either."

He blew the cork, poured, placed the caviar and the crackers and the knives and plates on the table, and raised his own glass. "I guess we can only drink to the future."

She drank. "What does my future hold, Mr. Hayman?"

"It'd probably look quite bright if you would like to call me George."

Now, why had he said that? Was it because, sitting there, knees crossed and heavy black hair flopping over her forehead and resting on her shoulders in relief at being released from its bandanna, she was a remarkably lovely woman? Was it because of the other beauty, the beauty he had seen lying on the floor of Roditchev's cell, and which had haunted him for nine years? Was it an offshoot of that ambivalent generosity that leads a confident man to want to embrace and protect any woman in distress?

Or was it merely because it was two years since he had held Ilona, or any woman, in his arms?

"I'm sorry," he said. "What I meant was, it seems rather silly to be quite so formal when we have to do a fair amount of traveling together."

"I would like to call you George," she said.

"Then be my guest."

"I would like..." She drank some more champagne, munched a biscuit, and got up to move restlessly about the room.

"Whatever you like, Judith," George said, "I'm going to see that you get it. For the rest of your life."

She turned to look at him. "Why? Haven't you enough responsibilities of your own?"

"None I can't cope with. Would you like to become my responsibility, Judith?"

Once again he received an appraising stare.

"No strings attached," he added. "I mean that."

She smiled. "There are always strings, George. One of them is called Ilona. She is probably the only true friend I have ever had."

"I meant..."

"I know what you meant," she said. "But if we went through the form, the reality would soon enough follow. That is a fact of life."

"And that would be abhorrent to you?"

"I think that would be rather nice, for me. I think I searched for that, with Michael. I have nothing else to look for now."

"Well, then..." Was he being a fool? An utter villain? If only he could be sure of his emotions. How could any man, married to Ilona Borodina, loving Ilona Borodina, even think of sharing that love? But how could any man, having seen Judith Stein on the floor of Roditchev's cell, having watched her and thought of her and worried about her, from a distance, for the intervening nine years, not want to take her in his arms and say, now you are safe, now you can live a little, with me?

And how could any man risk hurting so maltreated a spirit, all over again?

He got up without finishing the sentence, and held out the bottle of champagne. She glanced down at her glass, realized it was empty, came towards him, and stopped as the front door opened. They both turned to stare at Ivan Nej.

Judith slowly lowered the arm holding her glass. Her face had closed, the animation disappearing to leave it nothing more than a mask through which her eyes gleamed in twin pinpoints of hate and anger.

It was not possible to see Ivan's eyes behind his glasses.

He closed the door behind him and rested his hand on his holster; the flap was already unbuttoned.

George could only wait, but his heart was beginning a slow rumble into activity. For six years he had been forced into the role of observer. Six years was too long.

"Judith," Ivan said. He glanced at George. "One of my people saw you at the station, and telephoned me. Is that a farewell drink?"

"Yes," George said. "Will you join us?"

Ivan shook his head. "I do not drink on duty, Hayman. Well, I am sure you will wish to join your ship. You had better come home with me, Judith."

Judith glanced at George.

"We have certain matters to discuss," George said. "In private, if you don't mind. I will see that Judith gets to you safely before I leave."

Ivan smiled. "I think she should come now. Michael would wish to know she was in safe hands. He does know you are in Petrograd, Judith?"

Judith continued to look at George.

"Of course he does," George said. But he knew that he was not going to lie his way free of this one. And suddenly he did not care. His fingers wrapped themselves around the neck of the champagne bottle. Not much of a weapon against a revolver. But it was so ineffective that Ivan might not even consider it, just as he might not consider a forty-three-year-old American journalist to be much of a threat either

"I will telegraph him," Ivan said. "And tell him you have arrived safely. No, we will telegraph him together, Judith. He will be pleased about that."

"No," Judith said, speaking for the first time. "I am leaving Russia. Tonight."

Ivan raised his eyebrows. "Michael knows this?"

"No," she said. "Michael does not own me. It is my decision."

Ivan glanced at George. "Your doing, Hayman?"

"I intend to see that Mademoiselle Stein goes where she wishes to," George said.

"*Comrade* Stein belongs in Russia," Ivan said. "She is Russian, and this is her home. Besides, she is my brother's woman. He is fighting for the future of Bolshevism, while this trickery takes place behind his back. But it is my job to combat subversion. You will come with me, Comrade Stein, and I will see that you are returned to my brother."

"No," Judith said. "No." She looked at George.

He shrugged, and moved into the center of the room, slowly and carefully, the champagne bottle hanging at his side. "I don't suppose you have much choice, Judith," he said. "Ivan has a point. He also has the law behind him."

"You . . ." Judith stared at him, mouth open, color slowly draining from her cheeks.

"I *am* the law," Ivan said. "And I am glad you are showing some sense, Hayman. I would not like to have to arrest an American."

"I would not like it either," George said, and turned to face him, swinging his arm as he did so, the champagne bottle an extension of his fingers. Ivan saw it coming and ducked, drawing his pistol, but the liquid was bubbling out of the neck of the bottle and flying across his face, and George still managed to strike him a glancing blow on the side of his head. Ivan fell to his hands and knees, and his spectacles came off. He turned on his knees, and George swung his foot, in turn, in a perfect punt that caught Ivan on the wrist and sent the revolver arcing away into the far corner of the room.

Ivan turned again, well aware that without his gun he was no match for the big American, but Judith was already throwing herself across the room, to seize the revolver and turn, also on her knees, to face her enemy, the revolver held in both hands, her face twisted with passion.

"No," George said.

She hesitated, her head turning up to look at him, while Ivan sank back on his knees and slowly reached for his spectacles. His face was composed, but his hands trembled, and George remembered Peter telling him that Ivan had seemed afraid to join up, back in 1914.

"He murdered my mother and father," Judith said.

"And many others. But *you* can't murder *him*, Judith. Not if you want to turn your back on all this."

She gazed at Ivan Nej; her fingers were still white on the trigger. "*Can* I turn my back on all this, George? Will he let me?"

Ivan put his glasses on his nose.

"I think he'd better come with us," George said. "Give me the gun."

She sidled round the wall, reached his side, and gave him the weapon. Ivan's sigh of relief was audible.

"I presume you have a man outside, Ivan," George said. "You are going to tell him that you are accompanying us to the ship. And there you are going to stay and have a drink with us. And then you are going to forget to leave when the ship sails. Oh, don't worry. We shall put you ashore in Stockholm. You'll get back in one piece. If you behave."

"Why should I do this?" Ivan asked, but he was having trouble breathing.

"Because I am going to be at your side until you are in our cabin on that ship," George said. "And if you don't behave, I am going to blow you apart."

"They would hang you," Ivan said. He licked his lips. "And her. They would hang you together."

"You won't enjoy the sight much," George pointed out, "looking up from hell."

Ivan gazed at him. Everything depended on how much of a coward he was, how much he wanted to live, to enjoy Tattie's beauty and his own booming career, rather than die for his pride and his honor.

Tattie, George thought. Might it not be possible to take Tattie away from Russia as well, to the safety of America and the protection of her sister? But Tattie would not want to go. Tattie was happy here, and this man was the father of her children. To attempt to take Tattie against her will would be to endanger Judith. It was as simple as that.

Ivan slowly got to his feet, stooped again, and picked up his cap. "One day," he said, "one day, Hayman, when we have carried our revolution over the entire world, you will have to answer to me. You, and Ilona, and your friend there. You will have to answer to me. I can wait for that day."

"I always figured you for a patient man," George agreed. "Shall we go? You first, Judith."

She hesitated.

"There's nothing to be afraid of," George said. "Comrade Nej isn't the stuff of which heroes are made. Heroes are not usually patient men. Out there is freedom, Judith."

And I'll be at your side, he thought. Hurrying back to Ilona. I wonder if you know, Comrade Nej, he thought, how many more important things I have to do with my life than worry about your revolution?

* * *

Sevastopol was a huge rubbish bin, its decay and its squalor increased by the August heat, its horror increased by the activities of the Red Guards, able at last to revenge themselves on those who had supported the Whites and who had been unable to get away.

But this had been the pattern all spring and summer, as Denikin had reeled back from defeat after defeat. Some had been close-fought, and near-run; others had been simple, and as the summer had advanced the simple victories had outnumbered the hard-fought ones, as the White morale had cracked and the White armies had disintegrated. And every victory, every village and every town liberated for the revolution, had been accompanied by the same crackle of the firing squads, the screams of women and the wails of suddenly orphaned children. But this was the tide of revolution. This was the decree of Lenin. And this was the way to victory. Final victory. Only in this way, Michael Nej realized, would he ever have been able to stand here, in a Sevastopol hotel, and realize that his mission was complete.

And only the poor had suffered. He could still see the smoke, seeping over the turbulent Black Sea horizon, that marked the last of the British fleet. On board those ships were enough tsarists to stock an entire court. On board those ships were the Dowager Tsarina Marie Feodorovna, mother of the late tsar and sister of the Dowager Queen of England, and the Grand Duke Nicholas Nikolaievich, ex-commander-in-chief of the Imperial Army, uncle of the tsar, and the logical claimant to the throne. Would he bother to try to claim it? Would he imagine he had any chance of success?

With them were several other members of the Russian royal family, including Prince Felix Yusupov, the architect of the death of Rasputin, which had first encouraged the Kerensky revolution, and his wife. Would *they* bother to continue to oppose Bolshevism, or would they now admit defeat?

And with them too was Prince Peter Borodin, his wife Rachel, and their baby daughter. What had Peter Borodin thought, Michael wondered, as he had crept on board his ship and turned his back on Russia and the men he had led so valiantly for two long years, defeated at last by his own valet? Where would Peter go? Well, he'd try England first. But not for very long, Michael thought; the British government was holding conversations with Lenin's emissary. France? It was a possibility.

Or the United States? To join his sister Ilona and her husband, to let Rachel join Judith in that happy exile. He realized his hands had clenched into fists.

But did he really wish he had managed to capture Peter? As a military man the answer had to be yes; of all the people on board those retreating warships, he supposed Peter Borodin might be the most dangerous in his antagonism to Bolshevism. But he would not have enjoyed having to hand Peter over to a firing squad, or worse, his own brother; since his absurd visit to Stockholm in the spring, Ivan had sought the destruction of Whites and tsarists with an almost pathological hatred.

Perhaps that was essential, for a policeman. It was not necessary for a soldier. He did not hate Peter Borodin anymore. He did not even hate George Hayman for having robbed him, successively, of the only two women he had ever loved. He even admired the man. And it was all for the good. Had Ilona remained in Russia, with little Ivan, he himself would never have been a revolutionary. Had Judith remained at his side, he might never have found the iron will to drive himself and his men forward, day after day after day, to achieve this final triumph. He could wish them all joy, and even, perhaps, look forward to seeing them again one day, when there could be peace and friendship between Bolshevism and the rest of the world.

Captain Gonarov cleared his throat, and Michael turned. "Yes?"

"Your call to Petrograd, comrade commissar."

"Thank you." Michael went into the foyer, picked up the telephone. "Comrade Lenin?"

"Michael Nikolaievich? Is that you?" Even Lenin sounded excited this morning. "What news, man, what news?"

Michael drew a long breath. "I have to report, comrade, that the British fleet has left the port, and the last of the White army has today surrendered. We hold Sevastopol, comrade. We hold the Crimea. We hold all Russia. Your revolution is complete."

An Excerpt From THE BORODINS BOOK III

FATE AND DREAMS

To Be Published in September 1981

The taxi squealed to a halt. "There's the car," Lupin, the driver, said.

"Is the street empty?" Peter Borodin sat in the back seat next to Tattie, who had temporarily run out of breath and had ceased wriggling and fighting. But he still held her wrists, which she had managed to get out from under the sacking.

"Looks empty," said the driver.

"We'll tie these, anyway. Come along, John."

John Hayman took the length of thick cord from his pocket, and hesitated. Suddenly he was not at all sure what he was doing here, and wished he weren't here at all. When Uncle Peter had read of the coming tour of Europe by Tatiana Nej and her dance troupe, and had said, "Good for her. She's coming out. We must be there to help her," it had all seemed tremendously exciting and daring. And there could be no question but that they were doing the right thing in taking her away from the Russians. But now, to be told to tie her wrists together . . .

He wondered if the Bolsheviks had tied her wrists together before raping her.

"For God's sake," Peter snapped. "Hurry up."

Johnnie drew a long breath, looped the cord twice around his aunt's wrists, pulled it tight, and tied the knot. The fingers opened and closed, and jerked ineffectively as the wrists pulled to and fro.

"Now let's change cars," Peter said, opening the door. "Come along, Tattie. Don't be foolish, now."

She aimed a kick at his leg, but since she could not see through the sacking she missed her target and fell half out of the car. He caught her easily enough and stood her on the pavement. She stamped up and down as the chill struck at her feet. They had hustled her from her dressing room at the Albert Hall so quickly that she was still barefoot and dressed only in her slip.

"Come *on*," Peter said.

John got out of the back of the taxi. Lupin was already behind the wheel of the small English Austin Uncle Peter had bought for this adventure, because of its inconspicuousness on English roads. But it looked even smaller tonight, like a matchbox standing on end. As they pushed Tattie up to the back door, Peter glanced up and down the deserted London street.

"You get in first," he commanded.

John got in and saw Tattie being thrust towards him.

"Catch her," Peter said.

She had tripped and was falling. Johnnie caught her shoulders, but her weight still pushed him against the far side of the seat. Peter gathered her legs and thrust them in, then slammed the door.

"But . . ." John protested. Tattie was half lying across him, head on his shoulder; he could hear her panting through the sack.

"There's only room for two," Peter said, getting into the front beside the driver. "Besides, I can keep a better eye on her from here. For God's sake, Lupin, let's *go*."

A gear grated. Even Lupin was nervous tonight. Then the engine roared and they drove up the street. "The Great North Road?" Lupin asked.

"Of course not. That's where they'll look for us. Stick to side roads and country lanes. There's no hurry."

John was wrestling Tattie around to sit her properly on the seat beside him. To get her straight it was necessary to hold her legs and pull them out in front, and she tried another kick, which caught him on the shoulder and once again pushed him against the side of the car.

"If you don't behave, Tattie, I am going to hit you," Peter warned.

"I think it's because she can't see, Uncle Peter," John said. "Can't I take off the sack?"

"She'll see where we're taking her, stupid boy," Peter said.

"Does it matter, since we're taking her out into the country?"

Peter hesitated, then shrugged. "I suppose not."

John unfastened the cord that had held the sack in at Tattie's waist, and cautiously lifted it over her head. Her face was hidden by a mass of golden hair, scattered every way, which a fierce toss failed to restore to order. She put up her bound hands to uncover her eyes, and blinked into the darkness of the car.

"You wretch," she said. "You abominable little wretch—"

"Now, Tattie," Peter said. "John was only carrying out my orders."

Tattie glared at the front. "As for you," she said. "When I get my hands free—"

"You aren't going to have your hands free," Peter pointed out, "until you promise to behave."

"Promise *you*?" She seemed to tense, like an angry lioness. "I'm going to have my hands free, one day." she said. "And then I'm going to twist your neck until it snaps!" She turned her head to look at John Hayman. "And then I'm going to fix you, too."

With a speed and a violence Johnnie had never suspected his uncle to possess, Peter leaned over the front seat and seized his sister by the front of her slip, jerking her forward with such force that she fell off the seat and onto the floor, on her hands and knees.

"You listen to me," Peter said. "This is not a game. As far as I'm concerned you're diseased. Because that is what Communism is, a disease. And diseased, you are a disgrace to the family, to the memory of the tsar, to the grand duke, and to everything we are fighting for. You are a traitor, Tatiana Dimtrievna, a foul, loathsome traitor. It is my curse that you also happen to be my sister. But I swear to you that sooner than let you go back to Russia, I'll kill you myself."

"They used a taxicab." Superintendent Dorrington of Scotland Yard sat at his desk and looked quite pleased. "We found it abandoned down a side street in Harrow. That's north London."

"And you're sure it was Peter and Tattie?" George Hayman had slept and shaved, and he felt better than he had the night before, when he and Ilona had learned of the kidnapping. But his mind was still trembling with the utter absurdity of what Peter had done. The dangerous absurdity.

Clive Bullen, Tattie's English lover, did not appear to have slept at all.

"Oh indeed, Mr. Hayman," Dorrington said. "There is no question of it. There are even traces of Madam Nej's, ah, scent."

"So where are they now?" Clive asked.

"Ah, well, they changed cars. We even have a wheel mark to go by. A small car, I'd say, an Austin Seven or some such thing. Unfortunately, as you will understand, there are an awfully large number of Austin Sevens in this country."

"Can't you positively identify the car?" George asked. "Get a license number or something? After all, it must have been stolen, or hired."

"Or bought, Mr. Hayman. I rather think a man like Prince Borodin would have bought the car."

"Well, then—"

"Under an assumed name, almost certainly. And quite a few of these cars are sold every day. We shall find out, of course. I have men looking into it now. But it will take time. Perhaps two or three days."

"Days?" George shouted. "For heaven's sake, man. Can't you put more people on it?"

"Doing what, sir, would you suggest?"

"Well, they changed cars in north London. That means they're heading north."

"Does it, sir?"

"It seems fairly obvious to me, superintendent. Now we know Peter can't get Tattie out of Great Britain, and he knows that too. Not if she doesn't want to go. So it stands to reason that he's taking her to some secluded spot where he can talk or bully her into going with him of her own free will. That means north Wales, or the lake district, or Scotland. But first of all he must get there. It's two or three days' drive, isn't it? So if you'd get your provincial police on to checking all Austin Sevens heading north—"

"My dear Mr. Hayman," Dorrington said. "I thought I had explained that. My men, and our provincial police, have more important things to do than gallivant about the country on wild-goose chases. My dear sir, Madam Nej is with her brother, and therefore is hardly in physical danger. Now, sir, if, as you suggest, he manages to talk her into accompanying him of her own free will, then there is absolutely nothing either you or I can do about it. If, on the other hand, she continues to refuse to cooperate with him, then you may rest assured that we will certainly find them in due course, when, should she then wish to prefer charges, we would of course take the matter further."

Clive sighed. "I suppose that about sums it up."

"Like hell it does." George turned on his heel and strode out of the office, slamming the door behind him.

Clive hurried to catch up. "Well, as the man says, Prince Borodin *is* her brother."

"You don't know the half of it, Bullen. He is also Prince Borodin of Starogan, and he hates the Bolsheviks the way you or I would hate the people who had murdered our families, because they *did* murder his. As far as he is concerned, Tattie is a traitor to everything he and his family have ever held dear. He has dreamed of getting her out of Russia for five years. I'm damned sure he has no intention of ever letting her go back."

"But . . . what exactly do you mean?"

"I'm getting my own people onto this, and we're heading north. I think Tattie may be in considerable danger."